T0115164

An American Dream
THE LIFE

Tony Thomas

authorHOUSE®

AuthorHouse™
1663 Liberty Drive
Bloomington, IN 47403
www.authorhouse.com
Phone: 1-800-839-8640

First published by AuthorHouse   3/17/2011

ISBN: 978-1-4567-3208-0 (e)
ISBN: 978-1-4567-3209-7 (dj)
ISBN: 978-1-4567-3207-3 (sc)

Library of Congress Control Number: 2011900906

Printed in the United States of America

Any people depicted in stock imagery provided by Thinkstock are models, and such images are being used for illustrative purposes only. Certain stock imagery © Thinkstock.

This book is printed on acid-free paper.

Because of the dynamic nature of the Internet, any Web addresses or links contained in this book may have changed since publication and may no longer be valid. The views expressed in this work are solely those of the author and do not necessarily reflect the views of the publisher, and the publisher hereby disclaims any responsibility for them.

INTRODUCTION

This is a story of real life, harsh realities of many young men in various cities and neighborhoods all across this country. Oh how the game of life can be so bitter, yet so sweet. It's internally deep. Sex, drugs, money, and violence are like essentials to a nutritious breakfast for black youth. It's survival of the fittest, and the struggle continues.

Prepare to laugh to the humor, cry to the loss and pain of these true to life characters, but ultimately to enjoy this novel of typical, yet powerful everyday American drama.

CHAPTER 1: The Jones'

It was the year of 1978, on a hot summer morning in mid August when two twin boys were born. However, some may look back and consider it a cold day in hell. These twin boys were born to an Italian-American mother and an African-American father in Winston Salem, North Carolina. The first born was named Antonio. The baby boy was, Sizalino. Antonio and Sizalino's parents were a typical young couple. They got together right after graduating from high school. In which Sizalino's mother, Carmen, got pregnant in the early winter months of '78, by none other than the playboy himself, Anthony Jones.

Carmen was somewhat of a drama teen. She was wild and adventurous. So Carmen's parents sent her to live with her aunt in North Carolina during her senior year because of disciplinary reasons. Shortly before being sent to North Carolina she was torn apart by the death of her father, a veteran from the Vietnam War. As a result, she became unruly. Being withdrawn from others, even running away to Washington D.C. where she got with a bad group of winches who had her doing drugs and not to mention, she was raped. This was unacceptable behavior for a catholic girl from Martinsville, Virginia. So Aunt Sissy (Sicilia) was the answer. She was a strict, no nonsense kind of lady and a firm throwback from the old days in Sicily, with all of the solid traditions. It was because of this transition that Carmen met the love of her life, Anthony. He was a true father figure type.

A few months into her pregnancy, despite her family's wishes, Carmen married Anthony (Tony). Becoming Misses Jones. She would erase the existence of her family name, Cruzano, especially since her mother would no longer have anything to do with her or her new family. Anthony was a wild country Negro, who grew up in the South fighting segregation. White people! In his early years of school, on into junior high, blacks went to separate schools than whites. He fought with whites for most of his life. His brothers, sisters, cousins, and uncles all fought along with him. It was finally a breakthrough in his second year of high school after a big riot of violence and injury had broke out from the previous school year. It was so disturbing that not only did it make the news and newspapers, but it also forced a change in all schools of the South. Blacks could now attend the same schools as whites. They were now entitled to equal and efficient education.

It was a new day for Anthony and all other blacks across the South. Anthony still had a grudge against most whites, but there was a stunning 5 foot brunette who had captured her attention. She didn't act like most of the other white girls who attended his high school. She was talkative and open to blacks. She even hung with some of the black girls and tended to seem just as one of them. At times she was degraded by white students for this, but she didn't seem to care.

Anthony did his research on this mystery girl, who he felt always gave him the eye, and found her to be a Miss Carmen Cruzano. An Italian-American! That explained it. She was somewhat a misfit herself to white folks. Well, he had to have her. He made an introduction and they were soon well acquainted. They dated for the rest of the year. Secretly somewhat, due to the forbidden wishes of Aunt Sissy and the fact that back then, interracial relationships caused serious drama.

After high school came the twins and eventually the marriage. Anthony moved Carmen and the twins in with his mom near Wake Forest. He got a job doing maintenance work but thought he did better supporting his family by gambling playing hoops almost every evening. Some he won, but most he lost. Frustration began to build. The pressure of living at home with his mother and complaints by Carmen that he was always running the streets with friends, chasing women and not spending enough time at home resulted in Anthony using his wife as a stress reliever, kicking off in her ass whenever he was in the mood. She eventually tried to leave him, but he somehow met her at her cousin Norma's in Newport News, Virginia, begging and pleading with her to come back to Carolina. Swearing he'd change, saying that his actions were a sickness from being an abused child himself. She agreed, and they eventually moved to Dallas, Texas, after Tony got plugged in with a job making $25 an hour; a job that his cousin Leon from New York hooked up, which also required Tony to fly to N.Y. every couple of weeks.

Tony and his family were living better than ever, until Leon got popped in the skull by a rival organization; right between the eyes, execution style. Tony flew to N.Y. for his cousin's funeral, and then vowed to plot vengeance. Carmen begged him to let it go, telling him he had a family. In all the while she was enjoying their good fortune; she hadn't even realized that her husband was engaged in illegal activities.

Shortly after Leon's demise, Tony found out that his mother had moved to Columbus, Ohio. She was following her sister's advice that raising her 5 children in the city, the last of her 13, would be best for her and the children.

The city offered convenient housing, welfare/social-security, and all the other false dreams that city life promises. It turns out that the

3

kids got into trouble, and stayed in it. Misses Jones' health had gotten dramatically worse due to stress and partially to age; and generally to a rough life. On top of all this she continued to chain smoke. She ate salty, greasy foods, and cursed anyone who warned her about it and the effects it could have on her high blood pressure.

After about a year or so, Tony's conscious broke down, sending him and his family to Columbus. When he arrived, he was informed that his mother was dying and that she was on a respiratory machine. Finally after a few months went by, she quietly passed through the end of the night. On the morning of April 10th, 1989, Misses Jones was pronounced dead. Tony was enraged. He blamed everything and everyone. He was distant from all of his family at the funeral, hating them for ever being born. He claimed that he was not their brother, because out of 13 children, he had his own father. He became so bad after his mother's passing, that he cheated on Carmen more than ever before. And brutally beat her with no remorse, having no conscious about it. He sent her to the hospital nearly every week. There was once an incident while they were living on 17th Avenue on the city's north side, where little Antonio drew his father's 44 magnum pistol out of the closet and pointed it right at Tony. When he coaxed his son to put the gun down, he savagely beat him, claiming that Carmen put him up to it. So he beat her as well, giving her a matching cherry nose just as he had gave their son. Carmen could take no more. She packed up her and the boys' things late at night while Tony was at work. She left him for good, exactly one year after his mother's death. April 11th, 1990.

CHAPTER 2: Young Murder

It was a windy spring night, in late March of 1993. I was walking down Joyce Avenue with my brother, Twin (Antonio) at about 1a.m.

"Hey bruh, you know pop's bitch of a wifey gon' rat us out for bein' out so late. Fuckin' wit you and ya lil' broad. And you didn't even fuck! I'ma cuss her homegirl out, though. I'm salty that hoe ain't slide through," I said.

"Yo, she got a fat ass, too. Don't trip about pop's bitch, though. You know she probably asleep, anyway. I'm telling you though Siz-o, the next time I get that bitch's panties down…" Before Twin could finish I cut him off.

"Yo Twin, check these niggas out creepin' up on the sly, all hooded up wit they heads dipped down," I said.

Twin just made a gesture down towards his waist where he had Tony senior's 44 magnum tucked under his N.Y. Giants starter parka. "Just be cool lil' bruh, they don't want no drama," said Twin.

As we walked past this unknown trio, it was something about the deceitful look in the short one leading the pack's eyes that told me this was going to be a night to be remembered. Indeed filled with drama.

Once they were about 12 feet past us, the little short wanna-be-thug muthaphucka who also seemed to be the oldest and wore a Chicago Bulls starter parka with a matching Kango, stopped and muttered some, 'Hey homey' type shit, along with a click-clack. As we turned after hearing this definite sound of a death threat, the walking dead man said, "You with the Raiders jacket on! Check it in, dog."

I looked wide eyed at my bruh, heart racing a mile a minute as he said to me, "run Siz-o!" As I did just that, he pulled out the 44 and started busting. The 3 stooges tried to dip but the tall one caught a soft leaded slug to the hip as he hit the pavement like a scene from 'Boyz-in-the-Hood'. In the midst of turning the corner for safety behind the church, I caught a slug in the shoulder. I continued to run as I heard a few more shots. After jumping the fence into the backyard of a neighborhood home near Joan Park, I collapsed. I was startled when I looked up and saw my twin over top of me. Thank God!

"Siz, come on bruh, we gotta get you to the crib." Twin said. I just laid there as I heard his voice. "Come on, bruh! You gotta get to a hospital. You gon' make it. You ain't dyin' tonight, bruh," he said.

Something in his words allowed me to rise. As we ran through the park we had shot ball in, gathered with associates, and mingled with so many cuties daily. Within a few minutes, which seemed like an eternity, we reached the crib as I collapsed on the couch once we got inside. I was losing blood like a slaughtered pig.

"Yo Ann! Call 911, Siz-o just got shot," Twin yelled.

"What? What happened?" Ann said as she turned on the light and came down the steps rubbing her eyes.

"Just call an ambulance and call my pops. Siz-o got shot, he need help." Twin yelled again.

"Oh my God, he's bleeding everywhere. Let me get my coat," said Ann.

Twin helped me get to the car, but shot back into the house to stay with my baby sister, Samicia. We pulled off from Republic Avenue onto Joyce Avenue as a police cruiser sat on the corner, while 2 officers doing paperwork with their dome light on just looked at us. Ann informed them that I had been shot and that we were headed to Doctor's North at full speed. The blonde female officer said that they'd lead.

"Y'all didn't just hear gun shots a few minutes ago?" Ann asked.

"Yeah, but we hear gun shots all the time," said the officer. It turns out that they had been on the corner the whole time, just 2 blocks down from a fatal crime.

When I got to the hospital I was rushed into the emergency room where I was put on a gurney. I laid there lightheaded, replaying the whole night in my mind. I was losing a lot of blood, though; and getting weaker by the minute. 'Damn', didn't these muthaphuckas realize that I had been shot?! I started thinking about all of that '911 is a joke' shit and the rest of those hood sayings that applied to most lower class minorities.

They finally wheeled me into an operating room where I was given an I.V. and some medical attention. My pops eventually arrived, followed by my moms. The doctor started telling my pops some shit about how it would be best to leave the bullet lodged in my shoulder, saying that it would be too risky trying to remove it. My pops wasn't feeling that, though. He wanted a second prognosis. Another doctor with more years of experience from another floor said he recommended that it be surgically removed because the bullet was liable to travel into my neck or elsewhere; being fatal. Pops almost choked the first doctor until mom and the other staff members stopped him. Just then the laws walked in. Can you fucking believe that they wanted to question me in my condition?! I was heavily sedated and my parents were against it as well as the doctors. Saying that I needed to get into surgery immediately and that I didn't need any traumatic reminder of the incident. I was too unstable. I was too high to tell the pricks anything. I was fucking dying, I felt! They rushed me off to the 5th floor to perform the surgery. As my parents walked out to the waiting room, praying for their baby boy, one of the officers said that there had been two other shootings in the area that night.

He said that one young man, a Jamal Stevens (age 15), had been shot in the side and was in critical condition at Grant hospital. The other man, a Jason Parker (age 18), had been pronounced dead at the scene from a gunshot wound to the chest. He died holding a 380 automatic in his right hand. The clip had been emptied. It was only when my pops heard the officer say that both victims were shot with a 44 magnum that he felt he could not take a normal gulp so the officer wouldn't see an evident sign of acknowledgement. He did not want to believe that his thirteen year old son could be responsible for such serious crimes. With his gun! What the hell had happened? He was sure as hell going to find out when he got home.

"Well officer, I'm sure my boys didn't have any wrong in this shit. Right now I'ma go in wit my ex-wife and wait while my son is in surgery. We'll get back wit y'all when he can speak to tell us what happened," said pop.

"Can we speak with your other son...?" Mr. Jones rudely interrupted the officer saying, "Antonio! And 'hell no' y'all can't speak to him tonight."

They continued asking questions like, 'Why were we out so late? Did we own a gun?' And a bunch of other bullshit questions. Pops got so pissed that the hospital staff asked the officers to leave for upsetting the parents of a patient in their care. The officers got pop to agree to bring Twin down to the station to make a statement by the following afternoon. Then, after apologizing, the officers left.

Moms asked pop, "Tony, what's going on?"

"I don't fuckin' know, Carmen. I've been at work," Pop said.

They did their typical, domestic arguing, and then finally came together to be at peace while waiting on my outcome. Hoping, wishing, and praying for the best. Especially pops, because he had a real good idea as to what had happened, and had silently asked God to see to it that this tragic nightmare was not revealed to the rest of the world. Damn his hot-headed son, Antonio! He had to get home. The gun... First, he'd see to it that Sizalino came through okay. And then, he'd deal with Antonio. These next 12 hours would be crucial.

CHAPTER 3: Recovery and Concealment

Six hours later I was out of surgery and placed in recovery. Mom and pop were allowed to enter my room after the nurse confirmed I was conscious. She told them that my speech would be limited because of the sedative still wearing off. My mother spoke first, "How you doin', baby?"

I nodded my head, letting her know I was good.

"Boy yo ass is lucky. Six more inches to the left and it would've been yo thick ass skull. I'm glad you alright, though. You coulda ended up like that other boy, six feet in the dirt. What the hell happened, Jerele? (Jerele was my middle name that most of my family called me because it was easier than Sizalino. My black half was the only family I really knew). And don't lie to me, I'm ya daddy." Pop said in a low, but very strained and serious voice.

My mother looked at me hesitantly with tears in her eyes. Just then it dawned on me. Twin must have shot and killed the boy pop was talking about.

"I don't know," I whispered as I shrugged. "We was walkin' home from Josheema's house and some dudes walked past us; after that, one of 'em pulled out a gun and told me to check in my coat. So Twin pulled out….. yo' gun, and told me to run. So I did," I said to pop.

"I knew it! Damn that boy. What the hell was y'all doin' at some funky winch's house that late for?" Pop asked.

I just shook my head and turned to look out the window.

"Tony, just calm down. What if he didn't have the gun? They…" Pop cut moms off by sayin', "But Carmen, the boy shot two people! One of 'em he killed! And wit my piece!"

We all just silently stared at each other for a minute. I had to think of something. I couldn't let my bruh down. Although we were juveniles, it would still turn out disastrous for my family, especially for my pops. So I came up with an idea. My pops was taking Twin down to the precinct later to make a statement for the folks. Our story would be that there were two other groups of guys out there that night on the same corner. Some words were being exchanged as we passed, and then, shots were fired. It was sellable because the Myrtle boys were notorious for gunplay in that area. I mean, fuck, we were only 13! Pops bought my devious idea after he got over the Good Samaritan mind fuck that he felt obligated to. My mother just gave a sigh as she looked off into space. We had our family pack. I mean, hey, it was justifiable homicide. As my mother and father hugged and kissed me goodbye, I was notified by the nurse that I would be released in 3 days. Mom said she would come and get me then. Pops assured me he'd be back after he and Twin visited the precinct.

After they left I laid there reviewing the tragic event as best as I could. I felt a strange sense of pain and rage. Sort of like my fellow thug brother, 2Pac. It was Twin and me against the world.

***

Pops finally arrived home to get the details from Twin, which he had pretty much figured out. Once things were in the clear, pop told him about the trip to the precinct that they had to make and the white lies they were going to tell to the laws. That's why they call them little white lies because they're made out to be innocent lies told by white people.

Pop told Twin that they had to make a stop to get rid of the magnum. He stopped by his job at General Castings to tell them that he wouldn't be in that night due to the incident with his sons. What a perfect playoff it was as he returned to his fire red mustang to retrieve the hand cannon wrapped in a dirty maintenance rag and carried over to a liquid metal tub. No one thought anything of it because it was his normal work area near the furnaces. The gun was no big deal to Pops because, like most black men, it wasn't registered in his name.

They arrived at police headquarters where shortly there after, they waited for the assigned detective to return from interviewing the other victim, a Jamel Stevens, who had got out of surgery just yesterday. Twin was sitting thinking to himself about how I had come up with the bogus, but logic story. Until he heard it from pop, he was a little shook. But ultimately the knucklehead was prepared for whatever. Focusing on the script to his story Twin entered the homicide detective's office with Pop after the Jones name was called. Once they sat down the detective said that no one was currently being charged with the murder of Jason Parker, or the shooting of Jamel Stevens, but that it was the same shooter of both victims. However, he just wanted to hear Twin's side of the story, as well as mine. He said that Mr. Stevens was claiming that he didn't know anything, which lowered his credibility and made our story sound logically believable. The detectives bought the story. They weren't happy, but that was because they didn't like the fact of having nothing. It wasn't because suspected anything. They told Twin and Pop that they could go but would need a statement from me as soon as I was released. It seemed that Twin and I were in the clear.

After I was released and made my statement, I returned back to school. The word was that the Jones boys were killers; some notorious young soldiers. The bitches were on my sling and my wood. They were all oohing and aahing about my shoulder. I was getting a head rush. And not just from all the girls but from all the love and respect. It turns out that the deceased was rather notorious himself at age 18. An around the way hood that everyone called, Puffy. Well, fuck him! And may he rest in piss. There ain't no love for those who oppose; me or mine. Puffy had it coming. In this life it's about moral and principle. Don't ever show remorse or mercy for fucking over anyone in anyway who fucked you over first. Rules are rules. But always repent and ask the Lord for forgiveness. Life is about survival. It's crazy! I learned all that at an early age, which is an attribute in this life.

"Hey yo, Siz-o! Wusup, boo?" said a familiar voice as we got on the bus.

That jazzy New York accent turned out to be Tyese's thick ass. Yep, the one who stood me up the night I got shot.

"What's the deal, baby?" I spat back

"I'm sorry about the otha' night. You wanna come by the house 'til my moms get home? She don't get off 'til 6 o'clock," she said.

"Ain't no doubt." I said as we got on the bus. I got my first shot of pussy that day. I put it in her life on her mom's loveseat. True thug passion after the storm!

CHAPTER 4: Young Menacing

The school year finally came to an end and junior high was over. Brookhaven High School was the next level. Honeys, sports, honeys, and more honeys. The summer was truly a breeze. It consisted of the usual bullshit; kicking it with the local losers, and doing nothing while everyone else was getting money. This shit had dawned on me at an early age, but at the time it hadn't quite registered all the way.

However, Twin and I did seem to have a ball whenever we went out to mom's house on the south side, which was in a respectable neighborhood but down the street from, 'the hood' where we would usually hook up with our two youngest uncles, Dustin and Miquel (pronounced Michael). Dustin, a.k.a. Dust, was a 16 year old hoodlum who felt that at his youthful age he was already an O.G. Well, at least our O.G. Miquel, who we all called Skins because he always wanted someone to slap him 5 on the palm, was 14.

We spent our summer days and nights drinking 40 ounces of malt liquor (which were usually attained by some criminal act of violence) and talking shit; we loitered in the malls because we were broke; and stayed into mischief just for something to do. Just like the time when we were

at Northland Mall Cinema and we didn't have any burnout money…
burnout money was just pocket money that we could jack-off. It was the
only kind of money that we knew of at the time.

Anyhow, we caught a few yankee-doodle white boys in the lobby
aiming to make Virtue Fighter rich. They were so into the game that
they didn't even see us surrounding them. Cinema intermission had just
passed so the lobby was empty. Dust sent Skins up to one of the yanks
to ask for some money. With Dust being the oldest, he always stage
managed all of the dirt. Thus far that is. Skins approached the yank
and asked for a quarter. We all cracked the fuck up laughing because
Skins was always known for being rather slow. But after Skin's request,
the yank just cut his eye at Skins and replied that he was broke. This
enraged Dust as he approached the yanks demanding that they come
out of their pockets. After the yank hollered broke again, Dust cold
cocked him and replied, "Bitch, if you broke then how you keep playin'
these video games?"

Twin stole the other yank as the third one ran behind the counter
begging for someone to call the laws. We quickly stripped them of their
goods: money, jewelry, Starter hats and jackets, and then we bounced.
On our way out the door Dust dropped a big ass white guy walking
in with his young, blonde beauty. It turns out that it was his mistress
because during our escape Twin and Dust were detained and the big
motherfucker claimed that they weren't the suspects. He was a fucking
United States Senator!

That summer was wild. And what was really wild about that particular
event was that a week later I was hanging out in the same cinema lobby
again, coming from my aunt and uncle's apartment who lived right behind
the mall, and at closing time there was this sweet, redbone beauty named
Nika waiting for her mom to come get her because she had missed the
last bus. I sat with her inside the entry doors, talking and flirting as I

told her of the events the week before. As I talked and finessed her, I was in her wet ass panties immediately after I knew her name. But then we saw headlights. It was her moms. She couldn't see in, though, but we had the advantage of seeing out. So before I could bust my nut I had to let Nika get up to catch her moms before she bounced, thinking maybe her daughter wasn't there. I got her info, though. I called her up the next day and paid her Cleveland Avenue residence a visit. I ended up finessing her moms, too. I finessed her to the point where she allowed me to stay the night with her 14 year old daughter. I had to return the favor by putting it in sweet, high yellow daughter's thick life. Not once, not twice, but three times that night. And it was truly a charm. It's definitely something lovely about that redbone pussy. Miss Nika showed her gratitude by making me breakfast. Before I bounced, for a trophy type souvenir I guess, she asked to wear my chain. I objected but left her with my flannel jacket instead. And she loved me for it; ate it up.

***

The summer was soon over with and it was time to begin a new school year. Twin and I were now freshmen in high school; at the 'Haven! Now, I personally never had a problem with school.....school work that is. I was always pretty smart. And so was Twin, when he wasn't being a knucklehead. But now that we were getting older, school was becoming a headache. Or somewhat of a job that busted your balls to the fullest with no immediate benefits. Once you get older, appearance becomes more important. The females start to look better, and they start to pay more attention to you. Peer pressure becomes a big factor. It's as simple as this: it's hard to concentrate in school when you're starving and trying to stay up with the latest fashions. Or at least when you're trying to avoid wearing the same outfit twice in one week.

Our pops was by far the cheapest son of a bitch on the planet. We were his last priority, financially. Twin and I quickly decided that we weren't with this being broke shit. Although we hadn't quite decided yet how we were going to get money. I mean, we were only 14! We were not old enough to work.

Twin had decided he would go live with my moms out west in Wedgewood projects where she stayed with a girlfriend. He'd quickly hooked up with a childhood friend named Corky who we used to bully as kids. Any how, to be age 15, Corky was getting it. He sold weight and worked the game full time. And, since he had a mother who didn't care he had stopped going to school. Plus, the money was too good to miss out on. He had got so straight in the game because his older brother sent all of the project fiends his way since he had graduated to brick boy status. By Twin being the savage that he was, though, he soon took over Corky's flow.

Meanwhile, I was still staying with pops and attending the 'Haven. I was getting dead tired of being broke, though; and hearing about Twin getting paper and having a ball. He would have Jeff, Cork's big brother, and the legendary P. Money (A.K.A. Mike P.) picking him up and dropping him off at West High School in Cadillac's and Acura's and shit… Whenever I went to Mom's for the weekend we'd kick it tough. Those niggas spent money like it was water. Twin would throw me money to buy shoes and to have some in my pocket.

My little sister had decided that she wanted to go live with moms, too. Pops didn't give a fuck. It just meant more time, freedom, and finances to dedicate to his bachelor lifestyle that he'd adapted to; especially since he had divorced his wife, Ann. His excuse for their fallout was that she'd started smoking crack. Her excuse was that he beat the shit out of her. I was eventually pushed out of Pop's house too, but mom said it would have to wait for another month or so until she found a place for us to live.

Which by then the school year would be over and I could finish out my freshman year at the 'Haven. The thought of West High School was so lame; or any other school for that matter.

In the meantime, I would wild out after school with my local homies from up north. We'd go to Friday Night football games or just chill out at Linden Recreation Center, where I blindly met the jazzy love of my life, Keysha. It was a cool, spring afternoon in late April when my nigga Ed and I were shooting pool and, across the room I scoped a chocolate, chinky-eyed little thing checking me out. Or so I thought she was. And so did my boy Ed. She was with another girl, though, a girl who seemed like a straight, loud mouthed rat. But my homeboy Ed was with it if need be.

We finished our game and then we bounced. Once we got out front Ed was juicing me up on getting at the two infamous hot girls. I wasn't with it so he slid back in to spit at them by himself. He came out rapping with the loud one, and then he told me to tell her that I wanted to get with her girl. So I told her to go get her girl's number, and if she wasn't with it then 'fuck her'. Yes. Young, dumb game but, fuck it! I didn't care, I was only 14. Baby girl came back out with her girl's number. Wow, I thought. Anyhow, I called her a few days later. We kicked it for a minute and then decided to meet up at the center we had met at a week ago. I found out that she was 17, which surprised me because she only looked about 14 or 15. I lied and said that I was 15.

When I got to the recreation center I saw a pretty, petite but voluptuous little cutie. Now her age was a little more believable. But most of the girls I knew of who were her age usually kicked it with a fast, hot bunch. All of who chased older guys with cars and cream. It turned out that she did have a crew, including a cousin, like that. But she kept her own secluded distance. Her hot girl cousin, Dionne, went to the 'Haven with me.

Anyhow, she wore some white short shorts and a white halter-top, which complemented her Halle Berry figure. Totally different from the loose jeans, t-shirt, and jacket I had seen days ago. I thought to myself, 'a girl this fine has got to have a man or either she's shaking a gang of 'em. But we talked for a minute and then decided to slide to the side of the building for some private intimacy; privacy away from Ed and Keysh's girl, and also, privacy from the rest of the crowd hanging out front. She was eying me up and down in my black and gold rayon shirt and black slick jeans. I slid up on her to feel her out. Ever since I'd seen her that day I wanted to kiss and hug her, and explore her body. As we got close and started to kiss, I gently caressed her ass. It was firm, but at the same time it was so soft that it melted in my hand. She complained of something poking her, and I instantly thought of my manhood. But it was my pistol. I removed it from my waist and set it in the grass by a tree that we stood near.

She looked wide-eyed as I resumed kissing her passionately and continued my exploration of her unique physique of dynamic curves. We broke it off eventually after Keysh's girl kept complaining about us being anti-social.

But we hooked up about a week later when I talked her into leaving school early to catch the bus over to my pops house. I was bored as hell while she flicked through channels watching soap operas and BET. I tried to game her and get her in the mood by putting my hands up her shirt and down her sweats, but she kept rejecting me. She was determined not to let me smash, which would only make me more persistent. We started communicating back and forth over the next few weeks. People at school began gossiping and saying that they heard I was kicking it with Keysha Berryman; Ben Berryman's little sister. I guess he was an older nigga who was supposed to be somebody.

Anyhow, I soon heard talk of Keysh supposedly kicking it with some older nigga, her brother's boy, Ken. A few days later my phone rang. It was someone screaming some, "don't be calling my girl" shit. I cussed the sucka out and then hung up on him. Shortly after that, my phone rang again. It was Keysh, who I was furious with about this corny ass drama. She claimed that she used to kick it with the chump and that he'd decided to check her phone book while he was over seeing her brother.

She tried to apologize but I wasn't hearing it. I cussed her out too, and then I hung up on her. A few weeks went by and I was out in Hickory Ridge Apartments kicking it with my homeboy, Bruce, when some loud mouthed nigga pulled up to visit a local rat. He instantly began arguing with her before he even got out of the car. When I asked who he was, my boy Bruce said that his name was Ken. My memory light bulb came on. The nigga was still cussing the broad out. And while doing so, I caught the voice. It was Keysh's ex. I briefed my homeboy of the drama and told him to go into the crib and get me the pump. It was Bruce's O.G. homeboys, Big Greg and D.J.'s crib. They were two maniacs! I put the gauge in my three quarter length leather jacket and headed Ken's way.

I called out to him, "Hey home boy, let me holla at you."

"Who dat?" he shot back.

He knew Greg and D.J. but he didn't know me. Once I was close enough, I drew the pump on him as I watched his body freeze.

"Yo dog, you need to be more careful about whose crib you callin' and tryin' to check about a bitch who ain't even yours, nigga. Yeah, you know who I am now, huh?" I asked him.

The nigga just stood there shook, looking death straight in the eye. I gave the clown a pass because for one, it was too many people out that night, and for two, I knew the nigga got the message. Also, I informed him that if there were anymore problems then I would let him have it. He didn't want that.

The shit got back to Keysh, along with everyone else, even at the

'Haven. Keysh was on my dick like drawls. I was said to be a no nonsense nigga, light-skinned at that, and street bullying a twenty some year old man.

Keysh and I started back kicking it again, all throughout the summer. She would come out to see me at mom's place in Lexington Green. I hadn't got the pussy yet but it was cool because I was getting a little pussy here and there from other girls. I was going to make Keysh my wifey. My time was coming. I had to get on my job. I had to set my mark and enforce it. Get my eyes on the prize and keep them there. My legacy would soon begin.

CHAPTER 5: Hood Stars

The following school year began, at Mifflin High School, because from my new address at mom's they wouldn't let me attend Brookhaven. Mifflin was truly lame. Although it was infested with bitches, it just seemed too uppity and high class for me; attended by a bunch of suburban kids, both black and white.

Twin was really salty because the move took him away from his hustling grounds out west. Corky was getting even fatter now that Twin was gone. Twin was soon broke and let the blues and social ills drive him to drinking 40ounces of Old English everyday and wildin' out with Dust. I on the other hand had decided to do what I had wisely heard before, make my own moves. My big homey Freeway and I started shooting out to the Arms projects almost everyday to set up some spots to move work. Bolivar Arms was a low income housing project out on the city's east side where my man Big Free had grew up at. This was all so simple since Twin and I had just got kicked out of Mifflin for the school year for fighting, inducing panic, and inciting a riot.

Twin had had a beef with some lame named Darryl because the nigga was trying to mack on his girl out in the Gahanna suburbs. A girl Twin had met at the mall and fell for a short while back.

However, we were grateful to get expelled from Mifflin; a.k.a. Lameville! Although I did take a liking to the chocolate brown, female counselor there, I was so glad to be out of there. I could've sworn that the sexy old broad wanted to come in for a threesome the day she took us home after the expulsion. I think she felt 20 years younger chauffeuring us home that day in her shiny gold Lexus. We were two young and vulgar, sculpted thugs. She wanted it, no doubt.

Once this bullshit surpassed and Free and I got our shit rolling out in the projects, everything was sweet. We would take our little breaks and kick it out at mom's house with Twin and Dust. We would buy liquor and weed for the weekend and invite chicks over; groups at a time. We even threw a big party in late January for Dust and Free's birthday at the Residence Inn. We kept fly little rides that we would constantly buy and sell. Nothing fancy yet, though, just mid to late model Buicks and Olds mobiles. But sometimes we'd get geek rentals. Only from the ones with hot shit, though, like the Mustang 5.0s, the Corvettes, and the Nissan Sentras or Maximas. We felt like we were the shit. We kept a fat knot and we kept all of the neighborhood bitches on our dicks, even some of the lames that went to Mifflin would jock ride us whenever we'd shoot up to the school to pick up some of their broads. They'd stare when we pulled up knocking the latest gangster rap, rolling something different every other trip, and then finally they'd say, "Yeah, that's 'Siz-o and Free'." And no longer was the rides stolen as they were before.

I would lace Twin with some pocket money and some shoes and shit whenever I could, just as he had done for me. But I could sense that he was a little salty. I felt him, but it would get greater later. Patience was a virtue.

I hadn't seen much of Keysh since school had started back. She too had changed schools. She was now an 18 year old senior at Linden McKinley High. I had heard she had given up sports, basketball and track, since she had got her leg broke during a game against Mifflin. We eventually hooked up one night when I got her over for the weekend with an empty nest. We kicked it for a minute but she still wouldn't let me hit it. She claimed she was on her period. So for now I thought, 'fuck it'. Through the course of doing my thing, though, I would swing by her momma's house to see her every so often but I made no progress in getting the pussy. My frustration was at its peak. 'Fuck Keysh'! The bitch could go off to college or the army or wherever. I no longer had the time.

***

Summer time was coming up and my moms was forced to move, once again, because of us wildin' out in her high class project complex. We extorted people, corrupted our peers, beat up innocent bystanders, pulled guns on security and shot at them the night they tried to regulate us for beating up mom's boyfriend after they came from the bar. The clown was asking for it by trying to get brolic with my mama.

However, most of the dirt was caused by Twin and Dust. I was hardly ever around. But them niggas did shit I didn't even care to know about. I think they both had death wishes. I had heard of them robbing people at local bars, robbing young neighborhood hustlers trying to come up, and I had also heard of them hooking up with a 28 year old federal ex-con named Shahiem. The nigga's sister lived in Lexington Green with her boyfriend where Shahiem was paroled to. He was fresh out of Lewisburg for bank jacking and he was looking to recruit and corrupt some young soldiers. He had quickly got him a crack spot there in the complex, which was unheard of in this suburban area, and put Twin and Dust down with him. They came up quick, having fiends write big checks for shoes, clothes, and jewelry. They were going out of town hitting licks, and eventually they hit a bank job. But Shahiem felt the heat and split on them with all the money. Twin and Dust were salty. The Feds were all over the complex asking questions and shit. My mama was stressed like never before. Especially after my little sister, Micia, took Twin's 380 automatic to school. I guess she wanted to be expelled, too, because she was kicked out of school for the remaining two months of the school year. Not to mention mom had to go pick her up from the detention center; a place that I had frequented a number of times at just age 15.

Mom was furious at us all. She called Pop in an attempt to help her put her foot down. She was truly fed up. None of us were attending school and we stayed in some shit. Mom had found a house out west on the Hilltop where her and her lame excuse for a man would lease to own. She thought that with her joke of a man being a painter and her working for Bank 1 for 5 plus years, she had it all figured out. She would soon learn that that wasn't the case. With her bright idea and new attitude to straighten us out, we were headed west.

My moms knew Pop didn't give a fuck; he got a kick out of knowing we were putting her through hell. He had his own life; being a piece of shit. As far as I was concerned it was just a stone in my shoe. I would get back on the paper chase somehow. I had to earn. I had to meet my quota. Just like any other businessman. I was determined to make this game pay. Numero uno, me!

CHAPTER 6: Still Grinding (A New Beginning)

Here we were, finally out in the wild-wild west. Mom immediately got us enrolled into West High School. It was only two months left in the school year, so I knew I could make it for that short amount of time. On my first day there I found myself in homeroom sitting next to a light, bright, bad ass Aaliyah look alike.

"Where are you from, Cali?" She asked.

I just gave her a smirk, then said, "Naw baby, I'm from up north; the north side here in Columbus."

Because she looked at me like I meant one of the states up north. She initially thought California, though, like all of these other west side jokers because of my image: Cornrows, khakis and locs. But I thought nothing of it. To me it was just a way to dress and save money. And it was gangsta!

I asked her, "ain't this school and this side of town mostly white people? 'Cause I ain't never seen this many white people before in my life."

"Yeah, mostly white people. I've lived out west my whole life. It ain't all white people, though! It is some blacks," said Miss Aaliyah.

"Yo, what's ya name, anyway?" I asked.

"It's Ericka. Ericka Fenton. And yours?" She asked.

"Sizalino. I mean, Siz-o." I said.

"Siz-o? What's that, French?" She asked. I stared at her for a minute, then said,

"No, it's Sicilian. I'm half Italian and half Black."

She told me that she too was mixed; with a black mother and a white father. It was hard to imagine. But she was real sweet. She agreed to show me around to all of my classes. And she seemed honored doing it. Wow! I was going to have to get back at her. She was in my homeroom, so I knew I would see her everyday.

I also met a very interesting, and very cute cheerleader named, Cristalia. She was a short, petite little redbone in my History class. She was high-spirited and very uppity like a white girl. And my goodness did she have the finest thigh and calve combination I had ever seen. She was BADDD! But my mind was on some money.

A few weeks later I was sent to the principal's office for having a necklace with an Uzi emblem on it. The racist, scary bastard said that I would be suspended for wearing it. 'Fuck him, his lame ass school, and a three day suspension. There was no need for me to come back. I had work to do. My moms flipped when I got home and told her what had happened. She called them up to ask for a logical explanation. They stated that they wouldn't tolerate that sort of thing in their school. Uptight faggots! Twin eventually stopped going, too. He was hardly going in the first place. He had hooked back up with Corky out in Wedgewood where Cork put him back in the game. But Corky had blown up like nitro. He was riding old schools with hydraulics, wearing big chains and blowing big weed. Twin wasn't trippin', though. He was just glad to be back in the mix.

***

Freeway and Ed began coming out west to kick it once the summertime rolled back around. Free told me that the crack game was lovely out in the 'Arms' and that we needed to get back out on our grind. I thought, cool, let's do it. Twin was out in Wedgewood getting it under the big dogs, while I was back out in 'the hood'.

The Arms was live, and prosperous, but it was too hot. And it was too grimy. I mean, we'd clown with the local homies and pigeons, even the ones from other hoods, but the drama was heavy. O.G.s were beefing from a decade ago, the police were harassing and whooping niggas, and there were shootouts and dead bodies all throughout the project circles. It was some wild, cowboy-outlaw shit. My run of fun ended shortly after midnight on a humid night in June. It's been said many times in this game to go with your instincts; with your gut. This was just one of the few times that I wish I had. The most critical one was yet to come.

Free and I had been killin' 'em so bad that past week, running through an ounce a day, that we decided to go up to Delaware, Ohio for the night. We knew some small town rats up that way who were expecting us at their fish house. A house full of pussy! Free and I had went and got some new gear and new sneaks earlier, but fucking around in the hood all day we had got side tracked. We started drinking at Mina and Ana's barbeque that evening once we returned from the mall feeling super-duper fly. So fly that we showed our ass by spending a few hundred bucks on a half an ounce of sticky, seedless evergreen weed.

Once we started smoking that it was all over. We decided not to hit the highway, but instead go to the local hood bar, Jasmine's. I wasn't really feeling that so I told Free I was going to shoot around to my hood rat Dana's crib after I checked the spot.

When I got to Dana's I blew a sticky blunt with her and her pothead mama. And then we slid up to her bedroom where I beast fucked her and busted my nut onto her ass and back.

"Turn that fan up, it's hot as hell up in this oven." I said.

After she turned the fan up, the black ass mutt asked me to smoke another blunt. "This bitch is a Hoover," I thought. Most hood rats never get high. No matter how good the weed may be. I told her to go and take a shower first because I wanted to fuck her one more time. But of course I tricked the bitch. Once I heard the water running, I bounced. I never stayed the night anymore since I began getting 4-digit money stacks again. Dana was bad, but her black ass couldn't be trusted. And she fucked with some older nigga close to 30 who still sold rocks and who was a drunk. The clown was in love with the hoe and was known to drop by drunk at any hour of the night. And I didn't even have my strap on me. This nigga was a giant, 6'4", 250 plus pounds. I wasn't with the possible drama.

I stopped by the spot on my way Jasmine's to pick Free up. He had just paged me while I was at the spot. Lucy's crack head ass still had some of my dope but claimed she'd be done by morning. I took what she had left to go slang around at the bar. After I collected and counted my cash, I dipped.

When I got around to Jasmine's, the police were all over the lot. No wonder Free had paged me 911. Selling the rest of my rocks was not going to happen now, at least not at Jasmine's. It was back to Lucy's. I spotted Free coming out of a crowd of spectators.

"Ay yo, what the fuck is up, dog? What happened?" I asked Free.

He got in the Cutlass then said, "Niggas started scrappin' and throwin' bottles. It was Mingo 'anem fightin' wit them Long Street niggas. One of 'em started shootin' up in the air like a jackass when he got outside to his strap. He probably got his ass whooped," Free said, as he cracked up laughing.

He asked me for the sack to roll us up a blunt as we drove away from the bar. I should've jumped on the highway and headed west, but instead I told Free to hold on for a few more ticks until we shot around to Lucy's to drop off the little bit of work I had. And then he could roll up. I drove through the project circles to see if I saw Marty or Danny Boy, but they were nowhere to be found. 'Fuck it', I just shot back around to Lucy's to let her get rid of what I had left. Damn, I wanted all of my money before I went in. Greed!

I looked over to see Free passed out and then back at the road to see a police cruiser headed towards me. Once I passed him to turn right onto Atchison Avenue, I saw him bust a U-turn. "Fuck", I thought. Once I completed my turn and stopped in front of Lucy's to get out, he pulled behind me with his lights flashing. As we got out at the same time he walked towards me as I began walking towards Lucy's door.

"Hey man, did you know you had your bright lights on?" He asked me.

I eased closer to Lucy's door as I replied, "Nah, did I? Damn, my bad about that. I didn't even know."

I was so high, I really didn't know.

"Hey! Come here, buddy. How old are you?" He asked as he quickly walked towards me.

As soon as my instincts said to run he grabbed my Pirates jersey and wrestled me to the ground. I quickly got back up and tussled with him where I slung him to the ground, causing him to break his flashlight. He was a persistent, energetic little Robocop. As I tried to run he jumped me again. Once he got me down this time he grinded my face into the street. I thought, 'fuck it', I'm beat. There was no further need to resist. He found the 4 grams of crack that I had, and then he radioed for backup.

Backup arrived in less than a minute where they put me in the back of their cruiser to ask me 50 questions. I was too high. And so was Free, because he was still asleep when the police banged on the passenger side window. They got a kick out of it, too. He finally woke up as they pulled him out of the car and searched him. They realized that he was clean and of age, so they let him go.

I was salty because I was headed downtown to the detention center for some bullshit. I hoped like crazy that they weren't going to try and keep me for a permanent stay. It was summertime and I had big plans. Maybe Free was right about out west being a goldmine. I would have to do my research when I got out. Hopefully it would be soon. I would have to make a power move now that I was exposed to the laws out in the Arms. The first step was getting out, though. And then I could proceed with my plans.

CHAPTER 7: A West Side Goldmine

A few weeks drug by before I was finally released. Mom came down to the detention center and pleaded at my hearing, as she had done so many other times, for me to be released. She swore to keep me out of trouble, so they put me on non-reporting probation. When I got home I was given a disciplinary speech by my pops. He tried to spit some senseless noise to me that I was not feeling.

Like every other hustler or criminal, I thought I had the game down packed to a tee. And this was just a careless mistake on my behalf. I was slipping, but it would not happen again. But who Pops really needed to be having a talk with was my moms and my little fast ass sister. She needed a foot in her ass, for real. I listened for nearly a half an hour while Pop shot off his nonsense and vile threats. I half ass acted like I was listening and that I understood, so Pop finally left. I instantly popped in Carlito's Way. I had been dying to see it. It was one of the videos that mom and Twin had gotten from Blockbuster for the weekend. It would help me to marinate and gather my thoughts. I had to gather a plot for some currency.

A few minutes into the movie the phone rang. I picked up, "Hello."

"What's up jailbird?" It was Free.

"Yo, what's good, dog? Yeah, I'm finally out of that bitch. I wish I was 18 like yo ass so I could've bonded right out. The police was clownin' you that night, nigga." I told Free.

"Yeah, I was high as hell. Fuck it, though," he said.

"Well, you know I ain't fuckin' around out there no more. I'm about to see what I can make shake out here. You feel me?" I asked Free.

"Aw yeah, I told you it's some cheese out west. And you can serve 'em scandalous. A nigga can make like $2,000 off a ounce!" said Free.

"Yeah, no doubt. Well shit, you know I'm only a few hours out, so I'ma kick back and watch this flick, 'Carlito's Way', then shower and eat me somethin'. I'll holla back at you tomorrow," I said.

"Alright my nigga, I'm gone," Free said.

"Peace!" I shot back.

I sat for a while looking at the tube, then I thought about Keysh. I hadn't seen or talked to her in a few weeks. So, I figured I'd call her up.

"Hello. May I speak to Keysh? Yo Keysh, wusup?" I said once she got on the line. We rapped for a few minutes as I told her of my arrest and release. She spoke of how she had told me about my activities out there and also how she was salty because I didn't go with her to her senior prom last month. She had agreed to pay for the tux and all, but I wasn't on no sensitive prom shit. I later found out that she went with some lame named Ron, who Twin used to kick it with and bully at Brookhaven, when I went over to her mother's house and saw the picture on the wall. Anyhow, we concluded the call with her telling me that she was coming to see me the next day.

The following day came and I got dressed around noon in a tan khaki shirt and pants, and some black shell top Adidas. I had my aunt braid my hair the night before after I showered. Her worrisome ass lived down the street. And she was always begging for a few 'illegal' dollars for cigarettes or beer.

Twin had finally fell through the night before by about midnight while I was dozing off on the couch. We chopped it up about my events out in the 'Arms' and how Wedgewood and the whole west side was a lick. A goldmine! I perceived it as the right move and had my mind made up. Now it was just about making it happen.

The phone rang and it was Keysh telling me she was on her way. It was wild when I thought about it, because here she was 18years old with no car, but I had talked her into catching the bus from up north to out west. She had taken the bus before to see me, but it was local, and on her same side of town. She had even walked to see me at Pops house before. I guess she didn't mind since she was a track star with legs like a stallion. And also, I knew she loved the attention of being seen. A flirt and a tease she was.

I was sitting on the porch sipping a cold 40 ounce of Old Gold and bumping 'Top Authority' when I saw Keysh coming up the street. I got hard at the sight of her. She was sporting some orange daisy dukes and a green and orange halter-top; and that mean ass walk. Fuck a dime, she was a quarter! She was 5' 7" tall, 135lbs, with those chinky eyes on her pretty face and mocha chocolate skin. She was small framed with C-cup breasts and a firm, fat ass. And she had a super small waist that made it hard to fit her jeans. She could've easily been a model. I had only been locked up a few weeks, but it seemed like it had been a few months once I saw Keysh. I was going to try like hell to hit the pussy.

As she walked up to the porch I greeted her with a hug and a soft kiss on the cheek because of her lip-gloss. I caught a few eyes staring our way as I briefly observed my street from left to right before we entered the house. I put on some music that was a little softer once we got inside. My girl, Sade!

My moms was gone to a friend's house, Twin was making moves, and my little sister Micia's fast ass was supposedly at her girl, Baby's. Still, I didn't appear too anxious or out of my hook up. Instead I was player, and just laid back. Although I indeed wanted to fuck, I was maturing. At nearly 16 I had had my share of pussy. I was now prepared to chill and kick it on an adult like level with my future wifey.

We sat at the dining room table having a typical conversation while I flirted every 5 minutes by trying to fondle Keysh from one body part to the next.. During which she'd sat on my lap. She would jump up to retreat back to her seat once my groping got her too hot. But things settled down after a while where she told me of her scholarship to Central State next fall. She said she'd postponed it for 14 more months because she wanted to have some money saved for a car and living expenses. She had started a receptionist job where her mother worked. We spoke about her virginity (still) and she stated that she wanted to be married first. I wasn't trying to hear that, but I didn't speak on it.

Just as she had proceeded with her usual bullshit about me supposedly fucking dozens of hoes, Micia and Baby walked in. Baby was a fine little, super light, but too young cutie; and also had heavy a crush on me. She eyed me for a second, and then gave Keysh a once over. Keysh caught the vibe and gave a sassy sigh as she rolled her eyes. Micia saw Keysh and instantly rushed her for a hug before even saying hello. She sort of intervened on my visit with Keysh spitting her childish gossip to her like she'd known her for a lifetime. When in reality, she barely knew her at all. Sill though, I guess it was the connection she felt from me telling her and my moms so much about Keysh and them feeling that I cared for her.

After about five to ten minutes of Micia running her mouth, mom walked in. Now it was really about to be some feminine, 'Waiting to Exhale' shit going on. Mom came to the table all high-spirited and got settled into a seat to converse after saying hello to Keysh and, briefly to Baby. Mom went on and on about how she knew I loved Keysh because the way I spoke of her and so on. And like how I needed to stay out of trouble and go back to school. Keysh didn't help the situation. She giggled with them and intently listened as they spoke. Embarrassing me for the most part, but it was cool. This was my mama. And maybe they needed this one on one. Or two on one should I say.

I finally dragged Keysh away into the living room. I was feeling the buzz from the malt liquor so it wasn't easy to stay focused. We picked up the conversation where we had left off at about the future and Keysh's plans for college, and marriage. I told her that I had some plans of my own. She gave me a sideways look and then pursed her lips. I stared back wide-eyed with a grin.

We debated over the next twenty minutes about going to a movie. But after bullshitting for a little while longer, it was too late. I wasn't feeling a movie no how. I had style and class, and having no whip was having no class. Even at age 15 I couldn't try taking a girl on a date without a car. I called down to my aunt Angie's to see if Dust was there to run Keysh home. It was too late for me to allow her to get on the COTA bus. Although she had truly loosened up after talking with my moms, more than ever before, she still insisted on going home.

Dust pulled up out front in his champagne Chevette and blew the horn. Keysh told mom and Micia goodbye, and then we bounced. Since it was late, although it was summertime, I gave Keysh my Carhart coat to put on. With her near nakedness and being anemic, she happily accepted.

During the ride home I played quiet and buzzed, when really I was sober and in deep thought. It was time to get on my grind. I decided that night that I would never live or exist being broke. I had work to do.

We dropped Keysh off as I gave her a very sexual, exotic hug and kiss goodbye. Dust and I chopped it and talked shit on our way back out west after we got a few 40s from the gas station. I needed to get drunk for the night, but this week I'd have the green light for some greenbacks. I got back home and called Keysh. I talked dirty to her until I passed out.

CHAPTER 8: West Side Suckers

The walls were shaking and any minute now my manhood would erupt to unload a very healthy dose of life into Keysh's warm oven of love. I had her knees pinned down next to her ears, giving her my true thug passion. I shoved my tongue into the back of her throat, and I shoved my love even deeper into her guts. She whined and moaned as I exploded my massive nut. Her eyes showed me that she loved it. It was then that I knew she was mine.

"Do you wanna hit it from behind, Daddy?" She asked.

"Yeah. But give me a few minutes." I said.

"What? Boy, get the phone. It's a collect call from Free, he in the county." It was Twin. I had been dreaming all along! And damn, was it intense, I had creamed all over myself in my sleep. I sat up to grab the phone. Head spinning and still trying to gather myself, I spoke, "Yo!"

"Siz-o, wusup? Man, these mu'fuckas ran up on me in Whitney Young comin' from Gina's," said Free.

"Oh yeah? So what they got you down there on?" I asked him.

"Drug possession! Some lil' shit, though," he said.

It was fucked up because I didn't even have the few hundred dollars he needed for his bail. After we spoke briefly about that, he said he was going to try to get his bitch Shenay to gather up the money by the weekend. I told him that I had him and to just be cool.

"Man, this is some bullshit. Somebody had to have told on me, because I ain't have no warrants," Free said.

It turns out that it could've been the bitch Gina's old man, who smoked primos, or possibly a geek who Free had beat for $20 that evening when he sold him a rock off of the ground. Free was always doing dumb shit like that. Like the time, back about 2 months ago when he saw Charlie Mack, a local project geek, cashing his county check at the corner store and waited outside to mug him for his ends in broad daylight. Free followed him down Sin Clair Avenue telling him to come up off of his ends or else. Charlie continued to play dumb and stubborn, so Free picked up a broomstick and started to whoop Charlie across the head and back. After it broke down to about 8-10 inches, and little Turkey stole him, some local rats rode by screaming, "Y'all can't even drop him!"

Wanting to show off and prove them wrong, Free hit him with a left hook and dropped him cold, using all of his six foot, 200 plus pound frame. He went through his pockets to find nothing but his I.D. We later found out that the ends were in his sock. The shit was funny, though. Me and the homies cracked the fuck up as we watched from across the street.

"Yo dog, the shit just said 60 seconds, get back at me by Thursday or Friday to let me know what ya broad talkin' about. My nigga, you know what I'm about to do, so never the less I got you. Holla back!" I said.

"Alright, peace," he spat back.

Damn, I thought. Now my ace lieutenant was locked up after I had just got out less than 48 hours ago. I had to get dressed and make some moves. Fuck! And clean this mess up in my pants. I handled my business and then headed to Wedgewood projects.

When I got there I instantly got some work from both, Twin and Cork. With Twin my dope was on the house, but I was expected to pay Cork back, which I could've said 'fuck him', but my morals said 'pay him'. Cork was a cool dude, too. I planned on going far in this world, and in it, a man needed solid alliances and good, trustworthy credibility. Now big Cork didn't know that I had got broke off by Twin, but no knowledge left the conscious empty.

Twin and Cork were on at least a few ounces so they had their own spots and personal clientele. I was stuck with the block, or more less, the building. 809 Wedgewood Drive was the notorious, on fire building that had cranked for years. What I soon figured out was that as many dudes who were hustling out here, everyone pretty much had their own spot or clientele. The building was headache money. Although sometimes it was good money, it usually resorted to being made risky and packed with too many hustlers. Plus the old lady who stayed downstairs would sometimes call the rental office. And it was rumored that she would even call the cops.

So, I soon found me a geek with runner potential and, who seemed to be like a money magnet because all the fiends would cling to him. I realized that he resided with a chubby young mother of four, his baby's mama, Jeanette, who originally just smoked weed but he eventually got her hooked on primo joints. I immediately made their apartment my spot. It was beautiful because none of these other local niggas had ever set up shop here. It was real low-key. I quickly charmed big Jeanette. I was young and attractive to her, I had got real cool with her kids, and I kept some chronic.

She would cook for me and braid my hair from time to time. And for a big girl she was pretty, but because of her weight and new bad habit, it wouldn't happen. I could never, ever fuck her! In all of my years of hustling, I'd never tricked on no kind of addict pussy. And it would hold true for the future.

My geek, Dino, was a headache; to Jeanette and myself. He was always geeking and begging even when no business fell through. But for the most part I'd tolerate it because he knew how to go out and get that money. He finessed the crack hoes and scared the male fiends, being six foot three and two hundred pounds. He was a black, ugly, toothless cocksucker with gingivitis. The man's breathe smelled straight like shit from the toilet. He truly had dragon breath.

After about a month, things were lovely. I would catch rides back and forth from Wedgewood to the Hilltop, steady stacking my ends. Twin started slacking and sometime hustling. He had recently realized that his troublesome girlfriend, Stephanie, was 4 months pregnant. Now that he was comfortable and moms would allow Stephanie to stay at the house, he just stayed at home smoking trees and drinking most of the time. Meanwhile, I had Skins and Dust running with me out in Wedgewood. I never did hear back from Free. Oh well, I still had to do me.

Anyhow, Skins ended up getting him a spot on the Hilltop at old man Bruce's. He had hustle and potential. Now Dust on the other hand just wanted to drink and be menacing. He was still my family, though. I had mad respect for him. He was my elder no doubt, but he was also loyal and thorough to the bone. And he was always good to have around. The guy was a fucking lunatic! He was known growing up as a knockout artist in his Main Street neighborhood. The guy earned respect off of that alone.

Well, here it was mid July, as hot as fish grease, and we were all unusually kicking it at mom's house. It was starting to get dark as we sat on the porch winding down while the music played. We were all high and buzzed; Dust, our homey Big Troy, Twin, who was inside with his baby's mama, and myself. Skins had just busted a move over to the spot.

Moms and Micia were also inside the house. Since mom's old man had bounced, leaving her with a high house note and some false dreams, she had been lonely as ever. Finding the bar and marijuana as her way to deal with the pain. So, often times she'd party with us.

Troy and Dust began to slap box. I guess they were jazzed up on the bud and felt like clowning. Dust was especially a fool when he got buzzed up. While I was watching them clown around I spotted a blue old school Chevy pull up in front of the house, and just post in the middle of the street. Dust and Troy stopped their goofing off to peep out the unknown ride. I stepped off the porch and spat out, "Who dat?"

One of the jokers asked, "Is Samicia in there?"

I put a mug on my face and said, "Nigga, who is you comin' over here at ten o'clock at night for my lil' sister? She 13!"

The clown speaking from the passenger's seat vividly looked familiar. I couldn't place him, though. "Oh, we ain't know that, dog. That ain't what she told us," the clown said.

"Well, yeah nigga, she 13. So ride out before I light y'all shit up," I barked.

The fools sat still there, glancing back and forth at each other, and then towards me. My flip mode rage kicked in. I pulled out the Ruger at about the same time Dust upped the 357. The Mossberg was sitting on the porch behind the couch, as it always was when we were chilling outside after dark. The lames slowly pulled off, which made me really want to let loose to motivate their ass. I would've if it wasn't my mama's house. Boy oh boy was my trigger finger itching.

I went into the house to let Micia's fast ass have it and to tell mama of her activities. Lying to niggas and portraying to be a little hoe, she was tripping. At 13 she was thick with a body and a cute face. I reminded myself to watch out for her.

***

The following week we were out in Wedgewood over at Corky's mama's apartment when I finally met my connect, Mike P. A.K.A. the man! He was only around 21. He had somewhat known of me as I had known of him. He had known Cork and his older brother Jeff for a few years now, but he had only been acquainted with Twin for about a year or so. It was funny because he didn't seem like the kind of nigga who was on bricks. But then again, at the time, what did I know. However, this guy dressed plain and rode plain in Pontiacs and Buicks. It seemed weird, but that's how it was.

We chopped it for about an hour in the parking lot, and then we exchanged hip numbers. Prices would definitely be cheaper now, but more importantly, this was an establishment of future longevity. I was looking for a connection to be large and affiliated. A man needed alliances in this business. Making it happen and doing it BI (BIG) was my mission.

While walking back over to Jeannette's I was in deep thought about the conversation I had with P. The nigga was something serious. He was the kind of guy that I needed to get close to. He said he saw potential in me that Cork and Twin lacked at our young age. Patience was the key, though. As I passed 809 where all of the niggas hung out at during the day, small-time grinders and even big-timers, I stopped to chop it and hit a few blunts. Everybody started oohing and aahing at some hottie coming up the street talking about, 'Ooh, here she comes'. She was bad! As I looked closer, though, my memory light came on. Oh shit, it was Miss Aaliyah; or better known as, Ericka. I gradually crossed the street to walk with her. All of them niggas saw this and their mouths dropped in shock. I smirked inside. As I slid up on her, she stared for a minute then spoke, "Hey Siz-o, wusup?"

"I can't call it, wusup wit you, Miss Aaliyah? You stay out here or what?" I asked.

"Yeah, I stay right here in 810 with my mom and my little brother. What about you, do you stay out here? I see you quit coming to school. Or you moved."

I smiled charmingly, and then said, "Well, you know, school wasn't working out for me. I'm cool, though. The only thing I miss about that school is seeing you." She smiled. "And naw, I don't stay out here, I just visit," I said.

"Hmm, so that's who you come out here to visit is them?" She gestured to across the street.

"Something like that. I see that they're all fans of yours," I said.

"Oh please, them fools ain't worth nobody's time."

I walked her into her apartment as we talked for about 20 minutes after I met her moms. We exchanged numbers and then I told her I had to bounce. She gave me a warm hug that sent me away hard as granite. I would definitely have to get back at her. She was light-bright, 5' 9", about 140 some pounds and stunningly beautiful with long jet-black hair. She had small breasts, a small waist, and a fat ass with big gorgeous lips. Her status was 16 and single. I had to get it.

When I got over to my spot there was a problem. Jeannette's older brother, a late twenty something year old hustler, was tripping on her about allowing me to do my thing over there. So I bounced back around to 809, but told her before I left to get at me. I didn't want to create problems for her, but if need be I would let her brother have it that one-way. And she knew that. But it was ultimately her decision. However, nothing would stop my hustle. Besides the fact of her brother having a point and me having to respect it, I think it was time to relocate anyhow. Yep, it was. The bitch did have kids.

While sitting on the porch steps chopping it with Skins, Dust, and Rose's crew, we saw the task force surrounding Bill's building across the street. That was Joe Kingsley's spot. We all instinctively split our own ways. Skins, Dust, and myself, ran down to welfare Debbie's. We were all dirty. After about an hour or two, and about 4 or 5 blunts, we went back out front. This time I left my work and my strap in Debbie's crib. It was calm and quiet out. We saw Rose 'anem walking up. They had bounced over to Miss Jackie's. We all rolled up and smoked heavy as we tried to figure out who got pinched. Old man Bill and two of Joe's little homies were arrested. The task wasn't no joke.

We saw Joe pull up with his bitch Shannon, riding his old school Nova. I guess he had heard the news and had started getting lit up when he did. They got out and walked up to politic with us. After about ten or fifteen minutes, they began arguing. She slapped him and called him a short dick bastard. We all laughed in unison. Joe caught feelings and started hollering obscenities. Some bullshit about 'fuck all of us' and claiming that we was plotting to fuck Shannon. During his jaw-jacking, a green Jetta pulled up. Bingo! It was the nigga in the blue old school. This is where I had seen him at. Tank Man was what they called him.

He stepped out and approached Joe. They was homies. I alerted Dust of their lame connection and about who the dude Tank Man might have been. I guess Dust felt he had been quiet long enough. And now that he knew this was one of the niggas from the other night at mom's house, he was ready to act a fool.

"Ay nigga, address who you talkin' about sayin' all that sucka shit," Dust said.

"Aw naw, I ain't talkin' about y'all Dust, these niggas know who I'm talkin' about," said Joe.

"Oh, okay then. As long as you ain't talkin' about my lil' brother or my nephew, then you cool," Dust spat.

Tank Man peeped us out, as I eyed him the whole time. He slid up on me pipe-riding a young killer. He apologized about the other night and swore he didn't know. I let him think it was cool. He blew a whole 50 sack of sticky green with me and my people outside of his Jetta. His status didn't impress me. Even with me being years younger I knew that I would surpass him in this game soon enough.

CHAPTER 9: Missing Keysh

It was early August, and the day before Twin and my 16th birthday. We'd arranged to have a big party at mom's place. I had got a call from Free telling me that he had been out for about a month now. I thought to myself, 'Why was he just now calling?', but I didn't speak on it. He spat out through the course of the conversation that he had been laid up with his monster mutt, Shenay, and that she was a few months pregnant. Wow, what a hex! That was a moral code of mine, never to have babies by a mutt. It was simple to avoid, 'Don't fuck 'em!' The irony was that Free had (bad) bitches. He was a pretty boy, lady's man. He was brown skinned with good hair; a G-Money look alike. I remember our days at Club Underground just like it was yesterday.

After chopping it for a minute, and telling Free of my minor two month success, he told me that he was going to fall through tomorrow night.

The following night came and the house was soon packed. Twin and I were dressed in similar fashion. I wore a black Atlanta Falcons t-shirt, grey Dickie pants, with black and grey Jordans. Twin rocked a brown Texas Longhorns t-shirt, tan Dickie pants, with black and brown

Jordans. It was funny because growing up and even now, people would say it was hard to tell us apart. We were un-identical twins! At the present time, he wore his hair short and faded, looking more like an angry Puerto-Rican than a bi-racial nigga. We both had the angry Ice Cube eyes, but I rocked the long plats.

Everyone was soon faded off of sticky, seedless weed, although a few people brought some commercial; and from an assortment of liquors and beer. I don't ever remember it being a fucking cake. Micia had a few of her little fast friends over, who all wanted to fuck me and Twin. Dust and Skins, along with some of my other aunts and uncles were there. Mom was as joyful and cheerful as she could be on her two twin boys birthday. Corky had slid through hitting switches with his big brother Jeff and a few of his fine female cousins. Big Free eventually showed up to show some love. His monster mutt and her sister had dropped him off, reminding him before they left that they'd be back in an hour or so to pick him up. 'What the fuck? How lame!' My main man, P., also made an entrance. My brother and I had got real close to his older brother Tone, too. He was as cool as a fan, kind of the O.G., uncle type. And he was a maniac. At 27 he had already beat a body and had had his share of drama. He only stayed a few blocks away, so we'd always be over at his spot toasty high. All he ever did was work on cars and, smoke and sell big weed.

Pops had showed up late with an estranged look in his eye; a look that I was very familiar with. I suspected he was getting high. I shook him off of my mind as he went on and on with moms about them getting back together and that kind of shit. I was sitting on the porch zoning out, feeling like Tony Montana when he was at his desk high, previously before his demise. At first I couldn't figure out what it was. Then it dawned on me when I saw Twin with his baby mama, Stephanie. There was emptiness inside of me, and it was Keysh. I hadn't seen or talked to her for a while now. Why, I didn't even know. We were too different.

It just wouldn't work. For about a year now I had been more persistent with her than anything in my life. Anyhow, she'd be off to college soon. It was time to let go. I would disguise my pain with currency. I had to get on my job.

"Baby what's the matter?" It was my mama speaking to me. My facial expression always gave way to my emotions; with my mama they did.

"Hey, ma! Uh, I'm good. What's Pop talkin' about?" I asked, trying to throw her off.

"I'm not thinkin' about that man. I tried to talk to him about your sister, and he's going on and on about me and him," Mama said.

I wanted to mention to her that pop looked high, but I kept it to myself. I walked into the house where there was major commotion. I was relieved to see that there were no problems, but that everyone was preparing to shoot out to the Continent Cinema to see 'Menace to Society'. I was definitely game for that. And looking at Micia's home girls, I was game to fuck one of them, too, especially Erica, because she had 'body'. She had tits, ass, and hips! Baby was pretty, but she hadn't quite filled out yet.

We all grouped up in different rides and bounced. The movie was gangsta, no doubt. We shot to the Waffle House and got our grub on. Afterwards, P. dropped me off at the crib. We had one of our many talks on the ride back out west. I was being bred to be a bread winner. My 16th birthday was now over. A lot would change by next August. I would use a whole year to test myself on my success. I was truly looking forward to it. It was time to hit the next level. I was ready.

CHAPTER 10: A Hustler's Focus

Out of the blue mom's ex- old man showed up. He had some biker looking guy with him who he claimed was his co-worker. And who was also, a good friend. I sat on the porch as I listened to them talk in the front room. He eventually got to his point when he told mom his friend was looking for rock; from her sons. I peeped it out when they walked up and the lame said, "Hey man, I'm glad you're over here."

Mom called me in the house to tell me of her ex's surprising request. I told dude to walk over to my spot down the street because I didn't want to conduct any possible transactions at mom's house. I had relocated to the Hilltop because I, along with a few other hustlers, had gotten too hot out in Wedgewood. They supposedly had pictures of me, but no name. S.W.A.T. had hit two more times since they hit Joe's spot, hoping to get the 'light-skinned guy with the plats'. Or so I heard. I did, however, keep my worthy clientele. I just had them hit me on the hip now, where I'd bounce around meeting them at different locations. Shit, I had dope fiends who worked at General Motors, at Bank 1, as construction workers.….and the list went on and on.

However, I had two questions for this white boy once I got him to the spot. First, I asked him was he the police, as I had Dust frisk him. Next, I asked him what he had. $40, he said. I served him, and soon after that we began to deal constantly. The candy was so good that he started bringing another co-worker with him. This geek got so strung out, so fast; he sold me his maroon 1990 Buick LeSabre for a quarter of an ounce. He originally asked for $1500, but his addictive habit made him submit. The ride was clean, too; with low miles. He claimed it was a gift passed down from his parents.

The first dope fiend yank' followed in his partner's footsteps by selling me his blue, 2-doored 77 Cadillac Deville. I copped some 15-inch wire rims with the vogues for the Buick from Skins Hilltop homey Lamont. And I had Dust steal me a nigga's whole sound system out of a Regal from up north. A few times I went to cop from my man, P., he was on some salty shit. It was revealed when I traded him the Caddy for a black, 77 Cutlass and said that I was going to buy some gold shoes for it. He was totally against being hot. And stupid! So I agreed with his philosophy and put my ideas to the side. I even sold him the Buick for a pack, which I had him put up for when I needed it or wanted it. I trusted him; he was my nigga. Plus, the Cutlass came with a booming system, so I was cool with that.

***

Mom had us going to North Adult Education Center to get caught up on credits because Twin and I weren't feeling West High School. Or any school for that matter. However, I attended North Adult for a while to floss my rides and game on some bitches, but after a month or so, it played out. It interfered with my business. In this life, you flew straight or you were a dirty bird. If you got it twisted, then that's when you got fucked in the game.

The winter banged so hard, I was running through a quarter key of rock every week. Sometimes 2 weeks. But I was supplying Twin, Dust, Skins, and even a few of his homies. I sold them all work and small amounts of weight, cutting into my profit. The problem was, as it was with every nigga with a good heart, I had too many friends. I was supplying weed and drinks every weekend when Twin and Free and everybody would want to kick it with bitches and get hotel suites.

However, I kept at least 10 stacks with P., no matter what. At 16, I tried to stay focused like a 30 year old business man. P. was always drilling me with the game. Sometimes we'd ride and have all day long talks, and kick it with the older crowd in pool halls or at the car lot. P. had an old man with a dealer's license open him up a legitimate car lot. That's when he told me about having more than one hustle. And also, he warned me of getting high and losing focus. He tried to keep me separated from my peers; mentally that is. He put me on a separate level than them. And they all saw that. They didn't like it, but they respected it. Just like everyone else that I had met through P., including the older niggas and bitches. P.'s sister Nikki, who was a few years younger than him, was always trying to seduce me. She was bad and I don't think P. really would've minded, but I steered clear of her out of respect. That was something I quickly learned about this guy, he was not an emotional sucka. He really could give two less fucks about a bitch. He was a real nigga! And he knew that his sister was a grown woman, with a child, and that I was clearly a mature young man.

We'd often go fuck with lil' bitches he knew, and he would straight set 'em out; for me or any of the homies. I mean, bad bitches, too! I would eventually do the same for him, returning the favor in a major way with a redbone, high school cheerleader.

The winter had soon come to an end. And I had set my mark. Having dope and game could get you really connected. I had a guy at Vance's gun store, a guy at Westland Mall's Footlocker, a bitch at Donato's Pizza, and I kept some professional check writers. I even had a guy at Sun T.V. I was kicked back at mom's smoking a sticky swisher, waiting on dinner to get done, when Micia told me that some girl wanted me on the phone.

"Yo, wusup? Who dis?" I spat.

"It's Keysha. What you doin'?" She asked.

I was in total shock. What kind of games was this girl on? The last few times that I tried to call her, I was shitted on. I was told that she wasn't there or not available. Her evil ass step dad had picked up the last time that I called and told me that she didn't want to talk to me and for me not to call back. 'Fuck 'em both', I thought.

However, according to her, someone supposedly called and told her step dad that that they just wanted to fuck her; saying their name was Siz-o. Some hating ass dick sucker, I guess. But she claimed that she didn't believe it was me.

So, here she was, 6 months later, calling me out of the blue after I had damn near forgotten about her. We sat and talked for a little while then she mentioned coming to see me. I thought, 'Uh-oh, here we go again'. Valentine's Day was coming up that week, so I just told her to page me when it was convenient for her. I gave her my hip number and she gave me hers, then we hung up.

I passed mom the swisher as I told her of Keysh's strange story and deranged mysteriousness. Mom was a lot happier these days. I had bought her a '92 Grand Am and kept her bills on point. Twin, however, was in constant conflict with Stephanie. She had had their son and had moved in. Not all the way in, because she had one more year of high school, but you may as well have said so. And Dust kept drama coming mom's way either with his bad ass pit bull, Duke, or the Franklin County Sheriffs serving warrants for him. Every time I turned around I was bailing him out for some bullshit.

My moms had got her a special someone, P.'s brother, Big Tone. I was happy for her, but cautious. This was my mama. Pops hated it. It was a real a shame what he had resorted to. But life went on.

***

A few days later I got a strange page. It was Keysh, all cheerful and excited. She told me that her sister was dropping her off. I said cool and I'd be home. I didn't even mention that I had two whips sitting out front. She'd find out soon enough. Besides, I didn't know how much of her shit I was going to take. I had grown tired of it long ago. It was nearly a year later, so I would give her the benefit of the doubt and see where her head was. If I felt the need to then I'd tell her to go fuck herself.

Meanwhile, I got dressed in a white North Carolina t-shirt with the matching windbreaker, some Pelle Pelle blue jeans and the Carolina blue and white Jordans. Hearing the knock at my door, I lit my blunt before I answered it.

"Keysh! Wusup, lady? What you got there?" I asked, noticing that she had her hands full.

She stepped inside and said, "Here, this is for you; and this, and this!"

I grabbed the balloons and set them on the table. Then I took the card and the Original Cookie box and sat down to open them.

"Damn Keysh, this is a pleasant surprise, I must say. You're far too kind," I said.

I was truly shocked. This girl was something else. This was definitely the next level. During our 18 months of knowing each other we had never bought gifts for one another.

"Hey, ma, look at what Keysh bought for me! Ain't she sweet?" I said to my moms, as she came down the steps.

"Aw, yes she is. Hi, baby!" Mom said to Keysh, as she read the balloons.

I opened up the box. It read, 'Happy Valentine's Day, SIZ-O! I love you!' Then I opened the card and read it. Still slightly overwhelmed, I broke off a piece of the cookie and bit into it. Maybe Keysh was going to be my wifey after all. She was mysterious, but I would figure her out. I was persistent like that when it came to what I wanted. I wouldn't jump the gun with her just yet, though. Patience was a virtue. I was almost for certain that I had her now, so I'd just gradually wheel her in. The pussy was now on marinate-mode. And I'd eat soon enough.

She sat on my lap smiling and giggling as she, mom and I talked for a while. I was as hard as steel with her soft, heart-shaped ass on my thighs. And I was getting nauseous from her seductive scent, 'White Diamonds'.

Mom was delighted to see her baby boy happy and in love. In truth I was her favorite child. I showed her the most love and respect. My other two siblings didn't really like it, but it was what it was. Mom smiled and spoke joyfully with us as we carried on for a good hour or so. Then, finally she said she was going around to Tone's to chill and get a sack of green. She smirked to ensure that she would not pay for it. My mama was really something. She was 34, acting 24; which she didn't look 34 at all. She told me and Keysh goodbye, then grabbed her keys and bounced. My mind began racing with thoughts. Damn, I didn't even have a bedroom! All three were occupied by mom, Micia, and Twin. I really didn't need one until now. I was hardly ever there, so when I was, I slept on the couch.

The basement was clean, but not bedroom clean. It was more of a lounging type of atmosphere; for social gathering. It had a couch set, a card table with chairs, the washer and dryer area, and a spot where my full-size waterbed used to be at that was now occupied by just my dresser and stand up closet. And of course, the stereo set.

I decided to take her down for a brief tour; where we could get relaxed and I could feel her out. Or perhaps, fill her up. My pager kept beeping so much within the hour I soon had a low cell. It was one of my homies needing some work and two of my exclusive fiends. The first time they rang me I called them back and told them to go across the street to my spot. That was over an hour ago while we were still upstairs. Going to the spot, minus me, meant having to deal with Dust; which they didn't like. They were always salty because he wouldn't serve them big enough rocks. Well, fuck them and their crying complaints. I was tied in a knot with Keysh. Or at least, I wished.

"Don't you want to call them back?" Keysh asked.

"Naw baby, I can't help them right now," I said.

She had that doubtful look on her face like I was full of shit. I played the stereo as we briefly discussed her going away to Central State in 6-7 months. I tried to speak positively about it, but in a selfish reality I wasn't too thrilled about it. I knew that if it happened, under the circumstances, I would probably never see her again. Talking about it made her a little uneasy, too, I noticed.

After we sat dwelling in our own thoughts for a minute, we began to kiss and hug. I tried to explore every inch of her body with my hands as we grinded hard against each other. It was about to go down! I felt that, although she was still a little shy, she was ready. I unbuttoned and unzipped her jeans, then raised her shirt to suck, lick, and caress her 38 C-cup sized breasts. I could hear her moaning and taking deep breaths. Here they were, her beautiful, brown 'Hershey Kisses'. I went to work. But my session was cut short by my annoying pager and finally by Skins entering the house hollering my name down the steps. Class was concluded for now, but I wasn't trippin'. Because I knew now that it was mine. It was just a matter of when I wanted it. Soon enough!

After seeing what Skins wanted (some work), I handled it then got back to Keysh. It was getting late, and after sitting quietly in the living room for a short while, she mentioned calling her sister to come and get her; saying that she would probably bitch about it, though. I told her not to trip, because I had a whip outside.

"Ha? You ain't got no license," she said.

"So what, don't jinx me! Let's roll," I told her.

She procrastinated for a minute by taking bites off of my cookie and fidgeting with things on the coffee table. She wasn't ready to go. Finally, she got up and I told her thanks for the sweet gifts, and then we exited the house and jumped in my grey Cutlass. I cranked the music up as we pulled off. It felt good riding with my boo shotgun. She was so damn fine! What was wild was that she was one of those women who acted like she didn't know that she was fine. But she definitely knew it. She just didn't show it. I liked that, though.

Staring into her eyes at a stop-light, I thought about one of the many dreams I had had of her. The one when I was called to the hospital where she was conceiving my baby girl. The light had changed; causing me to snap back into reality. We pulled up to her crib and sat there for a few minutes saying our goodbyes. I tongue kissed her passionately before letting her get out. Which she didn't want to do, it seemed. I had her.

"Oh, Keysh! Here," I said, handing her a fifty dollar bill.

"I don't want that," she replied.

"Why not? It's for Valentine's Day!"

"That's alright, babe. You keep it. Just call me tomorrow. You gon' call me?" She asked with a cute, half smile.

"No doubt!" I said, pocketing the Grant.

"Okay. Page me, alright?"

"Alright, cool!"

"Can I have another kiss?" She asked, with mesmerizing eyes. I gave her another deep, long, passionate kiss. She wanted it.

"Okay, bye-bye! I'll talk to you tomorrow?" She questioned.

"Bye, Keysh," I said, shaking my head yes. I watched her go in, and then pulled off. This girl was definitely special. She had captured my heart. I was in love. And I was certain that she was, too. Man, I was rock hard. I'd have to give it to her soon. It was coming!

CHAPTER 11: Bagging Keysh

Spring was, thus far, a breeze. I was working the west, while Keysh was working her 9-5. I had been busy trying to put new moves down. I had started to fuck with my man P.'s nigga, Nuts, on the green side; just some small shit, like a few pounds at a time. The problem with Nuts was that he smoked like a train. The nigga got money but he always wanted to party. He had just recently come home from Desert Storm in that Gulf War bullshit. He was a little older than my man, P. He was closer to Big Tone P.'s age.

Nuts had invited me over to his girl Hedricka's for a cookout a week ago. She stayed a few blocks from mom's house. In the last month or so, I hadn't spent much time with Keysh. And I could tell that she felt neglected. She had come over a few times to take Micia to the mall, trying to be in my mix. I wasn't fucking with no bitches, though. The truth was that I was chasing money more than I was some pussy. The money really made my dick hard. I was setting my mark, establishing a name and identity for myself. Affiliation was the key, and I would soon be made into my click. I was making all the right connections. I began to handle so much that I would have to have P. hold more money and weight for me. I couldn't keep but so much stashed at mom's house. I needed me a crib of my own. I thought of Keysh. No. She would be leaving in a few months. I needed me a good bitch, though, and she was just that. Last week she saw me counting out nearly ten stacks. I didn't know if that was good, but a few hours later while she was at the City Center Mall with Micia, she called to ask me what I wanted from Wendy's and what shoe size I wore. She had bought me the new Deion Sanders. She was surprising me all the time.

It was a late Friday afternoon when she called me, saying that she had just got off of work and was it cool to have her cousin Dionne bring her by. I knew Dionne had the hots for Twin, so I told them to come on through. I got spiffed up with a shower, and then I jumped into some blue Dickies with a red, white, and blue Braves jersey. Oh, and my new Deion's, courtesy of Keysh. I had just copped me an 86 gram Gucci Link, which put the icing on my smooth appearance. I felt like a cool million.

When I came downstairs I saw Baby sitting on the couch eyeing me. She was waiting on mom and Micia to go to Blockbuster and Kroger.

"Siz-o, let us get some money," said Micia.

"What? Who's us?" I asked.

"Well, let me get some money. I meant me and ma. We're going to Blockbuster and to the grocery store."

"Girl, how much you talkin' bout?"

"Umm, I don't know."

I gave her fifty bucks. Mom had money. The fifty was for her.

I walked out onto the porch where Corky and Twin was. I told him that Dionne's hot ass was bringing Keysh over. I joked with him for a minute about hitting her off, which he responded back by asking had I hit Keysh off yet. I felt like Tre' off of 'Boyz in the Hood', and like Twin was Cube. I hadn't hit. Although I felt that that was personal, I shook my head no. Twin and Cork gave each other a brief smirk as we puffed on a fruity sweet, blunt. Twin and I sipped on a 40, but Corky didn't drink brew.

Keysh and Dionne finally pulled up in her maroon Honda Accord. Twin spit a little game to Dionne, but then told her that he was headed out to UrbanCrest Projects. She played non-chalant about it, but she was really salty. She later bitched to Keysh about how she came all the way out West and Twin was leaving right after he said, hey! Twin didn't want to get caught up fucking with her while he had Stephanie.

After about another ten minutes, Twin and Cork bounced; followed by moms, Micia, and Baby. I suggested for Keysh to come with me up to Micia's bedroom. She did, willfully. I knew it. She had been ready, but it was just up to me as far as when. We sat on the bed where I started to kiss her and unbutton her sleeveless blouse. When I saw she was assisting me undress her, I stood up to remove my clothes. We looked each other in the eyes until our nakedness was complete. I was undressed first, lying in the bed with my missile on torpedo. I watched her calmly remove her lace panties and bra. She laid her voluptuous, pop bottle figure next to mine. After we began to kiss, I touched her moist pussy hole. She protested. Okay, cool. I thought, 'let's get to it'. I climbed on top of her, sucking her supple breasts and caressing her ample ass. Lord have mercy, she was heavenly! I put my bell head at the entrance of her wet, warm pussy. As I tried to penetrate it, she sighed in pain. The door was closed. She 'was' still a virgin! I gave her a look of shock. She stared back with a distressed face and said, "I told you I was a virgin."

"Alright, just relax. It's gonna be a little painful," I said.

"Duh!" She shot back.

I felt like slapping her, but I'd just beat her with my dick. My goodness, it felt like it was no entrance. I was 16 with 6 solid inches, but by far no porno king. After a little experimental shoving, I was pulled in with acceptance. It felt like I was going to come once I got my head in her tight little twat. I worked it about halfway in and started gutting her as she moaned and made fuck faces. I squeezed her ass as I dug in harder. I kissed her breasts, her neck, and then her lips. I raised her head above my shoulders and began fucking away the two years of frustration I had with the pussy. She moaned, biting her lip and pulled tightly on the back of my neck. My balls were about to explode. Both of them, it seemed. I rammed harder with solid strokes. I kissed her savagely as I shook and erupted; giving her a load of life. It was by far the greatest nut I had ever busted. I got up to go clean off. I brought her a warm rag, and then got dressed. She had a tragic look in her eye that I could not figure out.

Once she got dressed we walked downstairs. As soon as we reached the bottom of the steps mom, Micia, and Baby walked in. They kind of gave a look like they knew what had just happened. Micia began immediately talking with Keysh, but it was like Keysh wasn't hearing her. I rolled me a blunt, lit it, and then called Keysh out onto the porch.

"Girl, wusup wit you? You alright?" I asked her.

"Yep!" She replied.

"It don't seem like it."

"Well, you got what you wanted now. So you probably just gon' dog me."

"What? That's what you think? Girl, you trippin'! Come here," I said.

I held her tight. She had tears in her eyes, causing her eye make-up to run. I kissed her and told her let's go in the house to eat and watch us a new 'Blockbuster' release. It was no doubt that I had her now.

CHAPTER 12: A Hot Summer of Hell

I had decided to give the spot a rest for a while. My geek bitch Janice had been tripping lately, allowing other small-time dealers to steal a few dollars here and there on certain days that I had told the bitch we were shutting down for a minute to let the heat cool down. Dust and Skins had just whooped an unruly dope fiend in the back alley for popping up drunk and belligerent for the twentieth time. They said that Dust sucker punched him from the passenger seat, and then Skins cracked him over the head with a case of beer from the back seat. The poor bastard drifted down the alley crashing his new Daytona into some old lady's garage. And then he had a nerve to page them an hour or two later, after just making a police report, asking could he still come by to cop his forty rock. My nigga big Free had just knocked him out in the snow the previous winter and took his watch and necklace for the same ignorant shit. He then gained his consciousness and called to tell us that he had gotten mugged, but that he was on his way back over to spend. Dope fiend Mike, a born loser!

Anyway, Dust and Skins also ran with some primo smoking hustler from Alabama who was scheming off of the clientele and even beating

67

them physically at times. I was getting skeptical of it altogether. Plus, it always bugged my conscience that it was cattycorner to mom's house. I thought of this for her sake and the fact that I kept substantial amounts of money there and at times, coke. Not to mention that I also had Keysh staying with me. And she was now about six weeks pregnant. I couldn't stay out of the pussy.

The move in was put down after I slapped her up a month or so ago, telling her to go back home so my nuts could breathe. As far as I concerned she was in my way. She always wanted to be up under me. And she eventually stopped going to work. I mean, she had a little money saved, but it wasn't much. Plus, she was on her way to college soon. But she cried like a spiteful baby when I sent her on her way. I felt bad for a minute, because I had mad love for her, but I couldn't lose focus.

A couple of weeks later her loud mouthed, younger big sister, called me bitching; like I was fucking her! She was saying that I had wronged her sister Keysh and that she was pregnant. I instantly cut her off and asked to speak to Keysh. She informed me of the disposition, telling me she had been sobbingly emotional ever since she had left. Shocked, I invited her back over to stay. When she arrived she brought her mom, her aunt, her sister, and her cousin Dion with her. They came over to meet and talk with my moms and me. I guess they were supposed to be intimidating to me, in a strong, black-woman kind of way. Looking at them all together now, I could see where Keysh got her ass from. Her mama!

**

I had been in deep thought thinking about what P. was spitting to me lately. Serving his small-time clientele weight, but keeping my good rock star clientele and my green game on the side had worked out sweet. I was moving up the ladder a notch, and most importantly, relocating from the block. P. taught me that in this game you constantly had to move around and change numbers. You had to keep them guessing (niggas and the rollers). P. was molding me for the future, to be a major part of his cream team. A bigger and better life than what I was used to. The ultimate level of the game, moving bricks! A true American Dream. I would soon be ready. P. would always drill me, though, on not blowing blunts all day with my peers; or with his older brother, Big Tone. A.K.A. the Black Charles Manson! He'd tell me that if you remained focused with your eyes on the prize, then you'd excel and leaves those with habits at a stand still. If you yourself had habits, then you'd be the one with your feet stuck, frozen in concrete.

During my brief time of vacationing in my thoughts, I'd spend time away with Keysh, often spending the evenings out at a longtime friend of mom's house in Groveport, Ohio. A cool, down to earth, very tanned Caucasian-Navajo. She was half White and half Indian; and very sexy for her near 40 years. She also grew hydroponics weed.

I would take Keysh to numerous outdoor exploits, to have fun and enjoy her body while it was still in tact. I loved to see her in a swimsuit, always a two-piece. We went to hotel suites with pools and Jacuzzis, Wyandot Lake…We even went camping. Where we played hoop, swam, and fucked out in the woods. In fact we fucked everywhere. In pools, bathrooms, bedrooms, backseats…every fucking where! She'd play shy and hesitant, but she would always participate. I was in a zone. I had to have mine. Especially when I saw her in her swimsuit! That ass would say, 'Come fuck me, daddy!' And slinging sperm by the quart was of no consequence now, because the damage had already been done.

***

I had gradually and quietly got my new hustle style up and running. A few weeks passed by and things were cool. However, I was more paranoid now than ever. In this game, sensing heat was a natural instinct. But you can't smoke, shoot, or snort the game; you have to be born with the hustle. And you can't have a late start in this game, either. I feel that I'm an environmentalist. I can adapt to, analyze, and ultimately utilize my environment. Now I've heard it said that paranoia is a conscious, realistic phase of reality. Sort of like an instinctive warning of what could be. Instinct told me to make a move fast, before my world crumbled. One thing that I learned really fast was that you couldn't make any money in jail.

I thought of Keysh. Now that she was pregnant she could easily get me a place. College! Fuck it. All she had to do was get me the place before she took off; if, that is, she was going to go 5 months pregnant. I would talk to her.

***

It was Friday afternoon when I awoke to the sight of big booty Trish. She was a friend of Micia's from our old north side neighborhood, whom I had also boned a few times.

"Siz-o! Siz-o! Wake up, they fightin' out front," Trish yelled.

Boom, boom, boom! 'What the fuck?' I thought.

With Trish standing over top of me, I couldn't think straight, especially with this awakening hard-on. 'Where the hell was Keysh', I wondered. And did I just hear gunshots?

"Who?" I asked, as I jumped up.

"Dust and 'Tonio (she called Twin). Them speed sellin' yanks shot at Tone's car. You didn't hear it?" She asked.

70

Ignoring her question I ran out front with my Smith & Wesson clutched tightly in my left hand. Twin and Dust were walking back to the house, breathing heavy. Dust had an empty 45 Ruger in his hand.

"Yo, what the fuck?" I shot out. Catching myself in mid sentence, I realized that the beef was with the speed freak hippies from four houses down. They were a wild bunch of rednecks. Twin briefly explained to me what had happened, telling me the hippies had animosity towards us for being young niggas getting money on the block and, it was basically a stare down which had lead to words, then eventually the drama. I knew the cops were coming, so I told them to go next door to our older homey G's crib and I had Trish stash the heater.

Keysh and Micia had just pulled up in my Cutlass. They had gone to the grocery store for moms. She called from work to have them pick up some things. They say they left Trish behind because she wanted to chief and drink with Twin and Dust. A Hoover!

The laws arrived a few minutes later. Both the hippies, and us, denied knowing anything, regardless to the neighbors' allegations. No one was seriously hurt. And even though there were bullet holes in their house and two in the trunk of Twin's Regal, the police were eventually forced to leave with a flaky report.

Mike and Tone P. blew through, along with my Pops. Tension was still high in the air with the late June humidity. Moms soon arrived home from work. By mid evening we were all chilling on the front porch, discussing the drama while we smoked hydro weed and drank. Trish was pumped up off of the shit, reciting the whole story. I was still shocked and disturbed by seeing her. It was getting late and it didn't seem like she was preparing to go home. I looked on with discomfort as she spoke girl talk with Micia and Keysh. I knew Keysh wouldn't be all smiles and laughs if she knew what I knew, which was the real reason Trish was here, because of me. But Keysh threw a monkey wrench in her mix when she arrived. I was glad, too.

My mama was truly upset to hear what had happened. We saw one of the hippies pull up and decided to go and have a few words with them; once the laws were out of sight. They had been cruising the block all evening since the incident. Tone and Mike P., Pops and I, all walked down to their spot. When the hippie saw Tone, he froze. He knew of Tone and his younger brother, Mike.

These hippies were grown men just like Tone and Mike were. Once we all spoke, and the tension had been reduced, we agreed to kill the beef. Although, they were the ones who left the fight with a black eye and a few teeth in the minus from Dust and Twin's hand and foot work. One of them suffered a horrible stomp out once he hit the pavement.

Anyhow, it was agreed that the drama was senseless, and that we were both engaged in illegal activity so neither of us needed the laws on our back. Pops emphasized that we were teenagers, too. And along with the Pettways, promised that if there were anymore problems, then they would suffer damage that they wouldn't walk away from. They clearly understood. Now, although pops was in a drug addictive stage, he was still a 5th degree black belt, and still very dangerous. We walked back to the house feeling brolic and triumphant. I would never trust those hippies, but I knew that they knew what time it was.

I looked Keysh in the eye and she too knew what time it was. I told her to say goodnight to everyone and then head down to the basement. And that I would be down soon. She had recently altered the basement with a queen sized bedroom suit and a new 27" color TV; courtesy of me, no doubt.

Once P. bounced I blazed a blunt with the fellas. Twin said that he was about to bounce out to Gahanna to see his son and son's mom. My moms and Tone were going to smoke and chill upstairs in mom's room.

Dust was feeling himself, and had insinuated that he was going to try to hit Trish once Micia fell asleep. I laughed inside, and then headed downstairs. Keysh was in her pink, oversized ESLEEP shirt flicking through the channels. I undressed, and then thought to myself, 'I'd have that talk about a place with her' after we fucked.

"Take ya panties off....."

CHAPTER 13: Uncle Red's Release

I had rapped to Keysh about finding a place, in which she agreed to do the following week. She questioned the logic in it by the fact that I was 16, soon to be 17. Although she was 3 years my senior, it didn't seem that way to most people. As young as she looked, and at times acted, and as mature and on top of my game as I was, some would have thought that our ages were reversed.

She would act like she didn't think that I was, or that I could be serious about wanting to get a place. And then I would feel insulted and threaten to slap her. But she'd innocently reply that she was sorry and 'didn't know' as she spoke in her squeaky little girl voice; as she sometimes did when I yelled at her. Something she came up with to soften my manner. It often works, touching me so deep that I have to bend her over to show her how sorry I am. She felt that she had me ever since I sent her away with a foot in her ass and then she ended up sicking half of her female family on me, causing me to take her back. 6 weeks pregnant!

Anyhow, she hadn't spoken much on college or leaving in a few months. I think it was pretty much decided that she wasn't going. Being pregnant was already a major factor, but I really didn't think that getting a place would entice her to go away.

Sitting on the porch at mom's house, lost in my thoughts, I heard someone yelling my name from inside the house. It was Micia telling me that pops wanted me on the phone. After talking with him, I shot around to Big Sally's a few blocks away. Pops had befriended these two large Russian guys, Sally and Ron, about a year after we moved to Columbus, some 6 or 7 years ago. Pop said that Sally needed a half gallon of ice cream, which I understood, but he also sounded paranoid. Now even though he claims to have quit getting high ever since I put him on Front Street for knocking on my window at 5a.m. in the morning while I was stroking, he still never sounded this shook before. Paranoid people make me paranoid. In my own cautious manner, I whipped down a few blocks over to Sally's place.

In my coming of age and knowing Sally, we became pretty cool. Since Sal's house was so big and was equipped with a pool, I would invite the fellas over, along with our chicks and kids, to throw big barbeques. I would go out to the shooting range in Delaware with him and pops sometimes. And I even got in good with his neighbor, Mac. He was a 60 year old war vet who basically became my local gun store clerk. I bought everything from pistols and ammo, to Calicos and cleaning kits from him. Sally was a truck driver who, over the years had acquired some really nice weed and pharmaceutical connections, especially in Texas. He had tried to get me involved a few times but I said no. I was cool. Although I would sometimes have dealings with him on the greenside, and on the coke side, as well; like now.

"Ay yo, Sally! What's the deal, baby?" I said as I walked up to the porch, looking back briefly to scan the block. He didn't respond as he opened the screen door for me. Once I got inside, he instantly closed and locked the door. Pops was sitting on the couch. I could tell he was high. But it was a relaxed high.

"Sally?" I questioned, pointing at pops.

"Oh, I gave him a shot of nubaine. He fuckin' needed it! I'm gonna tell you all about it, but let's get this out of the way. I need a line and Kevin's on his way over for a quarter of this. I still gotta cut it, though," said Sally, as we walked towards the kitchen to the scale.

Nubaine! A pharmaceutical, downer drug you take by injecting it into your ass (usually) through a needle. It had pops looking like the dude off of the movie 'Weekend at Bernie's'. I served Sally, and then I walked back to the living room.

"Pops, wusup?" I asked hesitantly. Sally walked into the room and sat down to do his line.

"The fucking Feds, that's what! They hit my shit," said Sally.

Pops explained to me how 'the boys' picked him up at the post office and interrogated him for nearly 12 hours. He was smart by hesitating for a minute before opening the box when things didn't seem right around him. They thought he was on to them and was about to split, so they jumped the gun and grabbed him.

"He fuckin' kept quiet, too. Oh boy, I love your old man," Sally said, with sincerity.

'Wow', I thought. The Feds were real live drama. Even though pop had slipped up out of it, what had he gotten himself into? Sally assured me that pops would be cool there for the night. He'd let him sober up, and then drive himself home in the morning.

I drove quietly back around to mom's house with the words 'careful' and 'cautious' on my mind more now than ever. I crept inside and slid straight down to the basement. I didn't mention pops or the Feds to anyone. Keysh had concluded her conversation with her moms and then asked if I was hungry.

"Nah baby, just get what you want. I'ma smoke me a sticky, put my lights out blunt," I said. I still had a few colorful, fruity buds that I had copped from my cowgirl-Navajo chick.

"You sure babe, I'm about to call Donato's?" Keysh asked.

"Yeah, I'm cool, boo. Go ahead and get ya 10 inch pepperoni wit a side salad," I said.

"And a 2 liter of Pepsi," she added with a smile.

I blazed my blunt and when Keysh's food came, I smashed two slices and then fell into a deep sleep. I didn't even hit the pussy until the next morning.

***

Twin slid in from his son's mom's Gahanna residence at about noon and woke me up. He wanted to take a ride and have a talk about a new move that he had in mind. Okay, I thought; the boy's mind was back on the right track. Lying up eventually always gets old. I decided to ride to the mall with the knucklehead for some fits and some sneaks. Once I showered and got dressed, we rolled out in his champagne Regal with the earthquake knock. He kept his ride squeaky clean. And he had been trying to get me to sell him my chrome and gold Dayton's that I had bought for my Cutlass but was always too shook to ever put 'em on. I figured I'd save him the heat, too, by telling him no.

"Hey Siz-o, I've been bangin' 'em out in this new north side, suburban project. Freeway and his bitch stay out there. And you can bring a pack out there with you to serve work to all of Freeway's homies that always press me for small weight," Twin said.

So that's where Free had been. "Like that, bruh? I don't know, I'ma have to slide out there to see wusup.....that broad have Free's baby yet?" I asked.

"Yeah, she had a little boy. He look just like Freeway's ass," Twin said.

We arrived at the mall and slid in to blow a little change. Twin hit Champs and I slid over to the Oak Tree. After about a half an hour we met up near the food court. We grabbed some lunch and then I told Twin to keep an eye on my bags while I went into Lady Footlocker to grab Keysh a tennis skirt and a t-shirt. 5 minutes later I walked out and saw Twin sipping his drink and looking into 'Jacob the Jeweler's' display window. I nearly froze when I didn't see my bags on the isle bench. I approached Twin enraged and asked, "Bruh, where my bags at?"

This nigga just looked over towards the bench and said, "Shit, they was just right there."

He actually said it like it was no big deal. My Cross Color and short outfits, gone! I argued with this knucklehead all the way out to the car about not watching my shit. It was crazy because he acted like he wanted to fight about the shit. That's how he was, though.

***

It was a day to be remembered when the devil was set free from the abyss. We got a call at about noon from Dust and Skin's older brother, my uncle Ron. Red! He had called out of the blue a few months ago saying that he was due to be released in July. After 7 long years he had been paroled. He called from our Aunt Linda's, wanting us to come pick him up. He had got out of Lucasville Penitentiary that morning.

I told Dust and Twin that I would go get him since they were notoriously hot and had to ride with pistols. I had recently bought a white '91 Bonneville with maroon, velvet interior. And of course I added the knocks. But no rims; although I had a set of 17 inch KMC rims set aside for it. Skins rode shotgun with me. I had no license, but I didn't give a fuck.

When we pulled up the nigga was smiling at us as he hopped in after we stopped. Damn, he looked just like Skins. Just 10 years older, though.

"Ay man, y'all niggas is a muthaphucka! Younger than a muthaphucka gettin' paper! Y'all got the beats in the ride wit the pull out stereo," he yelled because of the music. Once we hit the highway Skins lit us up a blunt.

"Yo, this ain't shit, dog. We ain't hardly flossin'," I said.

"Aw man, y'all smokin' that damn dope, and I gotta go see my P.O. in the morning," said Red holding his fingers up to his nose.

"Y'all ain't got no guns in the car do y'all?" He asked.

"Naw!" Skins said as he laughed then gave me a distinct look.

When we got to moms out west, Pops was waiting on the porch.

"Damn boy, you used to be fat. What happened?" asked Pops. Not really expecting an answer.

Red replied, "Shit, stress! The penitentiary ain't nothin' nice, big brother."

"Yeah, I hear that. So wus been up, boy?" Pop asked.

"I can't call it," Red shot back. Red used to run with the Detroit boys, Straughter and Stutter Man's crew. Before he went to prison he had a red Mustang 5.0., with gold Dayton's. He was ballin'! But then he got turned out by some crack hoe named Peaches; smoking primo-rock joints. We still don't know what he did time for. As a kid I just kind of remember him disappearing right before his moms, my grandma, had passed away.

After Red got re-acquainted with everyone, he pulled me to the side in the kitchen to tell me that he wanted to get to work and on the grind immediately, assuring me that everything would be copasetic and that he still knew all of the old faces. We talked it over and both decided that he was ready. I threw him an eight ball of crack and had Dust and Twin drop him off out east off of Main Street. Our program flowed smooth for the next few weeks, with Red building up his clientele and fattening up my pocket as well.

CHAPTER 14: My Two Maniac Siblings

It was a hot, Monday afternoon and we were all chillin' over Tone's crib blowin' blunts. It was me, Skins, Dust, and Twin. Tone needed baggies to bag up some sacks and his girl Dee Dee was gone to the doctor's with his daughter. She usually made all of his runs. Twin told Tone that he would go for him because he needed a cold beer and some more Phillies. Tone shot him a few dollars and he and Dust bounced; shaking the block as they pulled off.

"Yo Tone, have you seen P. yet today?" I asked. Because I know he hadn't talked to him, Tone didn't believe in having a phone in his house.

"Naw, he ain't came out yet. You page him before you left the house?" He asked.

"Nope, I thought he would be over here. I need to holler at him," I said.

"He'll be here soon, I'm sure. It's almost 2 o'clock!" Tone said.

P. had moved out to the suburbs, but was usually in the hood by noon.

"Ay Tone, come out back and open the garage up. Hurry up!" Dust barked.

"What? Wusup?!" Tone shot back.

"Man, we just had a shootout with some niggas up at UDF gas station. The police might be lookin' fot the car," said Dust.

Tone ran out back and opened the garage for 'em to park the Regal in. After they came in we rolled up and poured some drinks as they explained to us what had happened. Dust, laughing as he always did when he told his part. It turns out that their opposers were some east side niggas who they had robbed, beat, and left stripped naked and bound out in Wedgewood a few months ago. We watched the evening news and they had reported a dispute between four young men that resorted to gunfire. Most of the glass got shot out of the store front from the niggas runnin' into the store for shelter. Twin said that they recognized the niggas starin' at 'em, and then one of 'em tapped the other one and said somethin', and then he pulled out a 9 and let off one shot. Twin said that him and Dust drew their pipes and commenced to dumpin'. All 15, 16 shots!

"With these cheap ass fuckin' throwaways we couldn't even hit 'em from that far away. I aimed right for the nigga's head!" said Twin. He had a Jennings 380, and Dust had a Bryco 9.

"Yo Twin, you would've got him if you had this," I pulled out my 16 shot Smith & Wesson 9millimeter with the beam on the trigger. Although I was kind of glad that Twin didn't shoot the guy. But then again.....the niggas may have still wanted to retaliate. P. stood up, then shook his head and told me he'd meet me around at mom's house in an hour.

"What the fuck is up with that nigga?" Dust asked.

"I don't know, but he stay on some sucka shit," Twin said.

"Yo, y'all chill wit that bullshit. Y'all know y'all stay in some hot shit.

Muthaphuckas don't be feelin' that," I shot out. These niggas always felt that they had something prove. P. was the wrong nigga for anyone to fuck with. And we were in his crazy ass brother's crib. These two niggas were some real hard heads. I knew that they were still buzzed up, and charged from the drama earlier.

"Ay, wusup wit ya dude at the gun shop, Vance's? You gon' hook us up?" Dust asked.

"Yeah. Take ya dope fiend Steve out there tomorrow, Twin. I'll have Paul give y'all the employee discount. Get y'all some reliable heaters," I said with a smile as I gripped my Smith 9'. I thought about sending them to my war vet, Mac, but if some dirt was done with the weapons and it traced back to Mac, it would be all bad. Plus, those fools would probably try to rob him. Although the news said that the cops had no license plate number, I told them to lay low for a few days.

I shot around to mom's to check on Keysh and wait on P. Here lately she had been craving all kinds of crazy foods, from White Castle to candy sprinkled donuts. P. came through and we chopped it up, and then handled our business. I bounced to make a few runs and set the spot straight. When I got back to mom's house, me and Keysh talked for a while, and then agreed to go look for a place in the next few days.

***

Twin had Stephanie over all night. They had been arguing for nearly an hour. Twin was cursing her for not being home for about a week. I knew it was going to get ugly soon, because Twin had been drinking all day. Toying with his new Glock and Tech he had bought earlier at Vance's. Mom was bitchin' about Twin yellin' and cursin'. Stephanie kept yelling from Twin slapping her and.....whatever else he was up in his room doing to her.

I had originally only came in to grab a pack that I had stashed for my lil' homey; who was around the corner waiting on me. 'Fuck', I thought. I ran upstairs to tell Twin to chill with the drama up in mom's house. I stood in the doorway of his room as I spoke my request. After I did so, the nigga had that look in his eye I has seen many times before when we would fight as kids.

"What? Nigga, you tryin' to check me?" He asked.

"Naw bruh, you trippin'," I said. "I don't give a fuck what y'all do, you just got mom buggin' out and....."

'Bamm!' The nigga stole me in mid-sentence. "Muthaphucka", I thought to myself. I ate it, though. And as the punch clearly got my attention, I grabbed him and pushed him back to get some space to swing, which I did; landing a lead left, and then a close solid right hook. My heart skipped a beat when I saw him go through and nearly out the window.

"Bruh!" I yelled. As I helped to pull him back in he lunged for my waist, taking me down into the hallway. After getting untangled with him and back to my feet, I pushed him back down as he tried to get up.

"Yo, fuck you, bruh. I try to talk to ya drunk ass and you gon' flip on me? Fuck you!" I said. And then I walked back downstairs.

"Haa! Haaa!" Stephanie had been screaming the whole time.

"Shut up, bitch!" Twin spat.

As I got to the bottom of the steps mom met me there, wide-eyed and pleading for an answer as to what had just happened. I walked to the clock on the mantle where I had the work stashed.

"Nothin'. Your son's a damn drunk. You deal with him," I told mom. The next thing I knew, this fool had hit me upside the head with his Tec-9. I heard my mama scream as I watched blood drip from my forehead. I was on my hands and knees trying to gain my consciousness as I vividly heard this knucklehead yelling, "You think you better than me? You and P. think y'all better than everybody. This ya favorite son, mama?"

He was fading out. I had to have been consciously unconscious for at least a minute, but when I came all the way through, I was enraged. All I could think of was killing him. As I stood up I heard his car door slam. I ran downstairs to grab...my 45 was the closest gun in ready reach.

When I ran out the side door and onto the sidewalk, he was pulling off. In the dawn of the evening, I emptied the whole clip into his trunk. I walked back into the house, afterwards. Not even acknowledging the blood running down my face. Mom was crying profusely with the phone in her hand to call me an ambulance. I sat on the steps holding a rag on my head as Keysh and Micia walked in. They had taken my black Cutlass out to her mom's house earlier and to go buy her some cute little cheap paternity outfits.

"Oh my God!" said Keysh with tears in her eyes. "What happened?" She asked as she sat beside me with her arm around me.

Just then the ER guys walked in. They quickly gave me some gauze stitches that stopped the bleeding instantly. Mom tried to explain to the laws what had happened to the best of her knowledge. I told them that I wasn't pressing any charges, so they bounced after getting their report; without an arrest warrant for Twin. No, I'd deal with him myself.

Mom and Micia left to take Stephanie home. After taking some Tylenol, Keysh and I went to lie down. I rubbed and kissed her belly for a while then eventually caught a hard-on after grinding on her ass long enough. We began to tongue kiss as I slid into her tight, moist hole. I slow grinded her, hard and deep for 10 minutes before I exploded and then fell into a deep, much needed sleep.

CHAPTER 15: Unforgiving Forgiveness

Red had came out to talk to me, on the business side and to hear about the drama with me and Twin. Red had quickly bought him a hatchback Horizon to get around in.

"Yo, I'ma put one in his ass when I see him. He can't hide out in Gahanna over Stephanie's forever," I said.

"Man, that's ya brother, though," Red said.

"Yeah, Siz-o, you know he fucked up. That's ya muthaphuckin' family, though, boy," Dust said.

"So what. Fuck him! I'm tired of his reckless, hatin' ass. All he wanna do is be a dumb ass drunk. That beef he had wit pop growin' up and...

shit, the beef he got wit his muthaphuckin' self is gettin' old. We about to be grown men! And it's half yo fault he the way he is anyway, Dust," I said.

"Fuck you talkin' bout? That nigga been crazy from Jump Street," Dust said, trying to justify himself. He knew he had an ignorant, egotistical influence on Twin ever since they we're younger. Those two niggas together were like fire and dynamite. Their history as a destructive duo went way back.

"Yeah, okay. What the fuck ever. I know he better stay his ass away from here. And shit, y'all act like what he did wasn't fucked up. He can't keep using that bottle as no excuse. What?" I asked Red.

"Naw, I ain't said nothin'. Y'all niggas is a muthaphucka," he said, shaking his head.

"Yeah, Tony be on some other shit when he be drinkin'. Like when he came to my spot that time and Mark said somethin' to him 'bout sellin' to one of the fiends. Remember that Siz-o? He came back here and got yo' Mac, and went back over there wit Dust and shot Mark's crib up," said Skins. A few months back Skins had came to the crib telling me some of Mark's biker buddies wanted to sell their last 2 pounds of green before they went back to West V. Skin told them that he wanted it, but that he had to run over to his safe house to get the money, which was where he came to get me to watch his back while he stuck the rednecks for the 2 pounds. Not really my thing, but I went with him, anyway. "Fuck those bikers", I thought to myself. Plus he told me that he didn't want to involve Dust or Twin because they would try to beat him on the lick.

Cork was at the house blowing some sticky, so we all three drove around to the spot in his Delta 88' hooptie. Cork had his Smith 9 millimeter with the beam. He had the black one, and I had the stainless steel one; courtesy of my guy Paul at Vance's. Everything went smooth besides Skins slappin' the fucking guy with the pistol. Just a reassurance though, that he was serious. It turned out to only be 1 and ½ lbs. So we all just took a half a pound a piece. It was some good commercial green, but nothing famous.

Anyhow, Skins tightened things back up with Mark, shortly after. I still think that Dust and Twin were pissed that they didn't get to stick the bikers. They had a passion for that shit. More so, though, I think that they figured Cork and I were very well off, and didn't need it; which we didn't. Shit, as far as I was concerned, they could have gone and did the lick if they were around.

Anyhow, after that they talked of robbing the spot with Skins and whoever else in it. They were really grimy like that, and as sad as it was I couldn't trust them. They were my blood, but they were unpredictably off the chain on the slimy tip. It was crazy, because they were totally different when they weren't around the other, but when they were together......It was ugly.

"So muthaphuckin' what he shot crack head Mark's crib up, fuck that crackhead!" Dust said to Skins.

"See what I'm sayin'? I'm gone," Skins said as he bounced.

"Hoe ass nigga!" Dust spat out.

"Y'all niggas is foolin', man. Siz-o, I'm out, dog. I'ma holla at you," said Red, while grinning. Trippin' off of his two little brothers! I walked him to the door. As I went back past Dust to go to the basement I said, "Now look at you, you ready to jump on your little brother, too, huh? For what, some dumb shit?"

"Nah Siz, but that nigga be on some sucka shit. That crack head mutha....." Before he could even finish I walked down the steps.

After talking to Keysh for about ten minutes, I heard mom ranting and raving upstairs about something. I walked upstairs to see Micia sitting on the couch with mom and Dust looking at her face.

"What the fuck?" I yelled. She had got jumped around the corner at her girlfriend Baby's house. And the little bitch allowed it; by three of 'her' friends! It turns out that after Micia pounded on the first girl that she fought, two other girls jumped in.

"Let's go back around there. I want you to beat all of these hoes asses, uno por uno! Yeah, one by one," I demanded. Mom said no. But I said yes. And Micia knew that I meant it.

"Sizalino Jerele! Wait," Mom yelled.

"We'll be back, ma. Dust, let's go!" I demanded.

He ran downstairs first to grab my 45 Ruger. Keysh insisted that she come, but I protested, just as mom did. Keysh immediately got on the phone to call a few of her cousins to come westward. We mobbed around to Baby's on Eureka Avenue. Everyone knew who and what it was when they saw my black Cutlass pull up.

"Micia, get out! Let's go! All of you bitches come out of the house," I spat. Baby's fat ass mama came out talking shit. A coke whore! Baby's older, tramp of a sister, was standing on the porch with her lame ass Cambodian boyfriend, Lo. He knew to stay in his place. Erin, the second girl of the three stepped down into the street hesitantly to squab with Micia. They instantly hit like pit bulls in the many thoroughbred fights I had seen. Erin caught Micia with a nice 2 piece which slid off ineffectively, though, because of the Vaseline that Micia had laced her face with on the way over. Micia quickly turned the tables and got inside on her with my coaching. She was shorter and a little heavier than Erin. After pounding her with a few good blows, Micia dropped her. The silence of the fight let it be known that it was over.

"Stomp that little bitch," shouted Dust.

So Micia kicked her a few times, non-chalantly.

"Now that ain't right," yelled Baby's mom. "Tasha, get out there and kick her ass."

Tasha was their biggest soldierette. And she was a little dike like, I might add. No, she was manly! She wasn't quite as tall as Erin, but she outweighed her and Micia by about at least 20lbs. Micia gave me a look that I knew meant, 'uh-oh'. But she didn't openly show it and neither did I.

"Handle yo' business!" I ordered.

After a brief stare down, they hit. This big bitch was throwing my, thick, baby sister around like a rag doll. Pulling her by the hair and pounding her in the face.

"Keep yo' head up," I yelled.

Dust looked at me as if he was about to jump in. I gave him a look that said, 'no'! Not yet, anyway. When she tried to slam Micia again, she used her own weight as momentum to swing Tasha to the ground. Where she banged her head on the cement and blasted her in the face, drawing blood. But she soon gained full consciousness and awareness to reverse the position on Micia. And that was it, "Bitch, get yo' fat ass off my sister," I said as I threw her dazed, and amazed at my enraged strength ass off of Micia, where she clumsily landed onto the pavement.

"Samicia, c'mon! Let's go. Any of you bitches or lames got a problem wit me or my little sister, y'all know where to find me." I barked.

Dust was sure to flash the 45 before he entered the ride. They were all disgustedly silent as we drove away. Being ignorant of course by poundin' 2Pac's, 'OUTLAW'! Micia had pulled some Sly Stallone shit off of 'Rocky' on the big bull. I didn't think she had it in her. But sometimes it's amazing how the influence of an iconic presence can motivate you with an extreme adrenaline rush. It makes me recall the time, not even 2 years ago, when Free came to my crib with his lame ass homey, L. We had just moved onto the 'Hill. L. wanted to hit with me because some Detroit niggas jumped him for fuckin' one of their hood rats. Free, or myself, didn't help his dumb ass. Not only was these big, grown ass men strapped to a tee, but we were running two different spots for these niggas.

Anyhow, Twin came out the crib juiced up yellin', "Hoe ass nigga I should beat yo' ass and then shoot you for comin' in front of my mama's crib disrespectin'. You too, Free. But I know y'all don't want it wit me," said Twin.

"Naw Tone, I ain't come out here on that shit, I'm tryin' to get some green," Free shot back.

"Yeah, whatever muphucka! Siz-o, get out there and whoop that nigga's ass. Cause if not then I will," Twin said.

I was high as a kite and really didn't feel like fighting. I didn't drink like Twin did, but ever since we were kids I had a hidden rage inside of me. So I shook my buzz and headed for the street. Once I stepped onto the battleground, L. said that he wasn't on it, but that he was just salty that we didn't help him. In all reality, though, how? No fuckin' way! Fuck him and his emotions. Stupid kills. That's the rules. He knew he was dead wrong, anyhow. Rule number one, never wake the dead and never shed light on the blind.

When we pulled up in front of mom's house, Keysh's sister and two grown woman cousins were posted up on the porch. They ran excitedly towards Micia to get the dirt. And once they got it they saluted her. They were still pumped and talking shit, though. Keysh carried on about how she never liked the little bitch Baby because of her crush on me and she didn't feel satisfied knowing that Baby didn't get it too during the brawling that had just took place.

"Girl, sit ya pregnant ass down somewhere," I said as Dust laughed and Keysh just rolled her eyes and carried on.

I went into the house to snatch up a few packs for some niggas I had waiting on some work around the corner on Wayne Avenue. They had been waiting since before the drama. As I came out of the front door to jump in my grey Cutlass, because I needed to switch up, I looked towards the corner to see bodies running to and from a crowd. It was Keysh's pregnant self and her cousins whoopin' Baby and her already wounded entourage. They pulled hair from these hoes heads, stomped, scratched and kicked their asses. It turned out that they were walking down our side street to Erin's house when Keysh 'anem spotted them. In the midst of the drama Dust and I pulled off to make our move just in time to miss the swarm of police cruisers. We made our run, then shot right back to the house.

The laws had just cleared out, which I was thankful for. I made it a point to stay out of their sight and to keep them out of my mix. 'Duck, dodge, and stat low-key' was my motto. Keysh and her people were still hanging out on mom's porch re-enacting their war story.

"Here goes a souvenir of your little bitch's hair," said Keysh dropping a nice strand of Baby's brown, stringy hair.

"Bitch, I will beat yo' ass! Fuck that lil' hoe, don't play me like that 'cause you pumped off of that lil' shit," I said after I stared her down and then walked into the house.

"Babe, I was just playin'," she said, quickly losing her humor and becoming teary eyed. She was like a little girl when I yelled at her or cursed her. She concluded her peoples stay and came quietly into the basement to analyze my mood. She apologized and I left it at that.

After I counted the little bit of paper I had just made I stashed it with the rest I had behind a brick in the wall leading to the front porch. I then began to discuss with Keysh finding us a place. In barely five more months we'd have a child to take care of. Time came and went so fast. Skins, and sometimes Dust, were running the spot fulltime now. My move would have to be made soon.

"I've got a few places in mind to look at, but you ain't had time to take me," she said. Damn, this girl was about to turn 20 and still didn't drive yet! Although she claimed that she could.

"Ya mom said she'll take me Wednesday on her day off," Keysh said.

"Aight, cool. Come here," I said, lifting her big blue Nike t-shirt. I kissed her stomach then grabbed the baby oil from in between the rest of her cosmetics on the nightstand. "You know, you ain't put none of this on in a while." It was her favorite fragrance. And mine, too. White Diamonds!

"I'm fat now!" She spat out.

"Shut up and lay ya little A-frame ass down so I can rub some of this over my son," I told her.

"You mean daughter," she corrected.

"Whatever. Ay, you can wear some of this this weekend when we go to the fair, 'aight?! I'ma buy you a cute lil' outfit," I said. She shook her head yes a she stared into my eyes. She wanted it. I was momentarily mesmerized, but shook her chinky-eyed gaze.

"Ay, where's my chronic at?" I asked.

"Oh, I put it.....pull that bottom dresser drawer out, it's on the floor," she answered.

"Yeah, I need to smoke me one after today's drama. Although that was some bullshit you said earlier, on the flipside though, it was some real shit y'all did whoopin' them lil' hoes that jumped Micia. You feel me?!" I asked rhetorically.

"That's my girl. That's why I beat that bitch's ass," she said arrogantly.

"Ya lil' pregnant ass out there fightin', you must want me to whoop you. Throw that Eddie Murphy RAW in for me while I roll this blunt. Where my sweets at? Oh, never mind," I said finding them in the nightstand drawer.

While I blew my blunt, Keysh went to take a bath, returning in a long red Tweety Bird t-shirt that I had bought her, and the matching white and red brief panties. Smelling like a new born baby. After clowning off of RAW, I turned off the TV to marinate with my boo. Looking at her, touching and smelling her, made me want to taste what had been mine for nearly two years now.

"Keysh, you gotta cut some of this!" I demanded.

"Well, I didn't know," she whined.

"We'll do it tomorrow, don't worry," I insisted.

I licked and sucked away as best as I had imagined and seen on TV and porn. Keysh moaned and gently rubbed through my plats as I reached up and squeezed her breasts and rub her stomach. I continued on until my dick got so hard that it couldn't get any harder. Then I plunged it into her as deep as it could go, as I did the same thing with my tongue into her mouth. I placed her legs above my shoulders, grabbed two handfuls of her mutant-like, oversized ass cheeks and fucked her as hard as I could. She screamed so loud, before and after she came, that I swore everyone upstairs on both levels heard her. Which wasn't likely because being in mom's house we both would try to be as quiet as possible. After the full excitement of hearing her holler, I too could feel it in the air. Or rather my balls…..and exploded a full, backed up load inside her walls. I pulled out of her gooey, wet pussy to allow her to clean me off, and then herself as well. With the combination of the orgasm and my chronic high, I was soon sound asleep. It was funny, because for years she would go on swearing that her pussy would put me to sleep and that I couldn't handle it. Like I said, funny!

CHAPTER 16: The Summer's Storm

A few days later I got a page from a 475 number. I called back to the shocked realization that it was Twin. He was at Stephanie's out in Gahanna. It had been nearly a month since the incident between us. He gave me pleading apologies and swore that he hadn't had a drink since that day. I accepted the knucklehead's apology and we called it a truce. It was about noon and I was headed to the mall for me and Keysh a fresh outfit to wear to the state fair. So I told Twin to shoot westward, ASAP. I would be waiting on him.

Mom, Micia, and everyone else at the house were happy to hear that Twin was finally coming out of hiding and that we'd squashed the beef. It was hard, because I wanted to bust his brains; or at least put hands on him, although the nigga wouldn't be an easy win; especially sober. The knucklehead was my other half, though. And I knew that he wasn't right in the head. I don't know to say that he was the body, but I was definitely the brain. He was my twin however the story went.

An hour later he pulled up, hot boy style, shaking the block in his supped up Regal. I guess he still had to show some ignorance. It was all to the good, though. The sun was shining bright and we were all about to kick it and make our presence felt at the Ohio State Fair. It was guaranteed to be off the chain too because X-cape and Mr. Bump-n-Grind (R.Kelly) would make guest appearances by nightfall to do a 2 hour concert.

Once Twin and I embraced, I rolled us a sticky sweet while Twin kicked it wit pops for a few ticks. I had been getting with my Navajo cowgirl quite frequently here as of late to stay stocked wit that fruity, fire chronic. I loved when she'd take the hour drive to come and hit me off because she'd blow 2-3 blunts out of her sack. I made the ride worth her while though, by buying at least a fat, fluffy ounce at $350 and by having a few $100 a quarter customers for her, as well. I had even bought an '88 Bonneville from her. It was a clean, cream color with tan interior. I ended up giving it to mom and had her give her Grand Am back. Fuck a car note!

After we blew our blunt, Red came through for me to collect and re-supply him. He hollered for a few ticks and then he bounced. My nigga Nuts called and said he was coming down to the house. He was up the street at his girl Heady's crib. Speaking of which, she would live up to her name. Nuts pulled around in his clean, 2-toned blue Fleetwood Caddy. The 4-doored short bodied one. Twin and I jumped in the whip, then we mobbed out.

Heading to Westland Mall we smoked and talked shit, discussing today's upcoming events. Entering the mall through the Lazarus entrance, Nuts got a page from P. He hit him back once we got inside. P. said he was out north getting dressed and that he'd meet us at mom's house in an hour or so. We quickly hit up Finish Line and Champs for fits and kicks, then got a little Scooby snack before bouncing back to the 'hood.

While getting dressed I had to listen to Keysh's mouth about how I didn't bring her anything to eat. I knew I was somewhat wrong, but I was a prideful Leo.

"Yo, I told you we were rushing. You can eat as soon as we get there."
I sympathetically told Keysh. She sucked her teeth as she handed me
my freshly ironed, green Nike short outfit. I had just copped a 24inch,
solid gold rope with the chronic leaf emblem. I was gonna rock a white
chronic leaf hat over my unbraided fro and my new green and white Air
Max Huaraches.

I had given Keysh a cold stare that lightened her pouting mood. She
was asking for it, as usual. I had come in late the night before from Tone
P.'s crib and hadn't hit the pussy. She needed it! What the hell, I thought,
I might as well. The fair would be full of hot hoes, so it was best to be
empty headed than fully loaded. It was something that I learned from
the old heads about Clubbin'.

A few moments later while I was drying off from my shower, I
watched Keysh reach for her skirt to put on. She stood in her white laced
panties and push-up bra. I grabbed her arm for her attention, and then
closed the door to Micia's bedroom. We had gotten busy in here before;
in mom's room across the hall, too. Just as I laid her down to remove her
panties, I heard "Sizalino!" it was my moms or Micia screaming for me.

Startled by the interruption, my manhood went limp. Keysh jumped
up and so did I. I opened the door and yelled, "Wutup?!"

P. was at the bottom of the steps. "Ay Siz-o, come on. Get dressed.
Let's walk up the block real quick. Skins say Mario trippin'," he said wit
a slight smirk.

Although it was a minimum of 10 of our comrades on my mama's
porch, ready to mob down to the state fair, only me and P. walked down
to the spot. After our discussion we came to the conclusion that Janice
had seen O. at the local corner store and invited him to come and sit in
the trap. She had been sort of upset at me lately for not being the full-
time general that I'm known for being. Things just weren't the same with
Skins and Dust running things. And all Janice cared about was having

her habit fed; a typical junkie. And O. could do that with ease; ballin'
bigger than me.

He cursed Janice out and then dapped us up before speeding off in
his clean ass old school Monte Carlo. All of the homies across the way
on mom's porch were amped up seeing this. Assuming that, and it would
go on for a long time being said as, young Siz-o had checked O; Mario,
the young killa from Gary, Indiana. The truth was O. was cool. He was
real and showed respect to real niggas.

Law 19 of 'The 48 Laws of Power' states, "Know who you're dealing
with." Be it a sucka, or a killa, etc. Thomas Cleary translates: When you
meet a swordsman, draw a sword. And do not recite poetry to one who
is not a poet. Strange thing was that the following New Year's O. made
a resolution at a local nightclub to rob every sucka on Columbus' West
side, doing a home invasion a week later only to get lit up like a Christmas
tree. R.I.P!

Now that we were ready to roll to the state fair, everybody jumped
in a ride. P., Skins, Big Troy and I rode in P.'s burgundy Monte Carlo
SS. Nuts, the homey E., and the 'M' twins rode in Nuts' Caddy. And
my bruh Twin and Dust rode in Twin's Regal Grand National. We all
pulled off of the block knockin'. Keysh and Micia waited for Keysh's
cousin Dionne to come and pick them up.

The State Fair was all that with R.Kelly and the just as freaky X-cape
girls. It was also tons of brick house babes there but of course my action
was shut down because of Keysh. Although P. hooked me up on the
sly with an Ohio State freshman. A redbone who was there with her
girlfriend and fellow student that P. was macking on. I was cool, though,
for real. My mind was on some money; as usual.

***

I had just awaken from a late afternoon nap, due to me being up half the night networking, when I decided to slide around to Tone P.'s to see what had been up, and also, to see if P. had been out in the hood today; because some days, he would be missing all day; a luxury of being hood rich.

When I pulled up I saw him standing out front with a 45auto in his right hand. I jumped out the car, conscious of my 45 Ruger in my waist.

"Yo, wusup?" I asked him.

"I just tried to blast one of them muthaphuckas," said Tone looking up and down the now quiet block.

He had been having a late evening cookout with just his daughter, his daughter's mom, and his homey George. Two jack boys with masks were coming to the door, knowing Tone sold trees to close friends and associates, to pull a low-key daytime lick. But the way Tone's crib was his backyard had a privacy fence which started on the side of the house next to the porch and front door. So when these niggas got to the door they could see everyone on the side of the house grilling and kickin' it, ruining their element of surprise. So being shocked themselves the cowards started shooting as they ran away. Hitting the grill and nearly hitting Tone's daughter. By the time Tone retrieved his pistol and took off after them they were gone.

Everyone was in shock as Tone's neighbor asked was everyone alright, and informed him that she had called the police. I stayed with him, discussing who it could have been and chomping on a steak while we waited on the boys in blue. We would later find out that the clowns responsible were particularly targeting Tone's brother P., with the knowledge of his status and with him often hanging over at Tone's. Some joker that he dealt with had obviously been running off at the mouth. After Tone gave the boys a brief report I bounced around to mom's house.

"Ay yo, I'll be at mom's house, but holla at me when you find out what's up. You already know what time it is," I said.

These jokers must not have known who they were dealing with. Tone P. was not known as the black Charles Manson for no reason. In just his late twenties he was retired from the game and putting in work. His younger brother was the nicer one.

"Hey, I'll be around there in about an hour. I gotta take my daughter 'anem home and call Mike. Ya mom home?" He asked.

"Yeah, I think. She was," I said.

"Alright. You still got some of that fruity?" He asked laughing.

"Yeah, a little bit; enough for maybe 2 swishers," I told him but suggested that we needed to call my bitch Connie for more. My Navajo, Meigs County connect. He agreed.

Later that night we all got lifted and discussed the drama from earlier. Tone, Connie, my moms, my self, and Keysh; who attempted to taste the fruity trees with us, making me threaten to gorilla slap her for trying to damage my son growing inside of her.

A week later some bud head old school nigga who Tone knew said that his chick told him that her girlfriend's dude was talking about he was gonna rob the 'Ps'. Claiming that he had attempted to already, but it went sour.

I got back to mom's house after making a few moves when she told me that Tone had just sped off with P. and Nuts. She said it was something about the guy who tried to rob him. I ran out of the house to go look for them, but after riding around for about an hour, I came back to mom's house. It was late in the evening when Dust, Big Troy, and my self were sitting on the porch drinking some 40s. We saw P. walking up the street really fast. When he reached the porch he asked me, "Siz-o, give me something else to put on."

I thought to myself, 'this nigga is 5-6 inches taller than me and outweighs me by at least 50-60lbs'. However, I got him a Bulls jersey of mine and a pair of Dust's tan Dickies. Both fit rather snug. He acted weird and spooked but without asking I knew what was up.

Shortly after P. left we saw the news and got some insight on the killing. 'Fuck him', I thought. But what was next? And what did the cops know? Time would tell. A few weeks went by and everything was cool. Until Tone's lifelong homeboy Rich, the getaway driver, caught feelings and informed the police that it was Tone. He told the whole story. His coward ass beef was that his skank ass chick Rhonda was fucking Tone. Because she copped trees from Tone on the regular and was a natural flirt, Rich had questioned her the day before; interrogating her, asking if she had fucked Tone. Tone never touched her, but Rhonda got a kick out of keeping Rich in suspense by not giving him a straight answer. So Rich's sucka ass just assumed.

Tone got the word that the cops were looking for him so he was no longer staying at his house. He had the perfect hideout on the opposite side of town at an old high school buddy's crib. The guy and his chick were honored, even under the circumstances, being the fact of who Tone P. was.

***

P. and I were getting harassed every other day by two local cops, West and Bernard. Bernard was an Uncle Tom black cop who went to school with Tone. He was the same stereo-type as Scarface's song, 'I'm Black'. A sucka who was punked in school, who never got no pussy and now had a grudge.

Mike was still using Tone's crib to network out of, so one day when we came back to the house from making a move it was a copy of an arrest warrant for Tone left on the pool table. An Arrest Warrant, not Search Warrant. But the house was torn up. It was a small amount of work inside of an old stereo that they didn't find. Still though, it was the principle. These fuckers were out of control.

It was about a week later when we had heard about O's (Mario's) cousins from Gary, Indiana trying to take over the sales at Mike's spot on Clarendon Avenue. Old man Ron had called Mike at about 10a.m. steaming mad, but at the same time shook. Mike told him that we'd be through after dark.

Mike called me down to the honeycomb hideout condo he and Nuts had at about 9 o'clock. They were watching 'Above the Rim'. Once the movie ended, "Yo Siz-o, you ready to roll?" P. asked.

"No doubt, let's ride," I said.

Nuts slid to his chick Heady's crib. We agreed to meet up at P.'s new car lot/body shop in the morning. P. and I pulled up to the spot about 20 minutes later. Checking our pistols, we exited the vehicle. When we got inside K.J. and Chrome were inside. Ron's scary ass had been letting them bang all day long like it was cool. Knowing the rules and how these guys got down, I was ready to blast if one of 'em even looked at me for more than 2 seconds. P. called K.J. and Ron into the kitchen. Five minutes later he walked out and said, "Let's bounce."

"Wusup?" I asked as we walked out. He said that everything was cool. We sat in the car for a few minutes and watched them come out of the house. P. said that he gave Ron an eighth of a key to pump. We waited for K.J. and Chrome to pull off and then we pulled off, too.

After we got a couple of blocks away we noticed a patrol car following us. We turned onto Sullivant Avenue and the fucker was still behind us. We stayed cool and drove up to my mama's street, Ogden Avenue, which we turned onto. P. drove right pass my mom's house. "Bruh, why you ain't let me out?" I asked.

He said he was gonna drive around to the next block where his bitch Evette lived. Saying that he didn't want them to see me being dropped off at mom's from the spot. I didn't give a fuck, but.....as we pulled onto Broad Street the cop hit his lights. "Fuck", we thought.

The officer came to the window and asked for Mike's license and registration. He claimed that he couldn't clearly see the 30 day tag on the hatchback window of the Nissan 300 Z-X that we were driving; due to the fog or, low visibility as he called it. He was a rookie, though. Just as he came back to hand P. his license and we were ready to pull off, the dicks Bernard and West blocked us in behind the other officer's cruiser.

Now it was 'Fuck', for real. These pricks heard Mike's name, his last name in particular, over the radio and came immediately to the scene.

"Yo, what the fuck?!" I yelled as they snatched us out of the car.

"Hey Mike, where's your brother?" asked Bernard. Patting Mike down while his partner searched me, Mike answered, "He at ya girl's house."

"Aw, that's real funny. We gon' get him," claimed Bernard.

West had told me to stand back against the wall as he ran his mouth about how he knew all about Ogden Avenue, Twin and me, and my uncles, while he flashed his light inside the car and then, "aah, what's this shit?" He asked.

He had found the Smith & Wesson 9 millimeter under my seat. They put Mike in the back of the cruiser while they searched the car. While Mike was back there, handcuffed, he ditched his Glock in their backseat. They arrested me for CCW, let Mike go, and towed the car. While Mike was telling me he was gonna go around to mom's and tell her and Keysh that I had got arrested, the cops were taunting Mike saying that I was his fall guy for the gun and a bunch of other bullshit.

However, what was now on my mind was a prior situation involving the gun. A couple of months back my homeboy Snoopy had overheard a sucka named Black Sauce talking shit about my man P. Some shit about him robbing P. if we came to his block.

Hearing this bullshit, Snoop and I rode down on him, pistol-whipped him and threw him in the trunk. He claimed that he never said it. And after a few minutes of his pleading, I gave him a couple hot ones; closing him in his own trunk. A weak nigga just makes me sick to my stomach, which is why I plugged him. He had it coming already for running his mouth, but.....however, I went through a number of court hearings over the course of a few months where I was denied any sort of release. This was my fifth trip to the detention center, but I never got a permanent sentence to D.Y.S. I was mainly being denied release because of ballistics showing that the gun matched the 2 bullets taken out of a Corey Anderson from 3 months back. Two things would work out in my favor; the gun was found in the car, a car that was not in my name or Mike's, and not on my person. And second, Black Sauce would not come testify against me or even say that I was responsible. Before these factors came about, I was facing juvenile life after my third hearing, which is when my mother and Mike hired attorney Louis Dye for me; a Jewish legend with reputed mob ties. By my forth hearing I was released on non-reporting probation after Lou took the judge out to lunch.

Meanwhile, my uncle Skins had just got arrested for drug possession prior to my release. In which I had to leave him with some harsh words after a visit with moms. The nigga was fucking crying over 6 months that he had received.

When I got home it was drama. Mom had spent a fair share of my money on the lawyer, bills, Keysh, and some other miscellaneous shit. I had to track down and collect my money from Twin and Dust for a quarter of a key that I had left behind before my arrest.

***

Keysh had been stressed out thinking that I wasn't gonna see my child until it was about 3 or 4 years old. And those dickheads Bernard and West had been tripping. They had been popping up at mom's using loud music complaints to harass Twin and Dust. Just pulling up and walking into the house! Two days before my release, they had the task force snatch my moms and threaten her to tell them where Tone was at or they would run up in the house on Twin. She screamed and cursed them, crying profusely, as they finally let her go after about an hour. The next day, one day before my release, they arrested Tone. They followed his daughter's mom to where he was hiding out at.

I had been out for a few days and I still hadn't seen Mike yet. It was about noon and I had just woken up when I heard someone outside shaking the block. I opened the front door to see Nuts and Twin in a candy painted white Grand Prix wit' Chrome 'Ds'.

"Yo, wusup?!" I shouted.

They were puffin' on a swisher blunt, attempting to pass it to me.

"No, no. Where y'all comin' from?" I asked.

"The barbershop, getting' a fresh slice." Nuts spat out while choking.

"Here, Siz-o," shouted Twin. It was the remaining 2 grand that he and Dust had owed me for the quarter kilo. The boy had been making moves in the a.m. and looked to be doing real good for himself. I know he made at least 3 grand or better off of the quarter chicken. I had been in jail for nearly 2 months.

Anyhow, I gave him a determined look and reminded him of how hot things were at the present time. He gestured that he agreed then told me that they had just talked to P. and that he'd be out west by nightfall.

They were gonna go to the liquor store in a few hours then we would all meet up back at mom's house by 'bout 9 o'clock.

I sat at the dining room table with Keysh, in deep thought. It was a weird feeling for a Friday night; usually a conscience night for grinding or heading down to 'Flyers'. 'Flyers' was one of the hottest clubs down on the Ohio State Campus. But no, tonight was gonna be a night of heated emotions, major discussion, and who knew what else. I sent Keysh down to the basement once everyone started to arrive. It was me, Twin, Dust, Nuts, Mike, and Big Troy.

We all began to get lit up like a Christmas tree, even Mike, which was rare. We discussed the witness in Tone's case, who was in protective custody. We discussed those 2 dick cops, Bernard and West; whom Dust spoke of killing. We discussed everything that would affect us all as a whole. After about 4 or 5 hours everyone cleared out. I went upstairs to tell mom that Mike said Tone had a hearing Tuesday for a bond reduction, where Mike would then get him out. She cracked a smile but stayed silent. She had been in her room in a depressed coma ever since his arrest. I thought of what she had been through in the last few months. I had to do something. And fast!

Tuesday came and Tone was released on a $50,000 bond, against the will of the victim's grandmother. Who watched Tone shoot her grandson on their porch in broad daylight. Execution style!

Thanksgiving was in 2 days, so everyone was preparing for that. I headed over to Mrs. P.'s once I heard Tone was released. We chopped it for a while. As I played a game of chess wit' Mike, Tone said, "Man, don't be letting my little brother drink no more. This knucklehead got pulled over going the wrong way on Terrace Avenue. Terrace is a fucking one way! You remember, the night y'all got drunk."

'Wow!' I thought. He was really twisted that night. We ended the game with Mike getting a slick checkmate off on me. The guy was like a black Bobby Fisher Jr. We stepped out onto the porch where Tone said, "Bernard's girlfriend is gon' set him up for me. You know I used to fuck her back in the day."

'Damn', Mike and I thought. But, 'fuck him'. The sucka deserved it. And either way, it would be no talking Tone out of it.

***

Thanksgiving came and went. And everyone got their grub on. The weekend passed and it was now a cold, rainy Sunday night. And one of Bernard's days off. His chick had told Tone that she'd leave the backdoor open after midnight. She couldn't stand the fake playboy, anyhow. She hated him. Tone took Dust and Twin along for the caper; two natural born killers! Twin sat and watched the street in a stolen blue minivan. While Tone and Dust snuck into the house. I hooked them up with a few German silencers. Courtesy of my man Mac's C.I.A. buddy. The plan was to say that someone broke into the house, and then shot Bernard when he woke up during the robbery. It went a little differently, though. Tone instructed Dust to shoot the broad. But Bernard was all his. As they entered the bedroom she raised up throwing them a head gesture towards Bernard. Dust aimed the 45 at her melon and, 'Pop!' As soon as Bernard rose up he got it, too; his brain splattering onto the headboard. As they exited the house Dust suggested shooting the two kids who were sound asleep. Tone shook his head and pursed his lips, signaling 'let's go!' They jumped into the van as Twin slowly pulled out into the wet, dark night.

The following day's headlines said that either the ex-boyfriend or a burglar were currently the only suspects.

About a month went by and Tone had his bond revoked. All because the victim's girlfriend said that he gave her a threatening stare at a local shopping center. The judge now denied any sort of bail, which was all straight bullshit.

Mike had got word from a downtown source of his that the witness, Rich Green, had went AWOL. And that he was back on the West side hunting for his slut Rhonda. Now all we had to do was simply find, and 'push the witness out of existence'. Because the grandma had already missed identifying Tone in a line up. She was 80 some fucking years old.

About a week later opportunity presented itself when we got a call from a local bar, 'SHOOTERS', telling us that Rich was there pushing some high grade marijuana. Mike and I arrived ten minutes later where we saw Rich in the parking lot making a transaction.

"Yo, just stay right here. I'll be back in one minute," I suggested as I gripped my bulldog .357.

"Naw, just chill. I'ma holla at this dickhead," said Mike.

I thought, 'WHAT!'

"Bruh, the other dude about to go back in. I'ma run up and blast him when he get in his ride to pull off and then we out," I explained.

We were parked in between two cars about thirty feet away from him. But P. suggested that he could talk him out of testifying. I wasn't feeling that. It made me wish that I was the boss calling the shots. But I had to trust and back Mike. It was his decision.

He stood talking with Rich for nearly a half an hour. I was paranoid; casing the lot for the boys in blue. Mike finalized the discussion, and then we bounced.

He later claimed to me he threatened to kill Rich's mom if he testified. The trial came two months later, after Tone denied a five year plea bargain for manslaughter, where he was sentenced to 15 years to life for second degree murder. It turned out that Rich went directly to the police after the threat that night and got his mama put in protective custody. Tone never stood a chance in that trial. And he would go on to be enraged at his younger brother for the next few years.

***

I had sat things straight in my house. I moved my moms and Micia into a condo up north in the suburbs. And I sent Twin out east to stay with Pops in a Town & Country townhouse. I had to keep him away from Stephanie, although he frequently visited her and his son out in Gahanna. His left hand, Dust, was doing a year in county lock-up for a CCW conviction.

I moved Keysh and my 2 month old daughter, Jewel, into South Park projects. It would be temporary, though, because South Park projects was just that; 'The projects!' Although it was said that it wasn't as bad as it used to be, but still.....I was still doing a little bit of networking but because of my circumstances, being that I could be locked up until I'm 18 if I get into any trouble, I attended night school at North Adult Education Center. It was cool for a while, whipping rimmed up hot rides and macking on more honeys than John Mickens (the Mack), but I chose another alternative. I attended a Columbus Works program during the day, Monday through Thursday, and I was obligated to get my G.E.D. by my 18th birthday; which was just 4 months away. Otherwise, they could extend my probation.

My P.O., who I had only seen twice, seemed pretty cool. He was a brother. Who, once he found out who I was, offered to take me to a Cavs vs. Bulls game up in Cleveland. I declined, though. It turned out that he knew and had grown up with my man P.'s north side homies, Fat Cat and Hollywood Rick. The Cleveland Avenue and 17th niggas;

whom P. had propositioned to take over the hottest downtown nightclub in Columbus, 'IMAGINATIONS'. And it was poppin'; wit' celebrities there every weekend.

***

It was the beginning of the summer and I had finished both, the program and my G.E.D. I had recently got a call from older cousin Mann from back home in Carolina. I hadn't seen him since I was 13. I guess he had got the word (from the family) that little cuz' was becoming a major factor up in the 'Bus. Yes, at age 17! But no, clearly not yet major. We talked about hooking up and who would come to visit who but just agreed we'd decide in the next few months. After my situation cut me loose and I was 18 years of age.

I had recently hooked up with my fat broad from Wedgewood, Jeanette. She had got an apartment in South Park, staying with a 30 some year old has been hustler. I immediately put my manipulation tactics down on the cat. Lane was his name. He was actually a cool character.

I was about to turn 18 and needed to get my weight back up. My pocket weight, that is. I had less than 20 stacks to my name. I got out in the mix and began to establish some stable clientele. I hooked up with a few old homies and associates, got Twin right, and got a few light-weight clients from P. My uncle Red had recently got his parole violated from fighting with his alcoholic bitch. The guy was good for making me a couple grand a week. He kept my stacks up to par through the 6 month transition I went through after my release. He went away owing me over a grand, plus a pistol. But I couldn't complain. He'd be gone now for a few years. I'll look out for him, though. It's in my blood to be real.

Lane was getting good money for me; nearly the couple grand that I had been getting' from Red. We worked on consignment. I trusted him as far as you could trust any nigga in the street game. But he knew what time is was. It was a 60/40 thing. 60 percent being respect, 40 percent being fear. I didn't like fucking with none of the other shiesty South Park niggas, so I let my homey Big Carl do the foot work; a high school nigga who couldn't get a record deal singing, so now he wanted to be down. He was a hell of a high school forward, too, from what I had heard and seen now on the court. And then there was my lil' homey, Darren, who's moms got high and braided my hair. I had a smooth, flowing program just in this project alone.

By late July I had given Mike 30 stacks to hold for me, I had another 10 stacks stashed away at my only 'square' aunt's house out in Whitehall, and kept about a half a key pumping in the projects. I had begun to ride just plain, clean rides. Like Buicks, Chevy's, and even 3-5 year old Hondas and Acura's. Cars; a hustle we all picked up on, courtesy of old man Bob. P.'s half Irish/half Italian car garage and used car lot owner. He came in very handy, with a dealer's license and all. He got a car lot where we bought and sold cars through him.

It was now the weekend of the Cincinnati Jazz Festival; an old head, but low-key hot boy event. P. and all of the older homies who had their weight up, had just recently stunted at the Block Party, The Coming Home, and the Black Expo in Indiana. I hadn't attended either of them, feeling that I wasn't ready.

I did however roll to the Freak Neak with all of them back in April. Which was where I peeped, after seeing all the stars and rides and shit, that I wouldn't attend anymore major events until I was major and had my status up. However, since it was 2 weeks away from my 18th birthday, though, I let the homies talk me into going; Twin and I. I thought, 'fuck it!' My status was up (enough). And it would be up even higher by the next summer. Where then, I would be ready to act an ass and stunt.

After an hour long argument with Keysh, she had her sister come and pick her and my Jewel up for the weekend. I kicked it on the phone with my new fuck friend, Goldie, while I got ready. She was a Black and Asian honey that I had met through Twin's bitch, Chocolate, a few months back. She was a year younger than me but she was very mature. And her people had dough.

Mike finally fell through to scoop me up in a shiny silver, big body Acura Legend with 18 inch blades; unheard of back in the mid-nineties. We rode over to the condo to meet up with everybody so we could all hit the road with Nuts in a navy blue Regal with chrome flakes and chrome and gold Dayton's. Hollywood Rick, Cat, and all of their crew were rolling in BMWs and Benzes. We shot to the 'Nati and did the damn thing. We got back to the city after the weekend was over and got back to business as usual. I kept hearing a lot about this nigga named 'Legs' from Atlanta that Twin had got acquainted with; and who Twin also claimed to be 'about that drama'.

The way I heard it Legs felt he was 'Big Willy' by having BONE Thugs-N-Harmony over at his place blowing trees and shit from time to time. I got a call from Twin saying that he wanted me to come through Legs spot kick it, which I wasn't feeling because he didn't mention anyone wanting any work.

However, I knew he liked having my presence felt at times around his peers. I was nine minutes younger but still like the big brother now, mentally and statistically. When I arrived, though, shaking the project square in my maroon Park Avenue wit' gold Dayton's and vogue tires that, I kept strictly on the north side at mom's, I peeped a white rimmed up Suburban in front of Legs' building. I got upstairs inside the apartment to find Twin, Legs, and three other niggas who I quickly realized was the rapper cats, BONE. No wonder Twin had paged me twice since I first talked to him. Legs and Twin both introduced me to them, with slight praise.

I rolled and puffed on a blunt off in the cut with Twin. He told me that the BONE boys had some fire green, too. He stepped into the kitchen where they were chilling at as Legs slid over to holla at me, "Siz-o, wusup, pimp?" I've been sending you a lot of bread through Tone, me and all of my little cats."

This nigga started running off at the mouth. Going on and on like he had this toy ass project on lock and shit like that. All Twin ever called me for was a few quarters and halves; short shit like that. This nigga was a joker; egotistic, no doubt. And what I couldn't understand was why Twin was having me supplying these clowns when he could've had this suburban apartment complex on smash himself. Especially since his Ace was coming home in about 60 days. O.G. Uncle Dust! But what I heard next really made me say 'fuck this Legs character'.

"What the fuck! Y'all niggas lacing ya weed wit yay?" I heard Twin yelling.

I walked to the kitchen entrance where I saw Twin wit his Tech-9 millimeter in hand. He kept either that or his Mac-10 in his cassette tape case that he always carried, which was like a backpack or a carrying case.

"Yo Twin, wusup?" I asked. Standing in between him and these rap star hoodlums.

"Siz-o, these niggas is blowing primo backwoods!" Twin shouted. I looked at him in aw.

"We was supposed to match blunts, bruh!" he said.

"Ay Legs, wusup witcha man? Why he flippin'?" Asked the one called 'Busy'.

Legs was stuck on stupid. He got high, too. I read niggas. And I knew this guy was a piece of shit.

I calmed Twin down and got him outside. He wasn't driving so I had him bounce wit me.

I was supposed to hit the club 'Imaginations' wit P. and Nuts later on; which I knew wasn't Twin's cup of tea.

"Ay bruh, that nigga is a junkie ass lame. Shake that nigga. But yo, slide down to tha club wit me tonight. It's Fat Cat's birthday, so you know it's gon' be poppin'," I told him.

"Oh, y'all niggas clubbin' tonight, huh? P. goin'?" He asked.

"Yeah, he comin'. Everybody goin'."

"Yeah, fuck it. But I ain't gotta get all dressed up, though, right?"

I shook my head, "Naw, that's only on Saturday. It's Friday, bruh. Yo, let's throw some PELLE PELLE on and step up in there. I got the jackets...the whole hook up. I got to go get a fresh twist, though. My braids is frizzed the fuck up. Oh, dig, Redman and Keith Murray gon' be there, too. They was just at Nuts' crib getting blazed."

Twin looked at me like, 'What!'

"Yo, you know P. and Cat brought dem niggas down here. Well, they man, Pace, did. He handles all that," I said.

We arrived at the club about a quarter after eleven, pulling up earthquaking the block and parking lot in P.'s grey Suburban. It was a duplicate to the one in 'SET IT OFF'. It was me, Twin, Snoop, and P. The line was going down the block. We walked right up to the door, as we heard all sort of murmurs from pointing broads to mean-mug niggas. P. threw Cat's brother, Barrel, a big-face Franklin at the window as we all headed straight back to V.I.P. It was packed wit bitches. And they were choosing. I macked on chicks from grade school to grown ass ladies 5-10 years my senior.

After blowing some frosty evergreen out back wit Nuts and my nigga Cooks, we grabbed a table and a few bottles of Dom P. It was still about a half an hour until Red 'anem performed, so I slid to the bar to kill some time by macking on LaDon. She felt privileged bartending V.I.P.; her and her sister, Lisa, who I overheard her saying, "Yeah girl, they twins. Siz-o a little taller and slimmer wit braids. I forgot the other one's name. I hear he's crazy, though," Lisa said.

"I think his name Tonio or something. They went to Brookhaven," said a smooth, brown familiar face.

Ah yes, it was Esther; Antoinette, and Erica. Erica Knott, who I now heard was a probation officer. These were the hottest senior chicks at Brookhaven High when Twin and I were just freshmen. I knew they looked familiar. I invited them over to our table for a formal introduction. After we got acquainted, we watched Red 'anem perform, then agreed to go get a room out by the airport at the Radisson Inn.

Twin was macking on Esther; he dug her since the 'Haven days. My man Nuts, 'The Mack', rolling a brand new blue Deville, got at Antoinette. So I immediately began to apply the full court press on Miss Knott. Who's style I truly dug. But she wasn't as enthusiastic about hitting the 'telly as her girls were. She seemed more polished with morals and all. However, she was feeling me, so I knew there was a way in.

My pager was blowing up as it always did when Keysh knew I was out partying or perhaps, creeping. I hit her back on Nuts' cell phone and told her I'd had a few things to take care of wit' P. but I would be home by morning.

"Yo Nuts, wusup wit' y'all niggas and these cellular joints?" I asked.

"Wusup, you wanna get one Monday morning or something? You know it ain't shit!" He said, while nearly choking on hydro' smoke.

We got checked into a presidential suite. Equipped with a full kitchen and a stacked 'fridge, a bar, fireplace, 2 bedrooms, and 2 bathrooms as well.

"Lil' bruh, I'ma holla at you in the mornin', you know what time it is," Nuts told me.

"That's your brother, too?" Erica asked me.

"Uh, yeah," I answered. Everyone thought he was my brother. Nuts was black and Italian, also.

I chopped it in front of the fireplace with Erica until 6 in the morning. Filling her out and dissecting her brain. After informing me she was tired and wanted to pull the couch bed out she said, "I never had a one night stand before. Siz-o!" she said with emphasis.

As she smiled seductively I thought, 'Damn'. It's about time. I slid in to make my move. I combined undressing her as well as myself while I fore played in between. She was dark and beautiful, with a petite flawless frame. I beast fucked her fine, state probating ass, using Gin as my burning fuel. Yeah, I plugged her raw; first, giving her a rough, but intimate, missionary half hour. And then, 20 minutes later, I went for round 2 by way of doggy style. Pornographically! Indeed until the sun came up. And did she have work. Her back and her hips were all the way into it.

I didn't get home until half past noon. Keysh was quiet, but she clearly had an attitude. I played with my daughter for a little while then held her until she fell asleep. I went to get a shower then get dressed when Keysh followed me into our room. Something was on her mind. As I moved shit around in the closet, frustrated, I suggested we needed a bigger place.

"Yeah, we really gon' need one now," she mumbled.

"What? Why you say that?" I asked.

"Huh? Oh, um…..I'm…..babe, I'm …..I'm pregnant?" Keysh told me that she was 6 weeks pregnant; saying that she must've slipped taking her birth control. I was shocked but excited. I hugged and held her tight, before laying her down for a loving injection. I could always sex Keysh full throttle after I had been out creeping; morning, noon, or night. It was just an infinite attraction I had for her.

I got showered and dressed then told Keysh that I had to go do some running around. But that I would be back in a few hours. She gave me a disappointing look then informed me that she needed to go to the grocery store.

"Damn girl, you need to get ya license so I can buy you a car," I said to Keysh.

But it wouldn't be until after the baby was born. I told her that I'd take her when I got back.

I returned home at about 7 o'clock, where I took Keysh and my little Jewel grocery shopping. Keysh made me her famous lasagna. We stayed in and watched a few movies, just chilling out. The next day, Sunday, we went to SEARS and got a set of family pictures taken. I had long ago promised Keysh, so we did that there. We spent the rest of the day shoppin' for Keysh some new boots and a new winter leather. We bought some clothes for Jewel; and Keysh snuck off and got me the new NIKE Dennis Rodman's.

On the way home I got a page from Lane. It had been a good weekend. He had me $2,000 and another $800 on the next pack. I stopped by to pick up the dough and told him that we would hook up tomorrow. Everything was always on consignment. Yeah, the American Dream was very much attainable. And I was just getting started.

CHAPTER 17: The Transition

"**Y**eah, who dis? Somebody page Siz-o?" I asked.
"Boy, it's ya daddy. Look here son, ya cousin Charley just graduated from college up in Detroit. Well, his graduation is this weekend. Uh, ya aunt Linda thought it'd be nice if I brought y'all. She ain't seen y'all since the reunion in North Carolina 'bout 5-6 years ago," my pop said.

I had a busy weekend ahead of me, as usual. I guess I could pass out a pack and collect when I got back. So, I thought 'WHY NOT?' I had never been to the 'D'; Aunt Linda 'anem had moved there nearly 10 years ago, to the infamous south side. I had heard so many stories as a kid about the rough city that they had moved to. My pops always wondered why they moved there from Carolina. It was something about a job that my Aunt Linda or her husband had got there, if I recall correctly.

We headed out at about 6 on Friday evening. Keysh, Jewel, and my self rode in my new '93 Acura Coupe. Pops rode with his vet chick, my sister Micia, and my Aunt Beth. It was really good to see pop clean and off the drugs. He had been sober for over a year now. No drugs or alcohol. I mean, pop was always cool, but I preferred him with just his natural high. After all, who wanted a junkie for a father?

We pulled up to Aunt Linda's about 8:30. Where we hugged, greeted, were introduced, and re-acquainted with everyone. 20 minutes later we followed Aunt Linda to the Holiday Inn where we were gonna stay for the weekend.

Aunt Linda told us that the graduation ceremony was at 3 p.m. the next afternoon so we would meet up prior to that. My cousin Charley was a real square egg. He was 23 and had just graduated from Eastern Michigan after 4 ½ years. He was a distant cousin, but still, he was my cousin.

The next day, after the graduation, I was introduced to Charley's wife, Michelle and her family. Her brother Mike, was there with an entourage full of pimps and hoes, it seemed. It's as if they were at a Player's Ball or some shit. Dude was cool, though. He had major polish. After we kicked it and conversed for over an hour, I felt that I liked his swag and intellect. He too had graduated from college and gotten a business degree at Michigan State. Although quiet as kept he was a Wolverine football fan, just like my self.

"Yo dog, my wife's cousin went to Ohio State for 2 years. He said that campus is poppin'," said Mike.

"Yeah, it do pop. But the city is jumping in more ways than one. Ya dig?" I told him.

I insisted that he meet my man, P. So he agreed to come down to visit by the following week. He was currently working for some small business firm while his wife Lashay worked at a local fashion store. She was a real prize; a light-skinned, honey yellow hall-of-fame beauty with green eyes. I mean, a true brick house, 5'7", 140 lbs. And fly as hell!

My new D-town cousin was indeed oil slick. He grew up hood crooked but had legitimized and educated himself. Now, like most of the other guys who fit this stature, he kept illegitimate associates. Who would stick by and soon follow him.

We spent the next few hours eating and drinking good before we eventually headed back to the hotel.

The next day we stopped by Aunt Linda's for an hour or so to say goodbye and congratulate Charley again before we hit the road.

I pulled into the city at about 5:30 p.m. And I knew that it would be a restless remaining Sunday evening. I got Keysh and Jewel, and all of our things inside the apartment and then checked the caller I.D.

It was about 20 calls from mom's number since earlier that day. I knew that I still had to check some traps and do some collecting, but I called mom's number back to see what was up. They knew where I was at, so…

"Mom, wusup? We just got back," I said.

"Oh, I don't know. Ya brother's been calling you; something about that dude, Leg or whoever," she said.

Twin got on the phone and told me something about dude sneaking in the crib the day before and hitting his stash. I told him to give me an hour and I would be over there.

"Babe, Carl's at the door for you," Keysh said. It was my big square homey who pushed a little work for me around in the project.

Siz-o, wusup boy? How was the trip?" He asked. I just looked at him for an eternal few seconds because he knew I didn't play that popping up shit.

"I saw the Ac' parked out front…wusup?" He hesitantly asked. I thought of taking him along on this drama ride, but not knowing him so well, and knowing how I got down I deferred against it.

"Yo, everything is good. Wus da deal?" I asked.

He told me that Lane and my lil' homey Darren was looking for me, then handed me a stack of money. I told him that I'd re him up in a few hours. I quickly met up with both Darren and Lane at a local Big Bear store to collect before I went to stash the near 5 grand that I had. I turned my pager on not even an hour ago and already it was beeping continuously. Damn, I still needed to get that cell phone. I would have to call Nuts in the morning to get the hook up.

I stopped by Pops out south to stash my ends in the safe that I had dug into the ground in his chick's garage. This 'Roselyn', was a mysterious broad. Pop said that she was a Mason, who drove a bus for COTA. I didn't feel her, but I didn't have to know her personally. I parked the Acura in the garage where I had my Bonneville at. I drove it out to Gahanna's suburb where my China Doll, Goldie, stayed with her grandma.

Fortunately she was home. I had her drive me 10 minutes to mom's townhouse in her Honda Accord. A ritual of mine never let anyone know what you're coming in. Be unpredictable; keep them guessing. I liked that she didn't ask any questions.

I went inside to holler at Twin, while Goldie waited outside.

"Bruh, this muthaphucka came over Friday night to sell me an ounce of green. I sold him a half ounce, too. And I know that bitch peeped me go in the laundry room to get it. So I know it was him. Ma said he came over here Saturday morning at about 10 o'clock for me. I stayed at Stephanie's, though. Bruh, I'm ready to go blow this bitch nigga's head off," Twin said.

"Yo, I told you to cut that square loose. Then you let him come here to mom's house. Damn, bruh! How much was it?" I asked.

"Some lil' shit; a few quarters and balls I was gon' bang. I blew down at his lil' bitch ass homey, D-Dub's last night. They act like they ain't know shit or where he was at," He said.

"And of course he ain't been at his fat bitch's crib?" I asked rhetorically.

Twin just agreed, shaking his head no. We were gonna catch up with this joker. I was gonna make sure of it. I told Twin to chill for the night with his son and son's mom. Once he ran out of work I would get him right.

"Check it, Dust'll be out in 36 hours. We'll put the word out on the low and find this fucker by Tuesday night. He's probably done jacked off and smoked up that little work by now, but we'll get him. Now let me go say hey to moms, and then we'll bounce. I got some people waiting on me," I told him. I returned back downstairs from seeing moms a few minutes later.

"Come on, you ready. Yo bruh, you thought about getting a place for you and Stephanie?" I asked him leaving out the door. I could see he was giving it some thought.

"Naw, I'ma have the bitch go next week to see what's up, though. Aw, I see you got lil' Goldie wit you," He said walking over to the driver side window of the Honda to say what's up.

We pulled out of mom's together, both heading to Gahanna. It was almost 9 o'clock and I still had a pack to go pick up for my people. It had been a few months since I fucked Goldie, and I badly wanted to punish her. But I knew the possibility of her grandma letting me in were slim, let alone doing my business. Being that not even a year ago, just a few doors down from their place, Twin and I upped guns at Chocolate's party on some lame Gahanna cats.

So I suggested to Goldie that we ride around to the park by her crib. I was pressed for time, but had to get mine. We had a quick 2 minutes of foreplay; kissing, titty sucking, and finger fucking. I had her petite 120 pound frame ride me for about 10-15 minutes, where she exploded on my dick. Twice! During her second nut I had to withdraw to keep from unloading. I instructed her to get in doggy, which we realized wasn't going to work in her compact Honda. So I laid her on the seat cocking her legs up and began to plug her tight, soaking wet pussy. I gripped her ass cheeks as I had her hold the back of her thighs. To make sure she couldn't scratch or bite me. Five minutes later I pulled out and shot a thick, snotty wad onto her belly. I assured her before I bounced that I'd be in touch. I stopped at a payphone before hitting the highway to call Keysh and then Lane to tell him to have everyone be over at Carl's to pick up at 10 o'clock.

I stopped by P.'s bitch's house to grab an eighth of a key out of my brick, and then I headed to Carl's spot.

Chapter 18: Setting Marks

I could feel things start to heat up, and some decisions would have to be made. Life was like a chess game, every move counted. Some moves took time, but others had to be made quickly; with precision.

I got a call from Pop about noon telling me that my aunt, his sister, Big Cynthia, had recently moved back in town a few days ago. And that she was looking to get in contact with me. My aunt Cint was like a legend. Back in the day she was a madam out on Main Street, beating up bitches and niggas. She also ran a number of after hour spots, as well as her cathouse.

However, sometime during the late 80s, she got hooked on crack and lost herself. She moved away to Alabama where her father's family was from. Where I heard she got clean and lived the square, country life with some older cat. I hadn't seen her since I was a youngster. I got her address from Pop and shot to her residence. Surprisingly so, she only stayed 10 minutes away from me and Keysh's apartment on the Hilltop. The infamous 'West Side'!

I parked in front of the house and walked up to knock on the door.

"Hey, are you Siza...Siz-o?" Some big-eyed white girl asked. I nodded my head yes and then she let me in.

"Cint, Siz-o's here!" She yelled.

Big Cint walked out of the bedroom in the back, "How you doing baby? Come on in and sit down. Oh damn, you done grown up. Last time I saw you, you was a little boy. You damn near six feet tall!"

"Yeah," I said as we went on chopping it for the next hour or so. She reminded me so much of 'Vera' from HARLEM NIGHTS. Always talking shit and ordering people around. I could see that she already had flunkies and hoes around her; after just being in town for only a few days. I bounced from Aunt Cint's at about 3 and headed down to our car lot to holler at P. My D-town cousin Mike would be here by Friday for me to introduce him to P. and Nuts. We were gonna try and do something big. I knew P. had been having some problems with his connect game; AKA, Fat Cat. P. wanted to deal directly with the man down in Miami, Cuban Manny. Cat, however, didn't want it to go down like that. Not if he could help it.

I killed a few hours that evening by taking Keysh and Jewel to Ponderosa Steakhouse. Nuts joined me along with his girl Heady and his daughter T.T.

"Bling, bling, bling," my phone rang. "Yo, wus good?" I answered.

"Siz-o! I know where this black ass nigga at. He hangin' at his fat bitch's house with that lame nigga Roc. The fiend Slim Jim told me that they went to the store or somewhere. But they'll be back, dude's car still there. They're in fat girl's ride. Me and the homies about to go around there. How long is it gon' take you to get out here?" He asked.

"Bruh, I'm having dinner wit the family right now. What time is it? Just....." he cut me off, "Well look, I'll call you back in bout an hour or two," he said as he hung up.

'This fucking guy', I thought. I sat quietly, staring intently out the window as everyone looked at me in wide-eyed anticipation as to what may have been going on.

"Siz-o, wusup?" Nuts asked me.

"Ain't shit. Yo, let's go outside and smoke while the ladies finish eating. C'mon," I told Nuts.

I gave him a brief summary of what was up as he assured me that if I needed him to just call. Our chicks finally arrived outside where I gave Heady $50 on the bill she had paid.

I dropped Keysh and my daughter off at home then I headed down to P.'s honeycomb hideout, where I waited for Twin to call. The knucklehead was so out of control, if he had only waited...

P. said he could send Snoop and 'Los to kidnap him and bring him out to the West Side junkyard; a venue that P. had his hand in where many men had disappeared. I was on my second shot of Hennessy when, at about midnight, my phone rang. It was Twin.

"Bruh," he said sounding exasperated.

"Yo! Wus good? Where......" He cut me off.

"Ay, where you at? I'm bout to come holla at you," Twin said.

I told him I was at one of P.'s spots, but to meet me at Aunt Cint's.

I headed over to her place and Twin arrived a few minutes after with his fellow gangbanging homey, Fat Boy.

He told me that as they were headed up the steps to Legs' chick's crib to do a kick door, their ambush was foiled. Legs and his homey Roc were in the apartment getting froze. It turns out that Roc had coincidentally stepped out onto the porch to get some air and smoke a cigarette when he peeped Twin , Fat Boy, and Big Ed (the Enforcer) creeping up the steps. The scary coward started dumping and they all began to blaze. Someone called 911 quick Twin suspected because by the time they got to the car the next project lot over they had heard sirens.

However, they made it up out of there. Twin was fuming mad; I could see it on his face. He kept speaking of different scenarios like, 'how they should've waited for them to come out' and or 'followed them.', and on and on.

I didn't really know his banging homies, and didn't want to. On this side of the game it was good to only fuck with a few, which was why I pulled him off to the side and asked him why he didn't wait until Dust got out the next day. He was too ashamed to even answer.

We parted ways from Aunt Cint's at about 1a.m. I told him to call me in the morning or by noon after he picked Dust up from county.

As I headed home I thought about how this situation needed to be resolved. And fast. I didn't like problems. And neither did the people I was affiliated with. Time played a part in everything. And it had to be utilized precisely.

The next day I didn't catch up with Dust and Twin until late that evening. Mom cooked a big dinner and afterwards we headed to the 8-Ball pool hall in the Short North. Where we had some drinks and discussed last night's drama. Dust was fired up and ready to put in work.

"Here y'all, let's toast this drink to Mista Legs restin' in piss," Dust said as we clanked our glasses. "Now watch this." He banged in the 8-ball on me as he said, "See, I ain't lost it. That's yo ass Siz-o."

"Nigga, that ain't shit. This Tang is beating on my brain. Plus, I just smashed you two games straight. C'mon y'all, let's bounce," I said.

***

I went to see P. the following morning to get reloaded. I emphasized to him how much of an asset it would be to both of us if he'd teach me how to whip my own work. He eluded me like he had done the last time

I had half jokingly, but seriously, asked him to. He'd tell me I needed to have my focus and stop smoking trees first. And also that whipping was a whole other side of life. Once you went there, it was no turning back. Well, I was ready to be all in. I didn't do shit halfway, I did it to the fullest. Some niggas stayed on the block with a pack for 10 years. Fuck that, GO HARD or GO HOME.

I left feeling rather frustrated and thinking of Straughter, my uncle Red's people from the D-town. He was one of the few cats left from Stutter man's crew. I had seen Straughter twice in the last 6 months. And he was steady trying to get me to cop work from him, telling me he had cheap prices; and that it was 'butta'. And he also emphasized how he had mad love for me. You know the game that comes with persuasion. We exchanged numbers, but I never intended on calling him. Now I was really contemplating on doing so.

I headed to my Hilltop trap house to distribute a fresh half of a key; 9 soft, and 9 hard. I paged all of my associates who were waiting on me. They knew that this meant to meet at the designated place. I called Twin and told him to bring Dust westward to pick up his pack. He had arranged to crank out of his sister Angie's apartment in the Short North. He was too hot in his original east side neighborhood out on Main Street. He had also hooked up wit some light, damn near white, mixed chick named Kelly who stayed a few blocks from Angie on 11th Avenue. His homeboy had hooked him up wit her in the county jail.

As I hung up wit Twin and walked into my spot, my phone rang. Ironically it was a yellow bone chick that I had met a few months back in Legs' project.

"Yo Robin, wus good? How you get my number?" I asked her.

"Oh, I got it from ya sister. I saw her at the carryout by my house," she said.

"Micia tripping", I thought. She briefly met Robin, though, when

I took her over to mom's place to bone. I'd speak to Micia as soon as I got a chance. She should've got the bitch's number for me instead. Thanksgiving was next week so I would see her by then.

I took down Robin's number and told her that I'd call her later. I was busy. She didn't sound happy, but I didn't give a fuck.

My cousin Mike was coming to town Friday afternoon. 48 more hours… P. and I saw this as an excellent opportunity to legitimize some of our dirty money. I mean, we had the car lot and garage and P. was working on copping a few old houses, but we were looking for something more solid; something to bring prosperity to the city, as well as to ourselves.

I chilled in the 'Park for the rest of the day; and Thursday as well, just marinating my thoughts. I needed to go over to P.'s to play a few games of chess. Something I really took to in Juvie'. However, I laid in all day wit Keysh playing card games, conversing, and fucking every other hour. I spent Thursday at my little dude Darren's blowing hydro and playing Play Station while his moms gave me a fresh twist on my braids. Me, Carl, and Darren gambled for 20s and 50s on Madden, NBA Live, and Knockout Kings. Later that evening I decided to take Keysh and my Jewel to meet my Aunt Cint. We stayed for an hour or so then went home where I helped Keysh with dinner. She loved that. The tacos were banging, as was the sex. I even talked Keysh into giving me some head. She was good, too; a natural. With time she would be great.

***

I was up by 9a.m. As Keysh and my daughter had a bath, I made French toast and Canadian bacon. I also made a number of calls and answered a few important pages. That fucking mutt Robin had paged me

5-6 times last night. I turned my phone off when I was at home. Nobody really called it. I basically only used it to answer my pages. The broad was geeking for something. And I had a feeling that it wasn't good. She was bad, but she had some of that loose pussy. And 4 kids! I checked in wit P., then ate my breakfast and got dressed. My cousin would be arriving at the Hyatt downtown in a few hours. He had reserved a suite the day before. We were all heading down to club 'Imaginations' later that night to get acquainted and kick it. Perhaps even celebrate, depending on the outcome. I had Keysh get ready for me to take her to her mom's for the weekend. I would be very busy. She wasn't excited about it, but knew all of what I had brewing so she complied and put a half smile on her face. I told her I would be coming to get her early Sunday afternoon. As she made sure she emphasized it to me, too.

After I dropped her off I went to drop off a couple of packs and pick up a few stacks here and there. I met up with P. at the car lot at about 1 o'clock, then we did a little miscellaneous running around. About 2:30 my pager buzzed. It read (614) 224-1111-705. It was a downtown number; the Hyatt, room 705. I called the hotel, room 705.

"Yeah, wutup?" An unfamiliar voice said.

"Yo, somebody page Siz-o?" I asked.

"Hold on, bruh," said the unfamiliar voice.

"Siz', wusup dog? I just got checked in. Uh, where you at? What time you comin' through?" My cousin Mike asked.

"Probably about what....." I asked P.

"Tell him about, 45 minutes to an hour," P. said.

"Yo, about an hour. That's cool?" I asked him.

"Yeah, that's straight. We gon' order some food and kick back. My dude, D-Lo wit me," said Mike.

"'Aight, do y'all thing. We'll be down in a few ticks," just as I hung up, the phone rang. It was my headache of a slut, Robin. I told her I would call her when I got up north by her 'hood; a 49 fake out move, because it wasn't going to happen today.

We arrived at the Hyatt an hour later. The valet parked the Infiniti as we entered the lobby heading for the elevator. I pressed button 7. When we reached our floor we slid down the hall to 705. After just one knock the door was quickly opened. D-Lo ushered us in. We all had a nip of Henny, except for P., and then got acquainted. P. and my cousin Mike hit it off right away. Within an hour I could already see where the whole thing was headed. P. had it somewhat planned. When I told him about my cousin and his wife he had for seen then what he was trying to do. All he needed to do was get acquainted with and fill my cousin Mike out. Our homey Cooks had attempted to open up a hip-hop clothing store inside of Northland Mall just last summer. It somehow didn't work out, though. So now P. felt that he had a golden opportunity here. He just had to invest the money and stay watching over his investment. Our investment! We all agreed that the proper arrangements had to be made, but within a month's time the wheels would be set in motion and our business would be opened. P. told Mike to come up with the name of the place and he would do the rest. He already had a location in mind; Mike just had to simply get a small business loan that we would pay for. Laundering 50-100 thousand dollars was nothing for us to have done. P. would set up financing my cousin and his wife with a place to stay here in Columbus. After making a few calls, particularly to his accountant, he could move on down to the 'Bus. By the first week of December all of the puzzle pieces would be put together; according to our calculations.

We left the hotel for P. to go get his hair braided and get fresh, just as I had to do, too. But we had reserved to have dinner at Mitchell's Steakhouse at 8 o'clock; only a few hours away. P. started to call and invite a few familiars to help occupy our 10 guest table. I decided to go ahead and get myself a suite for the weekend at the Hyatt, as well before we left. I just needed to go grab some gear and a few other things, and then come back and get showered and fresh. I decided to call Goldie while I was making my runs.

"Yo boo, I got a few hours to kill and uh, I'm headed back down to my suite at the Hyatt. Me and my peoples is going to Mitchell's at eight. You can come too if you want." I told her.

"Well yeah, that's what's up, babe. Me and my girls are supposed to kick it later, but I can kick it wit you now. I was wondering when you was gon' call me," said Goldie.

"Girl, you knew I was gon' call you. I been handling my biz, you know. Yo, bring you a fly lil' dress to rock. And maybe some cosmetics or something to get cleaned up after...you already know," I said, real slick like.

"How long you gon' be? It's room 612," I said.

She said she'd be 45 minutes; coming from Gahanna. We met up at the room an hour later. For round one she gave me a wild rodeo ride, bursting onto my dick like a water balloon. I finished her off in the huckle buck, skeeting my nut all over her belly and breasts. I went for round two after she sucked my limp dick back to granite rock form. This time I hit her with anger and rage; beast mode, from the back. We got cleaned up and headed down to the limo waiting in front of the hotel. Everybody had a ball at Mitchell's and ate real well. A couple of the homeys asked me what was up with Goldie and did she have a sister. She did, I told them, but she was only 16. Goldie was only 17, which is why I told her that she couldn't hit the club with us that night. Of course I could've got her in, but that wasn't my plan.

We dropped her off to her car after dinner, where I hugged and kissed her goodbye. She had a great time but was salty that her (our) night had been cut short. Especially with her knowing that I had the suite for the weekend.

Drunk off Dom', the limo dropped us off in front of 'Imaginations' at about a quarter 'til eleven. My cousin Mike and D-Lo stepped out rocking minks and dab hats. P., Nuts, and my self wore everything from Versace, to Louie, to Iceberg. All the bitches had on Coogi dresses and Gator heels. To say that we were fly was a major fucking understatement!

We headed to V.I.P. to get a few tables and some more Dom P. P. had LaDon send for Cat and Hollywood. They arrived at our table 10 minutes later, where we introduced them to my cousin Mike and D-Lo. We chopped it heavy for the next few hours. It turned out that Cat knew quite a few of the players and pimp niggas that they knew from the 'D'.

By the time we left the club I was in such a visual zone about the future that I couldn't even focus on any pussy. Although Hollywood had hooked up a handful of hoes for my cousin Mike 'anem, I was cool. The first thing that D-Lo said when he saw Kim was that he wondered how much dough he could get out of her in just one week on the track up in the 'D'. Yeah, it was pimpin' for real here. And Kim was a bad peanut-butter brown stallion, half Black and half Dominican. She was originally from Miami, but had come up to the 'Bus with Cat about a year ago.

I headed back to my room, catching a ride with my high school 'X', Nashaya, AKA, Honey, who I had flirted with half the night. She was salty as fish pussy when I didn't invite her up. I told her that I would call her, but that I was too drunk to do anything that night, which of course was just a fake out. I got up to my room and called Keysh. "Why not?" I thought. She really dug it. I let her talk me to sleep.

CHAPTER 19: The Migraine Headache

I woke up at around noon. I started to order a late brunch but decided against it. I needed to get on the move. So I got showered and dressed and then, checking to see if I had any messages (on the hotel phone), I noticed that the light was indeed beeping. It was my cousin from the floor up above me. I hit him back to see what was up. We kicked it briefly about last night before I told him that I had a few moves to make. But I would slide by his room in a couple of hours, perhaps to shoot over to the City Center Mall and or do some rolling through the city; in his Benz, no doubt.

I headed west to pick up and stash a few dollars. Nuts called me while I was rolling to tell me he had just copped some Evergreen Indo from Hollywood Rick earlier. I told him to meet me back down at the room so we could blaze. I still hadn't eaten yet so I told Nuts to swing by Kingro's to grab a pizza and some wings. I told him about rolling out wit my cousin for a few ticks, too. Which he concurred he would roll wit us.

I hadn't heard from Twin or Dust so I decided to page Twin. He was supposed to take Dust to get a pager earlier today. He hit me back as I pulled into the hotel parking garage. After hearing everything was cool, I told him to meet me down at my suite to rap a taste and to meet his cousin.

"Give me bout an hour. I gotta go pick Dust up from Angie's crib," he said.

"'Aight, hurry up!" I told him.

"Muphucka, I'ma be there. Y'all niggas went clubbin' last night?" He asked rhetorically.

"Yeah, hell yeah! But yo, Nuts is on his way down wit some frosty Evergreen. And we ordered some pizza and wings, so hurry up," I said.

"Yeah. I'm on my way," said Twin. As I ended the call the phone rang again. It was Robin, screaming that I shitted on her last night by never showing up. Damn, I had had it with this mutt. I was gonna give this hoe some killer dick tonight. Or worse!

We kicked it at my suite for a short while. Mike and Lo came down to meet Twin and Dust. I watched the look in these niggas eyes the whole time. At one point Twin asked me, 'What?' in a low toned voice. I shook my head to say 'nothing', but still I watched his eyes. I knew his and Dust's ways. Never had they violated against my word, though.

After smoking on some green and briefly discussing Legs' whereabouts, they rolled out. Nuts had just hollered at P. and told him what was up. He told Nuts that after we hit the mall and took a ride, to come by the 'West Side' bar. It was virtually ours, but front owned by our associates, 'The Twins'.

***

"Look bitch, do what you gotta do to get that nigga out tonight. And call my pager when he get there. I told you I got you; the nigga got some big paper stacks in the crib," Legs told Robin.

"Nigga, I been tryin'. You know dude think he the shit. He don't wanna give a bitch the time of day. We only fucked once at his mom's house. The nigga beast fucked me, too. Uh, he ain't got no cheese over there?" She asked.

"Naw, ain't shit over there. But I know it is at his crib wit his baby's mom. So make that shake. I'ma be waitin' for that call. Ya dig?" He hung up the phone; aggravated with Robin and his coke habit calling.

After a few hours of flossing the city's east and north side, and doing some no conscious shopping, we headed west to meet P. at the bar. We all had a few nips and politicked for a few ticks. Nuts tried to talk everyone into going clubbin' again but Mike and D-Lo said that they just wanted to head back to the room wit some pussy. Which P. supplied by calling Co-Co, Hollywood's baby's mom. Co-Co was like the youngest madam I knew. Although she didn't claim to be, she was; and so much more. Hollywood didn't mind her hooking up the homies and affiliates. At first D-Lo was tripping by saying, "I know she don't think a pimp about to pay for no pussy. I'm a superstar for real. Let me speak to Co-Co, P. Dog."

They hit it off right away. Joking and laughing for the next ten minutes or so. He handed the phone back to P. and said that he and Mike were headed back to the room.

"Well, check this out, I'ma go pick up Co-Co and these chicks and bring 'em down there. Hollywood's ass ain't gonna let her bring them down there by herself," P. said. He laughed, as they walked out the door, telling D-Lo that Co-Co did not charge any of us. It was a Cardinal Rule.

"Well, I'm out too, Siz-o. I guess I'm bout to go kick it wit Heady for the night. Hit the club, shoot some pool, or do something," Nuts said.

"'Aight, I'll holla at you. I'ma go check on a few things. You ready? Let's roll," I told Nuts.

I headed for the highway as I called my Aunt Angie's to spit at Dust. "Young Siz-o! Wusup wit you, playboy? I need to holla at you. Where you at?" He asked.

"Rollin'. Why, wusup?" I asked.

"It's about ole' boy, Legs. I paged ya brother, he ain't called back, though. Oh, hold on. This is probably him."

"Nah, nah, dig…I'm on my way. I'll be about ten minutes."

"Ay, dig, stop at the drive-thru and pick me up a pack of squares and a 4-'0'." Dust quickly asked.

"Oh, hell no! Nah, I got you. I'm on my way," I told him.

I hit the local corner store 'Kelly's' before I got to my Aunt Angie's. I slid in to rap to Dust and see what was up with the walking dead man, Legs. Dust said that my aunt's home girl, Passion, had told her some dark skinned cat who called himself 'A-Town' had been kicking it with her for the last few days. They had been getting' froze, she said. I had my aunt call her but she didn't answer. So she paged her. The broad called back just as Twin walked in. Dust explained to him what was up while Angie asked Passion what was up with the dude, Legs.

"Let me see the phone. Yo, wus good, home girl? Where dude at now?" I asked her.

Wusup? This Siz-o? Um, I ain't seen him since earlier. About six o'clock, I think. Yeah, I met him at 'Pam's' bar a couple a weeks ago. He might call me tonight. I'm at my girl's now, but we about to go out, though," she said.

"Well, check this out, home girl…that nigga call you or come through, call my aunt and she'll 3-way me. Do that and I'll shoot you a stack, ma. A grand! At least a couple hundred if it ain't him."

"Okay, cool. I definitely will. Angie is my girl. Hey, my girl Kizzi knows you, too," she said.

I cut the small talk and eventually concluded the call. I told Twin and Dust what was up, so all we could do was chill. I called Keysh and talked to her for a while, while we had a few drinks and blew a sticky blunt of Evergreen. I had a page vibrating my hip. I checked to see that it was 'The Headache', Robin. This was the perfect time to torcher her. I told Keysh I'd be to get her by noon then hung up to call Robin's worrisome ass. And I caught an idea while doing it. After kicking some x-rated game to this freaky hoe, I talked her into letting me and Dust come through to gang bang her. I tried to include Twin as well, but the hoe said all she could handle was two dicks at once. Twin said that he was gonna chill at Angie's in case the call came through, he'd be close. I told him to hit us if he got the call.

"Ay, bust a nut on that hoe's back for me," Twin said.

"Oh yeah, I am. I'ma bust one on her face. This bitch's bad ass kids better be asleep, too. It's after midnight!" I said as Dust laughed.

We arrived at Robin's crib 20 minutes later, smoking the end of a sticky Evergreen blunt. I grabbed the Trojans out of the glove box and the Ruger 9mm out of the stash. The bitch was in heated anticipation because she let us in before I could even knock. And I wasn't even banging the block. After a quick introduction and a shot of Tequila, the torcher began. Wit Dust in her back door and me in her skull. We trashed this hoe. We choked her, scratched her, bit her, yanked on her good ass hair... hit her in the ass, in the pussy. After she gave me and Dust head I went back for seconds. Not giving a fuck that she was screaming about how her throat was sore. If we was paying this hoe then we sure would've been getting' our money's worth. Damn, it was nearly 4 a.m. I had to wake

Dust up. I thought of U.G.K.'s new joint, '3 in the Mornin''. We bombed out and headed back to Aunt Angie's. I was ready to go pick Keysh and my Jewel up; go home and punish Keysh and then pass out. I would just wait though. I'd just crash at Aunt Angie's until the morning time. Then I would go and get my boo's fine ass. Somehow though, I had this Legs character on my mind. How strange?!

CHAPTER 20: The Stone in My Shoe

I awoke on my Aunt Angie's couch at about 9:30 a.m. No call ever came through about dude. Twin had already bounced to his baby mama's, so I woke Dust up to see if he wanted to be dropped off at his broad's; which he did. I called Keysh to let her know that I was on my way. When I got there I rolled me a blunt and called my cousin at the Hyatt while I waited in my car for Keysh and my daughter. I know my cousin and D-Lo were heading back to the 'D' that afternoon. I rapped with him for a few minutes while we explained to each other how our nights went. When we concluded our call I had a good feeling about the near future and what we had planned. I would grind hard for the next few weeks and spend only what I had to. I was about to call and check in with P. but then decided that would wait until I got home. I told Keysh that I would make her breakfast when we got there. She was so happy to see me; as if it had been two weeks and not two days. I was happy to see her too, though. I had my Sunday plans set for her. I told her a little bit about my weekend and some of the plans we had made. She believed in me, and really loved me. This was so important that a man's family trusted him, and loved him unconditionally.

When we got home, walking into the building, I noticed that the door was cracked. I thought, "What the fuck?"

"Keysh, go back out to the car. Come on, let's go!" I yelled.

"Why? What's wrong?" She asked.

I grabbed the Ruger and slid back into the building. I eased the door open and crept carefully through the apartment. No one was there. The place had been slightly ram shacked. I had almost forgotten that I had a short stack of 5 grand stashed, apparently not well enough, in my daughter's closet. But then I noticed the opened toy where the money once was. I went to where I had my 40 S&W Glock stashed, and there it was. The front door had been pried open by, probably a crowbar. I called P. and before he could answer I heard, "Uh, Siz-o. Siz-o it's me, Brenda."

It was my dope fiend neighbor who only copped at my spot over at Lane's. And she also had a fine young daughter who was infatuated with me. I peeked out the door, showing Brenda my pointing finger to hold on, as I briefly explained to P. what had happened. He told me he was on his way right over.

"Brenda, wusup? Uh, come in. Come in," I said.

"I wanted to tell you, babe that it happened last night. Whoever it was, they banged and banged on the door. Then it just stopped. But I can tell you, it was a red car wit a black top that they left in. It was backed in wit the engine running the whole time. The car looked like your grey car," she said.

"My Cutlass?" I asked.

She nodded yes. I told her to come by the spot later for compensation. It was official now that it was the nigga Legs. The red Cutlass was Roc's. How the fuck did he know where I stayed at, though? I would undoubtedly find out.

P. blew through to get the details as I explained to him what was up.

CHAPTER 21: Removing the Stone

The thing about nickel bagging junkies like this 'Legs' character was that they never lasted. And they were so predictable. My Aunt Angie called me at about eleven the following night with Miss Passion over at her place. I was out at the 'West Side' bar with a few affiliates.

"Yeah, so what's the deal?" I asked, slightly buzzed off of a couple shots of cognac.

"Here. You talk to her," said my aunt.

"Siz-o? Hey, he at my house now. He sent me to the store for him. So wusup?" Passion asked.

"Ay, where you stay at, On Summit Avenue, down the street from Angie, right?" I asked her.

"Yep, it's 1217. The back door will be open. He by his self now, the Dude Roc left," she said.

"Alright listen, I'll be bout an hour or so. Let him get nice and fucked up, ya dig? I'll see you in a minute. I got that for you, too. And uh, Passion, you know what's gon' happen to you if you ain't bein' 100 wit me, right?"

"Tsk. Yeah, I know. I got kids, I ain't on that. Angie is my people."

"'Aight cool. Just so you know," I told her.

I had got the hook-up at McKinley's Junkyard from P. before I bounced and then I called Twin for him to meet me at Passion's crib. Dust was already with him. I gave him the address and we met in the alley behind her crib twenty minutes later.

"What we got here? Mossberg pump, the Tech, Glock...this is a little too much but listen; y'all follow my lead and back me up. Now this bitch got kids. I don't think she'll be a problem so let me handle it. We are takin' this nigga to the dumping spot. He goes in the trunk wit me. Y'all gon' follow close behind. We don't want shit to get messy in here if it don't got to. Dust!" I said emphatically.

"I'm cool, man. Let's go," he said.

"'Aight, let's do this right. Go home and bang the old ladies. Y'all ready? Let's go get this cocksucker," I said as we headed for the back door.

As I opened the door I could hear music playing. It was Genuwine's 'Pony'.

"No nigga! My kids might come down here," Passion said while she grinded on Legs.

"Well, let's go upstairs, then," Legs told Passion.

"Not quite yet," I said.

"Bitch, don't you move. Hoe ass nigga!" Dust demanded.

Twin stood by the front door holding the Tech firmly. I said what's up and nodded to Passion as I handed her a thousand stack of fives, tens, and twenties. She looked amazed. I whispered in her ear for a quick minute then signaled for them to stand Legs up. He was spooked; and high as a 'New Jack' junky out of the Carter Apartments.

"Now Legs, just take us to the money," I told him as Dust frisked him, pulling maybe a grand or so out of his pocket and a healthy powder bag. I had him give it to Passion and gestured for him to keep the money.

Twin took a peek outside before we escorted him out. Dust smacked him in the back of the head with the butt of the gauge.

"Yo," I said through clinched teeth, "We don't want no blood trail. You feel me?!" We walked discreetly to our vehicles. When I popped the Buick's trunk, Legs knew that his minutes were now limited. Dust pushed his limp body inside.

"Come on, let's ride," I said.

It was the longest fifteen minute ride I ever took. But however, it went smooth. Our initial plan was to put Legs, along with the Buick, directly inside the car compressor. But we decided to have a little fun with it. So we popped the trunk. He plead with us for his life. And he insisted that Roc had the rest of the money. Which, I never cared about beyond the principle; the principle of the cowards coming into my crib. So we gave the lame an ultimatum, the compressor or the grinder. He still babbled on. I had decided since he never bled in the Buick's trunk I didn't have to smash it. I told Twin, "Bruh, this is yo' mess. Now y'all got…four hours tops to dispose of this piece of shit. In that little shack over there is a room covered in plastic. Make this maggot remember y'all on his way to hell before y'all put his ass in the grinder. It's a couple Carhartt suits over there for y'all. Use 'em, then burn 'em wit the rest of the trash," I said. Dust and Twin both had the look of death in their eye. I knew they were about to enjoy this work.

"Mr. Legs, look at you. Aw shit and he done pissed himself. You pitiful, dude. This is my city, nigga. You an imposter! How's it feel to know you about to die? You came into my house. Where my wifey and my lil' girl be. Rest in piss! I'll say what's up to Passion for you. Yo, I ain't gon' keep y'all from y'alls work, family. I'm out. Y'all call me for breakfast at bout 9 or 10 o'clock," I told Twin and Dust.

"Ay," Dust said following me to the car. "What's up wit ole' girl, the

Passion hoe? I saw you whisperin' somethin' to her. Do I need to go touch the bitch?"

"Nah, she cool. What I told the broad was that my people and myself, got her info; where her kids go to school, where her mama stay...that type of shit. To just pretend that she never knew dude, you feel me?" I said.

Dust was real thorough like that. I told him to call me by noon, and then I jumped in the Toyota Camry rental and bounced. I took a few minutes while riding home to imagine what they were doing to the soon-to-be deceased. I got to my place a short while later. I got inside and rolled me a little hydro' blunt as I flicked through the channels on the TV. Not watching anything in particular. I thought briefly about the night before where Keysh was sitting on my lap crying while I clutched my Glock 40. She was pleading with me not to go do anything crazy. I didn't feel invincible but I knew she didn't fully understand who or what I was. It reminded me of what P. would say, "Respect the State (laws), but fear the FEDS." Just then Keysh walked into the living room. She played like she was headed to the refrigerator for a cold, late night drink. Squinting, she looked my way and said, "Hey. What time is it?"

I said, "Wusup? It's bout...3.a.m."

I told her I had been at the bar with the fellas. And that I had to sober up for an hour or so before I drove home. She understood, saying that she started to call me, but...I told her that it was cool. I would go on for many years concealing my dark side of life from my family.

I rubbed Keysh's stomach for a while then gestured that we go to bed. We stopped in my daughter's room to check on her while she peacefully slept. Once we were in bed I told her that I had a place for us in Westerville, but we had to wait until the second week of January to move in; which was only a few weeks away. She could stay at her mother's house or my mother's house until then; whichever one. She was so happy, telling me how it would be perfect timing for my daughter's birthday party; and also, how she was scared to stay at the apartment at night alone. Everything was going to be alright. I kissed her, and soon tore into her juicy, pregnant pussy. Round 2 came an hour later and...Round 3 in the morning. But what else was new (in my bedroom)?

CHAPTER 22: The Business Firm

The New Year came in with a blast. And we indeed partied like it was 1999 instead of '97. We opened my Cousin Mike's store up, 'D & C's' Clothing/Fashions; D & C standing for Detroit and Columbus. And soon the profits would be coming monthly. I chose to let him and P. work out the particulars. A mistake, I would realize later on. No matter how much you trust someone, always be on the front line about your business. I was, however, still young and not yet fully focused. But life is a learning experience, and that's how the story goes. I mean, in a normal life I would have just been graduating from high school. Instead, I was living the good life of crime, fortune, and street fame. I had recently been initiated in what we, a select few, had constructed as the FIRM; or West Side's Finest! A criminal organization headed by me, P., and Nuts. With me being the youngest. We would later become something much bigger.

***

Keysh loved the new condo. She was so enthused with decorating it; and going all out furnishing it. Not holding back at all on the ten grand I gave her. She bought leather couches, an exclusive oak dinette set, a walnut almond bedroom set, a Whirlpool washer and dryer, expensive rugs and pictures, and colored bunk beds for my daughter; and our arriving child who was coming in just a few months.

I copped a 50 inch big screen from my man with the supercharged cable box equipped with all the pay per-view channels. I helped my mama and Micia get a house out by the airport near Sunbury Road. It was an $80,000 3 bedroom with a fenced in yard, a 60 foot driveway, and a big 2-car garage where I could keep one of my stuntastic rides in. Either here or at one of the many storages we had 'full access granted' to.

Twin had even got back with Stephanie a few weeks ago, getting them an apartment just five minutes down the street from my condo out in Westerville. The half of a key that I had fronted him had helped to obtain it, and so much more. He had a slight problem, though. He had just got my phantom first love Nashaya's B.F.F. pregnant. We had been kickin' it wit them real tough for the last couple of months. Nashaya had called me over to a birthday set for her girl Meko back in December, where I introduced Twin to her. So now he was back and forth from Meko's to Stephanie's.

Dust was a wild creature of human nature. He had to dwell and reside in the 'hood. Particularly the city's East Side. He had a place on Champion Avenue by the interstate bridge and a crack spot on Wilson and Main. He had been spending a lot of his free time at the Boy's Club over on Ohio Avenue; teaching the kids in the boxing program.

However, I had just recently found out about him disposing of the late Legs' partner Roc, not even a week ago. He told me that the morning that they had finished Legs off, he himself had crept over to Roc's place on Bryden Road and waited in the alley by the dumpster for Roc to come out to get in his car and go to the shop where he worked; where Dust was going to execute him. His plan was foiled because the guy never came out. He was probably frozen off coke from the night before. Well, Dust however, a few weeks later, broke into Roc's house in the a.m. hours. But this time Twin was with him. Dust was such a hypnotic dog thief that he had put Roc's pit bull in the car while they maimed and tortured Roc and his fat bitch in the basement after tasing them awake.

Meanwhile, with all that the New Year had brought, Nuts and I had manipulated a crew of guys to rob Moses' Jewelry store downtown. Now, Ali and Mo' were our guys; some cool sand niggas they were. We dealt with them regularly. We simply saw an opportunity and jumped on it. It was strictly business, though, and nothing personal. Nuts had got the inside scoop and a few of his 'Bottoms' goons to go along with my guy, a professional safe cracker and alarm disarmer, Bill. It all worked out sweet and on time. Bill, and his chick, Tammy, stayed next door to my Aunt Cint'. Tammy had owed down for some pills and 2 pounds of green. So I told Bill that if he was down to do this then he could get himself some start up money and squash his broad's debt with my aunt; who, of course, I supplied. Bill had been out of the Feds for nearly a year off of an 8 year sentence and had just got off of parole. Before his arrest, his crew was the best.

After a few days of coaxing him, he finally agreed. Now Nuts gave Bill the alarm code but Bill said he could tamper with it for a couple minutes to make it look as if it were cracked after some time. Nuts had been in the back of the jewelry store with Ali drinking, a few weeks before and heard him babbling the code to Moses prior to them all leaving. Shit, even if they had changed it Bill could still by-pass it. Nuts' goons were sent to help out with hauling, but Bill was clearly the brains. We supplied them with a repair van from the city, courtesy of P. The heist was taking place near midnight so they needed a good cover. A 24hour repair service! I mean, they couldn't be caught in a domestic vehicle in downtown Columbus. Most of it shuts down by nightfall. Nuts was in charge of seeing to it that the job was done that night. Once it was done Bill and Nuts' goons were to meet him at his Uncle Bobby Arms' place on the west side. Everything rolled smooth. Tammy took Bill to take the van back by morning and Nuts had Bobby take his goons back down to their 'hood. He headed out to his Vet broad Clara's place in Worthington when he woke, with the goods in tow. He called me at about 8, right when Clara was heading to work. I felt good when I got the call, and now I was anxious to see how much the score was. P. and I had got the 'OKAY" page last night at about 1a.m. signifying the job had been done. And now I was receiving the designed a.m. call. I arrived, coming from Westerville, by 9o'clock. Where I realized we were in possession of roughly a half a million dollars worth of diamonds and jewels, and also, a handy 35 grand. Nuts' goons were sent along as well, to make sure Bill didn't pocket any jewels or a red cent. He was drilled to do the same with them. They would all receive their pay when the time was right. Nuts and I would leave the stash here at Clara's and take the 35 cash with us. And in 3 days, if things remained copasetic, we would drive to New York to cash the jewels and diamonds in for their valued worth. Fat Cat had a Turkish jewel guy right outside of Manhattan. Which would be how we'd get hooked up with his cousin at Eli's in Columbus' Northland Mall. Nuts let it be known he was just gonna break his goons off with some work and perhaps a slick piece. A chain or a ring; not from the heist, though. Not any of the slick shit. We would squash Bill's chick's debt and give him 10%, and split the rest 3 ways between me, Nuts, and P. By the week's end we had completed our trip and became $150,000 richer. Everyone was heading down to 'Imaginations' to club and get loose. The LOX and Lil' Kim were gonna be there, so all V.I.P. niggas and bitches were gonna be there, too.

I really wasn't feeling Bad Boy at the time since my nigga Pac had got shot up out in Vegas not even 5 months ago. But I wasn't sweatin' them, though. Maybe I could get shit poppin' with Kim's lil' freaky ass. I was just kickin' it with the hoe at Misty's strip bar late last summer with my Jersey niggas; Coupe, Big June, and Jerese. I hooked up with them on the work side through their people I grew up with, Damon and Ty. All of the Jersey cats were hitting the V.I.P. with Siz-o tonight. They had paged me that afternoon for us to hook up on a half of a key of coke. Ever since P. taught me to bake my own cake a few months ago, after I nearly hooked up with Detroit Straughter, I had seen a new side of the game. With my money doing crazy flips.

Anyway, I got another series of pages earlier. It was Nashaya and Meko wanting me to get them in V.I.P. I told them to send for me once they got inside, and for them to bring some money. After concluding making all of my moves, I got fresh, clean, and crispy out at my new honeycomb hideout in Weldon Square. By 10:30 I was ready. I rocked a cream Pelle Pelle sweater and jacket, brown stonewashed Pelle jeans, and brown Gortex Timbs. Chocolate brown complemented my complexion. I wore my Cartier rims and watch with a diamond pinky ring. These rap niggas ain't have shit on this here 18 year old boss, nor did any other nigga, for that matter. I hit my braids with some braid spray, and then shot out the door and into my Acura Coupe; headed to go ball.

Nuts was 5 minutes away on the Hilltop getting gangster in a blue waist length mink, blue leather pants and gators. 'Yeah, it's on', he thought as he looked in the mirror before he bounced.

P. pulled out his Benz after he got super fly and headed to go swoop up his childhood homey, Terique. Terique had just got out of the Fed joint from doing nearly 7 years. There was nothing like coming home to your man being the 'Man'. P. had his all purpose chick, Hot Sauce, follow them in a grey Suburban with a few of her girls. We all pulled up around eleven. It was important to me that we all walked in together, representin', instead of straggling in separately like a bunch of hobos; especially on a night like this. One of North Side's Finest, Hollywood, met us at the door. We snapped a few pictures on the way in, and then headed back to V.I.P. Greeting affiliates and bitches on the way.

"Yo wusup? Its bout time y'all got here. Come on in here, man. Everybody lookin' good tonight, Bad Boy in the house now y'all. We bout to kick it," said our friend, Cooks. He was one of the heads for the North Side Firm.

"Well, get some bottles over at our table. Where are we at, back here?" P. asked pointing to our 2 corner tables where we got posted with just me, Nuts, and P. at one table, and everyone else at the other table. We wanted to rap for a few ticks about the jewelry store lick before all of the fun began.

"Now Nut, I know you kept some of them stones, right?" P. asked.

"Oh yeah. I told you I was gon' keep some, a hand full!" Nuts said with a grin. "That Turkish muphucka up in New York was geekin' when he saw these muthaphuckas. He said that they was damn near flawless. Shit...you see what we got for 'em. And I kept enough of 'em for us to split and get some nice pieces. So..."

"Oh, I slid down to the store with my lil' Dream Bug yesterday and bought her a little tennis bracelet. They was cool, all on my dick, though. 'Mike P.!' 'Hey Michael!' 'Hey buddy!'" P. said mocking Ali and Mo'.

"Ay, them sand niggas was salty; no, sandy!" He said jokingly.

"Fuck them Jew, Arab cock suckers. Yo, you know me and Nuts ate at the Italian Restaurant in Manhattan that all of the five families be eatin' at. Yeah, my Uncle John told me about it," I said to P.

"Aw yeah, y'all niggas is spaghetti connected, but can't be spaghetti made. Ain't that right? That's how it go?" P. asked.

"Yo, you on that?" I asked him gesturing a flexing threat jokingly.

Nuts just smiled with a smirk, as high a kite. We talked briefly about going to get some exclusive pieces made at Eli's Jewelry Store the first of the week, for ourselves and for our ladies. Valentine's Day was next week so we figured that we'd lace the bitches. Keysh would be geeked, no doubt. Nuts' girl Heady, we'd recently found out from Nuts, had lived up to her name. Nuts was sprung. P. had already had a couple baby mama's, his first an Italian woman from Steubenville, Ohio; but he was working on his third one with his new boo, Jereame. She was a super bad, butterscotch beauty that he had snatched from our home boy, Snoop.

We jumped back in the mix of the party. First, we stepped out onto the V.I.P. patio with the LOX and their man, Mase. Cooks and Hollywood sent the waitress to get everyone drinks and bottles while we blew the best of assorted colors and flavors of chronic weed. Suddenly, I heard a jazzy, familiar voice approaching; which soon began rapping. It was Miss Hardcore: Lil' Kim! After busting her flow, while puffing on a hydro blunt, she stepped to me. I felt somewhat like Goldie off of the 'Mack' when China Doll slid over to choose him. I had been eying her throughout her 16 bar flow, and she saw that…through her Chanel shades.

"Yo, I know you, right? Where I know you from?" Kim asked me.

"Oh, uh, probably from my man Chuck's strip bar, 'Misty's'. Last summer, it was my birthday," I said.

"Yeah, my peeps from Jersey invited me down here. That was yo' birthday, huh. Ty kept telling me about you. He wouldn't shut up. 'Siz-o this', and 'Siz-o that'. His sister used to come kick it in Brooklyn wit Larceny. That was my girl. So Siz-o, is this how y'all do it down in Ohio?"

"Yeah, I guess you could say that. Yo, you know you was pissy drunk that night. Wildin' out! You was feelin' it."

"I know. I was, right? Shit, I'm bout to be feelin' it tonight. You know what, I think I'ma write a song about y'all. Y'all pretty boy celebrities."

"Ay yo, I ain't hardly no celebrity, ma. I'm somethin' much different."

"Nah, I peep ya style, I peep ya type. You a pretty boy, thug nigga. You gangsta, but you a hood celeb'," said Kim.

She told me later on, after they performed 'All About tha Benjamins' and some of their other hits, that she had already prepared a 3 versed track in her head about a fantasy fling with me, Prince, and Dru Hill's Sysco.

We had a real wild night; so wild that it resorted to me heading over to Kim's suite at the Hyatt to fulfill her 4a.m. fantasy. She told me that morning when I bounced to look her up whenever. I was cool, though. It would be just a one time fling. I had my pager blew up repeatedly the following afternoon by my little honey bird, Nashaya. I had forgot she had told me that her and Meko had a suite at the Truman Hotel. I guess she was pissed by having to listen to Twin bang Meko all night with no dick of her own. Shit happens, though. I had stayed at the club after it closed choppin' it with tha fellas up until Miss Hardcore called me. She earned that title, because that's truly how she loved it. Anally hardcore!

***

We usually met once a month at a disclosed location to discuss business and all that pertained to it. But at this particular meeting there was discomforting tension. It was the end of April, well into the springtime, and we now met with N.S.F. and E.S.F. John 'The Cooker' Cooks, Richard 'Hollywood' Parker, and Stanley 'Fat Cat' Williams represented the North side. Michael "Money' Morrison, Thomas 'Gloves/

or Hands' Coleman, and Anthony 'Tony' Johnson represented the East side. Torrence 'Nuts' Barzini, Michael 'Mike P.' Pettway, and myself, Sizalino 'Siz-o' Jones, represented the West side. P. and I had been discussing our coke connection for the past month or so, which came through Fat Cat. P. was one of Columbus' biggest cocaine distributors. Also, he could distribute it faster than a speeding bullet. And with all of the heat that Cat had had on him lately, with the Feds and the D.E.A., his gambling debt out in Vegas, and all of our suspicions of his coke use, everyone was skeptical of his position. He supplied half of the city and over 60% of our outfit. P. had been suggesting to Cat to plug him in with the Miami connect. Which, the idea was appealing to all of us except for Cat, of course. He was not feeling it; he emphatically refused. And he assured everyone that his problems and our skepticism would all be straightened out in due time.

The meeting was over in an hour, but no one left it breathing any easier. It was nothing any of us could do about it, though. I mean, we couldn't just kill the guy. Besides him being our people, he was the one with the connection. For close to 10 years now he'd been distributing kilos of coke for the infamous 'Manny'. If we touched him it could be hell to pay. These Latin drug lords and their cartels could be as vicious as Nazis on some niggas. And it was rumored through Cat that this connected Cuban king pen of his had ties to the Columbian 'Godmother'. However, the Latin Americans didn't operate like the Mafia, with the whole wacking out a connected or made guy thing. All they cared about was the product moving. So it could be done, it was just that if.....if, was the question!

I stopped out by Windsor Terrace projects over my Aunt Angie's to see Dust. He told me that Twin was on his way over. We sat on the porch kickin' it for bout an hour wrecking on my drunk, junky aunts and uncles. Hearing the block thump we looked up to see Twin coming down riding his shiny, candy painted, midnight blue Firebird. He had his bangin' homey, Fat Boy, with him. Dust didn't really like the nigga. He didn't like too many niggas, period!

"Wusup? Wusup?" Twin asked us.

"Ain't shit; I need you to follow me to park the Ac'," I told him.

"'Aight. Well look, Fat Boy need some green. What you tryin' to get, a Q-P? Or a half?" Twin asked Fat boy.

What you gon' charge me?" He asked me.

I told the clown that we would have to see once we got out to my spot in South Park. I couldn't just send him out to the weed spot; my Jersey cats ain't know the nigga. I told twin to drop the guy off to his ride and come get me from Pop's bitch's crib where I was parking my Ac' at. Twin seemed salty about it but I didn't trust dude. I told him to have dude go to the project's 3rd circle and wait on us, because it wasn't no phone there at the spot. Once we left Pop's house I told Twin, along with Dust's approval, how I felt about Fat Boy. And then I asked him, "You ain't told dude about the junkyard or none of that, have you?"

"Naw, hell no. We done did dirt together, though," he said.

"Bruh, watch that guy. You feel what I'm sayin'?" I said.

"Yeah, nephew. We ya family, ride or die! That nigga ain't shit. You uh, know ya brotha just came from the gangsta's circle. What is it, The Black Commission, Siz-o?" Dust asked.

"Somethin' like that. It's rumored to be. You know not to talk to nobody about this shit. We supposed to deny it. So remember that," I told them.

We met Fat Boy at the tree house, hit him off with a quarter pound, and then sent him on his way. My Jersey boys blew a blunt of some exclusive shit with Dust and Twin. They called the shit G-13! My phone rang and when I answered it I heard 'Big Jaws' say, "Siz! Where you at? Keysh is about to have the baby right now. We're at O.S.U." Big Jaws was Keysh's sister.

"Yo, check it out; I'm in the 'Park. I'm on my way," I told her. "C'mon y'all, let's bounce. My son's on his way!"

I had Dust snatch a few fruity buds from Big June to roll us a blunt on the way to the hospital. I didn't smoke often, but I needed something to prepare me for what I was about to see. Watching my daughter being born a year earlier was a scary sight.

"Yo Dust, roll that shit up. Twin, open this muthaphucka up, we on the highway now," I yelled.

"Chill Siz-o. We gon' be there in 2 minutes," Twin shouted back.

"Here nigga. Go on and light that shit up, boy. Cause Keysh gon' kick off in yo' ass and nuts if you don't make it there in time," Dust said, clowning me.

*

It was 2 days later and I was back at O.S.U. medical center picking Keysh up. I helped her and my son down to the car. Yes, she had birthed me a son. Maxwell Julien Jones; named after Goldie off of 'The Mack'.

"So, how you feel, girl?" I asked her.

"I'm alright," she quietly answered.

She loosened up after a few minutes. And we kicked it all the way home, after we picked my daughter up from Keysh's mom's house. We talked about how we had a second child now and we discussed some future preparations. We also laughed at how blood shot all over my baby blue Phat Farm and my ghost white 'Js' when my son's big head came out.

"Oh, uh, how'd the operation go?" I asked her.

"Huh? Oh, I didn't get it done," she saw the look on my face and said, "Babe, I was starvin'! I would've had to wait like 24 hours until they would've tied my tubes. But I'ma go back in 2 months to get it done. I am, I promise."

We rode the rest of the way in silence.

CHAPTER 23: Getting Connected

The summer turned out to be very lucrative and exciting; going smoothly so for the next 2 years. It was now 1999 and business was all that it could be. The store was poppin'; it was even extended next door, strictly for the ladies. 'Fly Girl's Fashions!'

Our car lot was in full swing, just as our two maintenance garages were. The old man even had a towing company that we used. We were connected all over the city. At phone/pager stores, jewelry stores, pawn shops, car dealerships, restaurants, gun supply stores, shoe stores, and even with fucking clothing designers over seas. We were officially V.I.P. everywhere, kickin' it with, and courting stars, in many different locals and venues. Now, P. and Nuts had their hands in real estate but I had yet to get involved. Soon, though, I told myself. I was only 20 years young. But P. was truly in deep. He even had downtown connections that we all utilized at a price. He had narcotics detectives, state officials, and also, he had 3 lawyers: A Jewish defense lawyer, a tax lawyer, and a state lawyer. The coke business was smooth, no doubt; except for one problem. P. was talking about retirement due to all of the problems that were transpiring with our connection, 'Cat'. On the week after New

Year's, where my cousin Mike got into a scrap with 'Money' Mike from E.S.F. over breaking up a fight, and where a few affiliates, 'Hollywood' Rick, and myself had stomped and beat some loud mouthed clown down with fists and bottles; the Feds seized Club 'Imaginations' and a large amount of cash from 'Cat', hitting him with a huge fine and some non-drug related charges, as well. He wouldn't speak on any of it, but did say that the Feds were pretty pissed that they couldn't indict him on any coke. Hollywood, however, had been questioned by the D.E.A., but not charged.

Cat was now so fucked in the game, that Cuban Manny wouldn't even supply him. He owed nearly a mil', and had already screwed up two second chances so far this year. He had a $400,000 debt out in Vegas, a weekly coke habit, and moved around in different cities with different bitches for the last 2 months. Big Pace sat in with Cooker and Hollywood for N.S.F., but shit had gotten so disorientated. Pace had just opened a club in downtown Cincinnati and Hollywood seemed to had lost his marbles after the D.E.A. boys came to see him. Attending church and talking off of the wall. P. announced quickly that he would talk to him. They'd grown up together, so…he felt it was only right.

For over a month now everyone copped coke from anonymous sources; Mexicans, Jamaicans, out of state…or just stood froze until things got back organized. But 'would they' was what most of us thought.

For the past 2 years, at just 20, I had been everywhere and done everything. In Atlanta at the All-Star game, and at the Super Bowl watching the home team go down to Elway and the Broncos, in the Atlantic City Casino and peepin' heavyweight boxing brawls, jet skiing in Miami; lounging on South Beach. Kickin' it at the Expo, the Derby, the Latin Fest…Hitting the gambling boats in Indy and Cincinnati. Rolling to the clothing shows and fashion shows with my cousin Mike up in the 'D', out in Chi-town, D.C., and over in Philly, too. I had politicked with legends all over the states; pimps, 'hood stars, foreign killers, drug lords…it all just juiced me up to step my game and weight up.

*

"What time is it? Y'all hungry? Y'all want some cereal?" I asked my son. He shook his head, yes. It was past 10. Well, so much for getting an early morning quickie. I got up to go downstairs. My daughter was on the couch watching cartoons.

"C'mon Jewel and tell me what kind of cereal you want," I told her.

I headed out back to feed my dogs. I had pit bulls lined up and down my 8 foot privacy fence. I kept my bitch in the house with me, though. She was trained, of course. I named her Money. She was my red nosed, green-eyed bitch!

"Babe, you know ya mom called from Virginia last night about 9 o'clock. I told her I'd tell you that she called. She talked to the kids for a minute. Oh, and she said ya family's having a reunion down in Carolina next weekend. Ya dad's family was," Keysh told me.

I was glad to see my moms move to VA last year. There for a minute she was caught up moving substantial amounts of coke, dealing with all of her dike friends at the bars and at the phone sex spot; the sophisticated ones and the skanky ones. Twin took over all of her clientele. He was fucking half of them, anyway.

Keysh had been bitching a lot lately about us not going anywhere or doing anything together; and bitching also, about me not buying her anything. We had a half an hour discussion while I smoked a hydro blunt and drank some green tea with honey. I told her all of what I had planned for us this summer. We were going to the reunion, to Dollywood in Tennessee with mom's family and the kids, to Cedar Point and King's Island, and to an exclusive location or city for our birthdays in August. She was so on my dick after we talked that she came into the bathroom to pee before I got my shower, where I shoved my wood-hard dick into her pretty face. After about 20-30 sucks, I bent her over the sink for a 5 minute beast fucking; getting my quickie after all. I got fresh and Keysh got herself and the kids cleaned up, as well. With everyone fresh to death we all headed out. Keysh took the kids to get McDonald's and then to Chuck E. Cheese in her new '98 Mazda MPV minivan that she had worried me to death to get her. I told her to head back home when they were done and wait on me. We were going to the Steakhouse at about 7 or 8. I had some running around to do, and some shopping, as well. For the past few weeks I had been banging a green-eyed honey bone named, Sa'tia.

She was actually an escort chick in one of my affiliate's stables. But it wasn't like that with us. She was cool people. Game recognized game, no doubt. I liked her style, though. She had hustle. Not to mention a green Ac' Legend, a flawless petite frame, and the face of an angel.

I had a thing with Keysh, though, where if I was out playing and cutting up for a short while, then I would pop up on her with charm, good game, hard dick, and some exclusive gifts. So I hit the City Center Mall and bought her an adjustable tennis bracelet for the wrist or the ankle from 'Moses'. I hit up Lady Footlocker for some Air Max and a matching outfit; a tennis skirt and a Nike halter-top. I dropped by the Coach store for her a purse and a belt. Before I bounced I stopped by Victoria's Secret and Lens Crafters. Where I bought her some black Donna Karen shades with the mirror tent, like Lil' Kim 'anem wore. I grabbed me a slice of pizza and a soda from Sabarro's before I headed out to our store, D & C's to get her a cream Coogi dress and some matching Gator heels. I chilled in the back office with my cousin Mike for about an hour. Talking a little business and getting clarification from him that everything was cool between him and Money Mike from the fight that they had nearly 6 months ago. We discussed how everyone had been laying low and out of the way lately until things smoothed over. He said he needed to talk to P. and I assured him that I was going to speak to P. by Monday.

"Well yo, y'all getting mad busy, dog. Niggas is coming to grab their club outfit. I'm outta here, fam'," I told him.

He shot me a pound and said, "It's on. Be cool, dog. Have a porterhouse steak for me."

It was nearly 7. I hopped in my black Navigator truck and called Keysh to tell her that I was on my way. I arrived home at about 20 after 7. Keysh was finishing her hair and the kids were putting on their shoes. Keysh wore a fur turquoise Parasuco tube-top with Parasuco blue jeans. She was gorgeous, sporting a Halle Berry hair-do. "I'm ready!" She said.

"Yes you are. Yo, you laced for the reunion next week. Come out to the truck and help me with these bags," I told her.

She asked had I been out spoiling myself, and then I gave her doubtful look thinking, 'Did she just hear me?'

"Aw, you bought me somethin', daddy? Uh-oh," she said as she darted out the door.

Just last fall we had moved out to a west side suburb just past Westgate. It was a nice 3-bedroom house with the huge backyard and privacy fence; a slight upgrade from our condo. I popped the Navigator's rear door as Keysh and I grabbed 2 handfuls of assorted bags. She was so pumped. We went and had dinner where I informed Keysh that we were going to take the kids to my aunt's and then head down to Club 'Red Zone' for my man Ricky's birthday party. Ricky was my Cousin Mike's wife's cousin. He helped out with running D & C's and sold major weed. The party was a blast, though; aside from the usual drama that came along with Keysh going out with me, x-hoes and jealous hoes mumbling and whispering shit, usually causing Keysh to spaz out and sometimes slap bitches.

The next month consisted of enjoying time with the family, and taking a few trips. I took the whole family to Dollywood in Tennessee, and Keysh and I even went up to Canada for a few days. The reunion was cool, too. My older cousins were getting a little bit of money, but when they got a load of me they knew it was room for them to get their game up. Their country asses were off the hook, though. We talked a bit about opening a club or something along the coast of Virginia or the Carolinas. I told them to check into it and feed me back the grapes and info if they came up with anything solid. It was their backyard. I found out, though, that cars, lbs. of green, and houses were a lot cheaper down there. I also found out that a lot of my female cousins were some freaks. Hitting on me and Twin, and saying shit like, 'If we weren't cousins…'

*

Meanwhile, P. had been taking a lot of trips down to Miami. 2-3 weeks at a time; not his usual weekend or short week at our vacation house. He had told me once or twice that he was working on something. It turns out that he was trying to get hooked up directly with Cuban Manny. He had gotten close. Two days after I got back from Canada he called me over to his place.

"Ay, I think I'm bout to get the plug with Mendez. Some cats down there who knew dude, Cat, hollered at me in the Biltmore lobby," P. said.

"Oh yeah?!" I asked.

"Yeah, the one lil' short muphucka, a Cuban dude, I guess. He Mendez' nephew, his name's Jose. I got at him through this bitch that I was fuckin' with down there. Dude knew who I was and everything. Now check this out, you know they salty at Cat, 'cause he owe them all that paper. And he done fucked up their monthly flow and distribution. Them muphuckas know I'm the one pushing most of the shit, so…they bout to send some cats up here to do a coke deal with me. It's gonna be within the next couple of days," P. said with raised eyebrows.

"'Aight. Let me know wusup. I'm there! I'll be a phone call away," I told him as I got up to bounce. I gave him a pound then I slid out to my truck. As I climbed in I felt my hip vibrating so I answered my phone. It was my aunt Lee Ann saying, 'Hey baby! Hold on.'

I heard a click and then, Siz-o, wusup nephew. I got 60 days left until I get paroled. I'ma need to holla at you." It was my uncle Red.

"Oh, wusup, big head, fat muphucka!" I spat out.

"Shit, not no more. I done lost hella weight. But dig, I'm on ya aunt's 3-way and it's only a couple minutes left. You be cool, dog. I'ma call you as soon as I get released, 'aight?"

"It's on. Stay up. I'm out!" I said, and then closed the phone shut.

*

It had been 4 days and still no call, until the 5th day P. got a 10a.m. call from a 'K.Dee'. K.Dee was the cat that Jose said P. would be dealing with. K.Dee was one of Mendez' 10 Miami dealers, who also was a loyalist to the cartel. The story was that after nearly 10 years of being connected with the cartel, Manny never paid K.Dee much attention or gave him much respect because he wasn't the biggest weight mover, he probably moved the least amount a month, and also because he was a hot head, drama case. He was somewhat of a buffoon. Anyhow, K.Dee let P. know that he had 2 guys with him and that they were here ready to do business. He wanted to know when and where. P. ended up giving him his baby's mom's north side address and told him to meet us there at 3p.m. The deal was for 20 keys at 15 grand a piece, K.Dee's cut being $1,500 off of each kilo with 13.5 being his price.

I arrived there at about 2:30, as did Big Tone. He was our west side affiliate, Snoop's half brother. He was bringing 50 grand to buy 2 keys of 85% pure coke. P. had normally done Big Tone's coke cooking for him, getting him a minimum of 50 ounces back off a whole kilo. P. had nearly 200 grand of mine including the money I had invested in D & C's, so I was not there to purchase any of the coke. Not initially. I was there as my main man's right hand. I mean, this was only a step to buy the weight, quickly distribute it, and then get with Mr. Mendez for a constant plug; P.'s goal for nearly 5 years now. And I was with him 100%.

K.Dee and his crew finally showed up a few minutes past 3. We all briefly got acquainted, but the next ten minutes were very discomforting and awkward. P. and K.Dee did an exchange and inspection while they spoke cordially about their prior acquaintance down in South Beach. I stood quietly, peeping out the scene while Big Tone chopped it with K.Dee's two goons, who seemed a little antsy. K.Dee quickly assured the money's count was on point and said that they'd be on their way. I gave P. a questioning look like, 'Is everything good?' But he didn't confirm it. Tone looked at P. and asked, "Wusup?"

By the look on his face, after tasting a coke tipped finger, I made my way to the door before P. could even let out the words, "This shit is some woo!" I pulled out the Glock 40 with the 30 round clip as I ran into the street. But before I could let loose P. yelled, "Nah Siz-o, nah!"

It was like fucking a Top Model from the back being about to bust, and then having to pull out for some un-natural reason; unable to catch that massive nut.

"Them niggas is gone. Come back in the crib before the fuckin' neighbors see somethin'. I got dem niggas," P. vowed.

Big Tone was heated, but was compensated with 2 of the 5 real kilo bricks that were on the top of the pack. After Tone left, P. and I put the remainder of the pack, 90% woo, in the trunk of the Infiniti and headed westward in silence. My thoughts were 'What the fuck we gonna do?', because I was ready to kill something. But P., being the boss, stayed cool, calm, and collective. We headed over to Nuts' place, well, Heady's place, to give Nuts the grapes. This guy was beefing with his broad of nearly 5 years, and ready to call it quits all over some whore he had been macking on. I about flipped when I found out that it was some skinny beige bitch named Natalie that the whole city had had. Even my Jersey niggas; Coupe and Big June had gangbanged her. The hoe was also a carpet muncher, going both ways. She herself was one thing, but I flipped twice when I heard that Nuts was trying to wife this tramp up. "What the fuck!" P. and I thought.

Nuts had a truck out front moving furniture, clothes, his pool table...... We hollered for a few ticks, but after a short while there was nothing to say. Everyone was so in shock. Shocked that anyone would pull a shyster move on the West Side Firm! A coward ass move, I felt it was. But the source was Emmanuelle Mendez! It didn't come anymore confrontational than that. We decided to keep it on the low, and play it like a connection was still in the making; although P. had planned to put a hit out on K.Dee the following morning. I wondered to myself why he didn't take action directly towards Jose or, Mendez himself. Although I knew that would cause a war that none of us were most likely ready for. I was in no mood to go home or speak to anyone in my family circle (The Cream Team), so I turned my phone and pager off and headed north towards Gahanna to Goldie's crib off of Sunbury Road. She had granted me access and a key to her place nearly 6 months ago; where I usually kept 10-20lbs. of green in her garage. She never tripped, though. She trusted and worshipped me beyond recognition. I'd just went through a rough transition with her not even a year earlier when she'd had a miscarriage 3 months into her pregnancy with my child.

The house was empty when I arrived at nearly 10p.m. 'Cool', I thought. I turned the TV to Sports Center but didn't pay it much attention. I was too zoned out in my thoughts. Before I knew it, I had dozed off.

"Babe. Babe!" Goldie said to me. "Wusup? What you doin' layin' here with this?" She asked rhetorically pointing at my Ruger P-90.

"Chi-Chiwa!" I said to her as I opened my eyes and slapped her on the hip.

She slapped my arm and walked towards the kitchen, not feeling my attempt at humor of saying hello; in her native, Korean language. She didn't like me hearing her speak it to her people or my attempt to speak it either.

However, I needed to relieve some stress. So, first I rolled me up a pencil thin, hydro blunt. I sparked it up, then had Goldie make me a glass of Tang' and orange juice. I could tell that she was pleasantly surprised to come home and find me there, but I didn't want to tell her what had just gone down earlier.

"So yo, how was ya night? Where you comin' from?" I asked as she intriguingly stared at me. She was still in aw that I was at her place when she arrived at 1:30 in the a.m.

"We just went to lame ass Game Works; me, Kayla and Chelia. Them bitches was going to the after hour club on 5th. Fuck that shit! I had to deal with enough lame niggas at Game Works. I'm so glad that I came home. Why you ain't call my cell?" She asked me as I sat zoned out listening to her. She could tell something was wrong, but decided against prying and asking questions. And I loved her for that; for knowing her position.

"Nah. I knew you'd be in after you did ya thing. After you kicked it or clubbed it, or whatever." I said lazily. The weed was taking its toll on me, along with my second glass of Tang'. She just stared at me intently, and sort of seductively. At least that's how I felt at that point. I began to realize how fine Goldie looked in a one piece Capri jean jumper made by Baby Phat. She wore red Manolo heels and her hair stayed tight. The thought of her being advertised all night and now being here with me, made my dick as hard as iron. Damn! It had been nearly a month since we had got down. I was both slippin', and trippin'. She told me to head upstairs when I got ready, because she was going to bed. 'Not yet', I thought, as I grabbed her arm and pulled her towards me. I tongue kissed her with passion and licked her neck and cleavage. As I began to suck and bite in between her breasts she quickly came up out of her jumpsuit. Then I slithered out of my clothes even faster. Seconds later I had her flat on her back on the couch, legs in the air like a TV antenna. I munched on her sweet pussy until she came on my tongue. Then I put her on all fours and punished her pussy like she never imagined I would.

I relived that whole day's worth of stress, and after 20 minutes of pumping and thrusting I unloaded what felt like both nuts. We eventually made it to bed, but 6 hours later when I tried to get my morning nut, she protested. Saying that I had beaten her pussy up too bad; claiming that she felt the swelling when she walked to the bathroom during the middle of the night. As the sun came up I lay still with Goldie's body sprawled of mine. Caressing her perfect 130lb. frame, I thought about how she was first in line to be my wifey; behind Keysh. I had encountered a handful of stars, but I had only let it go so far with any of them because of Keysh. Keysh was a catch with good looks and a loyal heart, but lacked the independence and brains of some of my other ambitious chicks with careers and sufficient finances. At 19, Goldie had it all. With a wealthy grandmother who's finances were deep into the 6 figures. And there were many chicks who loved my distinct good looks, my thuggish charm, and my character. But it was mainly just my status and image that they loved.

Goldie's love was sincere; it was real. And she knew about, and understood, my thing with Keysh. I had also foolishly crept with a few of her girlfriends, who were all nearly as fine as she was. Gahanna had hoes, no doubt. But to her the gossip was only rumors. I never admitted to any of it, though. So.....

However, I guess my mind was only in such deep thought because it seems that when a man has any sort of tragedy he evaluates every aspect of his life. I shook my conscience to get up and take an a.m. piss. Between my bladder and Goldie's naked thighs on mine, my dick was as hard as granite. I slid out from under her and grabbed my phone on the way to the bathroom. I turned it on to call Keysh and my kids, and then call to check up on my dog, P. After I spat at my family for a minute, I told them that I was on my way home. It was only ten minutes 'til nine when I called P. to hear, "Siz-o, wusup? You got ya phone and shit off?!"

"Yeah, I been in my 2-3 zone since last night. I'm out here at Goldie's, though. Wus good?" I shot back.

"Man, this nigga Nuts just left here bitching about 50 stacks that I had of his. You believe that shit; after what just happened yesterday?" P. asked emphatically.

"Oh yeah? The nigga was on some panic shit like that bout them lil' ends? With the way we rollin' together?" I asked.

"Yeah dog. I'm telling you, the nigga had me pissed. I gave him that lil' shit, though. But check this out; dude hit me a few minutes ago," he said...."yo, where you...you comin' through?" He asked me.

"Dog, I'm on my way." I hung up the phone then bounced.

45 minutes later I was sitting on P.'s couch sipping a V-8 fruit juice. He told me that Jose was heading to Columbus later that evening, if P. agreed, to meet with us to smooth out the bullshit that had just took place less than 24 hours ago. P. said that he was game for it. We were to reserve 2 suites at the Radisson by 3p.m. Where, even with unarmed pre-conditions, our room would be strapped to a tee. P. wasn't taking any chances. I called Dust and Twin out to the hotel. And I gave them clear instructions to set the room ablaze if given the word.

But this didn't seem like no 'funny business' bullshit. There would be no motive behind it, for Jose or his uncle Manny. We made all of the proper arrangements over the next 5-6 hours. As soon as Jose's flight arrived he and his muscle took the ferry over to the hotel. They called P.'s 'throw away' cell from the lobby. I answered, and then invited them up. I told P. that they suggested we have dinner in the hotel's restaurant, but he declined. A concentrated 5 minutes went by and then there was a knock at the door. Dust answered it. After we all spoke 'Holas' and 'Heys' and shook hands, except for Dust and Twin, with equal agreement Jose's 6'2" 235lb. muscle, Ramon, frisked each one of us. Just as Dust did the same to him and Jose.

"Senor Pettway, I sincerely apologize for…" P. interrupted, "Jose, it's just Mike."

Jose nodded, "my apologies, Mike. Let me assure you that this cowboy behavior has been taken care of. That was not the way that my uncle, or myself does business. Tha K.Dee muda' phucka was calling him self taking revenge out on you for the money that Fat man owes us. It was not authorized by Uncle Manny or my self. That's why K.Dee's dead! We took care of him this morning; right before I called you. Now, what we're prepared to do is send you 50 kilos in 2 days; at 13.5 a key. That's a price of 675k. You have at least…half of the cash. The rest we'll do on consignment. If everything goes smooth and you've got rid of all the coke by the time we come get the rest of the cash then we will fly you down to Miami or Cuba to talk to Uncle Manny."

"When? When will y'all be comin' back up for the rest of the cheese?" P. asked.

"We'll be back within the first week of the month. And let me tell you Mike, if this goes smooth, and sufficient, then Uncle Manny will be willing to establish a monthly supply on a consistent basis; perhaps more coke, and perhaps at a cheaper price," Jose emphasized.

P. thought of how the first was still 21 days away. But also, about how difficult it may have been to get rid of 50 keys in just 3 weeks. But he knew he could do it. N.S.F. would buy 10-20 of the kilos, and so would E.S.F; especially at 20 stacks apiece. The rest he would distribute to his own, The West Side Firm. He nodded, yes.

"So, do you think that you're the man that we're looking for, Michael?" Jose asked.

"Yeah," P. nodded again. "I am."

For the next 15 minutes or so, they discussed the details of how it would all go down. From the distance I couldn't hear exactly what was being said, but I could feel that it was all good. No matter what race, nationality, or origin, body language and facial expressions, particularly in the eyes, was the key to reading someone. And this deal was for real.

CHAPTER 24: Crowning a New King

July was a good month. It started off sour with the jacking, but ended as sweet as sugar with the connection that we made. All three Firm Organizations saw growth and prosperity for the future. And P. was the new Black Caesar; a polished like 'Nino Brown'. Everyone loved and worshipped him. Nuts had apologized and begged for forgiveness. P. put him back under his right arm. The funny thing was that it always seemed to everyone that they were the duo and I was the 3rd link to our trio. They were closer in age, good into their 20s, and everyone who didn't know any better thought that I was Nuts' little brother. But the reality was that P. and I were closer. I had been loyal to him since age 15. We had been on late night drug runs together. We had put in work together and had caught a case (that we beat because I didn't rat) together. And I put in every dime that I had for more coke, even when I was already holding weight. Nuts and P. had beefed when they were younger and had gotten into fist fights. Nuts was Big Tone P.'s protégé. However, P. and I had made an agreement to keep a close eye on, but distant companionship with Nuts.

On August the 2nd P. flew down to Miami to meet Emmanuelle

Mendez himself. He had called Jose a few days before to tell him that we were out of coke. Jose was a little surprised, but glad all the same. However, P. and Manny hit it off so well that P. didn't come back until 3 days later; with those 100 birds(kilos) flying right behind him (next day delivery, that is). P. was about to be the biggest coke pusher in Ohio. If he got 5, possibly even 10 years with this plug then he'd have Russell Simmons status. I just wanted average millionaire status; and to establish a legitimate foundation for my family, perhaps a few businesses.

P. had given Manny the breakdown of our organization with our North and East side affiliates. Manny had a slight acknowledgement of the West Side Firm, but until now it had just been a myth to him.

"Yo, he was feelin' how we got shit organized and linked to the other Firms. But he knows that it started with the West side. Dude was cool, for real. Oh yeah, and he gave Cat a pass for me, as long as I agreed to cut him out of the operation. I just saved that nigga's life," P. said.

"Yeah? Damn, he done lost the club, the plug, and everything. I don't know how he gon' pay that debt out in Vegas. That's Mob cats he fuckin' with. Didn't they allow him to run that bill up cause of Donny Ray from Detroit?" I asked.

"Yeah, but that's on that nigga. I told Hollywood 'anem that they can't fuck with Cat now; only on some distant friendship shit, goin' down to the club to kick it and stuff. But yo, you got ya birthday comin' up. What, this weekend? Yeah, ya 21st! Twin's 21st, too. Ay, ya cousin Mike got a new spot. He know the owner of the club. It just opened last month. It's off da chain, too," P. said.

"Damn, no more Imaginations?" I asked knowingly with raised eyebrows. "Wus it called?"

"Studio 69!" P. answered.

*

We exited the expressway onto Morse Road, made a turn onto St.

Clair and pulled into a huge parking lot. So this was the place that was already nick-named the 'Nasty'. The parking lot reminded me of the movie, 'Player's Club'. We stepped out of our whips with all eyes on us. We all parked in the grass by the door. Fuck parking blocks away. This club was new to us, but we were always V.I.P.

Nuts was rolling in his blue Caddy STS with his cousin, Jimmy Green. My man Terique rolled his white Lexus with his little cousin Buck. My cousin Mike was in a gray Navigator with his 'left hand' Ricky, and his right hand from the 'D', D-Lo. They also had our friend from New York with them, NY Hicks. My man Big B., also from Detroit, who had just opened his own clothing store 'Mr. B's Big & Tall, was rolling in a maroon Cadillac Deville with his fellow Detroit Pimp affiliate, Biggs. It was only right for pimps to roll together. And me, I was rolling a new royal blue '99 Corvette with the removable hardtop off. Twin rocked a chocolate brown Coogi short set with the matching brown Timberlands. I rocked a sky blue one with sky blue Timbs. Everybody was fly and fresh. P. didn't step with us, though. He was staying out of sight now with his high status and all that. But we dug it.

Niggas and bitches looked at us in awe as we slid past them up to the V.I.P. fence. My cousin Mike and Nuts threw the security guy a couple Benjamins and then we all entered the back patio; without a pat down. We were the only ones who made that V.I.P. entrance that night. With the exception of Papa Joe and his crew, and our other Firm affiliates from the North and East side. After we made our way inside and retrieved a case of Dom. P. and various other drinks, Nuts quickly began hollering at numerous dime pieces shooting them to one or another of our crew members. He was always the life of the party; the vocal, smooth playboy. Just like with the door man earlier. He was more so my Ace in one way, just as P. was in another.

We had been partying and macking on females for about an hour or so when we peeped out some wild-eyed nigga staring intently. We knew it was niggas who were star struck and intrigued with niggas like us, but I sensed that it was more to it than that. My man Terique shrugged the nigga off saying, "Yo, some of these niggas be starin' on some homo, female shit. They rather get a autograph or blow a nigga than scrap!" 'No doubt', I thought; but this dude was on some other shit.

"Ay man, that look like the dude, or one of the dudes, from down at the Hyatt. Remember last winter at the 107 party?" Nuts asked me.

I did. And it was. It turned out that dude was one of the guys that Nuts' cousin from Youngstown, Ricky the Pistol, had got into it with in the Hyatt lobby of the 107.5 party back in February. We had beat and stomped them senseless.

"Yo, wusup wit y'all niggas and all of this tough guy mean mug shit?" Terique blurted out.

It was 12 of us, along with half the club, but only 3 of us stood out on the patio smoking a hydro blunt. It was me, Nuts, and Terique. These niggas were about 5 deep, and they were congregating around the security cats. They stepped towards us, with security following right behind them. Before the one leading them could speak Nuts threw his drink on him and swung the Dom. P. bottle at the closest nigga to him. Terique followed firing a quick 2 piece at one nigga and a 3 piece towards the next one, catching one on the chin in the process causing him to stumble backwards a few feet. Before I could swing a bottle or a punch, the bald security nigga stepped in between me and the 5th nigga. That's when my loco homey Paul crashed the security nigga, dropping him. The 5th one rushed me, as we tussled on the blacktop. My dude Ronnie P. kicked the nigga a few times, stalling his movement. As he stumbled to his feet, I reached mine and swung a hard left to his chin. When the nigga fell a gang of niggas began stomping him out. The guy with all the animosity from 6 months earlier had got all of his boys, and the security niggas, a memorable beat down.

Through the mist of the drama we made our way to our rides. The shit was wild. And my fucking blue Coogi was ruined. The following Monday I went up to D & C's to holla at my cousin. He said that he had spit at the owner, Rick, who told him that the whole security crew had been fired. A lot of people had the wrong perception of Rick. Richard Morton, a white old school club owner from St. Louis who was not new to this life; or 'the game'. And he regularly bought weed and coke from a few of our Firm members. He was so down with our organization, that he let us hire our own security team. We got the hook up from the N.S.F. and hired 'The Hammer's' WOLF PACK. It worked out real sweet. They had done all of the security for us wherever we went. And they were a ruthless bunch.

The following weekend I was hit with some wild ass news. At about 10:30 on a Friday night I was chilling at our 'West Side' bar when my phone vibrated on my hip.

"Babe, where you at? Ya Aunt Cint just got robbed!" It was Keysh. "She just called over here for you."

"Yo, listen. I'm right by her crib at the 'West Side Story.' I'm bout to go over there now," I told her.

"Well, be careful. The cops are everywhere. Somebody done got shot or somethin'," she said.

"What the fuck? 'Aight, I'm headed over there right now. I'll call you back when I see what's up," I said to Keysh, then hung up.

When I got around to my Aunt's crib, the siren lights had the block lit up like a Christmas tree. She was in the back of a police cruiser. I thought, 'What the fuck?' to myself. I watched an ambulance pull off as I stepped out of my truck to get the 411 from a few familiar patrons. It turns out that it was a few of the local, young punks who, when in the process of buying a 50 sack of green, pulled a pistol and hollered, 'give it up'.

Well, what a dumb stick up buffoon he was because as him and his partner ran out of the house, and my Aunt followed them out with her 9 millimeter Smith & Wesson busting, the dummy fell down and shot himself in the groin. 'Ouch!' I thought.

Anyhow, after 20 minutes or so my Aunt Cint was released from the police cruiser. She was not under arrest; she just had to make a statement.

"Yo, I'm glad you ain't get arrested. I thought I was gonna have to come and bond you out. What the hell happened?" I asked.

We went back inside where she explained to me all of what had went down. And also, how she knew that she was 'on fire' hot from what she had been hearing for the last couple of months. I knew she was moving more weed on the Hilltop than any other sole pusher. Or just as much. She was so spooked from the incident that had just happened that the following Monday she was ready to bounce back down to Alabama. 'Wow', I thought. I tried to talk her into staying but she had her mind made up.

My phone and pager had been blowing up all morning, but with such a wild night that had just passed and Keysh draining my pipe through the a.m. hours into the p.m., I had just got out of bed shortly before 1.

After Keysh and I got our private parts clean and brushed our teeth, we walked our naked bodies downstairs to get a cold drink and some brunch in our system. Since the kids were at Keysh's sister's house. Today was Keysh's birthday, so we had plans for the weekend and the house all to ourselves. As Keysh returned her many a.m. phone calls and I prepared breakfast, I heard my dogs out back barking, I guessed the

booming car system; which was a rarity in our Westgate neighborhood.
I didn't even do it. I looked out the backdoor to see Twin's black 'Hot
Boy' Chevy Impala, with the 20 inch chrome rims, at my gate awaiting
entrance. I could see Dust in the car, but there was someone else, too.
Fuck! Twin was tripping. This house, with my kids and my wifey, was off
limits. Twin had been here once before with Stephanie and the kids, but
never before had Dust been. I pulled back the curtain and aggravatingly
held up a finger signaling 'hold on'. What the fuck was this guy thinking?
Twin had lost it. I told Keysh to go upstairs and put some clothes on, but
to throw me my Coogi shorts first. I pulled them on and slipped on my
Timb boots, and then I slid out back to unlock the 8 foot gate. Calming
my barking killers down with a few 'shut ups' and 'sits!' I angrily walked
back to the house then yelled 'close it back' just as I got to the porch.
That's when I noticed the unknown passenger step out of the car. My
Uncle Red!

As I walked in the house I saw Keysh coming down the steps wearing
some sweats and a tee, and also, an angry scowl. She was sassy with an
attitude when it called for it. And Twin's disrespect had her ready to
express her displeasure; especially when she saw my uncle Red with him,
who she never liked.

"Oh, hell no! And he got that muthafucker wit him," Keysh was
ready to flip.

"Just be cool, boo. Go in the living room. I got this. Chill out," I told
her.

It had been nearly 2 years since I had hollered at or seen the nigga.
The first year he was gone I allowed this clown to blow my phone up
repeatedly calling his crack head wife; I had shot him $100-200 a
month, and had visited on 3 or 4 occasions. But once we moved, with the
combination of his constant ungratefulness and then hearing from Big
Tone P. that he was creeping with jailhouse punks, I had cut the nigga

off. His little brother Skins had become full-time with homosexuality up in South East Correctional Institution.

However, I figured that the nigga would have animosity. That's why I was flaming hot with Twin. Although I knew he didn't know the details to the situation.

"Yo, Siz-o! What's good, baby? Boy, you doin' it. This muthafuckin' crib is off tha hook," Red said emphatically.

"Wusup? Yeah, it's nice, no doubt," I said as I dapped him. Watching him peep out how my 5'11" 185lb. tattooed frame had grown. I was a few inches taller and about thirty pounds heavier than I was a little over three years ago when he left. Not to mention 10 times richer.

I briefly gave a 'wusup' nod to Dust and Twin with an intent eye. Twin had a good idea how discontent I was with the situation. He could tell through my eyes and body language. I made a mental note to holler at him about this later on. It turns out that he had been calling me all morning and afternoon for my Uncle Red, who had just got out that morning. No response meant to pop up at my fucking crib, I guess.

"Uh, excuse me but Tony, did you think it was necessary for you to pull up to our house wit'cha music playin' like that? And wit him?!" Keysh asked with much attitude.

"Yo, Keysh!" I called out sternly as I nodded towards the living room. Twin remained silent, as much as it bothered him to do so.

"Hey man, I know this ya crib wit ya family and all. That's my fault. But I told Tony I needed to see you, A-S-A-P. I need to holla at you," Red said.

I looked out the window at Dust fooling around with my dogs and said, "Let's step outside."

"Babe, you gon' deal with him? That scandalous bastard! And he's a faggot, y'all said. I don't want him nowhere near the kids," Keysh went on and on as we rode to the Clermont Restaurant for dinner, where afterwards we'd head downtown by the river to listen to a jazz band.

Keysh really despised my Uncle Red. She felt that he was belligerent and vain. And she didn't trust him. Plus, she remembered how he'd owed me money when he left 3 years ago and how unappreciative he was with all that I had done for him. Women were peculiar like that with sensing shit and never forgetting even the littlest things.

"Yo, don't even trip. I'ma just spoon feed the guy some kibbles to get on his feet. That's all. As long as he comes with my ends every trip, then....." I paused.

"Hmm," Keysh let out.

"What's that? What that mean?" I asked.

"Nothin'," Keysh said.

Little did I know there would be so much more friction with Red in the near future, much more than I could have imagined. I tuned the volume up a couple notches on the stereo to bump Biggie's, 'Pray For My Downfall', as we rode silently the rest of the way.

*

A month had gone by and things had been just like I loved them; as smooth as a baby's behind. Uncle Red was coming up, without a question. With me supplying him, with coke and numerous other connections; and his old east side neighborhood was a crack alley goldmine. But he had grown tired of staying with different hood rat chicks every other night. And technically, although he was paroled to his sister's address, he couldn't stay there. So he pleaded with me to find him a place to stay; someplace outside of the 'hood. Two days later, after hollering at a client of mine with a few properties, I helped him get moved into a 2-bedroom flat off of Agler Road. It was cool for two reasons; for one, I hooked up one of the bedrooms there for myself to crash at and crash pussy, as well. And for two, it was conveniently only 10 minutes around the way from

Goldie's crib near Sunbury Rd. I had been fucking and spending a lot of time with her lately. There had been someone else, it seemed, who wanted to seduce me, too.

My man Nuts' ex-girl Heady stayed two streets over from us. I saw her quite often either at the corner market or if I was riding past her house on the way to mine. Perhaps I was tripping, but it seemed that she was always trying to get me over to her place. Either for a barbeque or a drink, or for me to sell her some green; a quarter pound to a pound was her usual. I always spun her, though. The funny thing was that when I'd tell Nuts he'd encourage me to go kick it with, and deal with her.

In fact, just last week we were networking at our car lot when I told him we had seen her at the 'Nasty'/Studio 69. He told me and my Uncle Red that if we got a chance to fuck her, then to do it. And also, about how her pussy sprayed when she came, and so forth and so on. We were tripping; about how he put his ex out there and about the water work details, as well. My Uncle Red told me to fuck her. In the ass, as a matter of fact! The suspicions about his prison activities were not hard to believe.

Anyhow, a few weeks had passed, and with Nuts' encouragement and Heady's persistence I found myself pulling into her driveway on a fall's eve Sunday. I had foolishly returned her page to hear that her girlfriend was in need of an ounce of green and that she was fresh out. We quickly concluded that it would be just a quarter of an ounce for $100 with the exclusive kind that I had. She said that her girlfriend didn't seem to mind so I told them that I would be over shortly. Even though the circumstances were what they were, this still didn't feel right.

It was just two weeks ago when I passed Heady's house on my way home from my people's hotel party from the night before when she flagged me down to invite me over to her girl Gwen's barbeque later that afternoon. Later on, shortly before I arrived, I got a call from Nuts asking me where I was, because he had ran into Gwen earlier at the Great Western Shopping Center and that she had invited him to her cookout; where his ex Heady would be. So he wanted me to come pick him up and roll over there with him. The whole time we were there Heady was hitting on me in front of everyone. Nuts wasn't feeling that. Especially since she was just doing the same shit a week ago at the 'Nasty', 69 Club!

Anyhow, I wasn't on the soap opera drama, so I left the barbeque early; before all of the food even got done. Nuts ended up talking Heady into going to the hotel suite where he had a dyke bitch waiting. He figured that since she was drunk and talking off the wall then perhaps it was possible to get her to go the other way. Heady spazzed out though, by pulling her razor and threatening to cut both of them. She vowed that she never cared to see Nuts again.

Well, here I was walking up to the door to her crib. Finally! I had a bad feeling about it, though. Still. But damn, I was only there to sell a bag.

"Oh, hey! C'mon in," said Heady.

I slid inside and quickly sold her girl the hundred dollar sack. But she just as quickly insisted on smoking one with me, and asked me did I have a swisher on hand. I had 2, in fact. But I told her that we would smoke out of my sack. Heady made me and her girl, Sharon, a drink as I rolled up. We soon began puffing and surprisingly Heady asked to hit it. 'Wow', we thought. Heady never smoked! As soon as the blunt was gone, Sharon said that she was about to bounce. She thanked me and told Heady that she would call her the next day.

"Well yo, I'ma bounce, too," I said.

"Hold on. Are you hungry? I just cooked some steaks and cabbage and macaroni and cheese right before you got here," she said.

Ain't no fucking doubt that I was hungry after just smoking the first blunt of the day at 10 o'clock at night. "Oh, hell yeah!" I said.

I asked her where her kids were.

"Oh, I put 'em to bed right before you got here," she said, clanking dishes around in the kitchen.

Damn, she really had this shit planned out. I sat in deep thought on the couch while I flicked through the TV channels, stopping on ESPN for Sunday Night Football.

She brought me my plate where I quickly began to put it away. She always could cook.

After talking shit about Nuts for 5 or 10 minutes, Heady disappeared into the back of the house somewhere. A couple of minutes went by and, "Hey, you can come back here and watch the game."

"What?!" I thought. I slid towards the back room where I heard her voice saying, "I'm back here."

"Yo, this where you went to?" I asked slyly.

"Yeah, I had to put on my night clothes. Here, sit down. You want another drink?" She asked me, wearing a sly grin.

Hmm! Night clothes, she says. A black slip, nighty! That's singular, without an S.

"Yeah. Why not? I'ma roll this other blunt up, too. That's cool?" I asked.

She shrugged, "Yeah. I don't care."

I grabbed the remote and switched the TV to the game. Damn, this shit ain't feel right. This was my left hand man's ex-girl. Plus, she had been around Keysh many times before in the past 5 years or so. At each other's cribs and out of town together. Our kids were slightly familiar, as well. But it wasn't like they were the best of home girls all like that. It just worked out circumstantially because of my link to Nuts. I lit my blunt just as Heady walked in with my drink. She instantly laid across the bed and asked, 'let me hit that'. I thought, 'Wow, again?!' And then I thought about how voluptuously thick she was lying next to me. Her body reminded me so much of Keysh's. She was an inch or two shorter than Keysh, 5-10lbs. thicker and a shade lighter. She was caramel chocolate, and Keysh was milk chocolate. They were both equipped with tits and ass, and a small waist. And they both had seductive eyes, as well. They also had matching tattoos of a rose with their kids' names surrounding it on their calves (just by coincidence). Although Keysh was slightly bow legged and pigeon-toed. It was so ironic that I was thinking of all of this because Heady soon brought Keysh up, getting very emotional, asking personal, intimate questions. 'Cool, I'll keep it real with her,' I thought to myself. Therefore, she won't press me for no dick. So I told her, "Yo, Keysh is wifey. It is what it is, though. You know how we get down. Nuts and all of us."

Damn, did that just come out right? I asked myself. Instead of turning her off, I may have kind of told her that it was cool (to fuck/get down). She looked at me for about a good minute with those seducing eyes, and then she began to kiss me and feel for my manhood. I responded and fondled her tits and ass aggressively. My pipe was 'stone' hard. Something had to give. But suddenly, everything stopped.

"Wait! Siz-o, I'm on my period," she said.

'Good', I thought; and almost blurted out. Now I could leave and never come back.

"But...I can give you an intimate kiss," Heady said softly and seductively as she looked up into my eyes and back down to my bulging erection.

With my mouth idly open I raised my eyebrows as if to say, 'huh?!' Heady didn't need an answer or any confirmation from me. Before I could blink twice my dick was out of my sweats and into her hands and mouth. Within seconds I was fully extended, hard pipe jamming into the back of her throat. Ooh shit, this woman was an x-rated dick sucker. A man hood eater! And she allowed me to aggressively grab her head and face. None of that young girl, 'get off of me' shit. And damn, I was about to skeet. She began to do some sort of nibble sucking on just the head of my dick while she jerked the length of my silk covered shaft with one hand and tickled my balls with the other. I needed to put this broad on a home movie, porno film for my own personal entertainment; and perhaps, for some of my boys entertainment, too. This head was excellent, with a capital 'E'!

"Damn, baby. Shit! Suck this dick. I'm bout to cum," I told Heady.

She jerked my dick with power as she looked up at me with those seductive eyes. She greedily chomped back down on my meaty bone like a toothless baby snake, sucking and deep-throating me, 50 strokes per minute. I couldn't take it. I laid back on the bed with my legs hanging from the knees down, as Heady laid on her stomach next to me. As she milked and drained my pipe, causing it to virtually throw up in her mouth, I squeaze her juicy ass cheek thinking about how I'd love to pound her cakes. Repeatedly!

After that 20 minute suck off, I was convinced that she should've been in black porn. And she swallowed every drop. Cum thirsty like she'd been in the desert for a week. It was an uncomfortable scene after I busted my nut, so I told her that I had to go catch up on a few things. Make moves and slide like grease. She went as far as to tell me that she got off of her period by Tuesday or Wednesday. 'And', I thought. That juicy ass, though. I just might have to smash her. As I pulled out of her driveway and began to ride down the street, I debated rather or not I should tell Nuts. Maybe I wouldn't have to because I never planned to fuck with her again. Or so I tried to tell myself that. I hit the highway replaying the 20 minute porn scene I had just had with Heady 'the brain surgeon'. Yeah, I would have to get some more of that head therapy. No muthaphucking doubt!

CHAPTER 25: A Homerun Hit

It was a big weekend with the Jay-Z and DMX rap niggas here in the city. They were going to perform at the Schottenstien's Center and then the after party was going to be at the Valleydale ballroom. So, half of the women in the city were getting right and all of the guys were getting sharp for the ladies. I was kicking it with a couple hood star chicks in Brooksedge Apartments while my little homey's moms braided my hair. They stayed in the same building and looked up to my dude's mom like an aunt. They'd always keep me company when I'd get braided up or if I brought my son to. They knew every time I was coming because I'd pull up shaking the block. It was by design, no doubt. Two dreadful hours had went by when I remembered that I had to pick my platinum silver Impala up from a crib of P.'s over on Columbia.

"Kell! Wusup, are you almost done?" I asked.

"Yeah, I got two more braids to do. Why, you got somewhere to be?" She asked me jokingly. After her and the hood star bitches got a quick laugh she said, "Nah, I know you be busy. Ya phone and pager keep buzzin' and vibratin'. Just hold on. I'm almost done," she told me.

I called my homey Big Carl to tell him that I was about to pick him up from his spot on the Hilltop so we could go over to P.'s crib to get my whip. After I made that call I returned a few more important calls to get niggas ready and in position to get hooked up. In a half an hour's time Big Carl was following me in the Impala out to my pop's crib on the east side. I'd keep it out of sight for the winter while I had Chuck, out at 'Creative Conversions', customize it to the max. And by the summertime I'd be shitting on niggas.

Anyhow, as we got close to the expressway we peeped the traffic was on stand still. It was mid-day rush hour. I hit Big Carl on his cell and told him to follow me. We slid through the center of the city crossing South High Street on Thurman Avenue. 10 more minutes and we'd be there. We got stopped by a stoplight in uppity German Village just before we hit Parsons Avenue. I was in my Navigator, knocking Dre's 'Chronic 2001', track 13: BITCH NIGGAS! I felt a strange surge of hostile energy coming from the surrounding street. The music was blaring, so I turned it down to realize that all of these angry whites were enraged with my amplified rap music. They were at the corner bar staring and across the street, as well. As I anxiously waited for the light to change, a rather large 6 foot something asshole kicked the back of my truck's bumper by the tail light yelling 'turn that shit down'! I thought, 'what the fuck' and put my truck in park and hopped out.

"Yo, what the fuck is wrong wit you, dude?" I asked as I viewed my truck to see if there was damage. I was standing near the curb's edge when I turned to see this maniac 6 inches from my face yelling obscenities like a baseball umpire. Before I could get a word out the fucking guy grabbed me by the wrists, continuing to yell incoherently. My man Big Carl had hopped out of the Impala, but by that the time, off of an instant reaction, I had broke away from the dude's hold and dropped his big ass with a hard left hook. Two seconds later I saw some scary shit. As the man fell he had just missed the table set that sat out in front of the café and bar.

He hit the back of his head on the concrete sidewalk, splitting it wide open. Blood instantly began to flow from the back of his skull. I looked up to see people staring in aw, outraged at the incident.

I jumped in my truck and hit the gas. Big Carl followed closely behind me all the way through the straight shot to Pop's house. I called my uncle Red to come follow us from there to my crib to park my truck. After what had just happened I didn't feel comfortable riding in it until I found out what was up. I was a little worried, especially with my uncle Red saying, "dude probably dead, man."

I watched the news after I got dressed. At the time being they had no license plate number, an inaccurate description of me, and had said that the truck was black. It was gray, though, of course. I felt a little better now. For the past few hours I hadn't been able to focus or concentrate on anything, except for the situation. I couldn't even eat all of my Popeye's chicken. I took it that everything was all good, though, because they said that dude was alive and in critical condition. It was time to relax and go kick it now. Red and I jumped into my blue Cadillac Deville, rocking Maurice Malone jean suits and Timb boots. Simple urban wear for a night like tonight. Rap niggas at the Valleydale? Yeah, we were stepping correct, no doubt.

About an hour had gone by and I was still nursing the same glass of champagne. Well, not according to everyone else. But aside from a seldom sip here and there, I was pouring the shit out. For some reason the incident earlier was still fucking with me. There was a reason for this. After getting through the rest of the night I made it home to wifey; whenever there was a storm in my life, usually my street life, Keysh was my refuge. It was the only place that I felt comfortable when shit got wild. If I had drama, if I had put in some major work, or if I needed to strategize and make a move then I went to my home with Keysh.

Keysh shook me fully awake, handing me my phone. I knew just who it was by the scowl on Keysh's face.

"Yo, wusup?" I said as I looked at the clock read 15 'til noon.

"Siz-o. What's goin' on, dog? I need to holla at you A-S-A-P. What time you comin' out?" Red asked me.

"Uh...shit, give me bout an hour. I'll call you when I touch down out west," I told Red, and then closed my phone.

I wasn't sure, but I had a good feeling it was about the incident the day before. Within a half an hour I was showered and dressed. I hadn't told Keysh what had happened yet. But I did head straight to P.'s crib, after I called him to confirm which one he was at, to let him know what had went down. I called to tell Red to meet me at P.'s and it was indeed what I suspected.

"Dig, here go the newspaper, dog. I told you, dude died," Red said. It wouldn't be the last time that Red brought, or was a part of some bad news. We briefly discussed the fact that they didn't know anything; at the time being, anyhow. So there was no need to do anything but chill and act accordingly.

P. called me into the next room to tell me that we had a meeting on Monday out at the Cooke Road house. He was preparing to take a flight next week to Miami, then a private plane down to Cuba for a major discussion with Mendez. He wouldn't give me any details of what it was about, but I think it was partly because he didn't really know yet.

Coming out of the meeting, where we discussed more lucrative prices, profits and business ventures, and of course P.'s trip to Cuba that week, I got a call from my pops saying that he needed to see me right away. A call from my pops was beyond rare. However, I told him that I'd meet him at the McDonald's on Livingston Avenue before he headed to the Iron Pony to check on his motorcycle. It was getting a tune-up, he said.

Leaving our once a month meetings always had me concerned for one reason or another. And being the fact that the quarter of a million dollar home we met at was an old couple's who Fat Cat had known ever since the late 80s didn't make me feel any better. Being the fact that Cat was, not only no longer our affiliate, but he was said to be on a mad mission for a come up. He was doing dirt from city to city and now he was back in the 'Bus. Broke! His habits were crippling. Between big tricking, living large, excessively gambling, and an enormous coke and liquor addiction he had it all the way bad. The word that we had just got last week was that he was perpetrating like he had work, using his former commission affiliation. Either he would beat niggas with bullshit coke or he would rob them. P. had told everyone not to worry, though. And that the old couple was still friends of ours and of the North Side Firm's.

When I pulled into the parking lot to meet my pops, something dawned on me. My suspicions were correct. We exited our vehicles together and headed inside for a convenient food and beverage.

"Hey son, what's goin' on, man? These two detectives came by the house yesterday asking me about a Antonio Jones. Ya brother! Cause they sure as hell wasn't asking bout me wit this shit. Yeah, they said they wanted to talk to him, though. They asked me if he drove my truck ever. I said, no. So, uh, after a short while they left. Now what's goin' on wit dat?" Pop asked.

I explained to him in detail what had happened. After bout a half an hour we rolled out. What would happen next, I wondered. Although they didn't seem to have anything but a license plate number, I was still concerned.

However, a license plate number was all they needed to start some shit. The truck was in Pop's name, but of course it was mine. They asked about Twin because he was Antonio Jones Jr. and they knew Pop didn't fit the description that they had got. Pop was dark brown and in his forties. Not light-skinned and youthful. Who the fuck had got the license plate number? Some fucking Good Samaritan?! I wondered if I should have them touched. Nah, it was too late. I didn't even know who it was, and the laws had the truck's plate already.

P.'s was about to head south, and since I was told to lay low, Nuts would be handling all of P.'s affairs. I had a dummy address and P.O. Box, but I still contacted my lawyer to keep an eye out to see if I had any warrants pop up. This shit had me stressed the fuck out. Damn, why'd that hostile ass yankee have to die? Or let alone even provoke me that day.

I peeked down at my phone to see that I had 2 messages from earlier when I had my phone off at the meeting. As I exited the expressway on 11th Avenue to ride up Cleveland, I played the messages. They were both from Goldie. She was asking if she could see me later on after she got home from work. 'Why not', I thought. We hadn't kicked it in a while. I was on my way to Heady's house, though. She didn't have to be at work until later in the evening. So I figured I'd go get me some wet, wet. Some mother fucking Water Works! Yeah, I had been fucking her for nearly 2 months now. My man Nut was right, no doubt. The pussy sprayed like a Windex bottle. And she stayed cooking a nigga some good food. Yes sir! I would eat good first, and then crash that pussy from the back. Then I would shoot around to my crib to get cleaned and fresh, and in a few hours go fuck with my boo, Goldie, for the night. But of course I would have to spend some quality time with Keysh and the kids for the rest of the week. A nigga could have his cake and ice cream, and eat it, too.

CHAPTER 26: Cooked Beef

Although Twin had calmed down a lot and polished up a little more, he would never truly change. He was running two spots; him and Dust. One out east off of Main Street, near Dust's stomping ground, and the other one was far north near Cleveland and Morse Road. Actually, they moved it around to different complexes in that area. The clientele would follow them wherever they went.

However, I had heard about a number of shootouts that they were having with some of the north side hot boys. They had even pistol-whipped two of the niggas at a local bar parking lot. In broad daylight! Twin had recruited a few of his goons; Young Marvin and his big brother Hanseo, and his baby's mama's cousin, Lil' D. Dust had his childhood right hand; Soul man and a number of other wanna be thugs on his team. They looked up to Dust like the O.G. gang banging nigga that he was. Twin, too. The shit that I could never understand was how these gang banging cats would beef with each other. The niggas that they were beefing with wore the same flag/color. The beef had started nearly a month ago when, out of jealousy, the head nigga in their crew, Bernard, had an argument with Twin that escalated into a brutal scrap. They were all initially cool for the most part, but the liquor brings it all out of niggas. Twin and Dust's team were getting most of the money and had a majority of the local bitches on their dicks, even Big Bernard's bitch. It was how the game sometimes went.

Anyhow, the niggas was salty and basically should have stood down after Twin smashed Bernard's big ass. The nigga was 6'2" 230 pounds, opposed to Twin's 5'9" 170lbs; if that. Niggas pride can sometimes get the best of them, though. So for the past 3 weeks they had all been shooting it out. On sight!

It was Tuesday, October 31st. Halloween! P. had left earlier that evening to go down to M-I-A. I had found out that I had a warrant for my arrest, and my uncle Red was about to have his wildest 30th birthday. Dust and Twin had been hanging out east all afternoon. After they had checked the spot earlier they had begun smoking blunts and just rolling around in Twin's minivan. Shaking the block everywhere they went. They were riding dirty with one of the Mac 11s that I had got them at Vance's. But I had Chuck up at 'Creative Conversion' hook Twin's van up with the slickest of stash spots. They ran into Red at my aunt's crib, who agreed to roll with them up north; for some drama they'd hoped. When they got up north they went over to their hood rat chick's crib, Tyese. In the building next to their spot in Lexington projects. Shortly after they had a blunt and a few drinks, Tyese's girl Quita came in. Of course, she was jonesing to tap the blunt.

"Oh yeah! Let me hit that, Tony. Girl, you know them lame ass niggas was just up there trying to hit on me while I was doing my laundry. And I coulda swore that one of the dudes with 'em is a fag. Girl, he was gay as black Spanky that do hair," said Quita.

"Who the fuck is she talking bout, nephew? This bitch is crazy," Dust said, just coming out of the bathroom shaking his hands dry; and reaching for the blunt from Quita. Who pulled it back saying, "I ain't crazy, Dust. You are, though. And I'm talkin' about Mark and Dwayne anem's punk asses; all drunk and disrespectful."

"Who you talkin' bout, Mark 'anem who drive the yellow Nissan with the white interior?" Twin asked.

"Yep. They probably still up there at Dirty Dungaree's," said Quita.

"Come on, let's go," Twin told Dust and Red.

They jumped in Twin's crack head ace Slim Jim's little Chevy Beretta. It took 2 minutes to swing around to the bar, but they decided to pull into the back of Big Bear's grocery store which was beside the bar divided by a tall fence. They slipped through the fence into the bar's parking lot. Mark, Dwayne, and the big punk were coincidentally exiting the bar.

"Tone, wusup? This dem?" Red whispered.

He had a 2-shot derringer in the palm of his hand as he approached the faggot nigga.

"Hey, Red! Wusup, boo? When you get out?" The fag asked Red before Red smacked him across the face and then pointed the small pistol to his grill.

"Nigga, shut up and get yo' ass down on the ground," Red told the sissy as Dust and Twin drew down on the other 2 jokers. Lying in between cars, the niggas plead with Twin 'anem not to shoot them.

It was late in the evening, with a little daylight still. No shots were fired, but Twin 'anem did kick and stomp them in their guts and grills. After they robbed them of what they had on their persons, of course. Not because they needed it, but just for G.P. Just for the fuck of it!

They made their escape and headed back around to the project. Clowning about the drama that had just took place, Dust emphasized how he wanted to plug them all. Then, about how they may have been looking for some get back now.

"Dig, shit, you know that was them hoe ass niggas that shot up

Stephanie's car in front of y'all crib a few weeks ago. Nephew, these niggas gotta go. They some suckas for real, but it ain't no need to give some suckas a free shot at you, nigga. You feel me?!" Dust asked.

Twin had seen the niggas after his baby's mama took him to the steakhouse for Sweetest Day. They usually weren't that far up north, according to Twin, but when he saw them out his way he knew that they had scoped him. Because 20 minutes after he got home the shots rang out.

Dust's eyes widened, "Ay, I say we go stakeout their homey Rob's crib. That's where they all hang out at. And that nigga got the most money out of all of them. It be bitches over there sometimes, but fuck it! They can get it, too."

"Man, this nigga crazy! Look here…I'ma show y'all young killas how to do this shit. We gotta head back out east first. Let me go in here and piss real quick, then we can bounce," Red said.

"What the fuck is up with this fake ass O.G. nigga? You know I ain't never liked this muthafucka. Ay man, did that big black ass fag say that nigga's name?" Dust asked.

"Hell yeah. And he called his ass, boo," Twin said as they both looked on with skepticism.

*

Dust had excellent break-in skills but they felt that they had a better idea. Dust and Twin had done their scoping surveillance well into the a.m. and had gathered that at Rob's place he had some broad shacked up with him, and his homey Mark was there nursing his battered body and face. He had got as drunk and as high as he could get before passing out shortly after midnight. It was now shortly past 3 a.m. Rob had surely hit the sack with his piece of pussy by now and the youngest buffoon would be coming out of his hood rat bitch's apartment any minute.

"Man, I'm telling you nephew, I'm ready to go in here and get this hoe ass nigga. For real! I know Red wonderin' what the fuck is goin' on," said Dust.

Red had instructions to come directly to Rob's house when he got the 9-1-1 page, anytime between 2 and 6 a.m. They were originally going to kidnap Dwayne from his bitch's place and then take him to Rob's, have him knock and gain entry, and then bust in. But that could get ugly not knowing who, what, and where. So they decided to do it slightly different. The building door opened and out came Young D-Dub.

"There he go. Go ahead, creep up on his ass. Careful though, cause you know he got a pistol on him," Twin told Dust.

He slid out of the car, with the silencer on the Glock in hand. Twin put the car in drive and slowly eased up on D-Dub just before he could open his car door and asked, "Hey bruh, is this Heather Green Apartments?"

"Nah, nigga. What the….." He quickly recognized that it was Twin, but before he could get a grip on his 9mm Beretta, Dust put the silencer into his lower back and said, "Bitch ass nigga you better not move one more muscle or I'ma dig up in you like the hoe that you is! Open the door, nigga."

After he opened the door to get in Dust told him to slide over to the passenger's seat where he then slapped him upside the head; knocking him unconscious. Dust started the car and then pulled off to follow Twin around to the next apartment complex over to ditch the stolen car that they had. As they began to ride, Dust slapped D-Dub with the gun again. Just for good measure.

A minute later Twin parked the hot ride. Checking the perimeter first, they pulled D-Dub out of the front seat of his blue Ford Mustang and put him on the floor in the back. Twin rode back there with him, keeping the Glock pressed to his head.

"Ay, you page Red's fat ass?" Dust asked.

"Yeah. Hell yeah. He comin'," Twin said.

"Alright, we damn near there. You ready to do this shit? Yeah, it's time to show these lame ass niggas what time it is," Dust said. Seeing the familiar look in Twin's eye he had seen many times before. He too wore the look, and knew it well.

*

I had been up with Keysh all night long. She wouldn't stop crying since I had told her that I had a warrant for my arrest and why. I just held her and assured her that everything would be okay. I had it set up to go turn myself in with my lawyer the following afternoon, where I would pay a bond and be released immediately. It still didn't seem to soothe Keysh's tension and her worrying. We had finally put the kids to bed and I had to do something to calm Keysh's nerves. It was nearly 4 a.m. and I knew we both needed to get to sleep soon. So I began to kiss her gently on her smooth face and neck, tasting her salty tears. She moaned as she received my kisses, but still she held me so tight. I gracefully broke her vice grip then removed her yellow, cotton nightshirt. I instantly dug in, sucking and licking her sweet pussy. She cried quietly but moaned softly as she held on tightly to the back of my neck. I swiftly removed my clothes. And by the time I was naked Keysh was coming; plentifully like a waterfall. I climbed on top of her, injecting my love deep inside of her walls. I slowly made love to her at first, but then I began to smash her. With her legs resting on my shoulders I slammed my meat down into her stomach. Slapping and gripping the sides of her ass cheeks, I began to squirt massive chunks of cum into the warmth of her pussy. I yelled 'Keysh' repeatedly as I came. Just as, a few seconds later, she screamed 'Daddy! Fuck me, daddy. I'm comin', daddy!' We let off in unison and then instantly fell into a coma like sleep.

*

My locksmith guy, Gary, had hooked Dust up with the lock picking tools he needed earlier that evening. So in an instant he had the door unlocked where they could gain entrance. Twin had duck taped D-Dub's mouth so if he decided to scream. Although they assured him that they wouldn't kill him or his homies, and that they just wanted all of the money and work they had, they felt that D-Dub knew better. So they duck taped his big jibs anyway. Twin slowly walked him inside at gunpoint. Dust quietly closed the door behind them. As Twin held D-Dub hostage in the living room with an intoxicated Mark, Dust slid upstairs to scan the perimeter. He looked in both bedrooms; they were empty. When he reached the third bedroom at the end of the hall, voila.....there they were a snoring Rob and a caramel bone, sleeping beauty. Dust walked over and stood next to the bed. Looking down at Rob he gun butted him in the gut.

"Uhh!" He groaned. "What the fuck?" He said groggily, opening his eyes to find Dust staring down at him; a nightmare for any nigga to wake up to. He quickly sat up, but froze when he saw the silencer headed Glock.

"Nigga, wake that bitch up, and then let's go. Oh, and if she scream then I'm lettin' you have it. Ya dig?!" Dust told him.

"Alright. Cool. Just chill! Shay. Shay, wake up!" Rob said emphatically. When she looked up he shushed her. She looked confused, and then looked over at Dust and the big 40 caliber Glock in his hand and almost let out a scream. But Rob shushed her even louder and more emphatic.

"Now, get the fuck up and let's go downstairs. I ain't gon' say it again," Dust stressed. The broad got up wearing only a waist length t-top and thong panties. Rob had on just his boxers.

"Play ya hand right, nigga, and you might get to suck her pussy again," Dust said with a smirk on his face. Their plan was to convince these niggas that they just wanted to rob them for everything, but would not kill them if they were cooperative.

They got downstairs to find Twin sitting on a chair across from Mark and D-Dub. Twin gave Rob a nod and a smirk as he looked his bitch over. Rob got a sick feeling in his stomach. The kind of feeling you get when you know you're in deep shit. He looked at his boys on the couch with amazement. With his eyes asking, 'What?', and 'how in the fuck?!'

"Dust, come on man. Ay Tone, listen man, I know..." Before Rob could finish Dust hit him in the back of the neck with a stun gun. His body jerked as he hit the floor onto his knees.

"Shut up, bitch. Everybody get down in the basement," Dust demanded.

Once they all got downstairs Twin unarmed his black backpack from off of his shoulder and retrieved the duck tape. He quickly bound and gagged the broad, who was quivering from both fear, and the cold basement chill. She lay on the floor hog tied. Twin then smacked her on the ass and threw the duck tape to D-Dub and ordered him to tie up both of his boys. D-Dub scowled at Twin before saying...something incoherent. His intellect kicked in when he realized that his hands were not yet tied. So he ripped the tape from his mouth and said, "Fuck you, you light bright, hoe ass nigga. You do it!"

"Hoe ass?!" Twin asked, looking at D-Dub. As he then looked over at Dust. Pop! The silencer nosed Glock spit out fire, hitting D-Dub in the groin. He yelled out in pain. Dust went over to tape his mouth back shut, and then tape his wrists.

"Ay, this is Red paging me. I'm bout to hit him wit the code and go up here and let him in. Watch these lame ass niggas," Twin told Dust.

He headed up the steps and, five minutes later he came back down with Red, who astonishingly scanned the entire basement scene. Dust had him hold the Glock as he completed the duck tape job on Mark and Rob.

Dust began the interrogation on Rob, as Twin slid over into the mix, un-taping Rob's mouth for him to answer their questions.

"Now look nigga, we ain't gon' kill y'all if you tell us where the money and the shit at," Dust said.

"Man, ain't no money here. I swear. Tone, you know I keep my stash out at my mom's crib out east," Rob pleaded. Dust punched him in the eye, swelling it instantly.

"Here Dust, tape this nigga's mouth back shut. Now, come here. Get up, bitch." Red said untying the chick Shay's hands from her feet. He positioned her over the couch, and then reached into the black bag that they had brought and pulled out a rusted, ridged pipe. Shay tried her hardest to scream through the thick tape. It was no use, though. Red forced it into her pussy and began to pound her with it. Tears streamed down her face as she let out the loudest muffled cry.

"Nigga, you can end all of the bitch's pain as soon as you decide to talk," Red said to Rob. Rob just squeeze his eyes shut tight, agonizing for Shay. This enraged Red, so he pulled the pipe out and shoved it in Shay's ass. She was now nearly unconscious. Blood was everywhere. Red zapped her in the side and the ass with the stun gun. And with the metal pipe in her she shook profusely. He then punched her in the rib and jaw, knocking her completely out.

"Come on, dog. Stop! Please. You gon' kill her," Rob stressed; while his 2 homies looked more frightened than horror flick victims.

"Muthaphucka, where's the money and the shit at? We ain't got all muthaphuckin' night; it's damn near 5 o'clock!" Twin said. He had just come back downstairs from doing a brief search of the whole house. He had slid upstairs when Red's torcher began.

"Ay, I ain't find shit but what this nigga had in his pants pocket. $1300 and a lil' smoke sack of green," Twin told them.

What they witnessed next would fuck with their psyches for a very long time. And it wasn't much that could do that to Twin or Dust at this point.

"Alright, fuck all this shit. Dig, bring that bitch nigga over here!" Red demanded.

Dust walked Rob over to the couch, Glock jammed deep into his neck. Throwing Rob 5-6 feet towards Red, Dust stood back with Twin to observe what was about to be done next. Red grabbed Rob and bent him over the couch beside Shay. After pulling Rob's boxers down Red pushed his own pants down to his ankles and began to stroke his penis.

"Bitch ass nigga, you gon' talk," Red demanded as he became erect enough to enter Rob's behind.

In just a few seconds, Dust and Twin watched Red torcher Rob like he was a porno whore. Rob shrieked emphatically as he gestured towards the right wall.

"Hold on, man. Hold on!" Dust yelled, as he walked over to strip the tape from Rob's mouth. "Now, wusup?" He asked Rob.

It turned out that there was over $80,000 in the basement wall just under the steps. They threw it in the bag and quickly discussed the 4 executions about to take place. With never doing a murder with Red, they had decided that everyone would pull the trigger on the Glock; with Dust capping two of the bodies. Afterwards, they carefully exited the house and slid off into the final, dark hour of the a.m.

CHAPTER 27: Dark Surprises

The same light brown, wide-eyed assailant had me held at gunpoint as he smiled at me and let out a psychotic laugh. I thought about going for the gun, but decided against it. But what else could I do, though? This was life or death. I made my move. Pow! The gun went off, with the bullet hitting me in the neck. But before it could begin to burn, I was jarred awake with 'virm-virm-virm.' It was my phone vibrating on the nightstand.

"Yo." I answered.

"Siz-o! What you doin'? You still sleep?" Twin asked.

"Nah. I'm just layin' here. Wusup, though?"

"Ay, I need 9 of 'em. Paper."

"Alright. Give me a couple hours, I got you." I told him, and then I hung up. Paper was the term that we used for hard coke. Crack! Plastic was the term for soft coke. Powder!

I had recently moved to Reynoldsburg and no one had the address. So I had Keysh drop me off down in the 'hood to do some whipping for Twin, where Red would come pick me up at and then shoot me out to our residence by the airport to hook Twin up and have Keysh's Mazda van that I had previously been rolling, towed. It had been having some electrical problems, so I was having it sent to my Chinese mechanic.

A few hours had passed and I was out at my house waiting for our tow guy to come, as well as Twin. Standing in my driveway, with the wind and leaves blowing, I peeped an undercover Chevy Caprice and a Ford mini-van rolling by, back and forth it seemed.

"Yo dog," I asked my uncle Red, "you see this shit?"

"Huh? What?" He asked me as he appeared to talk on his cell phone.

"Dog, it looked like the rollers. This tow muthaphucka has got to hurry the fuck up!" Just as I said that the fat fuck pulled up.

He got out, briefly said hey, and then hooked the van up to be pulled onto the tow bed. As he pulled off, Red pointed left towards the end of the street. It was Twin coming down the block in his black Z-28. 'About fucking time', I thought. I was paranoid, no doubt. And I had my lawyer waiting on me in his office. I rushed Twin in and out, with no clue as to what had just happened 6-8 hours ago.

We jumped in Red's Buick and headed towards the highway. I called my lawyer's office to inform him that we were on our way when I spotted the ghetto bird in the air above us. It seemed that it was following us. 'Damn', I thought. A police cruiser was pulling out from every side street, following right behind us. Two cars, three cars...they finally hit the lights. We were pulled over on Hudson Avenue just before hitting the highway.

"Sizalino Jerele Jones?" The white haired man asked.

"Yeah, wusup?" I asked.

"You're under arrest. Put your hands where I can see them." He said.

I was taken into custody without incident. They never told me what I was under arrest for, but I knew. They took me downtown to be booked into county. Shortly after that, I was taken over to police headquarters for an interview with the investigating detectives; once my lawyer was present, of course. The cock sucking D's were alright. They got me an ice cold coke while I waited. All of the normal fucking proceedings followed. I was soon interviewed and then put in population. Locked up until my morning arraignment where I would post bond.

I was put in a small ass 12 man cell on the fourth floor. A few cats acknowledged me; some west side affiliates who had been going down to West 'V' to push work. They now all had Fed cases. I wasn't trying to kick it, though. My mind was in a zone. How the fuck did the laws know about my crib out by the airport? It definitely wasn't in my name. And how did they even know to put a warrant out on me? I smelled a rat. After an hour or so of mind bending thoughts I fell into a coma-like sleep.

*

It was early in the a.m. and I was headed to Heady's house. When I called her, after Keysh got the kids off to the babysitter, she told me that she needed to see and speak to me rather urgently. I had talked to Twin last night and he told me that Goldie said the same shit when he saw her with her girl that he was fucking the night before. By the time P. had picked me up from the county jail after I bonded out the night before, I didn't want to do shit but go to the crib; my crib out in Reynoldsburg with Keysh and the kids. I had to get cleaned up, kick back and get my head straight. I did, for the most part. But I still had a lot to figure out.

I pulled into Heady's driveway at about a quarter 'til ten. It felt a little weird because I hadn't seen her for nearly 2 weeks. And I didn't plan on seeing her. After a quick 'knock knock', Heady let me in. She got me a beverage, and we briefly talked about my pending case.

"Yeah, this shit is crazy, no doubt. So, what's up with you? What do you gotta talk to me about?" I asked her.

"Well, I missed my period a little while back, so I went to the doctor last week. And…he told me that I was pregnant. Six weeks pregnant. Well no, about seven weeks now." Heady said hesitantly as she looked me in my eyes. I thought to myself, 'was this bitch crazy?' What was she saying? Certainly she wasn't saying that I was the father.

"Oh yeah? So what do you mean? We used protection every time," I said.

"I know. It must have been that night when you said that the condom broke. You know, the night we met up after the club," she said. 'Wow', I thought.

We went on talking for nearly an hour before I rolled out to go catch up on some things. I rode westward in deep thought. And this goofy broad had the nerve to say, after clarifying that she was keeping the child, that she would keep it on the down low from my family and everybody as far as the child being mine. How stupid did that sound. As I exited the highway onto Sullivant Avenue my phone rang.

"Yeah, wusup?" I answered.

"Hey, baby!" It was my Golden Girl, Goldie. "I got good news. You gon' be a daddy!"

CHAPTER 28: Abundant Change

I sat at P.'s Weldon Square townhouse where we chopped it about the work that was headed our way; via Miami. We heard a knock on the door and P. sent Big Tommy to answer it. It was our friend Mike Lewis. He came in, grabbed a sprite, and then we began to discuss some business. After he realized that there wouldn't be any coke available until another day or two, he brought up a name that we hadn't heard for quite some time. Fat Cat! Who had really become notorious over the past 18 months or so. Mike told us that he had Cat waiting on him to call for 2 keys. We told him, 'don't do it!'

"Dog, I'm tellin' you, dude is on some scandalous, dope fiend shit. He just robbed Shawn Merlin about two weeks ago. You know, Shawn with the blue Caprice. Yep, he had a chick drivin' while he sat in the front seat. How the fuck you gon' get in the front seat? Shawn was trippin'," P. said.

"What? Straight up?" Mike asked.

"Yeah, Cat got him for his jewelry and everything. Hey, don't fuck wit Cat," P. emphasized.

It was nearly 3 o'clock and Mike rushed through the German Village traffic and into Thurman's parking lot. Thurman's café was where the lawyers and all of the other cockroaches lounged at during lunch hours. Cat was sitting in a red BMW, already waiting. He was in the passenger's seat, though. Mike took a double take to get a good look at the driver once he parked. He peeped that it was a light-skinned guy…it was Hollywood, Cat's right hand Ace. Mike briefly thought of all the shit he had heard lately about Cat, and wondered if Hollywood was on the same shit or what. He quickly pushed the negative thoughts out of his mind, thinking to himself, 'these niggas know better.' Plus, he had his Smith & Wesson 9 millimeter with 15 hot ones under her skirt.

"Young Mike, what's good, bruh?" Hollywood asked Mike as he got in the backseat.

"I'm chillin'. Wusup wit y'all?" He asked as he gave them both some dap.

Cat was intently quiet, Mike had peeped. Just get this shit over with, he thought to him self. It was a one time thing as far as he was concerned. P. and the Firm would be back in business within 48 hours.

"Hey, pull that seat down, Mike. They're behind the seat goin' into the trunk. You see 'em? You got 'em?" Hollywood asked. Mike retrieved the 2 bricks as Cat appeared to be counting the 50 stacks.

"Wusup, these all ten stacks?" Cat asked.

"Uh, yeah," Mike answered.

"Alright, cool. I'll holla at you. Get at me. Yo, let's get the fuck outta this hot ass spot. We the only niggas around here," said Cat.

"Oh. Yeah. Alright, peace!" Mike said.

He got into his car and quickly got back to what he had started in the BM' wit Cat and 'Wood. He easily opened the wrapped package to taste its contents. No numbness. It was rather sweet. Damn, he had just been wooed.

"Mutha phucka!" Mike said, opening his car door and brandishing his weapon. Mike Lewis was known for being a laid back dude. But he had always had it in mind that if he was ever played like a sucker then he could, and would, become a live nigga. And now was the time. He pointed and then squeezed the trigger. Shots rang out; endlessly it seemed, in the small German Village neighborhood. Mike emptied all 15 shots into the car, hitting Hollywood twice as he exited the vehicle to run with the cash. Four of the other 15 bullets went into Fat Cat's back and shoulder. Mike ran up to the crashed BMW to find Cat barely breathing. He reloaded his weapon to take off after a wounded Hollywood, who stumbled down 3rd street towards Livingston Avenue. All of the corporate citizens looked on in shock as they screamed and pointed towards the action. Just as Mike caught up with Hollywood's limp body, which had now collapsed, he aimed his pistol at Hollywood's face. And then he heard, "Freeze! Drop it!"

The cops were everywhere. He surrendered as he was told to do. Once he was cuffed and arrested, so many things went through his mind. Shit was about to get ugly, he thought. If only he had listened...

*

"Good evening. And thanks for joining us. This is 6 on your side. We have breaking news. We have a team live out on the scene in German Village where one man was shot and killed. And another man was wounded as well. Police have who they suspect as the shooter, in custody. Carol!" The news anchorwoman faded out.

We watched on as we got the details of what had just taken place a few hours earlier. It was Mike Lewis. He had made that move, anyway. And wow, Stanley Williams was found dead on the scene. Fat Cat! Shit had finally caught up with him. Also, the wounded assailant was a

Richard Parker. Hollywood! Here today, gone tomorrow. That's how the game went. Damn though, my nigga Mike was about to go away and do some joints. I felt for him, but it was what it was.

*

I was waiting for Goldie to get her pregnant ass home from work so I could get 10 of the pounds of green that I had at her house for my southern cats. I didn't have my house key because it was left in my truck, which the laws had at the lab for testing. They were some dickheads because I had already told them what had happened. However, I hadn't had a chance to get a key made, so here I was waiting. A car pulled into the driveway, but it wasn't Goldie's Jetta. It was…Red's Buick. I saw him and his little hood rat get out of the car. She had her arm around his fat ass; it looked as if he was wounded. I opened the door to let him in.

"Damn family, what happened?" I asked. His left eye was swollen and his mouth was split.

"That muthaphuckin' Dust. I'ma kill that nigga. I swear that's on my mama," Red said.

"Yo, just chill, dog. Ain't nobody killin' nobody. Now what the fuck happened?" I asked him.

It turned out that Red and Dust were over at my other crack head uncle Reece's place out in the 'hood earlier and ended up getting into it. It was some egotistical shit. Dust dropped him, though, with a 2-piece combo. Red was embarrassed, no doubt, getting dropped by his younger brother; although Dust was something like a monster on both levels of the game. Red portrayed the tough guy role, but he was really just a big loud-mouth. I read niggas all day, everyday. But I let him tell his story. Right now he was hurt, though. His pride was hurt, as well as his eye and jaw. It probably didn't take much for the fight to get started, being that Dust despised him. Just last month in a hotel where I was posted with some dime pieces having a player set, they had nearly came to blows over something simple. I stopped it then, but I wasn't around this time to stop it.

While looking over the damage that had been done to Red, my phone buzzed. This had to be Goldie calling. Nope. It was an unknown number.

"Yeah," I answered.

"You have a collect call from, 'James Dawson'." The recording said.

I pressed the one button to accept. "Yo. Wusup, dog?" I asked.

"Man, you see I'm up in this dirty ass county jail. These hoes got me with a pistol." Dust went on to explain how he had got pulled over riding with his chubby, white bitch Cammy right after he beat Red up. He told me how he felt that Red had called the laws on him; on the low, though. We spoke for 10 minutes and then I concluded the call. I couldn't even bail him out because he was already on probation. So, of course he had a holder.

Goldie had pulled up while I was on the phone. My uncle Red had let her in. She was going to ride me down to South High Street, with my pounds, to meet my people. But Red insisted that he and his hood rat chick could take me. So I kissed and hugged Goldie goodbye, and then we all rolled out.

*

It was Thursday afternoon and I was heading down to see Dust in the County. His lawyer had told him that he was going away to do at least a year. I stepped into the visitor's booth and after about 10 minutes or so, he came out. We discussed a few things and then he finally told me that he thought Red called the cops on him after the beat down. And that he thought Red believed that the pistol he was carrying was the murder weapon from the robbery that they had pulled at Rob's. Which, it wasn't. We got rid of all hot burners. But this was a deep conclusion that Dust had came up with. However, I kept a mental note of it. After I left from downtown I slid out to Heady's for a bite to eat. I was still sick at the fact that Heady was pregnant with my child. I had never had another woman pregnant before besides Keysh. Well, and now Goldie. Heady had moved to the far southeast side of the city, in a suburban condominium near the 270 interstate. It was really nice.

"Hey, Headster! What's up?" I asked.

"Nothing. What's up with you? You ready to eat?" She asked me.

I nodded yes. As I began to eat I went deep into my thoughts. As I often did. One of the things that I thought about was Keysh's brother-in-law, Big Fred and his people. They fucked with the green pounds; heavy. But they didn't deal with any coke. Their other hustle was a nightclub, the 504! It was a hot spot, too. And they had a little CD shop next to our store, D & C's. I had seriously considered getting out of the coke game. Like I'm sure every other hustler has. The few times that I had hollered at P. in the last 2 months he had deterred me from retiring. Stressing how he needed me and questioning what I would do if I did quit the game. The question was rhetorical but still, he asked. I hadn't pushed any work, though. Not hands on. I did, however, have a number of cats who would always try to push 20-30 pounds of green on me. The opportunity was there. But I couldn't go all-in just yet. So I just kept it the same with Fred and Mark as I had with my usual 5-10 pounds. In which, Heady pushed for the most part. I would seriously have to weigh my options going into this new year of 2000. The 'Life' was the shit, but I didn't want to push coke forever. I truly needed a way out. Heady was the one who would talk to me about my future. She'd ask me things like 'where did I see myself in the next 5-10 years' and similar questions as well. She was the only one of my chicks who would ask me shit like that. This was a good bitch that Nuts let go of. Sadly though, she could only be my mistress. If Keysh ever slipped, though, Heady could slide right into that number one spot.

CHAPTER 29: Evolution

The holidays came and went pretty smoothly. Business was beautiful. We had a big holiday sale at D & C's, which is where our New Year's began. We partied big from Christmas Eve to New Year's Day. My cousin Mike had his wife and his right hand man Ricky run the store for nearly a week while we went down to Miami to celebrate and attend a clothing show that my cousin Mike was going to be a part of. The four of us went, my Cousin Mike, P., Nuts, and my self. Big cuz' had some Caribbean and South American models, who barely spoke English, chilling in our suites waiting on our arrival. They were going to model in the show as well. My cousin and everybody loved having me with them because I spoke Spanish. It was an excellent attribute to have down in Miami where the culture was heavy at. P. had told everybody that we were going to be gone for a week, but in reality it was only going to be 3 days.

We stepped off of the plane shortly after our 12:52 landing time, around 1p.m. A light-brown complected man approached us. He was Hispanic.

"Uh... Michael? Mr. Pettway?" Said the stranger; pointing back and forth towards P. and my cousin questioningly.

"Woah, hold on 'migo. Oye, que pasa? Como se llamo?" I asked him.

"Yo soy el hombre de Senor Mendez," he explained.

"Oh. Okay. P., he say he one of Manny's guys. In English 'migo, in English," I told the guy.

"Si, gracias," he said with a smile. "Mr. Mendez would like for you to come by his suite at the Biltmore. In a little while, whenever you're ready."

"Alright, that's cool. Tell him I'll be by there in a couple of hours," P. said.

"Good, good. I will tell him. It's room 602, Senor. Buenos diaz!" With a smile, the man walked away into the crowd.

We took a cab to the Hilton hotel where we were staying and got checked into our suites. The desk clerk had a message for us. It was from the girls. It read that they were on the beach waiting for our call. Nuts called immediately as soon as he sat his things down. Twenty minutes or so passed by and then there was a knock on the door. P. was on the phone, Mike was in the shower, and Nuts was rolling us a hydro blunt. I answered the door to four of the most beautiful faces in the world. I welcomed them in where they introduced themselves. The dark Dominican one was Raula, the tall Argentinean's name was Martina, the little caramel brown Jamaican one was Nechelle, and the very light-skinned beauty was Tyzanna. She was from Brazil, but had been living in Phoenix for a year now.

We all got acquainted and loosened up with some drinks. I had brought my blender so I could make some exclusive mixes. Having a bachelor pad influenced me to be a gracious host to any chick lucky enough to be in my presence; in my home, or where ever. I was a good cook, as well.

P. broke things up a little by stepping out to go holler at Manny. I told Nuts and Mike to keep the women company because I was going over to the Biltmore with P. Once we got there we toasted a drink and then he told us about a club called the Plaque where it was supposed to go down tonight for New Year's Eve. 'All the way live' the way he explained it. This was the first (and the last) time I saw Manny. He was one cool, Latin Drug Lord!

That night we kicked it like we were supposed to. I was so drunk and loose that I fucked Miss Raula on the beach shortly after midnight. Beast mode! And we fucked in numerous, exotic positions. P. got with Tyzanna, Nuts got with Martina, and Mike snatched up Nechelle. It was wild because on the plane ride back P. told me how he and Mike switched up with their beauties. P. was officially a freak. I mean, this nigga runs trains and 3-ways on his baby's mamas. And he told me how he's had two of the 5 together before. He was my Ace, though. We were similar in the fact that we both had a weak spot for pretty women, but our true passion was the dough. And although Keysh had my heart, I wasn't fond of letting too many people know it.

*

We stepped off the plane on the second evening of the New Year. It was back to Ohio weather. And back to reality. P. had told me shortly before we left that our friends from up north and out east weren't very happy with the current arrangements. They felt that our West Side Firm affiliates were getting more love and benefit than all of them; on the coke prices, inside Intel with the laws and such, and all of our downtown political connections. P. was fair, though. He knew that N.S.F. and E.S.F. had a number of things going on on the side. But he didn't trip and make beef. He just told them that they had to pay for the services that they were wishing to receive. Which, of course they didn't like.

However, we all had some things going on besides our coke connects and group affiliation. Together we had car washes, car lots, real estate, rec. center programs such as boxing and basketball teams, restaurants, carpet cleaning and laying businesses, escort services, clothing stores, maintenance shops, a scrap yard, bars, and even after hour clubs. I had just got Red to start an after hours spot on the east side in Cherry Alley. But my cousin Mike had it in the works to open a club downtown. Club Red Zone! Opening night would be Friday the 23rd. The clubbing and partying was cool, but as P. and I had talked about, it was a lot of hostility and animosity going on in the city; particularly in the Commission (of ours).

Although we were the richer, or at least the most powerful family, we were the most hated. I mean, it was a large group of niggas out there who hated the fact that they had to respect us. I knew shit was going to hit the fan soon. I could feel it. A nigga just had to be ready. In my mind, I stayed ready. Chance favors the prepared mind.

A few weeks had gone by and things were still smooth. We helped my cousin open up the club, which was all the way live; and it seemed that we had worked out all of the kinks in our partnership with our north and east side affiliates. But that all changed at the tail end of winter. Nuts had a spot down in the west side's bottoms where he had a smooth program flowing. He would whip up a brick at a time and serve eight balls for $100, quarters for $200, halves for $400, and whole ounces for $800. it was mid-March on a Sunday night. Now, each day the dough was counted up and collected in the morning. But Nuts had been in Indiana gambling since Saturday evening. And since he didn't trust anyone to do the collecting, Sunday morning's pick-up would become Monday morning's pick-up as well. At approximately a quarter 'til midnight Dave, Nuts' spot runner, went to answer the door. It was the neighborhood homey, Bean. As soon as Dave let him in two niggas came from behind the screen door and the side of the house. One held a 9 millimeter Beretta with the extended 30 round clip, and the other robber held a Tech-9. They threw Bean to the ground and slapped Dave with the Tech. Big Hank came from the back room. Quickly seeing the threat of danger he reached into his back for his heat. But he was too late. The cat with the Beretta ripped off several shots with one squeeze, hitting Hank in the stomach and dropping him. They smacked Bean and Dave up with their guns and demanded Dave to tell them where the money and dope was at or they would plug him just like they had done his man, Hank. Dave quickly complied. He was certain from the looks of things that Hank was dead.

The intruders put the goods in a black sack, but before they left the taller one whispered to Dave, "You tell that bitch ass Nuts that we comin' for his soft ass. You hear me, nigga?" Dave just stared at him with rage.

A few seconds went by and then they finally left; with over a half of a key and nearly 15 stacks. Less than 12 hours later it was revealed who was behind the robbery. Bean was originally an east side nigga and didn't like how Nuts was getting it down on his Bottoms' block. Being that he didn't feel like he was eating the way he was supposed to. So he played the role through the course of the robbery; getting gun butted and playing the victim and all of that. But he never received one dime of his cut. The east side niggas did him dirty. By the early a.m. hours of Tuesday morning he was found dead under a freeway bridge near the Miller/Kelton exit. They knew that over the past few years that Bean was in Nuts' pocket; due to the fact that Nuts was fucking his sister. The streets have a way of catching up with you. Bean had played the middle for far too long. He had caused too much drama between the smaller east and west side crews.

Meanwhile, a few days later my younger homey Darren was leaving a work house of ours where he had just copped two bricks of coke. But as he left to get in his truck he was ran down on and gun butted. They snatched the two keys and some loose cash. Now we were really like 'what the fuck?' He said that they said his name before they knocked him out but he didn't see much of anything. This shit was as fishy as the sea because somebody felt that they had a license to ill; on W.S.F! But what happened four days later, the morning before our daily meeting, would shake the past week up to the third power; P.'s little suburb-star TA, a cinnamon honey who he had been on and off with for the past few years, had allowed a major jacking. She had a love and hate thing for P. It was no question. Most females let their hearts, and not their minds, control their thoughts and actions anyhow, which in most cases proves to be crucial. TA had stayed the night with P., a usual thing rather, but when P. woke up to leave he left her sleeping. Opting to tell her to just lock up and leave once she got up. She did just that, only $150,000 left with her. P. told me about it on the way to the meeting. I about flipped! He said that it was in a Shop-Vac, which didn't surprise him that she may have known about it considering the fact of how tough he fucked with her.

We entered the large house knowing that, although it wasn't time for war, it was time for battle; of some sort, with someone.

*

Tank Man stood stroking his dick through his boxers while he puffed on his blunt. Staring TA down, he said, "Here go yo' 10 gees, baby. 'Tis the season! They say springtime is the start to new beginnings." He handed her the stack of money off of the table and walked her to the door, slapping her ass on the way out. TA felt a chill go down her spine when he did it. And it wasn't because she was aroused.

*

"Good afternoon, gentlemen. We got some serious issues goin' on in this room today. I'm sure y'all all done heard about the past week's events. It's some real live bullshit goin' on that's been okayed by someone in here sittin' wit us," Nuts said.

He went on to talk about how we seemed to be getting targeted with jack moves and robberies and such. There were mixed comments ranging from who may have been responsible, to perhaps it was all happening because we had became too soft in our lucrative success. Everyone knew that P. was the man bringing the coke in, so the attacks would be limited. But 'fuck that' I felt. It was time to show some people what time it was. I told P. constantly that just because we knew who we were and what we were about, didn't necessarily mean that everyone else did. We walked soft and carried a big stick, but sometimes you had to show niggas who was boss. Show them who the big dogs were. Especially when you were indeed the Big Dogs! You had to act the part. Guard your yard and your pups. And bite muthaphuckas when it was necessary.

We made some ground before we left the meeting. And we were all quietly in agreement that E.S.F. was the ones behind the past week's drama. But the whos, hows, and whys, were all still a huge question.

*

I realized that shit really knew how to hit the fan when it hit after I got a call from Nuts the following week while I was at Car Audio checking on my Suburban's status. I had got it hooked up with the TVs and all of that. It was supposed to be ready by noon. That's what they told me the day before. But now they told me that it would be a few more hours. My uncle Red gave their asses a mouthful like he always did when they bullshitted any of us around. As he spit venom I stepped away to answer my phone.

"Yo, wus good, Nuts?" I answered.

"I don't know. You tell me," Nuts said.

"What? What the fuck are you talkin' bout?"

"You know. Damn, lil' bruh. You ain't even told me bout the baby," he said. I sat silently for a few seconds. Which seemed like a few days, and then finally I said, "Huh?"

"The baby, nigga! The baby that you and Heady bout to have in a couple months," he said with a slight laugh.

"Dig, where you at? You at mom's house? I'm on my way over," I told him.

I told Red to run me around to where Nuts was at. He insisted on coming in with me. Saying that he wanted to let Nuts have it and tell him about his self.

"Nah dog, go ahead; I'ma holla at him alone. I'll spit at you after I leave Car Audio. I'll have him run me back up there," I said. I laughed inside at how Red always wanted to be a loud mouthed tough guy. He was 30 some years old and had already done over 10 years in the joint; and he had a reputable rep. from over a decade ago. Why he wanted to be so proven, I didn't know. I guess it was because he knew that my crew and I were on a level of our own. We were high powered in the city of Columbus and beyond. Red wanted in. P. and I didn't feel that idea, though. But little did we know, Red was working through the cracks, slithering like the snake that he was. And his hunger had no limits.

*

I smoked a sticky, swisher sweet with Nuts, something I rarely did anymore. Anyhow, we chopped it up for over an hour before Nuts dropped me back off at Car Audio. He said that he wasn't tripping about me and Heady, but I could tell that he was salty. I could feel how he felt, in a way. On the flipside though, how could he be mad? I asked myself. Given the circumstances, he couldn't be. He forced me on the broad and had made a tramp/dike his main chick. My spidey senses told me to be on my guard with Nuts from this point on. When it came to niggas egos with females, shit could turn ugly real quick.

"Oh yeah, what all do you got to do? Cause we need to meet up wit P. about some business. It's some real shit. It's bout to go down," said Nuts.

CHAPTER 30: So Much Dirt and Death

"It was Ant. Tony Johnson. East Side Finest Ant! And the nigga just got knocked by the Feds," P. said.

"Get the fuck outta here! When?!" I asked, standing beside Nuts in shock somewhat.

"Last night. Yeah, the way I hear it is when shit was fucked up last year he had his mule shoot out to Cali' for some bricks and dude got knocked comin' back and...eventually gave him up. See how karma catches up to niggas. He's the one who had them niggas run up in Nuts' spot down in the Bottoms. But they thought that Bean was gon' tell Nuts, so you know...they put him to bed. Yeah, Bean's baby's mama was fuckin' Ant's right hand man, too. Oh yeah, and she told it all. But at first we thought it was Chuck 'anem. Well, ya cousin Mike thought so because of the shit that happened between him and Chuck years ago," P. said to me.

"Right; but that was some bullshit, though," I said.

"Yep. Exactly! Ay, and that nigga had Nevelle 'anem run up on Lil' Darren. That's who got him, Nevelle and the rest of them Choke-and-Kill cats. Ant's people! Check this out though, I just got the word that he gon' make bond tonight. And, that he done flipped. So, I'ma wait to meet wit Cooks and Ant's other 2 top dogs from E.S.F. in the morning. But right after that them Spanish-only speakin' cats will be here. None of them niggas gon' try to oppose me, Money Mike or Tommy 'Gloves'. That's their boy, but he gots to go. He in severe violation, they gon' have to feel that," said P. with stone, steady eyes.

"Damn, so Tone gon' go out like dat? He sent dude out west, what, that time when nobody had shit? And he done got caught the fuck up wit dat? Well, fuck that nigga. His snitch ass done had my shit robbed. Our shit! Ay man, have all them niggas touched. Are you gonna give them the word to plug all of his homies who did that shit?" Nuts asked.

P. looked at him with a smirk, "trust me, dog. Their info is all on paper. The contracts are signed."

"What about the 150 stacks? You know...the Shop-Vac stash wit Miss TA?" I asked P.

"I'm on it. But keep y'all ears to the street. I should have the shit wrapped up in the next day or so, wit her sneaky ass inside of it; right in the trick bag," P. said displaying a slamming motion.

I nodded and looked at Nuts. He nodded too and gave an approving gesture.

*

Red had been orchestrating a lot over the past few months. But shit was getting real strenuous lately. All of his old school east side homies had come under fire, but he didn't care. Red only gave a fuck about one thing. Red! He made a choice nearly 2 years ago when he stepped out from behind the wall. He was just simply not going back. Ever! He exploited this philosophy just 90 days out when he dodged arrest for drug trafficking in the old neighborhood. He did that with cooperation; cooperation with the local dickhead detective, Bo Walton. He was an Irish terrorist-like Mick. Red gave up a few names from around his neighborhood, but not us or anybody too major. He'd managed to keep his bullshit undetected for the past year and a half. But once he realized that there were benefits and longevity to ratting, he took it to a whole new level. The mischief that he had stirred up with us and E.S.F. had not gone as planned. So here he sat in a Wilson Avenue project house with some of his goons, getting them ready to go kick Nuts' door in.

"Alright, now listen…this nigga is major and connected. I mean, he right next to the boss. This clown is soft, though. But you can't slip on this 'cause if y'all don't kill this nigga then it's gon' be ugly. I was just at his crib a couple hours ago; the finger might get pointed at me if y'all fuck it up. These niggas ain't stupid. So Bland, B., y'all go handle ya business and let's get paid," Red told his goons. Twin always said that uncle Red was a manipulative Crime Boss. Boss! At least that's what Red thought of himself.

*

I had been rolling around all day in my Suburban, but I was not feeling it at all; although I was bumping X's 'Flesh of My Flesh, Blood of My Blood'. I realized why I wasn't in the flossy, kick it type mode when I got the call from P. telling me of Miss T.A.'s treacherous caper. I met with him down at the tire shop by Tommy's diner. He was getting new tires on his '86 Bronco.

"Come on; let's get us a quick snack," P. said as we walked over to the diner. Big Tom Woods stood by the door as we spoke and ate.

"M.P., what's good, gangsta? Talk to me," I told him.

"Scoobs called me earlier. I went out and seen him. This nigga told me that his muthphuckin' cousin Tank Man done took him down to Cancun and, been stuntin' as usual. But he told me how Tank Man got this new lil' bitch that he been bangin' who helped him hit this big lick. Some bitch that do nails at Suzie Wan's in Graceland!"

"Yo dog, that's all I need to hear. I'm askin' you; let me take care of this. My nigga, I got you."

After nearly a minute of silence, he said, "Yeah, you handle it." And then we got up to leave. Once we were outside I headed to my truck when P. said, "Siz-o. Get pipe wrench dirty on this one," I nodded and then hopped inside my truck.

I was headed to park it and get into something more non-distinct. I dialed a number on my phone. It rang. Twice, and then on three... "Hello," Twin answered.

"Wusup, bruh? I need you to roll wit me. Like, right now. You ready?" I asked.

Yeah, nigga! I stay ready. Come on; we ridin' clean in leather and wood? Or dirty on rusted rims and paint?" He asked.

"Filthy!" I said, and then hung up.

*

We followed closely behind TA's Acura Vigor, which was headed out to Pataskala in the suburbs. Twin was quiet the whole way, just as I was. It was something about when you got in that mode; it just wasn't much to say. We were coming up to a left turn onto her street so I made a quick stop to let Twin out so he could meet her at the door. We wanted no forced entry. We also wanted discretion, so we dressed as Mission Men; myself as a priest, and Twin as my mission aide. We wore cheap suits and a facial disguise. We both looked older with our fake beards and wigs. And our church-like, old Buick helped us to match.

"Hello Miss. I'd like to introduce you to your friendly, fatal father here," Twin said to TA.

"What?" She asked with an attitude.

"Yes, my child. I'd like you to kindly open the fucking door," I said flashing a silencer nosed 38 and then a smile.

She got wide eyed and started to say, "Siz…" before I shushed her. She unlocked the door and we entered behind her.

"Yeah sweetheart, you guessed right. Now, I don't want you to worry. If you tell us the truth, the whole truth, and nothing but the truth, then I promise you will live. But if I feel that you are in any way being dishonest then my assistant here will send you to meet the Almighty. Or the forever damned. Whichever one is ya destiny. Do you get what I'm saying?" I asked her.

She nodded yes, and the interrogation began. After nearly an hour, she told the whole story. With Twin's intent, heartless eyes on her the entire time. He and Dust were like emotionless machines. I knew Twin missed him. But Dust had nearly 3 more months until he got released.

"So damn, you and that joker thought y'all was gonna play my man like that? You told him where the money was, and then left the door unlocked? He creeps insides and snatches it up, then slides right out, huh?" I asked her.

"Siz-o, please; I'm sorry. But Mike has hurt me so many times. It was still stupid, though. Please tell him that I'm so sorry. I still got some of the money. It's up in my room," she pleaded, with streaming tears running down her face.

"Ooh, I'm sure that'll go well with the boss. Twin, go upstairs and get the dough. Where is it, in the closet you say?" I asked her rhetorically. Twin returned instantly with the short stack in hand. "Hey, where's the rest of the money at? Ya mans got it? You are a stupid bitch." I just shook my head. "Well, it's time to call the man. It's his decision, sweetheart," I said.

She sat in agonizing anticipation. I dialed P. up and after the third ring he answered. I told him that I had just heard a great bedtime story. Then I asked him if he wanted the storyteller to tell another story or go to bed as well. I stared at TA while I waited for an answer.

"Ay, that sounds like a hell of a story. Put that ass to bed and holla at me later on," P. said, and then hung up.

TA looked more nervous than a Farmer John pig.

"Damn bitch, that's cold. It's off to the next life for you. I promise you won't be lonely, though. We'll send you some company. Tank Man will be to see you," I said. And then I stood up and nodded at Twin. The silencer hissed, all six times into TA's chest. Twin quickly headed back up to her room to plant all of cult following documentation. When he came back down I asked him jokingly, "You gon' pull a 'Frank White' and bury her wit the 10 gees?"

He replied, "Fuck that! Not unless P. said to."

I shook my head no. We both shot grins at each other, then quickly turned them to straight faces; bouncing from the crib to the Buick, and then out of Pataskala, leaving a dead Tara Ayers behind.

*

Nuts had left a message with someone at the scrap yard, where he knew I'd be eventually, for me to come over to his crib in Westgate when I got done. After we got everything handled with the 'job', I parted ways with Twin and headed to Nuts' place. It was just past nightfall, about 9:30 or 10, when I gave him a call. He said that he had Toya and Bird over, doing each other, and asked me if I'd stop at Kingro's and pick up a pizza and some wings. I told the nigga jokingly that he was killing me, but I would do it. He assured me that it was appreciated and that he had a few bottles of Moet and Alize in the fridge. And plenty of hydro green!

"Oh yeah, and...well shit, we'll rap when you get here," Nuts said.

"Yeah, no doubt," I said before hanging up.

*

It was still hot and humid, even after dark. Ant didn't have to meet with his new boss, special agent Nichols, until 9a.m. where he would

236

tell Nichols all about the 'Commission' and our whole operation. They had offered to cut his 10 years in half to 5 if he gave up his California connection. Which he did, but ultimately he wanted to remain free. So he chose to sell us all out. Every single member! He had spoke with Tommy Coleman earlier, who had agreed to have dinner with him tomorrow night, along with a lengthy, thorough discussion.

After running around all day with his girl Tasha chauffeuring, they headed out to his house in Reynoldsburg. He pulled his Benz into the driveway, and then he and Tasha got out to head inside. All the while his mind was on the testimony that he'd give the next morning that would change his life forever, as well as his family's life. He was extremely nervous. But he had made his decision. And there was no turning back now.

An hour later the two South American assassins went to work on Ant's Benz, arming it with 10 pounds of C-4. Nearly another hour had passed and then they entered the home. After a few minutes of by-passing Ant's alarm. They were equipped with a couple of Glock pistols, but they were mainly accustomed to using their traditional metal; axes, machetes, knives, and chicken wire.

Ant couldn't sleep. And he knew why. It was his conscious. But as he laid there in deep thought, he felt something. Someone was in the room with them! By the time he raised up to reach for his Desert Eagle 44 in the drawer, the machete had swung towards his arm. Ant let out a shrieked scream as he watched his arm fall to the floor. The assassin backhand swung the machete at Ant's forehead, just above the eye. He was silent as he fell back onto the bed.

On the other side of the bed the second assassin had grabbed Tasha by the head, slitting her throat before she could scream. Although Ant's limp body lied still, they slit his throat, too. The first assassin nodded towards the boys' bedroom to the other assassin. When he came back, that's when the ritual began. They used the chicken wire to coil around Ant's penis and testicles, cutting off his whole package. The blood was everywhere. After some brief activity the assassins quietly left the house and eventually, the neighborhood. And in a few short hours, they'd be leaving the country.

*

I hated dealing with incompetent people at restaurants and places like that. The foreign fucks up at Kingro's can barely speak English. No wonder they can't get an order right. I was surely going to let Nuts have it about this shit once I got to his place. When I pulled up though, something seemed strange. P. had called me 20 minutes ago telling me that he paged Nuts, 911. Twice, after one normal page! He got no answer, though. I had just talked to him about an hour ago, so…maybe it was those scandalous bitches that he had over. I had just put one scandalous bitch to sleep! I hoped that it wouldn't be anymore tonight.

Anyhow, we all had keys to each other's house. Me, Nuts, and P., that is. So I sat the food down and went around to the side door. It seemed the most appropriate approach being that the dogs were out back and that the front door would be too obvious. I unlocked the door and crept inside, drawing my Glock 40 with its extended 30 round clip. When I came up the steps and around the corner past the kitchen I could see the two chicks on the couch, bound and gagged. They quickly gestured towards the other room, where I heard movement of some sort. The question that came into my head next was answered when I stepped forward, just enough to see Nuts bound and duck taped as well.

Damn, who the fuck had my nigga like this, I wondered. He was sweating profusely with tears in his eyes. But I could see that he was reborn with new life once he saw me. I heard the assailant coming so I stepped back behind the basement doorway. As soon as the dude entered the kitchen, to check the back windows and door I peeped, I came out and backhand slapped him with my pistol. I grabbed him as he fell, and then butted him again. I grabbed his Smith & Wesson up off of the floor and tucked it in my waist. I kept in mind that there had to be someone else there, maybe more. So I crept back into the den where Nuts was at and grabbed a pillow. They all looked at me with wide eyes as I walked back into the kitchen with it. I put it over the guy's face, and then grabbed the 9 from my waist and pulled the trigger. Pop! The shell flew across the floor. I got a knife out of the drawer and headed back to the den, but before I could untie Nuts I heard, "Ay yo, B. What's up?"

B's partner, I guessed, seemed alert to some chaos, pointing his gun at everyone in the room as he walked to the kitchen. Just as he came around the corner I stuck him 3 quick times in the side and in the gut. His arm went limp and his gun hit the floor. I got over top of him, pointing the pistol to his head.

"Who else is with you? How many?!" I asked.

"Fuck you! You bitch ass, pretty boy," he replied.

I backhand slapped blood from his mouth, and then I got up to go untie Nuts and the 2 chicks. Nuts jumped up to hug me before I could get to the girls.

"Siz-o! You saved my mu' phuckin' life, lil' bruh! These niggas was about to murder all three of us. Man, I owe you my life, bruh," Nuts said.

"Yo, it's cool, big bruh. It's cool. Now untie them and come on in here. Was these the only two?" I asked Nuts alarmingly.

"Yeah, it's just them two. You ain't see nobody outside?" He asked.

"Nah, they must've parked a little ways away. Ay…dude in the kitchen is all yours. How you wanna do him?" I asked Nuts, seeing the hesitant look in his eyes. "I know you ain't never kill nobody overseas in the Gulf, or here on our soil, but you about to send this muthaphucka on a mission. You feel me?!" I told Nuts.

He knew what he had to do. So we tried interrogating the clown for a few minutes, but he couldn't speak. He was choking on his own blood. I could tell that the nigga wanted to say something. Nuts looked at me and back at him. He stood over the dying man and rolled him over onto his stomach. Then he squatted down and lifted up the guy's head, pulling it back and breaking his neck. I thought, 'Damn!' That military training came right out of him.

We now had limited time to act, so I had Nuts to pull my car around to the garage to put the bodies in. We would take them to the dumping sight. It felt weird when I thought about it because as well as I knew Nuts he had never been there with me. I called P. and told him everything was cool and that we were on our way to see him. A decision had to be made about the girls and Nuts needed a Cleaner over to his place immediately. "What a fucking night!" I thought.

CHAPTER 31: Mom's Epiphany

I had recently started to have a cup of coffee every now and again. Ever since I found out how good it tasted with all sorts of exclusive creamers in it. So I had a cup, with chocolate truffle creamer, while I watched the news. My stomach did a little twist and turn when I saw it. Anthony Johnson and his girlfriend Latasha Wilson were found murdered. Over 24 hours ago, the news anchor reported. It was a chaotic scene when someone tried to back the Benz out of the driveway for the forensic vehicle and the coroner van to pull up. Some poor bastard was blown to pieces, along with a number of other police and E.M.S. officials, when the car bomb exploded after it was started. And then they reported that Ant's two sons had their throats slit in their sleep. They were 8 and 5 years of age. It was a dirty game. I felt sort of bad, and went into deep thought for what seemed like forever; until my phone rang. It was ten after six. A.M!

"Hello," I answered.

"Sizalino. It's your mother. Were you asleep?" Mom asked.

"Uh...no ma, I'm up. What's up?" I asked curiously. I was rather disturbed when I heard what she had to say; which was, that my baby sister Samicia, was stranded down in Dayton where she had went to see some guy. I dug a little deeper to find that, not only was the guy a straight loser, but that he had recently got out of Ross Penitentiary with Big Tone P; where Micia was going with my moms to see him and Tone. And now, worst of all, the loser had her pregnant. Also, mom told me that her car wasn't really broke down, but that this 'Chris' had taken it and left her and her son stranded at a hotel by the highway.

"Mom, is this the same guy that y'all told me about who was into church and all that? But who's really a low-life cockroach, and an ex-con?!" I asked.

"No, he seemed like a nice guy at first. He treated ya sister real good and then…" I cut mom off. "Ma, perverted Catholic Priests seem like nice guys at first, too. Now you helped to get her in this shit, mama. She's barely of age and now about to have her second kid. Her first son's father's a piece of shit, and now you helped her to get another one. Just give me her number. I'll call her," I told mom.

"Now you listen here, I am still your mother," Mom said. I sat quietly for nearly 30 seconds, and then mom began to speak about how she was coming to Ohio soon because we all needed saved and a bunch of other bullshit. She finally gave me the number and then I quickly concluded the call. I thought deep about how I had just spoken to my mother and how far down the arrogant path my life had taken me. All I ever heard from my family was how I thought I was above every one and how I acted like I was Mafioso and god-like. Fuck all of them mother fuckers, I thought. But I still felt somewhat bad about how I had just talked to my mama.

I immediately called Micia and let her have it; not even caring about her sympathetic crying. I told her I would be about 2 hours, and to stay her ass put. I went and got Twin and one of our thug-matic uncles, Steve. Steve was out of prison for about 12% of his 11 year adult life. Not counting juvenile bids. By the time we arrived at Dayton's Best Western

Micia's gray Nissan Altima sat in front of her room. As we walked towards the door, Chris walked out.

"Hey, what's good family? Everything cool," Chris said. So he thought.

Steve hit him with a right cross and dropped him. Twin kicked him a few times and then they picked him up. Micia stood in the door way with her son, trying to covers his eyes. But he kept moving her hands, eagerly trying to see the action.

"Look here home boy; you seem like the kind of guy who wants to live. So dig this, we'll find you when it's necessary, to see ya seed when it's born; If that's what we decide. And don't worry, we'll find. Wherever! Even if you've gone back to the can we'll find you. Now go on. Get out of here. Micia, get your shit, get in the car, and let's go," I said.

As Chris walked slowly by us, Steve punched him again, right across the jaw. He fell against the wall and down to the ground. "What? He was takin' too damn long to bounce. You know I'm a fool, Siz-o. Y'all know how I do, Tone," Steve said, laughing as we walked down the steps to the car. I just shook my head non-chalantly because I didn't give a fuck about Chris. Being beat senselessly or even dying.

Our friend Snoop had helped with finding the location of Tank Man. But two hired hands that came down from Detroit had picked him up. Tank Man had no idea who kidnapped him. The options were endless, but he knew that he had never seen these two men before. He was shaken out of his dreary thoughts when he felt the vehicle stop. The two hit men pulled his bound, black sack-headed body from the van. He mumbled incoherently, as his head continued to throb. They drug him into the grind room, where he was tied to a chair and unmasked. They beat his face with gloved fists for 5 minutes or so, and then P. was called in from the scrap yard's office, where he was accompanied by Nuts. They entered the small room as P. signaled for the two men to halt their actions and step aside. Tank Man looked up at P. and tried to widen his eyes. It was barely any use.

"What's up, lame ass nigga? Did you get to enjoy them hundred and some stacks?" P. asked.

"M.P.! Nah, dog; what the fuck you mean?" He asked P.

Who walked over to the man on the left and whispered something to him. The man went over to the metal stand and retrieved an electric saw. Tank Man's eyes opened as wide as they could. He watched as the man sawed off his hand from his wrist. The blood jumped in all directions, as his hand flew over by the metal table. He screamed out in agonizing pain as the other hit man punched him square in the face. He grabbed the saw from the other man and sawed off Tank Man's other hand. Tank Man began going into convulsions. The hit men both grabbed a small saw and began to cut tiny incisions all over his body. But soon after they began, P. stopped them.

"Alright, chill. We gon' let Tank Man sit here and think about his violation against the Firm. You fuckin' piece of shit! You ain't even worth my spit. Oh, and ya cousin Scoobs is the one who told me you did it; gave me the whole story. I know. Family values done went straight to hell, ain't they? Let's go y'all," P. said.

They all stepped outside of the room. P. signaled Big Tom Woods over from by the Lincoln. "Ay, go get the bitches," he said.

"The bitches? Thee bitches?" Woods asked.

"Yeah nigga! Them black ass, starvin' ass, Doberman pincher bitches; the ones out back in the kennel who only get fed once a week. They gonna love this meal that we got for they ass. Now go!" P. said.

"Damn, that's cold. You getting' rid of everybody, ain't you?" Nuts asked.

"No, not everybody. Just all of my enemies! Here come Tom now, let's go," said P.

The bitches went crazy when they got near the door to smell the blood. As soon as the door was opened P. said, "Now, you had yo' meal ticket, so now these killers about to have theirs'. Let 'em in Woods." They darted into the room and began mauling Tank Man's bloody body.

P. told the two hit men to call the Cleaner as soon as it was over, and then head back to Detroit. He thought about the statement that Nuts had made, 'Did he have to get rid of everybody.' However though, he felt that there was still someone else out there. Someone close in his circle.

*

Red was rather shaken after two days had gone by and he didn't hear from Bland and B. He knew somewhat what must have happened because Nuts was still alive and well. He recalled the conversation that he had with me earlier.…."Yo, dog, mu'fuckas tried to come and take Nuts out da game. They was searchin' the crib when I came in but Nuts said it wasn't shit there to find. Them niggas is stinkin' now, though."

"Damn Siz-o, y'all killed 'em?" Red had asked me.

I just made a gesturing look saying, 'I'm not speaking on shit, in detail!'

That mutha fucka's so secretive. They all are. Red thought to himself. So many things went through his head. He wanted the Firm to go down; one by one, or all at once. He didn't care. He also kept in mind that he had to keep his rat status on the down low. Detective Walton was a real dickhead who was so pushy that he didn't seem to care if he blew Red's cover. If ever he was discovered he could be killed and his reputation would be ruined. He really dug it all, though. At first he felt bad about his ratting. But then he saw it in a positive light. It had benefits, he thought. It could protect him and help him excel in life. In the game! And it could also help him get rid of the competition. The Firm! He had begun to try and mold and manipulate a few of the 'wanna-be' black, white guys who grew up under P. as his flunkies.

Red had got his weight up a little so I had mistakenly begun allowing him to deal directly with P. Particularly because he and P. had gotten real cool. Or rather he had spent quite some time on his knees; sucking P.'s toes and dick! Figuratively, that is. I had recently seen a side of Red that showed me he was the scum of the earth. And I could tell that he despised me now. Envy was an understatement.

Everyone had been talking for a while now about how Red wanted to be me, and how he mocked everything from my clothes to my cars. Of course, he hated hearing this. It was just a month or so ago when he had begun supplying my white boy Gonzo with a few ounces of powder cocaine every week; on the down low, no doubt, while I had been supplying him with pounds of weed.

Well, the problem was that Gonzo's baby's mama snorted coke. So, within the first few weeks the pack, and the money, had been coming up short. When I found out about Gonzo accepting the coke I was rather upset. Gonzo moved a little powder from time to time, but never consistently. And more importantly, he bought from me. So the moment I discovered this I had Gonzo give me what he had from my weed and call Red and tell him that he would pay him off in a week. I guess Red didn't like it so he called me talking rather crazy. I was at a Target store about to shop for some wife beaters and ankle socks when I said, "just stay right there, doggy. I'm on my way down." Then I hung up.

My partner Big Young'n and I shot down to the projects immediately. Big Young'n was my big 19 year old, 6 foot 4 inch, 270 pound enforcer who was always looking for some work; one way or another. I had been locked up in Juvie Hall with him a few years back, and had recently seen him at the Gusmacker hoopin'. I put him down with my team immediately. My hoop team and my Cream Team!

Anyhow, when we arrived Big Young'n asked if he could check, or perhaps pistol whip Red. But I told him to just chill, 'cause I would handle this nigga. I pulled the Glock out and asked him, "now what was you sayin' a while ago? Huh? What was you sayin'? I couldn't really understand you, family?"

He immediately copped deuces and twisted the shit all around, though. The nigga was a loud mouthed coward. It took everything in me to refrain from beating his fat ass that day. Red thought back about that day, and about how Twin had bitched him out numerous times, and of course about how his younger, beast of a brother Dust had smashed him in front of everyone who stood to watch that day in the 'hood. As he sat on the couch of his hood rat bitch's house his anger raged on and his thoughts wondered.....

*

It was a lot of eased tension in today's meeting. Money Mike from E.S.F. had Ant replaced with his longtime friend and associate, Charles 'Chuck' Long; with the approval of the Commission. We had finally got Fat Cat and 'Hollywood' Rick Parker's seats filled by Wayne 'Nappy Red' Redmond and Johnny 'the Boxer' Freeman. With Cooks now the head of their family. P. had recently acquired my Cousin Mike's accountant. He hired him under D.N.W. Motors, our car lot establishment. He assisted in a number of our illegal, white collar activities. Both of the other families paid for these services, as they did for a number of our services. We were all moving into the 'point of no return' lane, right along with P.; which concerned me because I never wanted to feel owned or obligated by anyone. But I was no dummy. I knew what this life was ultimately about and what it entailed. I knew the price that it came with.

I came out of my zone when everyone stood to shake hands, as the meeting concluded. It had all went well. Especially with us finding out that Ant never got to speak to the Feds. Sadly though, it wouldn't be the last that we'd hear about Agent Nichols.

I left the meeting feeling eerie, with my spidey senses tingling. But it was all a part of the game. Just as I got into my champagne Lincoln LS, P. called out, "Siz-o!" He jumped in to ride with me as Nuts' Caddy drove past us and blew the horn. We rode back out west as P. told me about his meeting earlier with T.B. and my uncle Red. After I asked what for, a feeling of shock came over me when P. told me that they were being initiated and upped to positions just under us. And this meant knowing about the Commission. I wondered what had come over my man with this decision. The boss! T.B. had been P.'s Ace since a youth, but Red clearly had to have charmed, or rather manipulated P. to make this move. I didn't like it, though. And I knew that it was a good reason that I didn't. P. and I would have to talk. And soon!

CHAPTER 32: Same Old Shit (Is This It?)

The summer had ended as smooth as butter. Twin and I, along with my cousin Mike and a handful of his D-town affiliates, had slid down to our vacation house in Miami for our birthdays. It was without question a blast. Manny sent us up a special gift from Cuba; 2 twin beauties, Eva and Ava! They were swappers, too. Well, swingers! Whose birthdays were in a few weeks. Virgos! They were one year our youth, turning 21. But by Monday afternoon we were back in Ohio, ready for business, which headed into the fall prosperously; but violently as well. It came with being on top of the game. Everybody wants a piece. Everybody wants to test you. That's just the way that it was.

By the time the holidays rolled into winter, I began to think about a lot of things. Like how everyone else was buying houses and properties, small businesses and investing. Over 30% of what I earned went into businesses that I didn't over see each and every month. Plus, I had blown a lot of money, which I always thought came with the game. Cars, clothes, and jewelry were a given. But then there were the 2-3 mortgages a month, living expenses, and 'the club'. V.I.P. was a must, everywhere I went. As were out of town trips. I naturally splurged on pleasure trips, as well as business trips. And also, I liked taking care of everybody. My family, of course, plus I had had two more kids in the same month back in June. There was Anijah Love Jones by Goldie, and Samone Moneyke Jones with Heady; both of whom I shared houses with part-time. Just like with Keysh, who knew nothing about either child yet. Plus, I had my own place. That was always mandatory. But I thought about how I should have been a millionaire by now. Instead, I was a thousandaire.

I had begun to have serious talks with my mechanic, Felipe. He was a cool Puerto-Rican guy who quit working for GM after 15 years to start his own business, which he wanted me to join. I was all the way with it, too. But I was dissecting the blueprint this time. I wanted to be all the way involved. Right after I beat my manslaughter case back in October we began to talk seriously about a life after 'The Life'. My plan was simple; open this car shop with Felipe and push a power weed game. More legitimate business would come but I had to start somewhere. I would get back what money I had invested in our hip-hop clothing store, D & C's, and the money that I had invested monthly into the club. And then I would give up my seat and position at the table in the Commission. It would be a big step, but I was going to do it. I could retire the game before I was 23. And Twin, I had to get a way out for Twin. The knucklehead needed me to come through. And my uncle Dust did, too. But I would have to talk to P. soon. I would let him know after the New Year.

*

The holidays came and went, and I was so glad. Things were as prosperous as they could be for both of my families, our family and my own family. With the exception of Twin getting busted and put on house arrest for a pistol, which was really nothing, because it could've been a lot worse. I had cut short a lot of my associates and affiliates. It was time to slowly step away. Aside from flying out to New York to watch the ball drop, kick it with the stars and bang the TOTALLY bad bitches, I had been rather distant from my crew. And yes, I said Total, the singing group. P. had dabbled a little in the Hip-Hop Industry with Flip Mode and Def Squad. Quiet as kept, P. could flow. And, Nuts' cousin Quan from Jersey knew Redman and Keith Murray.

Anyhow, I had Heady pushing green for me full-throttle. She would be the one handling that for me. She was a doll, and she knew everyone. She was perfect for the job. And I had my blackanese brick house Goldie networking and handing out flyers for the Ludacris after party that I was helping my cousin Mike throw. However, Goldie had put on a good 15 pounds after having Anijah, making her a thick 140lbs! And she used it persuasively in many ways. Niggas would kill to lick and taste her pussy. She made me feel proud that she was my baby mama. She was a bad bitch!

Goldie had been working on the guy who owned the building of the old 'Imaginations', now called the 'Chrome'. I was scheming to get it. And I had a silent partner who was banked up. My thoughts and visions were in overdrive as I sat on the couch at my home in Holly Hill. My vibrating phone brought me back to the present. I answered, "Yeah."

"Hey, babe, I need some ice cream," Heady said.

"Ay yo, you a freak, you know that?" I asked rhetorically.

"No silly, some white girl. I need a whole one."

"Oh yeah? For who?" I asked.

She told me that it was for her faggot, hairdresser friend, Jasper. But he never bought coke before, I thought to my self. I said 'fuck it', though. She could do it. She could sell to her long time friend of over a decade. Because I sure as hell wasn't selling him shit.

"Alright, I'll be through there in about an hour," I said.

"Okay, I'ma call him back now. I'll see you soon," said Heady.

"Yep," I shot back.

*

"No, I can't do it. He'll kill me if he finds out. I ain't fuckin' wit them West Side fools," Jasper said to Detective Walton.

"Yes, you are going to do this. We busted you and your boyfriend with 6 grams of coke and your other boyfriend Red's already told us that you buy marijuana from this, 'Siz-o's' girlfriend. So you're going to do it. We had a deal," said Detective Walton.

"But what if this muthaphucka find out? Y'all can't protect me. Nobody can then!" Jasper emphasized.

"We can protect you; don't worry. Now take our C.I. here along with you as your new boyfriend. Alright? He has to witness the sale. Got it?" Detective Walton asked Jasper. Jasper complied with a doubtful look on his face. He knew that this decision would change his life forever.

*

I walked into the house shortly before 9. It was a freezing cold, dark December night. I wanted to drop this ounce off to Heady, see my daughter for a brief moment, and then get on my way back to the house. I had my new piece Shenaya coming over for dinner and a movie, Chinese cuisine by the fireplace on my Mink Lion rug, and then a Blockbuster DVD of our choice. Followed by hot, sweaty sex! She was a junior at O.S.U. and a High School cheerleading coach...who worshipped the ground I walked on. She was my kind of girl.

I called Heady upstairs to get the ounce of powder and then I told her that I would get the money from her the next day. I told her to keep $100 for herself. As she walked back down the stairs and into the basement to serve her people, I walked over to my daughter's crib. She stared up at me and then reached for me. I grabbed her and lifted her up onto my chest. She was my Angel. Within a few minutes she was sound asleep. I placed her back inside her crib and headed downstairs to tell Heady goodbye and that I was leaving. I stood by the steps and yelled down to her, "Heady, I'm out. I'll holla at you tomorrow, baby."

"Okay, baby. Bye; love you!" She said. And then I slid out and jumped into my truck, heading back to Holly Hill to do my thing. Miss Shenaya!

*

"Siz-o! Wusup, dog? I hear you been networkin' to do ya own thing," P. said.

"Huh?" I asked. "What you mean?"

"Come on, let's rap back here. You know I hear everything, Siz-o!!!" He said emphatically with a smile on his face. We walked back to the store's office at D & C's, where we had a brief discussion about some of my future plans and such. I got somewhat upset at the shaky response I got about collecting the money that I had invested in the clothing store and in the bar of ours. I felt that P. was giving me the spin-off game, and I didn't like it. We eventually got to the initiation that was coming up after the New Year for Terique and Red. I told P. respectfully that I had no objection to Terique, but that I would object to Red. And I gave him my opinion on why I objected. Red had charmed the pants off of P., though. He was pushing to be his all out yes man. That was his ambition, his goal...to be P.'s, the top dog's tough guy, yes man. I left the store standing solid with my opinionated decision, and feeling rather unsatisfied with our talk. I felt that P. didn't respect or take my future business decisions seriously. He always tried to keep me 'in deep' with him, talking me out of pulling out numerous times before. But this time was different. He was sort of smug about it all, arrogant and defiant. For the first time ever, I felt a discomfort with my Ace, P. Now a for real live Boss of a major criminal organization and drug pipeline that ran all the way down to the coast of South Florida and into South America. The deck was stacked against me and I knew it. If P. was opposing to my decisions in altering my future, then it would be very difficult to make them happen. I needed out.

CHAPTER 33: Columbus Clipper (SCANDALOUS)

We decided to stay in the city for this New Year; a rarity for
us. But we decided to make this New Year of 2001 a special
one, and bring it in in our city, the 'Bus! We rented out the River Club
downtown by the Ohio River near the Arena District. It was one of the
nicest clubs in Columbus, used only for special events. Nuts was working
on buying it.

Anyhow, we invited a few stars and celebrities; we had Kid Capri come
D.J. and Drew Sidney as our host. She starred in the movie 'Uninvited
Guests' that my cousin Mike had a small part in that was filmed right
out in front of D & C's. We headed over to the Residence Inn for an after
party where we all had rooms at. It was parties going on in all 4 suites
but in my suite it was me, my man Ronnie P., a former O.S.U. football
player, and my notorious uncle, Red! We had some uptown Cleveland
strippers who I snatched from my girl Cheron, who was more less their
madam. The chocolate, Cherokee Indian Malika was with Ronnie, the
tall redbone Cream was with Red, and the thick, caramel snazzy one
of the bunch, Salt, was rolling with me. We got it in, drinking heavier

than we did at the club. Straight liquor, though. We smashed bottles of Crown, Remy, and Belvidere. As we unwound and headed in different directions to get our freak on, Salt was acting very stank. Causing me to cuss her out and threaten to whoop her. Everyone agreed that she had an attitude; all night! I even threatened to put her out. She was still talking strong. She had no idea who I was or what I was about. But I thought of a different approach to the solution instead of my normal gorilla tactics. She needed some dick in her life. And she was going to get it. We had an extreme fuck session. I banged her pussy out! We decided to go for round 2.

"I gotta pee, first," Salt whispered to me. I shook my head okay as I stroked my semi-hard dick. She came back a brief moment later where I attempted to inject her sandpaper dry pussy.

"Damn baby, is it the x-pills that got you all dried out?" I asked her.

"No! You got to turn me on. You ain't doin' it. You did it earlier. C'mon now," she said.

This bitch was trippin! I tried to enter her a few more times. It was no use. She began talking shit, like it was my fault. I wanted to sock her in her shit, but no. I had never hit a female in the face with a closed fist, so I wasn't going to let her be the one to take me there. I did her one even better. She got up to go to the bathroom as I portrayed to walk into the suite's living room. Once she got inside I walked back towards her purse. I reached inside where she had her Crown Royal bag full of her stripping pay and her tips. I thought of the lyrics from my nigga Pac's song SCANDALOUS, 'Before I let her get me I got her, went in her purse and took $100, cause I'm so scandalous!' Fuck taking a hundred, though, I took it all except for a few ones. And then I slid into the front room where Red and Cream were. All of the commotion had startled everyone back awake and moving around. That was a factor in my favor. About ten minutes or so Salt walked out of the back room in a rage.

"Which one of you bitches went in my shit? All of my fucking money is gone, $220!" Salt yelled.

Both of her girls swore that that didn't take it. I laughed inside as I watched them plead with Salt about how they wouldn't do her like that and so on and so forth. I could tell that Salt was the dominant, alpha bitch of their trio. And they somewhat feared her. I just shook my head as said, "Damn, that's fucked up. We got the Columbus Clippers in the house. Somebody's holdin' out."

Red looked at me with a grin and whispered, "Boy, you a muthaphucka!"

He knew I got her. The shiesty recognized shiesty. But I played the role. And after 20 minutes of Salt's boo-hooing and accusations against her girls, I said "I'm out!"

She begged me not to go, and then eventually asked for $50 for a hotel room. I told her I had to go, and then I bounced. I left her with the sight of her teary eyes in my head. Fuck that bitch, though. She was a nothing ass stripper bitch, with an ugly attitude that would forever get in her way in life. I had no remorse. I got the bitch for the hell of it because she wasn't shit. So she deserved to be got. I felt bad for a minute, but I quickly shook it off as I headed over to Heady's crib to get sucked off and then pass out.

*

I stared into his cold, dead eyes as he smiled at me with the most psychotic smile I had ever seen. My movement froze when I saw the huge hole in the barrel of the pistol that he had pointed at me. He began to laugh that same crazy laugh as I had recalled every other time...and when I jumped for the gun he pulled the trigger. 'Pow!' The bullet hit me in the neck, burning like fire. But before any real pain could set in, I felt myself being shaken awake.

"Babe, wake up! It's ya Cousin Mike. He's on the house phone." I drearily heard Heady say.

I grabbed the phone, "Yo!"

"Siz-o, ay, this stripper broad Layla said she think she left her bag in ya car; from where they rode wit you last night. Can you check ya ride and see if it's in there? They ready to leave my room now," my Cousin Mike said.

I looked at the clock. It was almost 1 o'clock in the afternoon! I told him I would check and then call him back. I got up and grabbed my phone from out of my pants pocket. I had 5 missed calls! It was time to get up and get on the move. When I got out to my car there was a Louis bag on my backseat floor. I shot it up to the hotel to my cousin and then headed to my house to get dressed. I was low on coke so I called P. to grab a few keys. He didn't answer both times that I called so I figured he was tied up and would hit me back soon. But a few hours went by, after I had got showered and dressed, and he still hadn't returned my call. So I rang him a few more times. And still, I got nothing. A half an hour later he called me back. We spoke small talk for a minute, about the night that we had both just had, and then he eventually told me that there was no coke. He said that 'we were waiting'. I thought, "what the fuck?!" There was some shit behind this. I had recalled the time just a year or so ago when he was salty at Terique for banging his bitch, the now deceased, TA and wouldn't sell him any coke. Some silly, goofy shit! It only lasted for maybe a month, (Terique had bought 2 keys from me) but still it was rather childish. I think this nigga was playing me the same way; probably because of my future altering plans. I played like I understood and then hung up. Like a champion chess player he had made the first move.

I got with my younger homey Darren and had him get in contact with his Mexicans to get 2 keys from them. He was in aw about it because I was Siz-o, one of West Side's Finest; one of the originals! But I threw him a curveball story and kept it moving. Things were going to shake up a lot over the next few months, I could tell. This would be a life changing year, and every move counted.

*

It was early February, and mom was up from VA. She called me and Twin over to Micia's apartment for what she called a talk. I thought, "Oh Lord!" Twin felt the same way, no doubt. Micia was still pregnant and miserable. She was due later in the month. With two dead beat dads for her sons, she was a in a major depression. When I arrived I greeted my moms with a hello, a hug, and a gold necklace with the diamond pendant. And then I told her that I had a dinner date soon. Just as Twin noted that he needed to get back around to the spot.

"You see? That's what I want to talk to y'all about. The Lord don't want y'all doing the type of things that y'all been doing; living the way that y'all have. I've been feeling something lately in my spirit about all three of y'all. So I had to come up here and try to get y'all to stop doing what you doing. Y'all need to change ya lives and think about ya futures. Ya kids need you, the women in ya life need you, and I don't want to see y'all dead and in jail," Mom said.

"What about Micia?" I asked. "What you feel about her?" Because I know that she wasn't referring to her ending up in jail or dead.

"I've talked to her, before y'all got here. We've talked. She's gon' straighten up, too," Mom vowed.

We went on listening to mom's testimony and preaching for nearly an hour before we broke it up with our awaiting obligations. We kept interjecting to change the subject and tried lightening the mood discussing positive things.

"Y'all think this is a joke, but I'm serious. The Lord's done spoke to me, and I've seen what awaits y'alls future if you don't change," Mom plead, with tears rolling down her face.

I had to get up out of there. Moms was creeping me out. I drove around to Goldie's in deep thought. Everything would be alright, though. I would go to dinner on Sunday with everyone else, and assure mom that everything would be okay and for her not to worry before she left to go back home. But I gave myself something else to feel bad about. I had to hear my pop's mouth Monday afternoon about how I missed the dinner at Olive Garden Sunday that everyone attended with mom. Twin, Stephanie, and their kids, Micia and her son, and my pops and his fourth wife, Nett were all there. And about how Twin paid for the dinner and bought mom a gift, an expensive art picture. I was out of town, up in Detroit with my cousin Mike at a clothing show. I assured her that I would make it up to her. Just as I had done with my pops after I listened to his yapping.

*

I noticed how, over the next few weeks, everyone started to act different. My treatment from everyone wasn't the same; from our public connections to our street associates and affiliates. I was fuming mad. I wanted to show someone what time it was. But it would be too many people to show. It reminded me of Nuts' words to me when I was on a younger, rampage… "You can't take on the whole world, Siz-o." So I chilled, and just evaluated everything. I knew the direction that I was headed in was not to the liking of a lot of the people who I knew. And that was a clear fact. I also knew that my life outside of the firm would never be the same. It would be better in one aspect, and worse in another. That's life, and you got to take the bitter with the sweet.

However, I had enhanced my connection with Fred's people. I was getting 20 pounds of green on every go around. And at $700 a pound there was plenty of room to make money. I didn't want to be too big, or do too much. Eventually, I could be getting more, but I wouldn't concentrate on that until I was done with the coke. Which I decided would be by June. It was a 6 month time frame that I gave myself since I made my decision back around New Year's. And June would also be the month that Felipe and I would open up our shop, 'Buckeye Auto Service'. I still had to work on getting back my invested money with the bar and the store, but if need be, I could wait until the year's end. Either way, my goals and dream were set.

I was chilling at one of my spots with my young killer, Johnson. He was hot and on the run, both from the laws and from P.'s spot runner, Otis. Johnson had just shot 'O' in a Hilltop neighborhood where they were both battling for block money. It's so ironic how the streets stir shit up, because Johnson was pushing my work, and Otis was pushing P.'s. So it instantly came about that I had Johnson shoot 'O'; which was far from the truth. But that's how it got dealt out. I had familiar affiliates of mine, and of P.'s, calling and asking me where Johnson was. It was chaotic. While we were sitting there my uncle Red called. He had two complaints: one was that his old bitch Tasha had kicked him out and he needed a place to stay, ASAP. The other complaint was that he needed some work; a nine pack, or at least 4 ½ because P. was salty at him for getting his little sister pregnant and wouldn't sell to him. It was true lies, but I didn't know it at the time. So I told him to call me when he got in town from West 'V' and I would hook him up. And then I told him that I would call Nuts and get him a crib through Nuts' Real Estate people by next week. Why I was helping this clown, I didn't know. Especially now that he was P.'s right hand yes man. It was after midnight and I told Johnson that I was headed to my house out in Reynoldsburg to see Keysh and my kids, and he could not come with me there. So he asked if I would drop him off at his son's mom's place; which I didn't understand because that was his legal address. But it's where he wanted to go. So I dropped him off and headed home.

*

I woke around 10 o'clock with Heady blowing my phone up. I got up and got dressed, and then I called her back while Keysh was downstairs making some breakfast. "Wusup?" I asked.

"Not a thing. What's goin' on wit you, mister? You just gettin' up?" Heady asked.

"No doubt. What's good, though? I see you done blew me up."

"Yeah, ya daughter been callin' ya name all mornin' and these dogs of yours need some food. Oh, and Jasper called. He needs half of what he had last time."

"Alright, give me an hour or so and I'll be there," I told her.

I thought then how Red never called me yesterday. He must ain't need that work that bad. I fed my two pits that I had there at the house, D-Bo and Saddam; and then I ate myself. My son loved dogs, though. At just a few years old he was more infatuated with dogs that he was with toys. He was my little man, and my twin most people would say.

I got over Heady's by noon, where she told me Johnson had called collect. So he must have got arrested and was in county. Damn, they got him! Felonious Assault or Attempted Murder, I'd imagine. I fed my two pits over there as soon as I arrived. They were all excited; to see me and to see their food there. The two that I had over at Heady's was a white one named Cain and a brown one named Tito. I went inside to wash my hands and attend to my daughter. Heady told me that the Jasper character didn't want that until later on. I had to go to one of my spots anyway, so it was cool. I called and talked to my cousin Mike about going to our sports bar later to watch the game. My Lakers were gonna be in a crucial showdown later with their Western Conference rivals, the Sacramento Kings. So I left Heady's to go do some running around before the game came on later and I told her to give me a call when her people, Jasper, was ready for that half. She said okay and, "I love you, Siz-o!"

*

Red had called me 4-5 times in the last few hours saying that he wanted 4 ½ ounces of hard coke. But he never got close enough to call and say that he was ready. He was bullshitting for some reason. And he was pissing me off. I headed back to Heady's after I watched the game to change my clothes and go meet my longtime homey/uncle at our after hour spot. He ran it for us most of the time. I was going over there to collect some money, check things out, and have a quick celebratory birthday drink with him. He was cool people. He had a daughter by my aunt, who he had split up with a while back, but he was still like an uncle to me. I had known the guy ever since I was 12 or 13. Heady had her homo friend waiting on that half ounce, too. She told me that he was there chillin; with his boyfriend.

Just before I pulled up Red called. He asked where I was at because he needed 2 ounces, instead of the 4 ½ he requested earlier. And he said that he was with his people from down in West 'V', so I told him to park around by the flower shop and walk to the house alone.

When I got inside I gave Heady the work in the kitchen to take down to Jasper and I walked upstairs to get changed. I threw on a white and orange Platinum Fubu t-shirt and some black, with orange trim, Platinum Fubu shorts; with the orange leather Timbs, of course. I went down into the basement to see my little girl who was surprisingly still awake. As I walked over to see my 2 ½ foot alligator in his octagon cage the white fag with Jasper said, "Hey, how ya doin'? Here you go." He handed me the $500. A strange feeling came over me. I looked this guy up and down and straight in the eye.

"Wus ya name, bruh?" I asked.

"Oh, Siz, this is Tom. My guy friend," Jasper said with a slight grin.

I despised faggots. But I didn't have to deal with or know them. So, fuck it. I was gonna tell Heady not to have them over again. I had a bad feeling about these two. My phone buzzed on my hip. It was Red. I answered as I walked back up the steps.

"Wusup. Where you at?" I asked.

"I'm walkin' up to the porch," Red said.

"Nah, come to the side door," I told him.

I let him in and he handed me the money. He asked if I had the tan colored work or the pure white. I told him that I had both. So he stressed that his people wanted the white. 'This fucking guy', I thought. Now I had to go out to the garage to get in the quarter key that I had stashed under the rims out there. I gave him a look that showed I was frustrated.

"Hold on, dog," I said as I walked out to the garage. I retrieved it and brought the bag back in the house, where I carried it upstairs to weigh out 2 ounces. I brought it back down to him and opened the door to let him out.

"I'll holla at you tomorrow, fam'," I said.

"'Aight, I'm gone," He shot back.

I closed the door and walked into the living room for a minute to sit for a few seconds before I left out. Something drew me towards the window. I looked out to see Red right in front of my fucking house leaned into the window of his 'peoples' car. I told this dumb bastard to park them around the corner. This nigga was crazy! And…it looked like the white Oldsmobile of the old couple who got busted late last year. Yep.

It was a light colored older man and a homely looking white woman. The hot couple from West 'V'! P. had told this clown about them a few months back after they got busted selling guns and they had got caught with some work. I was furious. But I wouldn't go out there right now, or call this dummy tonight. No, I wouldn't say anything to him at all. But I would talk to P. tomorrow.

*

My 20 year old college girl Shenaya had recently got an apartment near the campus, where I had been spending a lot of time at meditating and laying low. No one I knew had known about this place, which is why I came here so often in the last few weeks. My trust with even my closest affiliates was shortening. The walls were shrinking. Everyone was becoming so distant, even all of my chicks; they were like some of my best friends. It's like they all felt the 'Life' slipping away from me. Or rather, they all felt me sliding away from it. And ultimately, I felt more distant with Keysh than I ever had.

There was a meeting coming up in 2 weeks where Red and Terique were to get initiated. My plan was for this one to be my last. I was willing to talk with P. and the rest of the Firm to do what had to be done and get someone else in my seat. I figured it would either be Tom Woods or Big Tone. My Cousin Mike's birthday party was March 14th, the weekend before Monday's meeting. The rapper nigga Ludacris was coming to the city for that. I had to help promote it. Well, have Goldie do some networking for me rather.

It was the second day after Red was spotted in front of my place with Heady with the suspected informing couple that I slid out to our car lot to have the old man Bob get P. a message that I needed to meet with him by the afternoon or no later than the evening. The old man and I had a brief discussion, about car dealings and life in general, and a cup of coffee before I left the lot at about 10a.m. I shot out to Heady's to grab an ounce

265

of weed for Felipe, who I was about to go meet to go over some paperwork about the shop we were opening next month. An hour or so later, when I arrived at Felipe's place out by Eastland Mall, P. called me. He told me to meet him out at his baby's mom Jereame's house in Pickerington. I told him I would be about an hour, if that.

"Wusup dog?" I dapped P. up as I came into the house and shut the door behind me. He walked back in the kitchen where he stood idle up against a cabinet. "So, how's this meeting gon' go in a couple weeks? I know everybody got a lot of opinions about me steppin' down. Too early to retire at 22, huh?!" I said to P. rhetorically with a smile. This was my nigga, and I could see that he was really hurt about my decision. He stood still; quiet, and withdrawn. And then he finally spoke, "Yeah, everybody hear you steppin' away from the Commission. The Firm! I think its like, 'Is he allowed doing that? Just quit?' And like, 'Damn, Siz-o of all people?' You know you helped us start this shit; just a few years ago. So yeah, everybody's trippin' about it. But you know, ultimately they all gon' go with the way I feel," P. said.

"Yeah, I know. So wusup, bruh? You still ain't respectin' or feelin' my decision here?" I asked him. He was silent for at least a minute.

"I mean, nah, I can't say that I am. Siz-o, you know you been like my silent right hand. For at least five years now. I done known you since you been 14! We're in deep together; on a number of different levels. You gotta consider how this affects all of us. You gotta consider Manny!" P. emphasized. I didn't quite understand the consideration of Manny, but...I commented with this, "Well then perhaps we can do this, maybe we can script it as I'm semi-retired; sort of in still, but from the outside."

"Yeah, but that would have to be under some extreme circumstances..... health wise, family crisis, or some legal woes or somethin' like that. But you're just decidin' to pull out 'cause of what, some conscious belief or some paranoia or somethin'? Siz-o, we the Firm, nigga! We help make the laws around this bitch and control how shit go. It's cold and lonely on the other side. Why you wanna be on that side? You my muphuckin' nigga!"

"Oh, so I can't be ya nigga on the other side, as you put it? You can't feel me tryin' to separate myself from all the bullshit!? Dog, I done seen niggas faces in my sleep; dead muthaphuckas who haunt my dreams and shit!" I emphasized to P. as he saw me getting really worked up. "I know what the game entails and who I am. I'll never be able to escape who I am, and I understand that. You taught me as a youngster to stay in reality and know who you are and what you're doing. But you also taught me to have ya own hustle and make ya own way. So why would you oppose me doin' this? You like my family, bruh. You are my bro'! You and Big Tone will always be my family. He's forever Step Pops! All I'm asking is that you let me slip away and just be a Firm affiliate. A friend! I'm not asking to be let go to go all the way square. No, never! But let me do my own thing. I understand a lot of what's linked to all this, and to me. So I'll still pay homage to the Commission. The Firm will get its cut. And you'll always be my Ace. So what do you say?" I asked P.

P. looked away from me, and then right back into my eyes. "I'll make it happen. We'll talk again before the meeting on the 17th, but I'ma make it shake for you, Siz-o," he said as he walked over to give me a hug.

"Good, dog. Good. Show ya nigga some love. It's us for life," I said as I embraced him. "Oh, there's one other thing. You know Fat Boy, my uncle…..." I explained the whole story to him. We ended up talking for nearly another hour before heading to Apple Bee's for a late lunch, where we were joined by his consultant, bookkeeping broad, T-Bone Steaks; as he called her. Tonya Parsons was her name, and she had nearly half of the ownership to all of P.'s assets. She was a powerful hidden gem, who would come into extreme power in the near future.

CHAPTER 34: My Life (Evaluation)

I felt things warming back up over the past week or two, with everyone from my Firm partners to all of my family members and affiliates. My uncle Dust had got out a few weeks ago from doing his usual, a year (for the gun). I immediately put him in a classical 88' Monte Carlo SS. It was royal blue with the wood wheel and wood grain interior, and it had the factory aluminum 17 inch rims; with the 350 rocket engine, no doubt. I had had it for nearly a year just sitting. I got it from a nigga who owed me for a couple of ounces of coke back then. And Twin, who was really starting to ball, had given Dust a few ounces to get on his feet. Twin had gotten closer to P. over the last few months, buying a kilo directly from him every other week. I kept my distance from uncle Red and advised Twin and Dust to do the same. Although I didn't tell them what I had seen and suspected. It was hard enough for me to even believe that it could be true and I didn't know for sure. But I learned long ago to go with my first instinct.

The party had been arranged beautifully. Goldie had done a great job for me and my big cuz'. He informed me that he would like to use her services further in the future. I had no problem with it. In fact, he had even hired her to bartend at our sports bar. However, we all stepped hard into V.I.P. that night at the ValleyDale ballroom. Every female affiliated with any of our Firms was dressed in Coogi or some other sort of name brand New York or European Designer. All of the fellas wore Coogi, Versace, or Louie. I was stunted out wearing an all brown Coogi sweater suit with chocolate brown Timbs, and my Cartier diamond studded shades, with the ring and watch. And I even pulled my 99' extended Suburban with the TVs and beats out to allow a 6 member entourage of females to ride with me. Keysh rode shotgun, of course. My cousin Mike had pimps, players, and gangsters from all over the country and mainly from Detroit, come to this extravagant event. It was one of the most live parties I had ever been a part of. In the end, as a surprise guest, we had the top player in the rap game, Too Short; fall through to perform a number of his hits. My cousin Mike was ecstatic. And he showed extreme appreciation throughout the rest of the night.

Red stayed along side P., as his certified yes man. His eyes stayed intent the whole time. We hadn't said much to each other lately, but I made it a point to speak cordially to him every so often, as P. and I had discussed. Twin even seemed to be having a great time, which seemed so weird because he never hung out much with my circle. But I think he was starting to enjoy it now that he was experiencing it first hand. We had really become a lot closer. He treated me more like the big, little brother that everyone perceived us as. Giving me, and my crew, love and recognition like never before. He was on top of his game, though. He now sold small weight and ran a spot from the distance. I watched him glow in a white waist length fur coat and hat, while he had Dust shining as well, in a gold Versace button up, black slacks and gators, and a black and gold dab hat. The night was epic.

Keysh and I left the party once it closed at 2:30 to head straight to the house to have un-adulterated sex. We sent all of her girls their own way with different girlfriends and niggas. We called the house to check in with the baby-sitter, her little cousin, and tell her that we were on our way home. After I shook hands and gave a gang of pounds and hugs, I congratulated my cousin Mike and headed out. When Keysh and I got home, we had some of the best sex of our 6 plus years. It was memorable.

*

I was awakened with a dreadful phone call. After my phone rang 5 or 6 times back to back, I answered it to the annoying sound of my uncle Red's voice. It was 11:30 a.m. and this guy was hollering incoherently.

"Yo dog, wusup? Hold on, hold on...what happened?" I asked him.

"Man, somebody broke in the crib out here on Nashoba. They got in my closet upstairs and took damn near ten stacks. They tore yo' room up...man, you need to get out here. How long you gon' be?" Red asked.

"Dog, I'm on my way," I said frustratingly and then hung up.

"Babe, what's wrong?" Keysh asked.

"Nothin'. I gotta go. I'll call you in a little while," I told Keysh, getting up out of the bed to get dressed.

"What that fat piece of shit got you in now? I can't stand that fat bastard!" Keysh went on mumbling obscenities with a horrid look on her face. I felt her anger, though. I couldn't stand the guy either myself. But I had to go check this out.

I arrived on Nashoba Avenue about half past noon. Red was pacing back and forth in the dining room until he saw me walk in. "Siz-o, wusup? I think I already know who did it," he said. "I already called the cops, they on they way."

"What! Why the hell you do that? Do you realize who we are?" I asked him.

"Aw, shit, that ain't gon be shit nephew. They just gon' dust for prints and shit," he said non-chalantly.

This guy was something else. The house was in his sister's name, my aunt. Who lived in Whitehall and had done this for me as a favor. I wondered who this guy had had come over in just those short few weeks, because the only person who had been over for me was my college chick Shenaya. My uncle Red however, had had quite a few people over from my acknowledgement. So the options were endless. After I done a quick review, I realized that the only thing missing of mine was my 357 Magnum that was under the couch, a couple of my Coogi outfits, and a measly $500 that I had in my top drawer. My room was ransacked, but the bullet proof vest that I had under my mattress was on the floor with a bunch of clothes. What kind of dummy would have left that behind? It was easily worth $500 or better. I thought about the Glock 40 and the quarter kilo of coke that I had stashed under the refrigerator. I went to retrieve it…bingo! It was still there, the gun and the brown paper sack. Red didn't know about this stash spot or its contents.

The other missing items were about 20 of the DVDs that we had, a few of Red's leather jackets, a gold bracelet, and the supposed 8 gees that Red claimed were missing. The cops finally arrived and to my surprise it was Officer West, the deceased Bernard's partner, and some rookie that I'm sure West had put under his corrupted wing. When I saw Officer West it was like seeing a ghost, after all the time that had passed. He didn't seem to realize who I was right away. I made minimal eye contact, though. They asked a few basic questions like when did we think it happened, did we suspect anyone in particular, and whose name was the house in.

"Uh, it's in my aunt's name, sir. But she recently moved out last month and let me and my uncle here take it over. She found her a boyfriend. You know how that goes," I said to West.

"Uh yeah, I guess so. Well, we can send over a team to dust for prints; I don't know if they'll find anything, but…it's up to you guys. I'm gonna need your names guys, for my report here," said Officer West.

I looked at him and quickly said, "Jerele Jones."

"Jerele Jones, Jerele Jones! You look familiar, buddy. Do I know you?" West asked peculiarly.

"No, I don't think so sir. I'm an honest citizen," I said to West as I walked over to the couch to sit down.

"Hmm. Well then…and you're…Ronald Dawson, the guy who called it in?" West asked.

"Yes officer, that's me," Red said with a calm tone.

I denied a 'team' as West stated to come and dust for prints. And I told him that there was nothing major missing and that it was probably just some kids. I said that the following afternoon we would install a security system, so they could be on their way. It was a relief for me to get them out of there. I couldn't believe that they walked right over the bullet proof vest lying on the floor. And I also could not fucking believe that this nigga even called them! I gave him a look to let him know that as well, as he told me of his suspicions of P. having someone break in while we were at the party; which sounded ridiculous to me. Red stated that he and P. had a huge beef last night after an argument over egos and some shit along those lines.

"I told that nigga he thought he was all that but he wasn't shit to me. And I called his mama all kinds of bitches and told him that I'm fucking both of his twin sisters and got both of 'em pregnant. Yeah, I told him all that. Fuck him! I'm telling you Siz, that nigga had somebody break in here last night cause he knew I was goin' over to his sister's house for the night. And you know the nigga salty at you. You feel me!?" Red said emphatically.

I just listened to him, but he sounded absurd. I told him that I would go talk to P. immediately by nightfall. Red disregarded his initiation and everything that was supposed to take place on Monday morning. The guy was truly off of his chain link. I found it to be impossible that P. would have someone break into a venue of ours; of mine! For what? Certainly not over any egotistical argument that he may have had with Red? Everyone knew that Red was just a big loud mouth who couldn't fight. At least everyone in our circle did. There was an angle here that I couldn't see. And I needed to dissect it further.

*

It was ten 'til eight, and my thoughts were still in overdrive with all that I had taken in since yesterday. I got dressed in a black and grey Versace suit and threw on my black velour, Versace loafers while Keysh made me coffee. She didn't exactly know about the Firm or the Commission, but she sensed that I had severe involvement with the streets and the underworld of illegal activities. She wasn't stupid. She felt my uneasiness and my stress like it was her own. She handed me my coffee and asked, "you okay, babe? Is everything alright?"

"Yeah, I'm cool. Don't worry, everything gon' be alright. 2-3 months from now we gon' be in a position to expand on some legal business and earn some legal dollars. You know? For us and the kids; maybe move south or somewhere else by next year. What do you think?" I asked Keysh as I sipped my coffee one more time and kissed Keysh goodbye.

She tightened her lips to kiss me and shook her head yes. We walked downstairs together and hugged before I left out the door. I assured her I would see her in a few hours and that I loved her. Once I got inside of my Cadillac STS and started to drive I got back into my thoughts, which flashed back to my meet with P. last night. I told him the ridiculous story that Red told me and he just brushed it off, saying that Red was just blowing off envious steam and that he had called and apologized earlier that evening. I thought, 'what'? What was going on with these two? I know P. had a way of not panicking or letting shit get him rattled, but he was ignoring Red and his antics foolishly. I didn't understand P. anymore. The power had him blind, and delirious. He especially had me baffled when he said he checked Red out through his downtown sources and Red had no connection to any sort of cooperation and his dealing with the hot West Virginia couple was harmless and nothing to worry about. It was all just too weird.

Once I got inside the 'Roadhouse', as we notoriously came to calling it, short for the Cooke Road house, I felt more uncomfortable than I ever had. And I usually always felt somewhat uncomfortable, but now it was way more intense. It got started just about ten minutes after everyone arrived; enough time for everyone to get coffee and water, and pastries. I saw Red, who, after talking with P. last night, I realized that he would finally make it to the 'Roadhouse'. He would indeed still be initiated. I think that P. felt that if he pulled out on initiating Red, then he would look bad for almost choosing someone that he had hand picked to join our Firm, and the Commission. So the small penalty that Red had committed with his insolence was just that, a small penalty. And it could be overlooked.

Everyone took their seats and we got started. There was some discussion between P. and some of the E.S.F. members about their requests to acquire some of his available services with his downtown corporate connections; some of their smaller scale members had run into some rather deep trouble. It was a brief discussion about the possible acquisition of P.'s, of our South American assassins and some discussion about the upcoming cheaper coke prices that everyone loved to hear about. And then, what I knew was coming, came.

There was a particular spokesman for each firm: Kevin 'the Cooker' Cooks was the spokesperson for N.S.F.; the deceased Anthony Johnson had been replaced by 'Money Mike' Morrison; and I, after Nuts being our spokesperson for nearly the first year, had become spokesperson.

Cooks spoke out, "So we got this thing wit my man Siz-o. Now wusup wit dat?" Cooks asked, nodding towards P. who looked my way with raised eyebrows, signifying me to speak.

"Well gentlemen, for my own personal reasons I've chosen to step down. I know a lot of y'all are thinking why or perhaps what's going on, but it's nothing other than me just deciding to go in a slightly different direction. I still got love for each and everyone of y'all in this room. It's nothing personal against any of you or our outfit as a whole. Now P. and I have spoken quite a few times about this in the past month or so, and we've decided that I will remain an affiliate and an associate to this Commission. It just won't be as deep of an involvement as before, and of course I will forfeit my seat to whomever you all choose to put in it. With that being said, I..." I was cut off by Nuts.

"Siz-o, you know you steppin' down from a position of power too, right? Why would you wanna do that if you still gon' be a part of the Firm? Man, I don't agree with this Siz. You should think about this, bruh. Who gon' sit in his seat?" Nuts asked looking towards P.

"It's already been decided. The decision has been made that Red here will take Siz-o's seat as one of the three heads of our West Side Firm. He is Siz-o's blood uncle who has also been alongside of him for the past couple of years; putting in work and earning with our Firm and this Commission. Siz-o brought him to me a little over a year ago, y'all are all familiar with him now. He's hard headed and loud enough to be heard from here to New Orleans where he's from, but he's solid and a good earner," P. said as he laughed, causing everyone to laugh with him; everyone except me and Nuts.

And this clown wasn't from New Orleans, he was from West Virginia. I can't believe what I had just witnessed. Nuts was enraged. He never liked Red, who was pleased out of his mind. The look on his face showed it all. It was his first time stepping foot into the 'Roadhouse' and here he was being initiated as a head of our Family Firm. In my seat! I know some of his East Side affiliates from E.S.F. had lobbied to help get him on board, most likely Tommy 'Gloves'. They'd known each other since the mid, late 80s.

"So, Red will get sworn in in place of Siz-o as the third head of our Firm and Terique as a lieutenant. Y'all come on over here." P ordered. He had our Firm advisor Frank Tillman read the scripted document, "Ronald Dawson, Terique Bynes, do you swear to this Commission that you will..." his words went silent in my head as Nuts and I watched Red and Terique get sworn in to 'Our Thing'; what we created not even 5 years ago! I was happy for Terique. I always liked him. But I could feel in my heart and soul that my uncle Red was not right for this. I just knew it. And I'm sure Nuts felt the same way. Frank's words chimed back in, "... on your lives, so help you God!" It was finished. Red was in power.

*

"I'm glad you got in contact with your people over in Federal. I woulda been a fuckin' dead man. But now I got Siz-o on the fishhook to get pinched and I got my foot in the door of the fuckin' Commission! You gotta hook me up now, Bo. I want a fuckin' raise and some more compensation," Red demanded to Detective Walton.

"Damn Red, I can't even argue with you about that partner. You the man! But there might be a problem with the trafficking charge sticking on Jones ya nephew. He wasn't even present for the first sale and with the second sale he came into the room after the drug swap but our officer handed him the money, which he allegedly looked surprised by. Now we can try and indict and arrest the girlfriend and get her to turn on him, but that's not likely with the story I hear. So..." Bo hesitated.

"Yeah, but look at all that y'all got on him. You know he sold me two ounces and you got the 2 sales he was involved in. Plus, didn't you say that you got some other guys buying from him or something?" Red asked desperately.

"Yeah, we do. And one of 'em you know: A Kevin Soleman. The other guy we caught with 2 ounces of crack back in November who says that his whole family buys from Jones, two of his brothers and even his dad and dad's old lady. But, none of em will wear a wire. And by them not being C.I.s their word alone won't hold up in court. So it's shaky. You know this nephew of yours is pretty banked up and connected. He'll hire Myron Shwartz or Belli or one of those other high profile Jew lawyers and they'll eat what we got alive. At best he may get a few years. I don't think that's what you want and I know that's not all we want. Jones is a career criminal. He been doin' this since he was a young'n and you know it. The Feds would love to get a hold of him and convict him. So that's why I don't want to fuck this up. But you got a much bigger ship to sink; this fuckin' Pettway and his Commission," Bo stated with intent eyes.

"Yeah, I know. I can't get discovered though, Bo. You got to protect me. I need every resource available and I need the green light to do what the fuck I need to do out here in these streets. It's me against a whole lot of them," Red said emphatically.

"We gon' protect you brother. You see how I had them Federal boys cover up that paper work for you, didn't you? I got Agent Nichols to back us up and he's ready to get involved on this investigation as soon as you gather enough information about these firm fuckers and Pettway and the whole gang. So do what you got to do. We got your back, brother," Bo told Red. Somehow, Red knew better. But he was going to ride the wave for as long as he could. He could help take down the Firms and then get financed to go ball in another city. He had big dreams, but would they be fulfilled? The Commission was a huge task to tackle. And soon, he knew that he would be forced to wear a wire; and or a camera. He got out of the blue Ford van in the City Center Mall's parking garage and walked into the mall. He'd stop by Sabarro's to grab a slice of pizza…no, 2 slices, and then head to the front entrance where he had his old bitch Tasha waiting to pick him up on High Street.

*

It was two days after the meeting and everything seemed so ominous. Nothing felt right. I was pulling up to the place on Nashoba to get my things and take them over to Heady's. After the break-in there was no way that I could stay there ever again. As I parked I saw Red pull up like someone on a HollyWood movie, screeching his tires as he stopped. He hopped out hysterically.

"Yo, what the fuck is up? What happened?" I asked.

"I just saw the nigga 'O' leaving out of the house while ago as I pulled up so I followed him. The nigga started shootin' at me!" Red said.

"O, O…" I said as I continued to think to myself.

"O, man. You know the nigga who Young Johnson shot up a couple months ago. P.'s nigga!"

"Oh, for real? Get the fuck out of here."

We stood in the front room of the house talking for nearly an hour.

Red had another wild theory that P. sent 'O' over to our place specifically for him to get at me on the creep; to retaliate for Lil' Johnson shooting him and to rub me out for stepping down in the Commission. Red emphasized that P. felt that I was expendable now. And that I was turning my back on all of them. It was all so crazy. I couldn't see it, though. In less then a week, after being initiated just a few days ago, Red was accusing P. of some major accusations.

I called P. after I put a few items in the truck. As I waited for the phone to ring I saw the same blue Chevy Lumina sitting up the block that was sitting there last week after the first break-in. It was very strange. P. finally answered and then I calmly gave him the story that Red and I had agreed we would give him, which was that we saw his boy 'O' leaving the house as Red pulled up. He said that he would check with 'O' and get back with me. And also, that if it were true then 'O' would take a permanent nap. I closed my phone and just sat there. Red had already left, but I still saw the undercover cop car sitting up the street facing my direction. After about another minute or so, I pulled off.

*

"Listen to me son, I told you not to have anything to do with ya aunts or uncles on my side of the family. Ain't none of my brothers or sisters shit! They all talk about you, cause they can't be you, or you won't give em the time of day. Well, uncle Kirk was over on Oakwood earlier next door to where Keysha's people stay at, and said that Red was over there tryin' to be all up on Keysha and talkin' shit about you. Talkin' like he was all that now. The muthafucka's dirty! I can't stand that fat muthafucka. That's why I beat his fat funky ass all of them times that I did." Pop was going off.

"Hold on, so you said that he was talkin' shit about me and he was all over Keysh? Nah, that can't be right. He fucks wit her little cousin's friend. She's like, 18. Was it a young, light brown thick girl wit her?" I asked my pop.

"Son, it was a lot of people out there when I got there. He was gone already, and I didn't really pay attention to who else was standin' out there. I saw her, though. Keysha," said Pops.

"Well, I'm bout to go see; I know right where he at. I heard he been talkin' lil' shit here and there from different people, about me and Twin. I'll holla at you later pop. I'm bout to go find this joker right now," I told pop and then I left. I had just given Pops over 3 grand last month to put a down payment on a nice house off of Livingston Avenue. The basement was finished so I turned it into a cozy little second home. Well, more like a third or fourth home.

*

I pulled up to Red's slum of a hideout on 18th Avenue. He was sitting on the screened-in porch with some little young tramp smoking a Black & Mild cigar. As I walked up on the porch a big black fag walked out and said, "Red, baby where yo' toilet paper at?"

I looked at him and then I looked at the fag, then I looked back at him. I shook what my mind was thinking and said, "yo, I need to holla at you, fam.'"

"Huh? Oh, uh, go in the house real quick Amanda. It's, uh, it's in the hall closet Big Reece. Wusup, Siz? What you doin' out this way?" Red asked me nervously.

"Nigga, you was just over by Keysh's cousin house, over by where uncle Kirk was at? What's this shit I hear Kirk say you was talkin' bout me?" I asked him intently.

"Huh? Aw, man you know that damn drunk ass Kirk be on some bullshit; hatin'! I was just talkin' my typical shit, nothin' venomous. Nigga, you my muthaphuckin' nephew! And I wouldn't see shit happen to you, you know that," Red said.

I just looked at him with doubt and disbelief, and then I said, "so what's wit the shit bein' said that you was all up on Keysh?" I said as my eyes scowled and tightened.

"What? That's my fuckin' niece! I was over there fuckin' wit lil' Ciara. That's some bullshit Kirk's drunk ass done said. Wait until I see his old ass."

"Right; what else has been goin' on?" I said, quickly switching gears on him. His tension eased a little as he went on talking small talk. I rapped for a minute and then I slid up out of there. The big sissy tried to come out the door right before I left, but Red shooed him back inside. What the fuck was with this guy and this big punk, I wondered. Red was a weird older nigga who, as far as I was concerned, was better left in his own world.

I was focused on making my goals for the near future a reality, so I concentrated on all that pertained to it. I noticed that the mentioning of a discussion about my money that I had invested in both the store and the bar kept being blown off by P. and by my cousin. So I made a mental note to myself to demand that we meet and talk about when I could collect, and the specific amount that was owed to me. I would see both of them sometime this week. I had been meaning to talk to Keysh lately about starting a hair shop or something. Her sister and her younger cousin could both do hair; exclusively! It could be a good investment if she was willing to put in the time and effort to make it work. Keysh! I needed to talk to her about this bullshit with Red I had just heard. I would mention it when the time was right.

*

"Oh, Michael, this shit is so stressful. Why can't you be in the illegal immigration and human trafficking business? Then I'd know that da shit would be prosperous and would run smoothly," said Mr. Mendez.

"I don't know what to tell you, dog. All I know is traffickin' white girls. You feel me?!" P. asked Manny with a bright, diamond studded mouth.

"Yes, yes. This I know. So what are you doing about your friend, Siz-o?" Manny asked with curiosity and his usual, heavy accent.

"I don't know yet, this is the first time that we been faced with something like this since we started the Commission. I mean, we not the Italians, but it only makes sense that unless it's a good reason for it, then you in for life. Death or prison is the only way out, right? Siz-o's my guy; he helped me start the Firm. We done been through a lot. I don't understand the nigga. I mean, at 22 years old? What the fuck he been thinkin' bout?" P. asked rhetorically.

"Well, I like Siz-o. And I know he's your friend. He's 'our' friend. But he can't just get out...or demote himself, so.....what are you going to do?" Manny asked.

P. thought about it for a short while and then said, "It's a few of the Commission members who've already suggested that we get rid of him. But most of 'em is just wondering what's goin' on? Cause mostly everybody like Siz-o. He don't beef unnecessarily, he earns good...he just saved Torrence's fuckin' life! Nuts. The nigga is loyal as fuck! And he makes all the guys in his circle loyal, and keeps 'em under control. Cause that nigga always keeps some maniacs on his team, includin' his twin brother and his other uncle. Not Red, but Red's younger brother, Dust. The niggas will flip on anybody if Siz-o give 'em the word. But they all respect the nigga and his word. Siz-o's a good leader and he's loyal. He done showed me that since he was young. Him and Nuts got that Italian blood runnin' through 'em. He my true right hand and I'ma keep him on my team. I got an alternative to the situation. I'll take care of it," P. assured Manny.

"Okay Michael, you take care of it. I got to be at the docks in less than an hour. Come on, I'll have Ramon give you a ride back to your vacation house. You call me when you get back to Ohio tomorrow, okay?"

"Oh, for sure. You ready? Let's go," P. said as they got up from off the couch to leave Manny's beach house.

CHAPTER 35: Falling Walls

I had made my decision to stop all of my cocaine activities and involvement by June, so I had 2 more months to earn money the one of a kind way. It was any and all sales at this point. My young nigga Poo had been hitting me every other day for 2 or 3 ounces of crack, but I hadn't heard from him in nearly 2 weeks. He had just called me saying that he had something for me, and then asked could I meet him somewhere. I suggested the Popeye's on Livingston Avenue in 20 minutes, since he seemed to be in a hurry. I had someone else to go meet, so I needed to make it quick, too. I pulled up in my new, black 2000 Suburban, where Poo pulled in right behind me in a maroon Cherokee.

I watched him walk towards my truck as I watched another guy follow him. It was one of the hottest niggas in the city, Sonny Jackson. He had been suspected of getting busted by the laws and going to work for them. This had been said about dude nearly 2 years ago. I quickly signaled for him to walk back to their jeep. Poo looked surprised as he pointed back towards the Jeep to Sonny. He got in my truck where I asked him, "Ay, what you doin' wit him? He's hot as fuck!"

"Huh? Who, Sonny?" Poo asked.

"Yeah, dog. What's up, though? What you got?" I asked him.

"Oh, me and my dude just hit this Mexican for a whole brick. I only want 20 stacks for it," Poo said.

"What?" I asked. I raised my shirt up to grab my 30 shot Glock 40 and pointed it at Poo as I shushed him and grabbed for his shirt. I patted it and then raised it up.

He looked surprised as he held his hands up to surrender. "Siz-o. What's up? What's wrong?" He asked.

"Dog, I don't know nothin' about no bricks. Get out. Get out!" I said even louder with emphasis. He quickly exited my vehicle and then I quickly exited the restaurant's parking lot. That shit was a set up. Damn, my lil' nigga! My phone rang, breaking into my deep thoughts. It was my homey Big Carl, who I had been waiting on to call and come meet me to get his pack. "Bruh, you ain't gon' believe this shit I just witnessed. I'll tell you about it over at the house. Meet me at Heady's," I said, and then closed my phone.

I met Carl at Heady's and told him about my suspicions with Poo. After we politicked for a half an hour, I gave him his 4 ½ pack and then I slid around to Dust's spot by Wilson Avenue to give him his 4 ½ pack and give his homey Soul Man an ounce. I felt relieved to be done with my work; all of my running around was stressful. Especially after meeting with Poo and seeing Hot Boy Sonny with him. And then hearing his ridiculous story! It felt good to be heading home. Yeah, I needed to see Keysh. I wouldn't ask her anything direct, just the indirect obvious.

*

"So what's up? What you wanna do about Siz and the money that y'all got invested wit us here and at the bar? He said he on his way up," My cousin Mike asked P. They sat together in the back office counting money that had been made throughout the past month. They were breaking up what Mike would take to the bank and what P. would take as a monthly cut. I never had any idea how any of this went. They kept me out of it. I didn't know what Nuts knew, but he had a piece in on the 100 plus grand that we all three had invested, too.

"Uh, just let me holler at him back here when he come in. I'll holla at him," P. told Mike. My cousin Mike just nodded, as he put the money in his floor safe and walked out of the office and onto the store floor. P. saw me walk in through the glass window that was a mirror from the outside wall.

"Wusup family? What's poppin' wit you?" I asked my cousin Mike. He gave me a pound and told me that P. was in the back waiting on me. I slid in the back as I gave P. a pound as well, and then grabbed me a bottle of water from out of the small refrigerator before taking a seat. An hour passed before we were done speaking and I must say that it went well. We went over some serious figures for the first time; which put my $40,000 that I had invested at $50,000. 10 grand into the bar over 2 years and 30 grand into the clothing store over 6 years. We supposedly only gained 5% on our investments for each year, so it was a measly profit, but money that I didn't plan to even get back. It was especially a blessing to hear P. say that he would take care of the percent that I still had to pay to the Firm. I would collect it by late January, so that was money that I had for the New Year.

I gave P. and my cousin Mike another pound before I left. I wondered why in the hell Keysh hadn't got here yet. I had told her to meet me there to buy her an outfit for the Mob Deep after party, and so I could give her a stack for the mortgage payment and the bills. I walked out of the store and saw Red's fat ass sticking out of Keysh's Infiniti car window!

"Uncle Red, wusup?!" I said as I scowled my trademark frown.

"Oh, what's good nephew? I'm just clownin' wit da kids, Jewel and Max's bad asses. Keysh told me you was in there. What's goin' on wit you, playa?" Red asked hesitantly.

"Ain't shit up, just handlin' my business. What's up wit you all up in my people's ride? You know we don't do that," I said, still wearing my scowled frown.

"Aw shit, this my niece nephew, quit trippin'. Ay, I need to holla at you. It's about P.; and his boy 'O'. Meet me at the after hour later on tonight, I'll tell you about it then," Red's slimy ass said.

I mugged Keysh, too. And then I got in to give her the money, along with an ear full about Red's fat ass being all up in her car and supposedly all up on her the other day. She denied that it was any of that, and said that he was over there seeing Ciara. She claimed that whoever was saying that was just trying to start some shit. But she also admitted that he was talking his usual Big Willy shit, which would naturally, but indirectly, down my character. Keysh had been getting salty a lot lately, though. We hadn't spent much time together in the past year and I think she began to hear about a lot of my other lady friends. But I don't think she had heard anything about my other two kids, or she would've said something. I know I needed to tell her but…then what. I had to wait for the right time. Little did I know, though, that Red was spitting venom to her behind my back; about me fucking other females! Which I know she pretty much suspected, but surely didn't need to hear. You must keep snakes out of your grass, this I know, but I had no knowledge of it at the time.

Keysh was becoming bitter and more distant than ever. We had really grown apart, while my son and daughter were growing up. They were my heart and soul. I mean, what more did a man need; a beautiful little girl, an angel! And a handsome little sequel, a mini me!

"Well anyway, before we go in I got somethin' to show you," Keysh said leaning over towards the window and looking back at me. She peeked into the backseat to see if the kids were in their own world playing or if they were in our mix being nosey. Once she saw that the coast was clear she said, "Look!"

I looked down into the back of her Baby Phat jeans to see SIZ-O JONES tattooed on her right ass cheek. "Woah!" I thought. I was speechless.

"Damn, when you get that done?"

"Yesterday. Me and my sister went together. She got a panther on her leg," Keysh said.

We discussed a few things for a few minutes and had a couple of quick laughs before we went inside for her to get her an outfit. Red was in the back with P., which was good because I didn't want to see his fat ass. My man Ricky clowned with my son, as he usually did when he saw him. At just 3 years old, going on 4, my little man was a charmer to both the girls, and the guys as well.

After Keysh bought her leather 2-piece out fit, that I knew she would hurt everyone with, I walked them out to the car where she said, "I don't even know if I wanna go tonight." I looked at her questioningly. "I'll...I'll tell you about it tomorrow. You gon' come over to my mom's? You know it's her birthday."

"Yeah, definitely. Have a good time tonight; if you go," I said as I smiled. She smiled back and told the kids to wave goodbye to me. I waved back as they pulled off.

*

"Listen, Your Honor, I have two informers buying from this guy and we have a secret indictment on him already for trafficking. Which, it's a little shaky but if I can get the warrant to search his house then I am certain that there's a substantial amount of drugs there. I've also been listening to his phone conversations for the past few months when he's on his cell phone or on a cordless telephone. Now I know that can't be used in court because I didn't have a court order to get a tap, but trust me Judge Barnes, I know what I'm doing," Detective Walton assured. "And I have someone on the inside."

"I don't know Bo, isn't this Jones guy one of the ones who's involved in the criminal organization that Special Agent Nichols and the Feds were investigating just last year and the Johnson guy that they got a hold of was murdered in the middle of the night before he could testify the next day; him and his family, in a brutal set of murders? This Jones is high-powered. You better know that you have something solid on him to be able to get him, and get him good!" Judge Barnes said.

"Your Honor, I have Intel that tells me that Mr. Jones has just moved some belongings of his from a residence on the city's West Side to the residence on the city's South Side where I suspect that the drugs are. He goes to and from this house every time he does a transaction with one of my informers. They've helped me build a case on him. Please, Your Honor, don't let all of this hard work go out the window. You're the only Judge left who can grant me this search warrant. Now along with it and the indictment that we already have on Jones and his girlfriend Gills, we can make something stick; maybe get the girlfriend to roll over on him and anyone else who she knows, or better yet get Jones to roll over on his crew." Detective Walton stared intently at Judge Barnes, desperately waiting on an answer. He would get the one he wanted.

"Now listen to me Bo, if you fuck this up and make me look like a goddamn idiot, then it's your ass. Do you understand?" He asked Detective Walton, who nodded assuredly. "Alright, now give me the damn warrant." Judge Barnes signed it and then Detective Walton marched out of his chambers, headed to get his man.

"I need a surveillance team ready within the hour and all first and second shift officers in the 6th precinct to be ready to respond to an arrest warrant and a search warrant when I call. The subject is a Sizalino Jones and the residence is 1802 Linwood Avenue. The time is now 10:10 a.m.," Detective Walton said into his police radio.

*

"Good mornin' babe. It's supposed to be 85 degrees today. It's gon' be nice. Springtime is definitely here now," said Heady.

"Oh, yeah. Ay, go to Kroger and get some meat to throw on the grill. Pick up some other stuff, too, like some sides and some chips. Call some off ya people and I'll call some people. You feel me?! And go ahead, take the Impala, too. Cause I ain't gettin' up yet to let you out. I know ya truck in the garage," I said to Heady.

"What? You gon' let me drive the platinum Impala? Okay." Heady jumped up to put on her clothes. She made numerous calls to her friends and family members as she got ready and headed out the door.

"Don't be bangin' my system either, girl!" I told Heady playfully as I handed her $200. Damn, it was already near 11 o'clock and I had just remembered that I told Keysh I would stop by her mom's to talk to her and see her moms. It was cool, I could get up and get dressed and then shoot out north for about an hour while Heady got everything ready. I got up and went to hop in the shower. I called Keysh first to let her know that I'd be by shortly. She said okay and, "I love you daddy, I'll see you in a minute."

I got dressed in a powder blue North Carolina short set and some white and blue 'J's. Heady walked in just as I was ready to leave. "Babe, I gotta drive that more often. Niggas was sweatin' me! Asking me was that my car and was it my man's ride," she smiled as she handed me the keys. I smiled back sarcastically as I smacked her on the ass and walked out the door.

I got out to Keysh's mom's about 15 minutes later where I hugged and kissed my kids, just as I had done the same with Keysh. I said hi to everybody and told Mrs. Berryman Happy Birthday. Keysh and I had bought her a new dinette set and had it delivered to her on Friday.

"So Keysh, talk to me. I see you made it to the party last night; I knew you was gon' go kill 'em in that leather joint," I said, looking her up and down seductively. And then my demeanor quickly turned serious. "What's up?"

"Oh, um, I know this is gon' be crazy to hear, and I know you think I got my tubes tied.….but I didn't. I'm so sorry." I stared at Keysh wide-eyed, waiting to hear her say the inevitable. "I'm pregnant. 8 weeks pregnant."

"What? How…this is crazy. Hmm," I sighed. Keysh looked at me questioningly. "Well, I guess we gon' celebrate," I said, as Keysh smiled cheerfully. "But this is it, Keysha Naomi Berryman. I guess I'm gon' really have to marry yo' ass now," I stated playfully. Keysh shook her head yes, as tears ran down her eyes. She hugged me tight, and wouldn't let go. I told her that I would try to make it back later but that I had to go now. "Okay, babe. I'll see you later," she said.

I headed back to Heady's in a daze. I was happy, but discontent. This would be my fifth child. My third in just a year! I would be 23 in 4 months, this had to be it. I got my focus back as I got near the house and began to ring everyone. "Come on through, I got some liquor and a case of Dom P. And we got plenty of barbeque!" That was all that needed to be said, everybody was on their way.

The cookout was a blast. We played cards, shot pool, swam in the pool and ate like farm pigs. Everyone left full and drunk. It was nearly dark out as my man Terique was leaving. He asked me to go to the strip club with him and my cousin Mike and a few of our other associates. I declined though, because I was on another level now; trying to get all my money and stay focused between now and June, which brought me to all of the calls that I had to return. My uncle Dust's homey Soul Man had called wanting an ounce of crack. He had been calling me all day. Heady had gone to take a few people home, so I told her kids to keep an eye on Samone and come lock the door, I'd be right back. I had Soul Man waiting for me around at the Shell Gas Station. As I got into my car I looked down the block a little ways and saw, what I thought was the same undercover Lumina that had been hanging out everywhere it seems, that I was at. I got in the car, stashed the work, and backed out to leave.

As I got to the end of the street to make my turn, I saw flashing lights coming towards me. I didn't pay it any mind, though, and turned right onto Frebis Avenue. The flashing lights turned behind me! I turned off of Frebis to see if they would keep going but they stayed on my tail. "Oh shit," I thought. There were a number of undercover police cars ahead of me blocking my path...and now there was an officer on the bullhorn, "Sizalino Jones, put your hands out of the fucking window, now! You're under arrest."

Three things went through my mind: shoot it out (because of all the possible things that I could have been under arrest for); ram through their road block and take them on a high speed chase with my LT-1 engine that the Impala had; or just surrender. I thought about the faces of all of my little angels: Jewel, Maxwell, Anijah, Simone, and my newcomer with Keysh, due in 7 months. I put my hands out the window, "Alright, alright. What's the problem, officers?"

They held me at gunpoint as the arresting officer walked towards the car, opened the door to get me out and then said, "You're under arrest! We've got your ass now. You're going down. It's all over," said the Indian looking asshole officer.

"What the fuck am I under arrest for?" I asked.

"Shut the fuck up?" said the asshole officer. This son-of-a-bitch had a real aggression issue. He was really uptight. I didn't want to make a false move, because he seemed like the type of cop who was trigger happy and on the edge.

"Do you have any drugs or weapons on you?" asked another officer.

"Nah," I answered.

The officer walked me to the back of the police wagon and said, "You are under arrest for drug trafficking on…" he read from some documented paper he had in his hand, "January 18th at, 1802 Linwood Avenue." He was distracted briefly by another officer who signaled for his attention. The officer held up my beautiful 30 shot Glock 40 and in the other hand, the ounce of crack. In the background I could see the Indian asshole, staring at me intently. He said it again, "Yeah, you're going down, man."

The mellow officer who read me my charges sort of motioned with his hand to the Indian looking officer to 'cool it'. He asked me to step up into the wagon. As I did so, looking through the cluster of cars and EMS vehicles, I saw the blue undercover Lumina. "Who in the fuck was that in that car?" I wondered.

I sat in the wagon for about five minutes, with my mind racing a thousand miles a minute. The wagon door opened and the officer said, "Siz…uh, Jones, come on out here." He directed me to go get into the police cruiser where two officers stood waiting to put me in it. When I got inside we pulled around by the house into the warehouse parking lot that was a street over. The officer in the driver seat read me my charges: Felony 2, aggravated drug trafficking; Felony 2, drug possession; and a Felony 4 gun spec. CCW.

"Now these are some serious charges here, Bud. But you may have an even bigger problem. They're going around there to your house to tear your place up looking for more drugs. You may just wanna tell us where everything is, 'cause I know you got a lot of nice shit in there…" the officer said, pausing for a moment.

I just looked at him, "What? Man, I ain't got nothin' to say to y'all. Get me downtown!"

They both looked at each other in defeat at their attempt to get me to be their singing buddy. "Fuck them!" I wanted to shout. I began to listen more intently to their radio as I heard the name Hedricka Gills and, something about an arrest warrant.

"There's ya girl there, man. They just arrested her now over at the house. They're over there fuckin' the place up. Ain't your kids over there?" The officer said.

As bad as I wanted to ask questions to have much of my curiosity answered, I stayed tight lipped. It was best to remain silent, because any sort of communication attempts to open you up and may let some incriminating shit slip out. I exercised my right to remain silent. I'd be sitting in front of a lawyer in the next couple of hours.

An hour later I was downtown at the county jail being processed. After that, I would get my one phone call. I got processed and then had a seat on the bench. I thought hard about all that had just happened; the 'how', the 'who', and the 'what'? I also wondered if the Feds were going to pick up my case. The thought of that really had me worried.

"Jones! Phone number 2," said the Deputy.

I walked over to the phone and gave the Deputy Keysh's cell phone number. It was close to midnight so I figured she was asleep. I listened to the phone ring about four times, and then she answered. After a few seconds for them to clear me to talk, I spoke, "Keysh, these muthaphuckas got me! I'm downtown."

"I know. Are you alright?" she asked.

"Yeah, I'm cool. How did you know? What'd you mean, you know?"

"Ya uncle's over here. He got over here about an hour ago. We was waiting on you to call."

"How in the hell did he know?" I wondered to myself. And what was he doing out at my house in Reynoldsburg? "What? How did...never mind. Anyway, they got me down here on some drug charges, State, not Federal. But I don't want you to worry. I'll explain everything to you tomorrow after the arraignment when I bond out. Alright?"

"Okay. I love you! I'll see you in the morning," Keysh said. I said the same to her and then we hung up. Damn, I hated this stinking ass county jail and all that came along with it. It would be hours before I got upstairs, so I was about to sit in the holding tank forever. I would get a much clearer picture painted for me in the morning at the hearing. Keysh knew to contact my lawyer between now and in the morning time; any of the two I had used in the past, Dye's office or my other Jew, Brantz. Wow, Heady had got arrested, too. And they ran up in the house. There was a rat informer in this situation, and whoever it was had better crawl into a sewer and stay there for an eternity. Time would reveal all.

CHAPTER 36: The Revealing

P. had just got dressed in a black Armani suit over a black, tight fitting silk shirt. He had thought about how he'd planned to set me up the next time I came to grab a brick, or perhaps two bricks from him. I had begun to take it slow and sufficient lately so that is all that I would get each time was 1-2 kilos. He wasn't going to set me up directly through any law enforcement link, though. He was not the police at all. He was just going to have someone call in on a hum bug to say that I pulled a gun on them just to get me pulled over. I stayed with my heat so it was buyable. Therefore I would get arrested and have some substantial time on my hands for a substantial amount of coke. If I went away then I would be out of the mix for a while and still a member of the Commission's West Side Firm. I wouldn't be able to branch out on my own and get out from under the Commission. And I would have plenty of time to think about my awkward decision to leave the life. P. felt that in a strange way, he was protecting me; from a bad decision and also, from getting murdered (by my own outfit). Because before they would let me out, that's what they would do.

He left his house to go pick Red up and then go down to Brantz' office so they could ride over to the courthouse together for my arraignment.

*

Red was extremely tired. He had only been asleep for a few hours. Detective Walton was on his back all night and all morning after I had got busted about his concentrated mission to take down the Commission. But Red, although his envy against P. was gigantic, knew that if he took P. down along with the rest of the Commission members, then there would be nothing left. No, he had to get rid of P. in another way; because he was after what P. had, the ultimate accomplishment of all. The Money and the Power! He just had to keep his deception on the down low. He had been getting really nervous lately, but he was in too deep. And there was no turning back. He knew he had lost something in this here game, but he had to be an all out Savage; a low down snake who cared for nothing or no one but himself. He would utilize the State police, and even the Feds, along with the Commission members to get what he wanted. And one of the things that he wanted was calling his cell phone right at that very moment, interrupting his thoughts, "Hello."

"Hey Red, it's Keysh. You wanted me to call and wake you up. Ciara gon' stay here wit the kids, but I'm bout to head down to the courthouse now," said Keysh.

"Oh, alright. I'll see you down there. P. bout to come pick me up. Ay, you gon' give me a ride after that? I'ma need a ride to my car," Red said.

"Um, alright, sure. I'm just so stressed out about Siz-o."

"Yeah. Well, you bout to be blown away."

"Huh? What do you mean?"

"Aw, nothin'. You'll see. I'll see you down there in a little bit," Red said, and then hung up.

It was absolute chaos out in the court's hallway. It was packed with my people and Heady's people. Keysh was having small talk with my pops when she spotted Heady's sister Ribbon just 12 feet away. "Uh, hold on Mr. Jones." She walked over to where Ribbon was and said, "Hi. What you doin' down here, girl?"

"Hey Keysh! Heady and Siz-o got arrested last night. You didn't know about that? Or..." Ribbon stopped in mid-sentence, realizing that Keysh had no idea.

"Yeah, I know Siz-o got arrested. That's why I'm here. But what you mean him and Heady?" Keysh asked.

"They got arrested together on this drug case. Keysh, they got a daughter together, too. I'm sorry if you didn't know."

Keysh was in shock. Her whole body became numb. She couldn't fathom what she had just heard. It couldn't be. Mr. Brantz came out of the courtroom doors and said, "Keysha, Mr. Jones...tell Michael and everyone to come on in, he's coming out now."

I walked out of the back chamber and into the courtroom. Brantz had told me before we came out that I had not been charged as of yet with any of what had been found inside of the house. And that we would just come out and plead 'Not Guilty' to the charges and then wait to hear what the bond was. I would then, of course, go back to my cell pod and wait to be bonded free.

"Your Honor, I would like to ask that my client be allowed bail at a minimum amount as possible. If you look at the circumstances in which my client was arrested under they are very shaky. And also, my client has no arrest record or convictions I should say. As you know, both cases that he had come before this court were dismissed. So…" Brantz was cut off by the magistrate.

"Excuse me Mr. Brantz, but I must inform you that your client is being asked by the prosecution to be held without bail for a number of disclosed reasons."

"I beg your pardon, Judge? You know that under the State Law in Ohio…" Brantz was cut off again. "I am aware of the law Mr. Brantz, and so is the prosecution. This request is indeed being given by the Federal government. So, we will meet again in a few days where you will be presented with the information that you need to hear why your client is being held and, of course, to request bail then. This hearing is adjourned. Next case…"

Just like that I was denied bail. You talk about unconstitutional. Brantz came back into the holding cell where I was taken to and assured me that he would get to the bottom of this. It made me feel a little better to hear that but I would feel even better if he showed me and got me the fuck out of here. A couple of hours later I was back in my cell pod. I knew Keysh would be to see me in a little while, but I called her anyway. I wanted to know what P. and everybody had to say, too, so I would get an update from her on that or have her 3-way somebody. The old school nigga wit the ponytail finally got off of the phone. I dialed my home number and it finally rang. On the third ring Keysh picked up. "Why, Siz-o? I just want to ask you that, why?"

"Why what? What are talkin' about? I asked.

"You know what I'm talking about, Siz-o. Ya fuckin' daughter wit ya Bonnie bitch, Heady. This bitch done got you caught up? I'ma kill that bitch. And then I'ma kill you."

"Keysh, just calm down. Don't fall apart on me now. I need you."

"Oh, you need me, huh? Fuck that, man. I can't believe you. I can't believe you, Siz-o!"

"Keysh, listen to me…we'll be able to talk about all of this shit soon enough. I'm in this shit hole hemmed up on fuckin' dope charges wit no bail! I need to know that you focused and with me on this shit or if I'm on my own. Now are you wit me?

"Yeah, Siz-o, I'm wit you. But I'ma still kill yo ass. And I'm not playing! I'ma get that bitch, too," Keysh vowed. She told me that she'd be down in a few hours and then we concluded the call.

At about 6:30 the Deputy called my name, "Jones!" They escorted me out to the hallway where I was placed in a standing booth with my visitor, Keysh. I saw my son and daughter in the background playing. They ran up to the glass when they saw me, past a scowling Keysh, and said "Daddy!" I waived hi to them and then turned my gaze towards Keysh.

"What's up? Are you gon' say somethin'?" I asked her.

After about a minute she exploded like fireworks. Going on an emotional tirade about Heady and the baby, and even about my activities out in the streets and how it was about to take me away from her and our kids. She began to cry uncontrollably about me having no bond and about my uncle Red telling her that I was going down. Hearing this pissed me off really bad. She calmed down after a few minutes of silence and went on to tell me that she had gone down to talk to my lawyer a few hours ago and he said that he would be to see me later on. It seemed like maybe ten minutes had past when the Deputy yelled, "Times up, Jones!" I felt crushed leaving away from that window. It seemed like they were leaving out of my life for an eternity. Back to my stinking ass pod I went.

"Hey buddy. How ya doin'? Have a seat," Brantz said to me. I sat down on the hard cold chair. "Okay Siz-o, I've talked to Michael. He just brought 10 thousand over to my office to represent you in this case. It seems pretty wild. This bond thing's first, though. Now this is a case where they are stressing how you are a threat to the informer and even to your co-defendant, Gills. That's your girlfriend, right?" He asked me.

"No, she's my daughter's mom, though," I told him.

"Okay, well, this is the typical bullshit that they might throw out there to keep you locked up, but there was some sort of request from a Federal figure which we'll find out about at the hearing on Thursday. We don't know if the Federal government will pick this up, with the dope and the guns that they found inside of the house, but it could just be some string pulled by Walton. Bo Walton, the lead detective in your case," Brantz said to me, seeing the confused look on my face. "Yeah, he's a real asshole! But I'll have all of the information that I need before the hearing. Now you haven't talked to anyone have you? Any of the detectives or…" I cut Brantz off, "Hell no, you know I haven't. They attempted to, but you know I didn't go for it."

"I know you didn't, but I just had to ask. Alright, well just sit tight for a few days and I'll see you at the hearing. Unless something we're not prepared for comes up be ready to make bail. Okay?" Brantz asked as I shook my head yes. "Alright, I'll see ya man, take care."

A few days passed by and my bond hearing came. My lawyer actually got me a pretty decent bond at $50,000, the 10% being $5,000. I had to agree never to be within 100 yards of the informer, Jasper, and they tried to say that I could not go within 100 yards of my co-defendant Heady either; until my lawyer argued that we had a daughter together. I was released by 7 o'clock in the evening. I couldn't get out of that county fast enough. I had called Keysh and told her that I was out and she could come and get me. I stood by the Certified gas station for about ten minutes when I saw Red's white Cadillac pull up at the light. Ciara and Keysh were in the car with him. I was not happy about this shit. I walked over to the car and hopped in the back with Keysh, who was tight lipped with an attitude. Red said, "What's up, nephew?" I just nodded back. He knew not to press the issue for me to have to say too much.

We rode to the liquor store to get a few bottles. Red was 'Big Willy' buying the bottles and all the snacks. We were having a barbeque out at my house in Reynoldsburg. I just wanted to get there and see my kids and have some alone time to talk to Keysh. Red told me that I was supposed to go meet with P. in the morning, which I suspected. I didn't have any of my two phones. The laws had taken my phones, my house keys, they were on my car key ring for the Impala, and they took the Impala. They were seizing it they said. I would have to go over to the house that they had run into the other night and, see and speak with Heady, too.

Shortly after I got home and saw my kids I called Twin and Dust to come out to the house. Where, of course, they ran Red off. But before I let him go I stepped outside to talk to him first. "Ay dog, what's this shit you tellin' Keysh that I'm goin' down and, 'I'm through?' She don't need to be hearing that. What the fuck is wrong wit you?" I asked Red.

"Ah, man, it wasn't even like that. I was just sayin' that them muthafuckas had some shit on you and it wasn't lookin' good," Red said.

"Nah, you be lyin' unc'. You always twistin' some shit around. I know you ain't bout to tell me that Keysh is lyin'!? I know you, nigga. I done seen you run all that deceptive bullshit on everybody else. This me, though. Dog, it sound like some hatin' ass, envious shit. I'ma be one-hundred wit you," I said. I put the nigga on the spot. I was so tired of his sucka ass... and my rage was sparked at the thought of his slimy ass possibly tryin' to charm my woman. I did not play when it came to Keysh! And this nigga knew that I knew how many niggas' chicks that he had bribed, and paid, and bad mouthed their men to them to fuck; weakening them up so he could creep in while they were vulnerable. That's some snake ass shit! I was ready to bomb on this nigga. And he felt it.

"Man, you know what nephew, I'm out of here. That's some bullshit I ain't even gone speak on," he said.

"Yeah. Whatever nigga! As a matter of fact, don't call or come back around my kids or my chick no more, family. And I mean that," I said to him as he walked to his car. The nigga was foul and he knew it. If he crossed me again then I would smash him. And that was on everything. He didn't have anymore passes. I went inside and told Keysh what I had told his fat ass. And I told Ciara that if she wanted to fuck with him then she had better do it else where.

Twin and Dust finally arrived and shit loosened up. We had a bunch of shots, Hennessy and Remy, and talked some heavy shit. Just like old times. I told them what had happened earlier with me and Red.

"I ain't never liked that soft muthaphucka. And Dust, I know you ain't never liked him," Twin said.

"Hell no, I don't like him. Pedophile ass fag! I wanna rob his bitch ass. I'm salty that nigga ever went on that lick and did them murders wit us, Tone. I don't trust that nigga. But he blasted one of 'em, too. That's why I made his ass do it, 'cause that nigga can't go tell shit wit out tellin' on his self," Dust said.

"What the fuck is y'all talkin' about?" I asked. They filled me in on the robbery/homicide from nearly two years back, and about how Red raped the deceased Rob and everything. I was thrown. I needed another shot after hearing all that. It got a little quiet when we saw Keysh pass by to go to the kitchen. She grabbed something to drink and walked back down into the basement where the girls were. I looked at the microwave clock to see it read 1:33 in the a.m. I hadn't realized that it was that late.

Twin waited for Keysh to go back downstairs and then asked me, "You think you gon' be able to get out of doin' any time on this one, bruh?"

"I don't know bruh. Maybe, but I doubt it. Cause I still don't know what they gon' do about the shit in the house. I ain't got charged wit it yet, but that's over a brick and a half. Some was hard but most of it was soft. And then there was the guns...that faggot muthaphucker set us up. That fag that Heady know," I said as I stared intently at the wall.

Twin and Dust were as high as kites, and buzzed off of the liquor. They asked me, "Who do we have to kill?" I told them I didn't know yet, but I was gonna figure it out. I walked them to the door and gave them a pound and a hug.

"Y'all niggas be careful, 'aight?" I said, and then I closed the door. I walked to the basement door and said, "Keysh." She came up the steps after I confirmed for her that my brother and uncle were gone. She said goodnight to her little cousin and her friend, and then came all the way upstairs with me to our bedroom. We talked for about an hour or so. She made me promise her that I would not touch Heady anymore. I promised, and then we had some hour long sex before we fell asleep.

I had an attitude filled morning with Keysh and fifty questions from my kids. I slid out of the house at about 10:30 to head to P.'s house on the west side. I had to go by Heady's afterwards to see her and my daughter and to see what they had found at the house. She had been out for a few days now since she made her bail at the first hearing.

When I pulled up to park outside of P.'s house I saw an undercover car parked a few houses down. I got out of my truck to walk up to the door with my face looking the other way the whole time. I rang the bell and waited. P. opened the door up and then the caged screen door, where he greeted me lovingly saying, "Siz-o, what's up my nizzle?! You see the Feds down there?" He gave me a pound and a hug and then he let me in.

"Them muthaphuckas been down there for the past few days. They ain't gon' stop shit, though. I ain't doin' shit here, anyway. What's up wit you, though, dog? I know you glad to be up out of there," P. said.

"Yeah, you already know. Why in the hell is the Feds around here?" I asked; my mind still on that.

"Shit, I don't know. Maybe cause you just got busted and I fuck wit you? I mean, not that you done flipped, because I know better, but just for the simple fact that they may be onto all of us."

"Yeah, you right. This shit is crazy, dog," I replied. I went on to tell P. all about my arrest and me getting busted. It was some major forces working behind it all. I could feel it. P. had already set up a freak accident in the making for the informer Jasper's daughter. He was going to have someone run her off the road on her way home from work in the late p.m. hours. It would be nearly, but not completely, impossible to get to Jasper with the protection that he was under. Plus, it would just point right to me, so we decided to get the next best thing to him. 'Daddy's little girl!' Or in his case, a faggot's little girl!

After a two hour discussion I told P. that I was heading over to the house on Linwood to see what was up, with Heady and everything else. Hopefully she was there because I didn't have a phone at the time and I didn't have a key.

"Alright, dog, see what's up wit her because I need to know if we need to get rid of her. I mean, I know she ya kid's mom, but the Commission is much bigger than her; and you, and me. You feel me!?" P. asked.

"Yeah, no doubt. But I got her, don't even worry about that," I told P.

"Alright. Get you a phone today and call me later on tonight. We'll shoot up to the bar and chop it about some shit, just you, me, and Nuts."

In these trying times that sounded like the best idea that I had heard in a long time; just the three of us where it all started. "Cool, cool. I'll see you later on tonight, dog," I said. And then I discreetly slid out of the house and into my truck. I pulled off the block, not even looking back Agent Nichol's way.

*

Red had been in Twin's ear for the last few days about how I was hot now and so was P. But that he wasn't because he always kept his distance from us and that he had his own circle outside of ours. They had bumped into each other out east a couple of times, near Dust's spot or just in the neighborhood. Twin basically paid him no mind and was rather offended by his comments. But on the third occasion where their paths had crossed Red found an opening.

"I got some of them new square Kicker 12 speakers for sale; they in a nice box, too. About like this," Red displayed with his hands the speaker box's size.

"Oh yeah! How much you want for 'em?" Twin asked.

"Ah shit, you know, for you the low. Just give me $300. They're $350 a piece, brand new; that's wit out the box!" Red said.

"300? Alright, cool. Where they at?"

"I got 'em up at my young bitch's crib way up north by Shrock Road. I'll call you later on," Red told Twin. He pulled out of the Church's Chicken parking lot thinking to himself how lovely the Kicker's were going to bang in his white '93 Astro mini-van. AKA the ice-cream van!

*

When I turned onto Linwood I noticed the notorious blue Lumina backing out of a driveway about 5 or 6 houses before Heady's, blocking my path. The dickhead detective looked into my driver's door window and said, "Hey! Bo Walton, chief detective of narcotics. I'm sure you remember me. I was wondering if we could talk," he more or less asked.

"Man, for what? What should we talk about?" I asked.

"Well, I figured maybe you might wanna give me your cooperation and have those charges you got disappear. If not, then you're going away. And you will be charged with the dope in the house, too. I'll make sure of it. So what do you say, you wanna take a ride with me up the street here?" Detective Walton asked.

I looked him in the eye for a good ten seconds. "Fuck you! You have ya lawyer contact my lawyer. And if you come around or try to contact me again I will notify my lawyer; and you know how the rest of the story goes from there. Now you have a nice day. Excuse me," I said to the dickhead as I drove around him. "Fine," Bo thought to himself. That was just fine.

"Hey, Head. How you holdin' up?" I said to Heady as I walked in the door and saw her in the kitchen. She was a soldier, I knew, but even this was hard for her.

"Oh, I'm cool. Here go this damn warrant and the shit that they took out of here," she said, standing in her robe next to the sink where she had just made coffee. She looked at me for a good while and then reached her arms out to me. I hugged her tight, putting my hands inside of her robe to caress her smooth skin. She wore nothing under her robe but cream laced panties. I got rock-hard instantly, but quickly thought about the promise I had made to Keysh. So I pulled away and asked where Simone was.

"She's upstairs takin' a nap. The other two is out west over Margaret's house. I'm bout to go out there later on. I had to get some sleep, though. I see you out; they finally gave you a bond?" Heady asked rhetorically.

"Yeah. They on some real live bullshit. That fag ass Jasper gon' get it; soon enough. Ay, would you believe that dickhead detective on our case was just up the street tryin' to pull me over to talk to him? He must've thought I was one of them duck niggas," I said.

Heady stared at me with her mouth wide open and then said, "What? They crazy! These fuckin' police is off tha chain, man. I can't believe this shit."

"Yeah, I know. What they charge you with?"

"Drug trafficking! They ain't charge me with nothin' in the house."

"Aw, yeah, me neither. Oh shit!" I said, as I looked at the seize document that the police left. It only showed 437 grams of cocaine methamphetamines, and 110 grams of crack cocaine methamphetamines seized. I ran down the stairs into the basement.

"What? What's wrong?" Heady asked. She followed me downstairs. I hesitantly walked up to Zilla, my 2 ½ foot Alligator's tank and said, "They didn't fuck with none of the gators."

"No, I don't think. My mom and dad said that the police said they're legal to have all the way up to 4 feet or 6 feet or something; dependin' on what state you in. Why?" She asked, looking curious. I lifted up the heavy concrete rock and set it down. My stepdaughter Talia usually handled this big bastard. However, I picked him up by his front legs, like I had seen it done many times before, and carried him over by the laundry room where I sat him down and quickly placed the big board back over the doorway. I took a deep breath and then I reached inside of his dirty octagon shaped tank up under all of the little rocks and came up with the plastic packaged brick. They didn't find it! I'm sure they never thought to look there.

"Wow, that was in there?" Another rhetorical question asked by Heady. This was $25 -35,000 that I had chalked up as a loss. There was a little bit of light at the end of the dark tunnel, I guess. I instantly thought of a safe way to get it out of here. The cops had fucked the place up a little, but not too bad. So I would throw out the dinette set, which had a slightly bent chair and a slightly discolored table top, and have a new one brought over to Heady by my big white dude, Lurch. He pushed work for me, usually a quarter or a half a key at a time, but he also drove a furniture delivery truck part-time with his buddy, Dave. So I'd have him come to pick it up in the next day or so when he delivered the new table and chair set. For now, though, I grabbed some duck tape and taped it under the gator tank table.

I took a deep breath and then grabbed Heady by the arm and said, "Come here. Let's sit for a minute. We need to talk."

A short while later I left; in deep thought about everything. My life had never been this complicated. It came with the territory, though. The game! It was a bitch! Sometimes it was a good bitch, and sometimes it was a bad bitch. But it was a bitch! I think Heady and I had a great understanding about everything. She was tough, and I knew that. I'm a great judge of character. And her character was solid, and loyal to me. But she was bothered by the fact that I wouldn't, and couldn't let go of Keysh. She was my heart and soul. And Heady acknowledged that; but hated it all the same. Through all of the shit, my mind would constantly key in on one thing, though. And that was the reality that more than likely, I was going to prison. What the Commission and my Firm could do to help me remained to be seen. It would be very interesting to see how it all unfolded in the end.

*

Keysh had been acting so stank lately. I knew the acknowledgement of Heady and my daughter Simone was eating her alive. I got up and got dressed to go see the bond probation officer that the courts had assigned for me to report to as a condition of my bond release. When I got dressed I asked Keysh if she wanted to come with me, but she refused. So I went out and jumped in my truck to head down to the probation office. They wanted me to drop some urine once a week or once every two weeks while I was out on this bond.

I parked on the side of the huge building where the parking meters were and shoved $2 worth of change into mine. I hated going into this building. And when I got inside it reminded me why. I went to sign in and let them know that I was waiting for my assigned officer. A few minutes later an officer Mouts came out of the back and hollered, "Jones!"

"Yeah, that's me," I said raising my hand and standing up.

"Oh…hey, come on back. So how's it going?" He asked as he opened the door to the back office for me. But before I could speak I was rushed and wrestled to the ground by a big security officer and now, the Mouts guy, who jumped in to help get me down and hand-cuffed. "You're under arrest, Mr. Jones. You have the right to remain silent…" He went on to say, along with the rest of the Miranda rights bullshit. They had arrested me for the dope in the house finally, which I knew was coming; because I wasn't going to cooperate with shit. They could kiss my dick and the Pope's. Over the next few hours I went through the same processing bullshit that I had just gone through not even two weeks ago. When I finally got my phone call I called Keysh. Who was hysterical, and immediately talking about killing Heady.

I got upstairs to my bunk and went straight to sleep; awaiting my arraignment in the morning. I did not look forward to it, seeing that I had a big Felony 1 and 2 possession charge. My lawyer had been notified of the hearing and they had let Keysh come and get my truck and all my other property. This shit was beginning to be fucked up. But what could I do.

The morning arraignment came and I was stunned with the result. The bond was a half a million dollars; with the percent being 50 grand! P. was prepared to put up a house. We didn't want to show and use 50 stacks, none of us did. But they denied me a bail again! I was going to have to fight for a bond. It was my visiting day so Keysh came right back down to see me by 1 o'clock. I was so tired of this shit, and so was Keysh. I wanted to kill that fucking detective. How these bitches wouldn't give me a bond I didn't know. I had to wait for my lawyer to come down later on in the evening. I was stressed the fuck out! Keysh wore a cute little skirt outfit to cheer me up. But I couldn't fucking touch her, so it didn't really work. Her phone rang and when she answered it she heard, "Ay where y'all at? Where Ciara at?" It was my uncle Red. Keysh told him that she didn't know and that she was visiting me, and then hung up.

"What the fuck!? Dude callin' ya phone for her?" I asked rhetorically.

"Yeah, she gave him my number cause she ain't got no phone," Keysh said.

"Well, I don't give a fuck. I told that clown not to contact or go near mine, so y'all better figure out somethin'."

"Hmm!" Keysh said sarcastically. She took advantage of being a smart ass every chance that she could ever since she found out about Heady. I wonder how much crazier she would get if she found out about Goldie and Anijah. However, we concluded the visit on a positive note and then I went back to my cell to wait on Brantz to come see me to tell me what the fuck was going on with my bond.

I sat in my bunk fuming mad while I thought about what Brantz had told me. They had no evidence of me being involved with the informant Jasper's daughter being ran into a guard rail the night before, but yet and still they held it against me by denying me bail. I told Brantz that he had better get me a bond by the end of the week, or it was going to be trouble for him. I didn't care who he had to bribe or what he had to do. They had nothing on me, so therefore I wanted my fucking bond. I sent word to P., too. Get me the fuck out of there! I eventually dozed off by midnight, right at 'lights out'. I was a grown ass man dealing with lights out by 12. I had to get the fuck out of here!

*

It had been nearly a week that Red had sold Twin the Kicker sub-woofers; right at his place with Stephanie and his kids off of Shrock Road. Red had made up the idea that he had a chick that lived in the area. Through topical conversation he had found out that Twin needed a key of coke. So he pressed; trying to get Twin to buy from him. Twin had entertained Red for a short while by asking what his price would be for a whole key and or a half of one. Red hung on to it and had his mind set on selling Twin the work that day. The whole day went by and Twin never called. Red was pissed.

*

P. hung at the car lot office waiting on a few things to shake including Twin's phone call for his half key. Red walked into the office where P. was at and said, "What's up Big Dog!?"

"Ain't shit, just workin'," P. said.

"Aw, yeah, that's what's up, playa."

Red was being his usual slimy self, slithering around in the a.m. It was his job now to stay in P.'s mix, which was easy with his new upgraded status as a top member of W.S.F. He sipped his coffee as he sat quietly while P. spoke on the phone and did a few things around the office.

"Where Stube' at? Old Steubenville Bob?" Red asked.

"Oh, he at the car auction. I was gon' go wit him, but I got too much shit to do. Wednesday the best day to go anyway," said P. His phone rang, for about the 10th time in the last ten minutes. He answered, "Hello. Tone, where you at? Okay, check this out, meet me around on Central. I'll be about 5, 10 minutes 'til I get around there. Alright, cool." P. stood up said, "Ay Red, stay here and watch the office for a few minutes. I gotta go around here and holler at Tone real quick."

"Oh, 'aight. Who you gotta meet, Tone? Big Tone, or…"

"Nah, Twin Tone."

"Aw, my nephew! Okay then," Red confirmed. "So Twin was copping the work from P.," he thought to himself. He assured P. that things would be cool until he got back. And then P. left out the door to go around to the house.

*

Soul Man had talked with Red many times before about a 'favor for a favor' ever since Red came home and they were going in together to buy work from me. Soul Man had more so grown up with Dust, they were a few months apart, but he had known Red like a brother too as well. They both worked for Detective Walton now, but Red felt that he was the 'big wig' undercover. He had manipulated Soul Man against his will to do this jacking; using the fact that Twin had fucked Soul Man's little hood rat bitch, who hung with Dust's hood rat bitch, Keyonna. Soul Man was rather fearful of Dust, and Twin as well. But Red was a good manipulator, and he had influenced and enticed Soul Man with this robbery in so many ways. He told him that it would be untraceable, and that he would reap a substantial reward. So here Soul Man was, casing Twin's crib with his other childhood goon, Revis. His conscious was really bugging him because he had already helped to set me up. He liked me, I was always good to him, but for him it was about saving his own ass.

It was a few minutes past eleven, and Red would be pulling up soon. Soul Man was really nervous. Red had talked Twin into letting him come through to grab a sack of weed for his non-existent lady friend. Soul Man and Revis had to be ready when Red pulled up. Red tapped on the car door and said, "Come on," shaking the life out of Soul Man. They followed Red and his white accomplice to the townhouse's back patio.

"Now y'all remember the plan? He got brick money, he just copped today. But remember to leave some of the dope in the house, alright? Now Jay, you gon' watch the door," Red said to the white boy holding the shotgun; one of P.'s white boys that Red had now corrupted and put under his wing. "Y'all two niggas gon' go in the house. Y'all ready?" Red asked rhetorically as he knocked on the door.

Twin answered, "What's up muphucka? It took you long enough," Twin said as he walked back towards the living room. Just then Soul Man and Revis came from each side of the door and rushed into the house, holding Twin at gun point.

"Where's the shit at, nigga? And the money?" They asked. Soul Man was high out of his mind, froze off of powder.

Twin couldn't believe what he was witnessing. Who the fuck had the audacity to rob him? They had to been scoping him, and waited on Red to come to the door to pull the jack move. His Mac-11 was in the Entertainment stand and his pistol was in the couch. There had to be a way to get to one of them.

"Nigga, where all the shit at?" The shorter assailant (Revis) asked.

Twin was shaken out of his thoughts by the assailant's emphatic question. "Ay man, listen…I'll tell you where it is as long as you don't fuck wit my family."

"Yeah, 'aight, nigga. Now, where?" Revis asked.

"Upstairs. In the closet in my room, in a Jordan shoebox in the back of the closet," Twin said. He was pissed at the fact that he was slipping like this. He should've had his pistol on him or in hand when he answered the door like he usually did. He thought about all of the times that he had a gun pointed at someone and all of the times that he used his gun. 90 some percent of the time! He realized that the assailant was bringing Stephanie down the steps at gun point and threw her on the couch.

"Tony, what's going on?" She asked Twin.

"Just be cool, baby. Just be cool. It's gon' be alright," Twin told her.

"Shut that bitch up! Tie her ass up and use that duck tape," Revis told Soul Man, who ripped the phone cord out of the wall and used it to tie her hands behind her back. And then he duck taped her mouth shut. "Watch they asses, I'll be back."

All Twin could think about was how could he get to one of the guns; because he had every intention on killing both of these cowards. But it seemed impossible with the tall nigga staring at him intently with a Beretta pointed directly at his face. Twin could see that the guy was scared. Damn, he needed a distraction. But one didn't come. The guy upstairs was coming down. The other guy looked towards the steps. "Could he do it?" He thought to himself.

Little Tone got up out of bed after he heard all of the commotion. He walked towards the window. When he looked out he saw a white man holding what looked to him like a rifle or a shotgun. He had seen plenty of guns in his 7 years, being his father's child. He looked back towards the hallway and listened for a minute. It seemed quiet. He figured that he had to be dreaming so he lay back down. In another minute he was once again sound asleep.

*

I tossed and turned in my sleep. I didn't know why. I knew that I hated jail, but this disturbance of my sleep seemed really deep for some reason. It seemed spiritual. I arose all of a sudden, looking around to see everyone asleep. It was weird because I kept hearing some sort of demonic howl or moan. The shit was creepy, like something I had never experienced before. The only thing that compared to this was when I was at my house one night, about 2 or 3 months ago, and it was past midnight...I was up late because I couldn't sleep but felt that I was hearing voices. Demonic voices! And when the girl who I had over at my house came down to check on me, her voice sounded demonic when she spoke; just as mine did when I spoke back. It was the weirdest thing that I had experienced up until now.

Suddenly, though, the sounds stopped. I lay back down, but although everyone was asleep, it seemed too quiet. Like the world itself was quiet. It nearly scared me to death. And I could feel that God was telling me something was wrong, and that there was a reason for all of this. There had to be! A minute later I was back asleep.

Twin had reacted on a slightly different idea than the one he originally had, which was to get to one of his guns, but there was no time for that. So he jumped Soul Man and went for the Beretta. But it quickly turned fatal. Twin knew that this was the end of the line, for him or the two assailants. Either he would go for the gun, take it away from Soul Man, and kill both of them and save his self, and his family. Or either they would win the tussle and most likely kill him. He lost the tussle. He never really got a good grip on the gun, and because of that Soul Man was able to push him back, where Revis shot him from about four steps up. The 38 slug hit Twin in the upper right chest, digging through him and coming out of his back left side. He fell down by the front door and immediately began to bleed to death.

The loud popping sound nearly scared Stephanie half to death. She tried her hardest to scream through the duck tape, but no sound came out. Instead, tears streamed down her face like a bad plumbing leak. She looked at Twin's limp body and then at their masked faces; studying them from their eyes, to their noses, and even their head shapes.

"Now turn over bitch!" Revis told Stephanie after he had kicked Twin a few times. He turned her over onto her face, with her knees on the floor and her upper body over the couch. She knew she was going to die, so she said her prayers. A few minutes passed by, and then she opened her eyes. It seemed quiet. They were gone. She got up to check on Twin and tried to untie herself as she did. The tie up was an amateur job; she got free in less than a minute. When she checked Twin's breathing it was really slowed, barely existent. She was in a dazed shock, as she stood kneeled over him and cried. And then it dawned on her to call the police; and an ambulance. She got the phone plugged back in the wall and then was able to call.

"Yes, hello! Yes, this is an emergency. My boyfriend's been shot. Please hurry!" Stephanie pleaded.

"Ma'am, you say that your boyfriend's been shot?" asked the dispatcher.

"Yes, please hurry up. He's still breathing. Hurry!"

"Okay, ma'am, what is your address and telephone number?"

"Bitch, just hurry up and send somebody!" Stephanie said, and then she hung up. She held on to Twin and rocked with him. She heard the steps creek and looked up to see Little Tone staring at them from the bottom of the steps.

"No baby. Go back upstairs. Please!" Stephanie told Little Tone. She saw the tears well up in his eyes and the shock in his little face. "Antonio, please go back upstairs!" She yelled.

*

I was nearly out of breath it seemed. But Twin was just ahead of me like usual. He was always a little bit faster than I was. We finally ran to a dead end, though. Where it seemed like from that point I was taken out of the scene and became a spectator. I looked down at the action taking place where I watched Twin get stomped and kicked repeatedly. My body jumped and jerked as the kicking took place. I felt like one of the evil Crimson Twins from G.I. Joe; when one would experience any pain the other would feel it, too. It was frustrating because while Twin got kicked and stomped, all I could do was watch. I could do nothing but watch! And then, it just stopped. It had to have been a nightmare. I opened my eyes and leaned forward. I saw the lights on, so it must have been close to breakfast time. "Wait a minute," I thought. I was hearing it again, the creepy, demonic howl and moan that I had heard a few hour earlier. I opened my eyes wider as I looked around the cell pod. It felt like I was all alone, even with the sleeping inmates inside the pod with me. I couldn't possibly go back to sleep. I sat up for the next hour trying to figure out these never before spiritual happenings. I knew it was a reason for it, and that's what scared me. I finally dozed off, missing breakfast and being woken up instinctively at about 8 or 9 o'clock, where I was lured to the phone. Everyone must have gone back to sleep, perhaps because it was a Saturday.

I picked up the phone and called Keysh. The weekend had came and Brantz still hadn't got me out yet. He had to file some sort of motion; I was still pissed off about being stuck in this shit hole. The collect proceedings went through and then I heard, "Babe…"

"Keysh, what's up? Why you sound like you do? And why you ain't sayin' nothin'?" I asked Keysh. She was still silent. "Keysh!"

"Huh? Babe, I gotta tell you somethin'. No, I think you better have your uncle tell you. You ain't watched the news or nothin' yet, have you? Well, hold on."

"What in the hell was going on?" I wondered. The news! I heard the line click and then I heard, "Hello. What's up, nephew? Yeah, man, hey… ya brother's dead, man. He got killed last night," Red said. I had to have still been dreaming. There was no way my muthaphuckin' brother was dead. Not Twin. Not Antonio Tomas Jones! No, it was just a bad dream. And I would be awake soon.

CHAPTER 37: The Demise

Dust was enraged. All he could think about was murdering someone's whole family. The laws would've given him life if they knew all of what his mind was thinking. He had scooped up his sister Angie's gangbanging boyfriend to roll around with him and investigate, and terrorize, anyone who he even thought may have had something to do with Twin getting murdered. They had no luck, though. There were currently no leads. Stephanie said that they had on masks, and that it was just two of them, one was tall and the other one was short. They took his cell phone, which was a minute phone, so the cops couldn't trace the number. The conclusion was that whoever came to rob him, had probably called first. And that's why they took the phone, to cover up who they were. Stephanie didn't know because she was asleep. Dust had talked to all of Twin's little homies and associates and none of them had seen or spoke with Twin in the last day or so before he passed. Stephanie vouched for that. This didn't guarantee anything but all of those guys worshipped and feared Twin. And Dust felt that he read people's characters just as good as I did.

The robbers only got about 5 or 6 ounces of crack, but they also found the 20 stacks that he had stashed upstairs. They left about 2 ounces of crack up in his room, but they never went to the basement where he had a quarter key of crack hidden in the washroom. Twin always copped his coke hard because he couldn't cook it. So here the police were having a field day with more than 10 ounces of crack, and a whole lot of questions; questions for Stephanie and anyone else who they knew who knew him. They came to me in the county jail trying to get me to answer some questions for them. I had been put in solitary confinement because I was ready to snap. I couldn't be around anyone. I couldn't watch the news.

I sat in my single man cell in a zone. I reminisced about so much, like about how Twin and I ran home at 1 o'clock in the a.m. after he shot it out with those Myrtle Av' niggas. I didn't even know that he had Pop's big hand cannon. It was the first time in a long time that I acknowledged Twin was my big brother; but he was. He gave the world hell out here, because we lived in a world of hell. Hell on earth! And he definitely gave those Myrtle niggas hell that night. I laughed to myself, thinking about how he crippled one with a bad, prosthetic hip for life, and murdered the shooter. The other one got away but, that's where it all started it seemed. It was no turning back for us after that. Here it was nine years later and my twin brother was dead.

I had intentions on calling him just a few nights ago after my mother told me that he said he had my back with anything I needed and that I should've called him before I called anyone else. But I didn't call. Of course I used that to make my self feel worse. I didn't believe in self inflicting pain, although I really felt like doing it inside of my isolated cell, but I would rather make someone else feel my pain; as soon as I got out.

*

The family was in an uproar. We had family members come up from Carolina, Georgia, and Florida. Even my people from up in Michigan came down. It was an issue with where everyone would stay and who got along with who…it was also an issue with the funeral arrangements. It was a given that I was the only one who could pay for everything, but I had been on suicide watch for the last 2 days, with no communication. I was told that I would be able to use the phone and receive a visit the next day, but not until then.

Red finally insisted that he would pay for some of the service but mom refused. And so did dad. They really didn't even care for him being there. P. and Nuts finally contacted Moms and took care of everything. They even told mom that I would be out by tomorrow because the lawyer finally got them to give me a bond; on sympathetic terms for my brother's death, and a deed to one of P.'s houses.

I got put back into a 12-man pod the day I was supposed to be released. Everything was signed and paid for before noon, so I was expected to be out by the evening time. The wake was 6-9 p.m. so I would make it to the showing of the body. But before I knew it, it was damn near 9 o'clock. I still hadn't got released yet! Everyone was yelling and hollering at the New Jersey Nets and Boston Celtics Eastern Conference playoff game on TV. Soon, it was over. And so was the chance of me getting out. The phones had just shut off and it was about to be lockdown soon. The fucking prison system truly did what they wanted to do. How in the fuck was I supposed to be released by nightfall and here I was spending another night in this hovel? I picked up the novel 'True to the Game' that I had got from my homeboy and read it until it put me to sleep.

"Jones! Let's go, you're out of here," said the Deputy.

I had no idea what time it was, but I knew it was early. It took nearly an hour for me to get out of there. With my release call I called Keysh, who came all the way down from Reynoldsburg in the pouring rain to get me. I walked over to the Certified gas station to get some gum and a newspaper while I waited. I had to get away from that stinking ass county.

Keysh pulled up a half an hour later driving my Suburban. It was already past 10 o'clock and the funeral was getting ready to start. I had on the Tommy Hilfiger outfit that I got arrested in that had sat in a knapsack for a few weeks getting wrinkled and mildewed. I needed a haircut and a shave. It was all bad the time frame that I was working with. I figured that I at least had enough time to get to the house and change. Keysh told me that my moms and everyone was waiting on me at my pop's crib before they went down to the funeral home.

We finally got to the house where I saw that the kids weren't ready and Keysh wasn't getting ready.

"Ay yo, why ain't you gettin' dressed?" I asked.

"I'm sorry babe, but I'm not going? I got into it wit Stephanie last night at the wake cause of the way she talked to mom. She was talking stupid to ya mom so I let her ass have it. I know she going through what she going through so…I just better not go," Keysh said.

"My Goodness," I thought. "Oh well." I wanted her and my kids there but I didn't have time to argue about it. I threw on a black tight fitted Versace shirt, some black slacks, and my black Versace loafers. I started to throw on a hat, but decided to just rock my un-groomed do and face. I kissed and hugged Keysh and the kids, and then I darted out of the house.

Ten minutes later I arrived around at Pop's house where everybody embraced me and badgered me about barely making it out and, not answering my phone. My older aunts were like that. But I never even turned my phone on when I got out. I called mom back from Keysh's phone when she picked me up, so I figured I would holler at everybody when I got to them.

We arrived down to the funeral home shortly after 12. Mom and

Micia were so broke up on the front row that they didn't want me out of their sight. Pops was in a quiet rage with all of his Club Brothers, and so was Dust. Everyone said that he hadn't said much to anyone since it all happened. I broke away from mom and Micia briefly by telling them that I had to go help greet a few people and speak with Dust. I hadn't spoken with him yet.

"Siz-o! What's up, dog? You hangin' in there?" said my Cousin Mike. He and P. stopped me on the way to go holler at Dust. I hugged and shook their hands. "Yeah, fam'. I gotta be. You know? Now M.P., I know you helped Pop construct the guest list, right? Only family and close associates?" I asked P.

"Yeah. Only me, Terique, Nuts, and Red are the only ones from the Commission; from the West Side Firm," P. said.

Red! I cringed at that name. Where the fuck was he, I wondered. "Alright, well I appreciate everything my nigga. I'ma go scream at Dust real quick."

"Ay, Siz-o. You know we gon' find out who did this…" P. said.

"Yeah, I know," I shot back.

When I made it over to Dust he gave me a pound and a hug, but didn't say anything. I saw that his eyes were blood shot red and his blank stare was intent. I told him that I was gonna go check the door and then I got up. When I got to the door, I saw Chocolate in the lobby. She nodded hey and then over towards the lobby chairs. It was Goldie. I walked over and gave Chocolate a hug and then I made my way over to Goldie, who I held for an eternity.

"Damn, baby! I'm so sorry," she said. I just nodded, and kissed her before I walked back inside. I scoped everyone who was there. It didn't appear to be anyone who didn't belong, so I relaxed a little. I went back up to the front row with mom, pops, and Micia, and then the ceremony began.

We rode over to the cemetery in stretched limos, where I was asked a series of questions by mom. As we got to the end of our discussion mom told me, "Now, I don't want you getting into anymore trouble behind this. You hear me?" Mom asked. But of course, I didn't.

"And you know I can't stand that 'Red'. He's a dirty bastard! He's gon' try to tell me that all this happened to you and ya brother cause y'all didn't listen to me and ya daddy when y'all was younger; or somethin' stupid. I told him to get the fuck out of my face, or I'd hurt him. I don't like him and I don't trust him," mom said.

"I know ma, I know. Don't worry about him," I told her.

We got my brother buried right next to my grandmamma. And then there was the get together at dad's house where it was plenty of food and shoulders to lean on. Keysh ended up coming through and she and Stephanie apologized to each other. After a few hours everyone parted ways. My cousin Mann and his girl, along with my cousin Junior and his girl, came to stay at my house for a couple of days until they headed back to Carolina. All that my cousin Mann kept saying to me was that he would come up with some of his country boys and barbeque fillet anyone who we pointed the finger at. I told him that his intentions were appreciated but it would get handled soon by my people. I just needed to know which direction to send them in.

*

Red saw Dust a week later over at Big Bird's place down the street from Dust's spot on Wilson Avenue where he told Dust what he had heard; which was that some local hood rats supposedly had heard about someone killing Twin. That was all that Dust needed to hear. He hopped in the car with his fat bitch and shot around to where the broad stayed at.

He walked into the building with a familiar feeling that he had been here before. And when he got to the door he realized that he had. It was Soul Man's bitch's apartment. He knocked, with the 9millimeter Ruger by his side. After the second knock there was an answer. The girl opened the door and asked, "Um, Jimmy, right? What you doin' here?"

"Bitch, I wanna know which one of you hoes was bumpin' ya gums about what happened to my nephew. Now who was it?" Dust asked.

"Uh, excuse you! Nigga I don't know shit about that," she said as she tried to shut the door. But Dust put his foot against the door. Two niggas walked towards the door. "Who the fuck is that, Michelle?" He asked.

"It's some nigga named Jimmy who know Soul Man. He askin' bout his nephew that got killed," she said.

"Oh yeah, Siz-o's twin?" He asked, trying to whisper.

But Dust heard him. And kicked the door open. "What you say, nigga?" Dust asked, raising his weapon. The two niggas tried to go for their guns, but Dust opened fire; hitting the chick in the chest first with the first shot. Her screaming stopped instantly. He aimed for the bigger guy first, hitting him with a throat and face shot. And then he quickly put two in the face of the shorter nigga, who got a shot off that went right over Dust's shoulder but missed. The whole building was quiet. Dust quickly checked his clip, not knowing if someone else would come out of the wood work. He had 6 shots left. He knew that he missed a few times, but it happened. Darting out of the building and into his girl's ride, he slid up out of the neighborhood headed to find me.

*

Soul Man walked into the Sun Star café on Main Street where he found Red sitting at a table in the back with Fancy: Born, Luther Vincent. A notorious homo prostitute! Luther excused himself to let Soul Man and Red talk.

"Ay man, do you know somebody just went over to 'Chelle's and killed her, Marquel, and Revis!?" Soul Man said to Red. "...in broad fuckin' daylight!"

"Oh yeah? Well, just chill. Here, sit down. You want a drink?" Red asked.

"Yeah man, get me a shot of Hen'."

Hearing this reminded Red that the walls would cave in soon; with him right in the middle of them if he didn't do something to cut the trail off from coming to him. He had got rid of Twin, not intentionally because the plan was not to kill him. That's why he tipped Dust off because he knew that Dust would go crazy and go do what he did. Red was rather upset at Revis and Soul Man for killing Twin. Regardless of the robbery, Twin was still his nephew. But these kinds of things can get out of control, and when you're dealing with drug addicts like Revis and Soul Man were, then the odds of that happening were extremely high. But he couldn't stop now. It was better just to roll in the direction that things were headed. Red felt that I would be gone soon, too, and out of his way. And soon, so would Dust. But for now, Soul Man was the next target. So Red played like he didn't know anything.

Red signaled for the bartender to retrieve a Hennessy and another Grey Goose.

"So listen, man…Don't be panickin'. Just be cool. Now, that bitch Michelle was runnin' off at the mouth the other night at the after hour and somebody took that shit back to the wrong people. So I'm tellin' you, just be cool," Red stressed to Soul Man.

"Yeah, but what if one of 'em talked before they died. We don't know!"

"Listen man, stop panickin'. Ay," Red nudged Soul Man's arm and said, "Nigga, I got somethin' that's gon' relax you for the night. Especially since you lost ya bitch, 'Chelle. I got two lil' young bitches from out West that's gon' meet us at the room. Come on, let's head over to the Capitol Motel and get a room. And then I'll call 'em. Oh, and I got some new Columbian flake for you, too. I'ma throw you a whole quarter for you and these hoes. They get froze, too. Let's go!" Red said, and then they got up to leave the bar.

20 minutes later they arrived at the motel where Red made Soul Man get the room in his name claiming, "I don't got my ID on me."

Soul Man didn't have a problem with it. They got inside of their room where Red insisted that Soul Man do a line before the girls arrived. Of course, there were no girls. Red made that up. Soul Man prepped his coke for a thick line to sniff, never aware that it contained rat poison and battery acid. He took a deep whiff, and then another. A few seconds later he began to shake, and then he quickly became paralyzed. He was truly frozen now. Red got up and quietly left out of the room.

*

"Nigga, I blasted all them muthaphuckas! The bitch, too! I don't think nobody knows shit either," Dust said. We were out back of my white boy Gonzo's crib. "And if they do then more than likely it was that fat ass Red's bitch ass. He the one who told me that the bitch was sayin' to people that she knew somethin' bout Tone getting' killed."

"Well, listen to this…Little Tone said that he looked out the window that night and saw a white man standing by the door holding a shotgun; a white man wit blonde hair. Now ain't that crazy?" I asked Dust. "All the evidence the police had and they don't know shit."

"Shit, maybe it was them bitches," Dust said half joking. "You say that's all they been tryin' to ask about ain't it, dope information? Askin' y'all who he got his dope from and shittin' on his name sayin' he was just a drug dealer and shit like that?"

"Yeah, them bitches tried to come at me in county for questioning. They want a muphucka to do they job for 'em. Oh, guess what the latest is…Red sayin' that he heard that P., of all people, had somebody go out there and kill bruh to send a message to me not to snitch; while I was in county lock-up. You believe this guy!?"

"I don't know dog, I don't trust P. But if I found out that it's true then, boss or no boss, he will get it," Dust vowed. I felt the same way. Not that I believed my Ace had any doing in my brother's death, but 'anyone' who did, could and would get it.

"I want that fucking cowboy bastard locked away for life! I'm gonna put an arrest warrant out for his ass right now!" Detective Walton said.

"Naw, naw, listen Bo, just chill. Not yet," Red stressed to Detective Walton.

"Well, why not? Your little bro's a menace, man!" He said with his radio ready and in hand.

"Listen to me, we got a live witness. Yeah, Marquel Conley, he just got out of surgery yesterday. He got shot in the throat and in the jaw. He made it, though. Now, they say he may not ever be able to talk, and that he might have some brain damage but he will be able to function soon enough. Plus, I need my little brother for one more thing before you send him away. Trust me."

"Alright, Red Man. You better be right," Walton said, putting his radio away.

*

I had been up at the clothing store since the afternoon politicking with P. about every topic we could think of. This was my Ace, and we both knew that I was about to go away for some time, most likely ten years or more. Brantz had told me that they were trying to indict me on an M.D.O. charge, a Major Drug Offender!

P. told me how ridiculous it sounded what Red was saying that he heard, but he was always saying and supposedly hearing ridiculous things; although this was a very serious thing that he had said. I read people, and I could feel that P. had nothing to do with Twin getting killed. It wasn't P.'s style. I knew how he operated, and how he had things done. Most of the time, either I done them or knew how they were being done, and who was doing it. The thing that happened to Twin was an amateur job, not a professional one. Red was a character, which most people felt just shot off at the mouth like a broad, but often times Red had an angle. I was still weary about him, and suspected a lot of deceit in his character. I thought about how he should have been watched closer, and kept more distant from our thing. Now that he was in, it was rather difficult to restrict him; which made me think to ask P., "Ay dog, let me ask you, what made you pick Red to sit in my seat at the top of the Firm wit you and Nuts?"

"Well, half of it was sincere judgment, cause the nigga got some solid qualities…but the other half of it was cause I was salty at you for even steppin' down. And I knew it would aggravate you and Nuts. So it was like I could make a solid decision and in a way, make it get to y'all that I did it. See, I can control Red when he get all spaced out. You know, when he be buggin'?"

"Yeah, but…I know he's my uncle, but I've never had a good feeling about dude. He's just too slimy and sleezy. I've seen the nigga in action, first hand. You know he's always played that role wit me like he'd never fuck me over like he tries to do everybody else, but what makes me any different? That nigga's a spiteful, envious hater. He just doesn't do certain shit right out to certain people, me being one of 'em, because he knows better. But dude is a slime bucket."

"Yeah, he tried to get at two of my baby's moms behind my back."

"You see, so why would you want a nigga like that in our thing? As deep as he's gotten in?" I asked.

"Man, I ain't sweatin' that shit. Fuck them bitches! But hey, guess who we've heard orchestrated Tone gettin' killed? We gon' handle it, though, so be cool. I got an ax crew comin' from Brazil in a few days that's gon' fillet this muthaphuckin' piece-of-shit, pig!"

"Pig! Who's that?"

"Ay, is the dickhead detective on yo' case, that Walton muthaphucka! He's as dirty as a shit eatin' fly."

My blood began to boil, flame boil! I couldn't control my rage. P. watched my facial expression and then he said, "Siz-o, they gon' chop-suey his ass. Don't even worry about it."

"Yeah," was all I said, staring straight ahead. I gave P. a pound and a hug and then I got in my truck and bounced.

I had spent the rest of the day with Goldie. It was my daughter Anijah's birthday tomorrow; just as it was my other daughter Simone's the day before. Goldie and I had took Anijah to the park and then to AppleBee's where we had a drink. I had begun to get a summer cold of some sort, perhaps from swimming a few days ago at the King's Island Beach all the way into the evening time. So Goldie insisted that she make me a spicy stir-fry dish once we got to her place. We stopped at the store first for a few things, including some condoms. We couldn't be making anymore little Anijahs. We got home and I immediately had a stiff drink of Remy. I rubbed off on Goldie, just as I had on all of my other females, so she kept a few bottles at her crib.

My food finally got done and I smashed it. It was the bomb! Goldie and I headed upstairs to kick back and watch a movie. A new release called Ocean's 11. She put Anijah to bed and got changed into a pink 2-piece pajama set; she called it. It was a thin top with spaghetti straps and it showed her flawless stomach. The bottoms were skin tight booty shorts. I loved it!

We both downed another shot of Remy before we lay down. It was quiet for a long while, and then Goldie finally spoke, "So what's been up, babe? What's been up with you and Keysh?" She asked sarcastically. Because it wasn't like she really cared.

"Yo, I'm not on that right now, boo. I got a lot of shit on my mind, you know?"

"I know, baby. I'm sorry. Are they gonna send you to jail?"

"At some point, I'm sure they are."

"Oh my God! Anijah ain't gon' have no fuckin' daddy for what... some years?"

I took a deep breath and said, "what do you want me to say Kimishah?"

She quietly began to cry. I held her tight. And then I began to kiss her; all over. She moaned and began to kiss me back. I slid down and removed her bottoms, where I began munching on her sweet, wet pussy. After my ten minute meal she was starving for my entrance. I sexed her slow and hard for nearly half of the night. It was like heaven. She was heaven! But damn, Keysh made everything so complicated. Goldie was wifey material. And I knew that I needed her on my team; in general and for this stretch that I was about to do. We sat up having some heavy pillow talk until about 5 in the morning. We talked about kids, we talked about the complexity of Keysh, we talked about the future, including the near future of going to King's Island or Cedar Point in the next few days. I finally drifted off; right after Goldie did, prior to sunrise. I held her tight as she lay on my chest with her legs crossed in between mine. We slept in peaceful harmony.

*

Staring at this silly joker, I wondered how many times he was going to kill me. This re-occurring nightmare never changed. I watched his insane eyes as he smiled psychotically with his gun pointed at my face. It always seemed so easy to go for the gun but when I did, pow! Right in the neck; every time! It burned really bad, I recalled, just like when I got shot nearly ten years ago. Just as I began to fall, I sprung up off of the pillow. I looked around the bedroom, and then over at Goldie, who was sleeping as peaceful as an angel. I heard a buzzing noise towards where my pants were. I got up to grab them and retrieve my phone, and then go take a morning piss.

I dialed Dust's number back after I saw that he had called 5 times. "Yeah, what's up?" I asked.

"Ay, I hollered at fat ass Red this mornin' at the Wilson corner market and you ain't gon' believe what he told me. When you comin' out for the day?" He asked, speaking in a low toned voice.

"Uh...probably in the next hour or two. I'll call you when I get out by your way, alright." I told Dust, and then I walked back into the bedroom where Goldie was sitting up in the bed and asked me, "Babe, you want some tea or some breakfast?"

"Nah, I'm cool, boo."

I dialed Red's number to see what he had heard. "What's up Siz?" He answered.

"Shit, chillin'. What's the word? What Dust talkin' bout?" I asked.

"Aw, man...where you at? Can you come by my spot on Bulen?"

"Yeah. Here in about an hour."

"Alright. You ain't hollered at P. yet, have you?"

"No. Huh-uh."

"Okay, that's cool. Just come on through," Red said, and then we both ended the call.

"Ay baby," I yelled down to Goldie. "Go ahead and make me some green tea."

"Okay," she yelled back.

*

I walked into Red's place where I saw a few goons sitting around; waiting to be told what to do, I guess. "What's up, Siz-o?" They said in unison.

I nodded back and then said, "where Red at?"

"He ran around the corner real quick. He said he'll be right back," said the goon.

"Alright then, I'ma wait outside."

I sat in my truck for about ten minutes before Red finally pulled up. He hopped in with me. "Siz, what's up, nephew? Ay, the word is that the cop on yo' case is the one behind ya brotha getting' killed. A Detective Wilson, or Walton, or somethin'? They say he a dirty muthaphucka; got his hands in all kinds of shit out here," Red said.

"Oh yeah! That piece of shit! How you hear that?"

"We heard it from P.'s people from downtown," Red lied. He was the source who told P.

"Well, he a dead pig, then."

"Yeah, and listen to this, I've been havin' dude watched for damn near a week now. He goes over to this spot on Ohio everyday at about 4 o'clock. And he drives a green Nissan. We think it's where his partners that he got snitchin' and workin' for him operate or somethin'. I know P. got the contract on him, and them niggas in comin', but I figured I'd tell you, just like I told Dust. Cause if a muthaphucka killed my brother, either one of 'em, I'd be at that nigga. So...what you wanna do?"

"I'll tell you what I'ma do. I'ma call you in 2 hours, that's about an hour before 4. You gon' be ready, nigga? You down?"

"Fa sho' nephew. Whatever you got in mind."

I went and got with Dust to fill him in and then to go and make the proper preparations for Detective Walton's demise. We had a blue Econoline van with the tinted windows and we had a black one that we kept in a garage for these kinds of situations. Well, not to go and kill a cop, but to portray to be cops or S.W.A.T. if it was what a job called for. We were going to put on all black with phony S.W.A.T. tags on our backs and kick in the fucking door of this particular residence. Red was having the place watched to see who came and who went, particularly Detective Walton. I went to where I had a small arsenal of weapons stashed at. I grabbed a Calico and two AR-15s, plus a few Glock pistols. If this was my demise then I would be going out spilling somebody's blood for my brother's. And I had a dying thirst for Detective Walton's blood.

Dust and I pulled into the alley next to a garage two houses down from Walton's spot. Red had just told us that he was there, according to his goon. And the green Nissan was parked on the street. But now Red wasn't answering his phone. He was supposed to meet us in the alley to hop inside the van and get suited up to go in the house. We waited for five minutes and then we said 'fuck it'! We were dressed down in all black, wearing vests and Hi-Tec boots. We put on our masks and cocked our assault weapons. I handed Dust a Glock and two clips, and then I said, "Yo dog, if we don't make it up out of here for some reason, then…"

He cut me off and said, "Nigga, I ain't hearin' none of that bullshit. We gon' go in here and kill all of these muthaphuckas. Whoever in here! You know I don't leave no witnesses. We'll drive over to the old abandoned factory by Williams Road, as planned, and then torch the van; and the clothes and the guns. Aight!?"

"Yeah," I said hesitantly. But then I thought about the fact of why I was here. This pig muthaphucker killed my brother. Or at least he was the white man outside the door. He had to be. Or at least he was the one who had it all done. No wonder the cops acted like they didn't know anything. I thought about Keysh and my kids. And the fact that this was not how P. had ordered it. But he would have to understand. He could pay them out of my money. I didn't care. We tried Red back one more time, but there was still no answer. I couldn't wait to hear what his excuse was going to be for this. Fuck it, though. "You ready, fam? Let's go!" I said, and pushed open the back doors. This was going to be one fourth of July to remember.

Red sat down the street in his Lexus near the Wasserstrom parking lot. Purposely not answering us, and just waiting for the script to unfold. He had just sent his white boy Jay over to the house on Ohio to take Detective Walton his weekly cut of what Red earned. Yes, Walton was putting a taxing on Red. He had to, he felt, since he was taking the risk of allowing Red to freely conduct illegal business. The Federal Agent Nichols had a huge hard on for the Commission so he was always monitoring Walton's supervision of Red's activities inside of the Firm and the Commission. I was a few inches taller and about thirty pounds heavier than I was a little over three years ago when he left. The pressure was enormous.

However, Red's white boy Jay was the one actually outside watching the door when Twin's murder took place. He had no idea then, that Red was an informer. But now Red had him blackmailed, just between the two of them, because Walton had no idea about the robbery/homicide. Red just made Jay think that he did. So he made Jay go to work for him and Walton. Red was supposed to take Walton his cut, but Walton didn't think anything of it because Jay was like Red's right hand informer now. And so Jay had no idea what was about to happen.

"Where in the hell's the Red Man at, dog?" Walton asked Jay as he locked the door behind him.

"He had to take his baby's mom to the hospital so he sent me. I got this bread for you, though, dog," said Jay, trying his hardest to sound cool; just as Walton did.

"Man, he done had me here waitin'. I've been shootin' the shit wit Sid here for damn near an hour." Sid was the old Jewish home owner who was under Walton's guise for a few years now. Walton busted him for a few ounces of heroin and agreed to wipe his slate clean if he gave his full cooperation. He was just a 56 year old addict who happened to score a few ounces after he got his income tax check. Walton was on to the dealers who Sid bought from and followed him after he copped and pulled him over for no brake light. However, he kept the heroin, giving Sid just a few grams for usage.

"It hasn't been an hour," Sid smiled at Jay and said.

"My fault, Bo! My fault!" said Jay.

"Yeah, well hand me that envelope and…"

Bam! Walton was cut off by the back door being kicked in. He quickly reached for his Smith & Wesson. A voice from the kitchen yelled, "Police, everybody get the fuck down! We got a search warrant."

"Damn, a search warrant!" Bo thought to himself.

Boom! Now it was the front door. "Police! Everybody freeze!" I yelled, as I entered the house with the AR-15 aimed at Detective Walton. He didn't want to, but he surrendered his weapon. Dust sensed the calmness, and came around the corner. He asked Walton, "How many? Who else is in the house?"

"Nobody. Nobody!" He yelled. I nodded to Dust to go check the upstairs while I held the three of them at gun point. He quickly came back down and nodded back to say that the upstairs was clear. I signaled for everyone to sit on the couch. Once they did, Dust immediately shot Jay and Sid in the forehead. They were out of the picture. Detective Walton was petrified when he saw this. He knew now that it wasn't any kind of police agency that he knew. And where was the rest of the cavalry? Just two guys?!

"Detective Walton, you remember me. And I know you remember my twin brother, right? Antonio Jones?" I asked as I raised my mask up.

"Oh shit, Siz-o Jones! What the fuck is this? And what about your brother?" he asked.

"No time for a story, 'Bo'? I just wanted you to look me in my eyes before you died. This is for Twin, bitch!" I said before pulling the trigger back on the assault rifle. About 10-12 shots quickly jumped into Detective Walton; spraying him from his guts up to his face. He died instantly. I looked at his dead body for what seemed like an eternity. And then Dust grabbed me by the arm and said, "Let's go, boy."

We ran out and jumped up in the van and then sped off; heading for the dump sight to get rid of all the evidence. We rode in silence, in anticipation to get it done with. I felt redemption just as I could feel that Dust did. It surprised me that the maniac didn't squeeze the trigger, too. Twin was his Ace. But I guess he figured that he would let me get the vengeance for the both of us. We made it to the warehouse and blew the van and all of the evidence with a quiet, plastic explosive that was provided to me by my war vet, Mac. We got into the old SUV that would be destroyed by morning at McKinley's scrap yard. I was full off of redemption, but empty on emotion. I felt totally ruthless.

*

I didn't attend any of the last two meetings, partially because I wasn't a top member of our Firm anymore, and second, I was out on bond for a drug case, which sat me out of attending any activities in any meetings. It was against the rules. P. wanted to speak to me immediately after the meeting, so I had Goldie drop me off at the Roadhouse where I sat outside in the gazebo until they were done. I had been 'sent for'. I had a good idea what for. But I still had to wait and have P. bring it up.

"Come on, Siz-o! What's up?" P. asked he asked as he put his hand on my shoulder. "You alright?"

"I'm cool. I'm cool. Yeah, I'm good," I said. We hopped in his Crown Victoria and drove away from the estate. As we rode he asked me did I see the news yesterday. "...the news about dude gettin' killed? The detective on ya case?"

"Yeah," I said. There was no need to bullshit wit the boss. "I saw it. You know I saw it."

He nodded, knowing that I was apart of it. "So you know I already paid them guys to come up here. 50 stacks!"

"Yeah, dog. You can take it out of my money. I woulda told you ahead of time, but it was just so sudden. I was in a fucked up mind frame; zoned the fuck out."

P. nodded again, understandingly. "That was slick how y'all done it, though; like that one time in the summer of '97. But they don't got shit, though. They been investigatin' a lot of the shit that he was tied into, too. But they are buggin' about the impersonations of their own. You feel me?!"

I nodded yes. But I was so numb that I couldn't really feel anything. P. told me that everything was cool, and not to worry about anything. Just to lay low and spend time with my family. The Commission was strong and in my corner. I was still one of the most respected members of the organization under the circumstances. I felt reassured after we had our talk. P. dropped me off over Goldie's sister house off of Morse Road. Keysh and Heady were pretty upset with me lately. Since my arrest, I had been spending most of my free time (in freedom) with Goldie. I realized that she was the one that I really wanted to be with. But I knew that it was too late.

*

"Okay, babe, my mom said that all the paperwork is done for her to co-sign on the house for us. You about ready?" Keysh asked, yelling up the steps at me.

"Yep, give me bout 2 minutes to put my shirt on and my Timbs," I yelled back. Keysh and I were about to go look at the new house in Whitehall that I was putting her and the kids in. It was time for a change; we had lived in Reynoldsburg for nearly three years. I came down the steps and told Keysh to head for the door with the kids so we could lock up and leave.

"Come on, buddy. You ready to go see ya new house?" I asked my son. He just looked up at me with that bright smile and nodded yes. He was such a charming little guy. Keysh's stomach was showing all five of her pregnant months. I had nearly forgotten she was pregnant with everything that had been going on. I had been in a zone. But I felt good being with my family. It was one of the best feelings in the world. As I walked down the driveway to the truck, holding my daughter's hand, men in all black with guns came out from everywhere.

"Freeze! Put your fucking hands up! You're under arrest. Get down on the ground, now!" An angry sounding man said.

I let go of my daughter's hand and put my hands in the air. After they yelled for me to get down on the ground two or three more times I complied. I was so fucking embarrassed that my kids had to see this. I scowled hard and then I yelled back, "What the fuck for?"

"You're under arrest for the murders of Officer Steven Walton, as well as a Sidney Stern, and Jason Davis. Now get up, let's go!" The dickhead said as he got me up off of the ground after he cuffed me.

Keysh was crying and going off. Cursing and screaming at all of them. It hurt so bad for my son and daughter to see this happen. I stared at them as the laws took me away to their unmarked police car. They were terrified! My daughter's face was streaming with tears as she tried to climb Keysh like a jungle gym, determine for her to pick her up. My son stared at it all with a quiet rage in his eyes. Those memories would stay stuck in my head for many years.

I rode down to the precinct already thinking of the future and how many years that these vultures were about to get out of me. And would I ever see the light of day? I had to harden my mind up, though, because it was getting ready to get real. I had to be sharp. I would listen to all of what they said, but I wouldn't say anything. Within 24 hours I would see my lawyer. How in the fuck did these bastards even get wind of my involvement was the question. I swear I wished that I had an AR-15 in hand when those bitches blew down on me; I would've shot it out with them. I know my kids were there, but that's how I was feeling these days. I was on the edge. I wondered had they caught Dust yet. Who the fuck ratted us out?!

Dust didn't have an address, just a phony P.O. Box. My address was not in Reynoldsburg with Keysh though, and they still found me. But the fucking laws were resourceful. Dust got wind that they were looking for him, he didn't quite know for what, he had done a number of things lately, but he had moved around a lot in the last few days since he found out that they were after him. Hew knew that it was bad, and when he found out that they had me, he made his mind up. He was strapped with a 30 shot Ruger and the other un-used AR-15 that we used in Walton's murder. He was moving real slick like with his big white girl. She had a tinted up ride and a father who was a terrorist like cop. He didn't like Dust at all, but as far as he knew his daughter was no longer involved with Dust. Dust vowed to kill his crack head sister Kim and his crack head brother Reece because they both had given the police information about his whereabouts; mainly for the crime stoppers money and also because he wouldn't give them any crack to stay hush-hush. That was family for you, though.

CHAPTER 38: The Departing

"So you're telling me that these clown ass cops got an anonymous tip? That's how they were able to get a warrant to arrest us?" I asked Brantz.

"Yeah. And that's great news unless; whoever tipped them off knows more that what they should. Now only you know that. But the cops are saying that the tip they got wasn't your names, but information that led them to your names. That sounds kinda funny but it could be true. What do you think?" Brantz asked.

"I don't know, man. But they gotta have somethin' more solid than that, right? You talk to P. yet?"

"Yes, I have; but probably not in the details that you may be thinking. And you're right; they are going to have something more than what they have now. And they'll have to provide it to me very soon or else the Judge is going to drop the charges. Now, some not so great news is that your indictments came in this morning for your drug case and they are indicting you on an M.D.O. spec. which you know carries a mandatory 10 years if you're convicted in trial. So we have that to fight. But from what I looked at we have a strong case with that. And we may be able to get a suppression order for the dope the found in the house and charged you and Hedricka with. I'm gonna have to look at the evidence again. So..."

"Brantz, listen to me. You tell P. to find whoever this is who's leaked this information. That's the only assurance that my uncle and I have. I ain't goin' to trial wit the chance of them muthaphuckas comin' out at the last minute with some fuckin' star witness. You know? This is my fuckin' life we talkin' bout here!"

"I know Siz-o, I know. I'm gonna get right on it, buddy. Don't...well; try not to worry too much. I'll talk to Keysha again and tell her not to worry too much either. I'll tell ya what...I'm going to file a motion for a fast and speedy trial, which is 90 days max, and ask that the prosecution provide some solid evidence within a week, or else I'm suggesting to the Judge to throw this case out by the first of August. And believe me; Judge Connelly will not allow these charges to stand as they are. I got a pretty good relationship with him. His daughter's married to my cousin Tom. We all play golf together. So just hang tight man, I'll see you in a few days." Brantz shook my hand as we stood up and walked out of the visiting room together.

*

P. was pissed. He didn't like the idea of any leakage in 'our thing'. He was eager for Brantz to obtain the evidence that the police had to arrest us for the triple homicide. We were very thorough and rather professional. P. had seen my work for years, and knew how the whole hit was set up. The police had just caught Dust. They kicked in the door of a hotel that he was staying in at 6 in the morning. He had no chance to reach for his gun; especially not the rifle. Lucky for him it was in his girl's trunk. He swore, though, that Red had to be the one to tip the police. It was the first word he sent around to my cell pod once he made it to the fifth floor. And, for me to send him some tunas and party mix around to his pod. Everyone was thrown by his accusation at first, but then it began to make sense. Red had just gone down to Florida about a week ago for a quick, much needed vacation, he said. But he was only supposed to be gone for 5 days. It had been 10! No one had heard from him. This clearly concerned P. I myself didn't want to believe it. But it was the only scenario that made sense.

The confirmed word was out…that since Red was the only one who knew about the murders, and was supposed to have been involved in them, and had gone AWOL, he was indeed the leak. So now Brantz knew that the prosecution had a weak case. We were set to go to trial by October. The prosecution knew that they had no case, but they were praying for any little thing to shake for them. First they tried the 'roll over on your partner' method, trying to get Dust and I to admit to it and just get natural life, while the other got a death sentence. And then, when they quickly saw that it was a no go, they tried to press us for an alibi. Mine was solid; I had spent the day with Goldie for my daughter's birthday and had stayed all night with her. Her and her neighbor had signed an affidavit saying so, and saying that my truck was parked outside of her house all day and all night. P. had paid the AppleBee's waitress and hostess to swear to the court, and sign an affidavit as well, saying that I was at the restaurant with Goldie and my daughter from 4 to roughly 5:30 on the evening of the murders. And the prosecution had no physical evidence linking us to the crime.

Dust knew that Red's mouth was the slow leak now, without a question. Dust was indicted on the two murders of Michelle Robinson and Revis Moore. And also for the attempted murder of Marquel Conley; who couldn't be competent enough to identify Dust or speak about anything. The gunshot to his throat crushed his windpipe permanently and the one to his face had him in a vegetated state. So Brantz said that case was beatable, as well. All they had was a word-of-mouth tip. And the accusation that Dust had got the word that Revis Moore was one of the gun men in Twin's murder, so he retaliated. That was their motive.

Our trial was in 2 days. I sat in the visiting room with Brantz as he shuffled through some paperwork. I felt rather numb. This trial was going to decide the rest of my life. I felt confident in a way, but unknowing as well. Brantz told me that on my drug case he never filed the suppression motion because the prosecution was willing to cut me a deal for a 6 year plea bargain, which was supposedly fair since they had me on the sale, the ounce possession, the guns/gun spec., and the school zone spec. if I agreed to the 6, then Heady would only get a year for her trafficking charge. I told him to get it to 5 years and I would plea to it.

Brantz reached into his pocket a pulled out a very tiny cell phone and handed it to me. "Here," Brantz said. "I gave the Deputy a hundred bucks. He knows. It's fine, go ahead."

I called Keysh and spoke to both of the kids for a few minutes, as we said a prayer together before my trial in 2 days. I told Keysh to call and tell my mama that I said hi, and I love her. She told me that everyone was praying and that they would all be in court for my trial. After that I called P. We chopped it for nearly ten minutes. He told me that business was smooth and everything was going well; our legal and illegal business. They still hadn't found Red yet. I was tripped out about how he said that they had heard that Red supposedly got plastic surgery and had grew dreadlocks. All of it was supposedly, though. He also told me how Red had been in his ear right after I got arrested about how he heard that I was talking to the cops and giving cooperation. P. told me that he just blew it off because he knew better. And that he just figured it was Red enviously hatin'. But he should have taken it more seriously. I vowed to myself that if it was ever a possibility, if he could last as long as I was in jail, then I would kill my uncle Red. And where ever he was at, he knew it, too. But I doubted that he would last through my first year. However, we concluded the call with P. wishing me luck and saying that he would see me at the trial. Brantz and I went over my entire case, both of them, and then we concluded our final visit before trial.

*

"Everyone please rise for the Honorable Judge Connelly," said the Bailiff.

"You may be seated," said the old Irish Judge after he walked in and got seated in his chair.

Dust and I were dressed in exquisite suits. I wore a grey pin-striped suit and vest, with a black dress shirt under it and a black cloth rag in my breast pocket. Dust wore a brown Versace suit with a thin, cream V-neck sweater. He even got his afro shaped up and tapered. We looked out into the courtroom and saw Mom, Micia, Pops, P., Nuts, and Keysh. My kids were, by no means, allowed to be present. I looked back for a double take and on the other side of where every one of our other people sat, I saw Goldie. Her adorably chubby cheeks were red and so were her eyes. I could tell that she had been crying all morning and probably all night.

Our trial was televised, I guess since a cop was killed and because it was a triple homicide; on top of Dust's separate double homicide trial. But the courts had decided that Dust's double homicide case would be tried a week after this trial in a separate court in front of Judge Fais, who was something like a terrorist.

The trial finally began. I thought of all of the movies that I had seen where trials took place. I thought that they seemed scary on TV; being on trial for your life was something ominous. The courtroom felt dark. And all of the opposition seemed like demons and devils, out to damn you forever. It made you really want to reach out for God. But did we deserve mercy I wondered. A question that I've asked myself for many years now was 'Will God forgive us for all that we've done'? All of my associates and affiliates that I've ever asked said 'no'! And their 'NOs' rang in my head repeatedly.

The trial lasted for only 3 days. Throughout it I kept hearing Brantz tell my numb, seemingly blank mind, that we were in good shape. And that it would be impossible to convict us on what they had. He also kept saying that he couldn't believe that they actually went through with the trial. He still couldn't even understand how they ever got an indictment. "They must have a star witness or a key piece of evidence or something." And then he would say, "But they can't because they have to give me everything that they have." I was ready to strangle him. It kept making me feel like Red was going to walk out into the courtroom any day now to testify. P. assured me that wouldn't happen but, they still hadn't found and terminated him. Tomorrow was the day, though. The verdict!

Mom, Pops, Micia, and Keysh all came to visit me the night before my trial verdict. They kind of all took turns in the narrow booth. Plus the visit was usually so short. But most of the time they would give me at least a half an hour. Keysh told me that she was with me no matter what, and of course, that she was praying for me. Micia told me to keep my head up and said what mom and everyone else was saying, which was that Brantz said that it was looking good for Dust and me. Pop told me that he was hoping for the best and then he whispered to me that he hoped they hurried up and found and killed the cockroach, Red. I assuredly agreed with him. Mom stepped into the booth last. She sat quietly with her eyes closed as she prayed in front of me for nearly 3 minutes. And then she spoke, "Your brother's watching over you, and so is God. You're gonna get through this. You gon' get through it! I just know it, you got to. I don't know what I'll do if you don't," she broke down crying and nearly fell as Pop caught her. Right then the Deputy called my name, ending the visit. I couldn't stand seeing my mama go through that. I said bye and walked out of the visitor's booth. They all waived back and said, "We love you! See you tomorrow." The Deputy walked me back to my cell pod. He was one of the few cool Deputies. Farrell was his name. "So you got the big day tomorrow, huh?" He asked.

"Yeah, live or die!" I said.

I could tell he wanted to ask me if I really did it; if I really murdered Detective Walton and the other two men. But of course, he didn't, nor could he. He had caught a lot of static from the other Deputies for showing me special treatment throughout my stay in county. He was half Italian and half Irish. So was I. Well, half black, 3/8 Italian, and ¼ Irish. He told me the funniest joke that I had ever heard about the subject of being both Irish and Italian, although he didn't mean to tell it as a joke. But he said that by being both Irish and Italian he was always fighting with himself. I always reminded him of it when I saw him.

I lay in my bunk that night in extremely deep thought. I thought about off the wall stuff like was Twin in Heaven or Hell, like mom talked about, and was there really even a Heaven and a Hell. I felt really bad about how all of this was affecting my kids. It was a trying time in my life; a real live trial and a true tribulation. But it was what it was. And it was like P. and I always talked about, I knew just who I was and what I did for a living. So I would have to accept what consequences came with being who I was. No one else was going to walk in my shoes for me. And if this was going to be my fate for avenging Twin, then so be it. Just as long as my uncle Red met his maker before it was all said and done with. I finally dozed off by the time it was 4 o'clock count.

All of the days of deliberating, cross-examining, and proof of evidence by both sides were over. Today was the day. The verdict! I said a silent prayer in the small room that I got changed in. I let the Deputy know that I was ready and he escorted me to the courtroom. I walked in and sat beside Dust and Brantz. All I could think of was how I wanted to kill Red, with whatever the verdict was. Because there was no way that I was ever supposed to be charged or even confronted about my work. We all worked so hard and got linked to too many of the right connections to stay safe for something like this to happen. But when you allow weak links in your circle then this was what happened. Uncle or no Uncle I knew that Red wasn't cut out for our thing. I could read that he was not solid and loyal. P. made the bad call ultimately on choosing this guy to get involved in our world. My thoughts were interrupted by the Bailiff's words, "All rise!"

I stood up and then I briefly looked back into the courtroom to see all of my friends, family, and associates one more time before it all began. I took a quick look at Dust and Brantz and gave a firm nod of confidence and hope.

"We are gathered here today to hear the verdicts in this case. Has the jury reached a verdict?" Judge Connelly said.

"Yes we have Your Honor," said the red haired woman in a tight blue dress. The Bailiff grabbed something from her and handed it to the Judge. She went on to read the verdict, after the Judge Okayed it. "We the jury, find Sizalino Jerele Jones Not Guilty for First Degree Murder in the murders of Steven Walton, Jason Davis, and Sidney Stern."

I felt the entire Courthouse Building lifted from off of my chest. I put my cuffed hands on Dust's shoulder in an effort to hug him. He presented a Kool-Aid smile but it was an incomplete one. The courtroom erupted; mostly for joy from all of my people. But some of it was from the victim's families, who knew that the State had a weak case in the first place. The Judge pounded his gavel, "Order! Order in my court!" When it quickly quieted down, he said, "Alright, now can the jury please read the verdict for the other defendant, Mr. Dawson?"

"Yes Your Honor. We the jury, also find James Neal Dawson Not Guilty for First Degree Murder in the murders of Steven Walton, Jason Davis, and Sidney Stern," the woman read.

The courtroom went into frenzy. It felt like the O.J. Simpson verdict. Now Dust went all the way crazy. He jumped towards me with body bumps and shoulder pounds, as he did the same with Brantz. We both shook Brantz hand repeatedly. He smiled as we thanked him and said, "Yeah, it's too bad I can't take you guys out for drinks yet." We both agreed, but were still happy as children in a toy store.

The prosecutor was disappointed, but he knew that what they had was shaky. There was just so much pressure on the State, though, to try and get a conviction once there was a finger pointed at us that they had to try as hard as they could and use what little they had to try and convict us. Thank God it wasn't enough. Where in the hell was Red? There was someone else sitting in the courtroom who was more upset with the verdict than the State was; the Government. Agent Nichols! He was Red's new pimp. And Red was his bitch. Red had got with Agent Nichols behind Walton's back. Nichols found out about Red when he got involved with overseeing Walton's investigation of us, The Firm/Commission. Nichols and the F.B.I. were hiding and protecting Red better than the Bin Laden cat. In the last 2 months Red had given Nichols all of what he had on the Commission, in return for immunity and the right to sell keys of coke, anywhere else in the United States; for the F.B.I., of course, and under a totally different identity as well. Nichols smirked, and then got up to walk out of the courtroom.

*

A week later I got sentenced to 6 years mandatory for my drug crimes. It was the best deal they would give me without 'cooperation', they said. It was take 6 years or go to trial and get 11-20 if I lost. Heady got sentenced the day after me, getting just 2 years because of my plea bargain. Dust, unfortunately got sentenced to 18 to life for the two murders of Revis Moore and Michelle Robinson, and the attempted murder of Marquel Conley. The police had Conley, fresh out of his vegetation stage, point Dust out in a three man line up that they showed him off of a printed paper with their pictures on it. That was how they convicted Dust. I was already on the sentencing floor when I heard the terrible news. I called and talked to P. after I heard it. I had 6 to do, but I really felt bad for my rappy and uncle, Dust. P. had his baby mama bring me down some whites and magazines, and drop a thousand on my books. He told me that he was gon' hold me and my family down while I was gone and hold my cheese for me, too. He had over a hundred grand of mine. I had no where to put it; plus he was my Ace. A.K.A. the man! I had money wit my sister and wit Keysh, and I also had some money floatin' around in the streets, so it was all good. I told P. to have Micia drop 500 or so on Dust's books, too. He was gonna need it. And need more on down the line.

That night, once things wound down and I read some of the VIBE magazine, I lay in my bunk thinking about how these next 5 ½ years were going to affect me and my family. I already missed them…all of them. And I missed Twin. I still couldn't believe that he was gone. I wanted to call everyone, right then and there, although it was lights out and lockdown. I had two families, but all of a sudden I didn't care so much about one of them. I guess things were different once you get sent away. But I had lived it. The American Dream! I had done it all. Everything! I had been damn near everywhere and had damn near everything I ever wanted. I had been in the most lavish atmospheres, with some of the most exclusive people. I belonged. It was who I was. It was all I knew. A couple of hundred thousand really wasn't shit, though. Not when I knew that P. and Nuts were worth over a million. And so were half of the other members of our outfit. When the second chapter of my life rolled back around, I would get what was coming to me. The whole fucking dinner plate! But for now, it was time to do time. My Terminator story would come back around soon enough. I would, without a question, once again be back. A new and improved Siz-o! And already I couldn't wait.

*

Agent Nichols and his team had set up shop in an old church right down the street from P.'s place on the Hilltop. Red had hipped them to it. It was where P. often kept keys of coke and large amounts of cash. They had been doing their surveillance out of the church for nearly three months now. They were going right for the head man, the source of it all. Nichols had been having pictures taken of everyone, even the day that P. and everyone came out of the courthouse for my trial. He was in overdrive with the investigation. In the mean time, Red was down near Atlanta looking to set up shop for Nichols, to begin selling keys of coke to some new friends. He had no heart and he had no soul. He had set up his own nephew to get robbed and killed; set up his younger brother to do a murder bid; snitched on our man P. and our whole organization; and set me up for a major dope case and attempted to have both me and Dust do life in prison or possibly get the death penalty for the murder of his former boss and two associates. I would have to say that Red's favorite quote from the "48 Laws of Power" would be, 'I would rather betray the whole world first then to let them betray me'. His day would come, though. There was no question in my mind about that. As long as

I had breath in my body, he was a dead man. As soon as I got to the Pen' I got the tattoo, 'R.I.P. Red', because it was subliminally evident.

*

Agent Nichols followed P. to the Roadhouse but had to keep driving along Cooke Road because there was a guard at the entrance of the property. "What the hell was going on out here?" Nichols wondered.

Everyone arrived to the meeting virtually on schedule. This was the first meeting of the New Year of 2002. It was a cold, bone chilling day in mid January where it was 10 degrees outside, but there was no precipitation; just the normal wind chill around this time of year. Everyone got inside and got warm, and after coffee and tea was served, they began the meeting.

A few minutes after they got started, the subject of Red came up. "So we can't find this fat muthaphucka, man? Don't nobody know where he hidin' at?" Cooks asked. Everyone shook there heads no disappointingly. "That fat muthaphucka snitch nigga got my muphuckin' dog, Siz, locked up; and his uncle, the crazy one wit the funny colored eyes. Wasn't that Red's muthaphuckin' brother, too?"

"Yep. But we gon' find his ass. He got some fuckin' connected help, I know that. Mendez' people all up and down the east coast and still they ain't found shit. I expect his ass to be caught soon, though. Here in the blink of an eye. Well, put to sleep; fuck caught! But check this out, I wanna invest a hundred thousand for Siz-o; 50 in the casino up in Michigan and the other 50 back into the store and the club. Nuts have our accountant take care of that right away when we done here today," P. told Nuts.

"Alright," Nuts said.

"Speaking of casinos...there's going to be a host of casinos built here by 2004. So, by the spring we should know where they are going to be built. Nuts." P. said, giving Nuts the go ahead to take over.

Nuts stood up and began to speak. "What we gon' do gentlemen, is start buying property wherever this land ends up being. If we get the property and open up whatever businesses we choose before the casinos are actually built then the property itself, as well as the taxes, will be cheaper. So that's one of the things that we wanted to mention today that are rather important. The other important thing is these Africans that have come out of nowhere. Already they've opened up a bar and a lounge, where they operate of course, and they push some heavy weight, too. Coke! But their main product is the boy. Heroin! Now before we go and wipe 'em out, P. has a friend who is a friend of theirs. Her name's Ruth. And her best friend and cousin's name is India. They are African, too. Ruth's convinced P. that they are willing to talk to him to negotiate some business. Now of course they would buy their coke from us, but they're willing to cut us in on their heroin connection. The heroin market's not that big in Columbus, or even Ohio for that matter, but it is more existing than we know or realize. But of course we have to take a nine man vote to see if we are going to get involved in the heroin business. Even though we would still have to work out the details of what our cut will be and so forth and so on. So gentlemen, all who are in favor," Nuts questioned raising his hand.

There were seven raised hands at first, and then a few seconds later Big Pace and Money Mike's hands went up as well. "Okay gentlemen, I see that we all in agreement to get this money..." P. smiled, with that million dollar grin. "Alright. Now it's time for my man T.B's initiation. You ready to get sworn in, dog? I don't think nobody here's gonna object. Come on down here to the head of the table."

Terique was getting promoted to one of the three heads of the West

Side Firm. I was really glad for him when I heard it. He deserved it. He was loyal, thorough, and about whatever. And he loved P.; his childhood homey. Terique had been to the Federal Penitentiary before for over 7 years, where it was rough. He had it in him. There couldn't have been a better pick. I'm glad P. made the right choice; the choice he should have made last time. He was the boss for now. But nobody lasted forever. Soon, everyone's American Dream becomes an American Nightmare! I was in mine now. But just as well, nightmares don't last forever. And I would be awakened from mine by the time everyone blinked. I closed my eyes. "Now I lay me down to sleep, I pray the Lord my soul to keep, if…" I mouthed the words inside my head, and before I knew it I was fast asleep. My return would be memorable. But for now, my pain and rage would be my motivation. And I had plenty of it.